Vampires in Literature

BOOK TWO

Published by OffBeat Publishing, LLC; Troy, Ohio

First Edition, 2025

ISBN(paperback): 978-1-950464-79-1
ISBN(eBook): 978-1-950464-88-3

Printed in the United States

Clarimonde The publisher is happy to preserve and include Art/Compositions by P.A. Laurens, from a 1904 French Language edition. Color Engravings by Eugène Decisy. (Color unavailable in black and white edition.)

The English translation of **MANOR** is based on a translation generated by Grok, created by xAI.

Other books and publisher information:
ReadAdventures.com

Short
Stories

Vampires in Literature

BOOK TWO

Compiled by

Michael Toeset

&

Robert Kimbrell

CONTENTS

INTRODUCTION

Welcome to Book 2 of "Vampires in Literature." In this volume, you'll find a wide selection of classic short stories about vampires. If you're new to the series, we encourage you to look up Book 1, which serves as an introduction to this extensive collection and also presents some classic poetry about vampires. It's "bloody" good, if we do say so ourselves.

To enter the world of vampire literature is perplexing at first. Vampires *seem* modern. Books about them *seem* like a current concern in the publishing world, they *seem* like a subject matter that didn't take hold until the popularity of horror literature and film exploded in the late 1900s. But people have been writing about vampires since even before Bram Stoker introduced us to Count Dracula.

That, essentially, is the raison d'etre for this collection: To open up new worlds to lovers of vampire stories. And you'll find plenty to love in this short story collection, and in subsequent books in this series; in Book 3, we will begin offering full-length vampire novels that you'll want to sink your teeth into.

Not all of the stories in this book are technically "vampire" stories, but they are close to what we nowadays would consider *nosferatu*. We wanted to be as comprehensive as possible in this overview of early vampire literature and felt compelled to include the stories that live on the edges of the genre as well.

Early vampire literature wasn't just written by people you've never heard of, either. If you're a student of literature, in this collection you'll recognize names such as Lord Byron, M.R. James, and Stoker.

But at the same time, don't write off the authors you're not familiar with. You're in for a treat discovering vampire works by writers such as Uriah Derick D'Arcy and Victoria Glad.

In this book, we've gathered some of the best representatives of the genre. To aid the reader, we've provided a brief introduction to each tale, giving context and providing information you likely would have looked up yourself. (For we are not just editors here, first and foremost, we are readers, too!)

A good thing about a collection like this is that you can read it in whatever manner suits you best. Some of us prefer to read a story a week, choosing to read whichever story sounds best that day. Some of us prefer to read the collection straight through, in the order the stories are arranged. It's all up to you.

Just be sure to leave a light on once you're done reading for the night. Or will that cast too many shadows in which evil can lurk?

-Michael Toeset

"Our ways are not your ways, and there shall be to you many strange things."

— BRAM STOKER, FROM DRACULA

DRACULAS GUEST

BY BRAM STOKER

The Irish Bram Stoker (1847-1912) is likely well-known to vampire fans, as he wrote what's considered the first masterpiece on the subject, "Dracula." Stoker also wrote several other famous horror works that can easily be found today, including "The Jewel of Seven Stars" and "The Lair of the White Worm." But his legacy is directly tied to Dracula and vampires, through his novel and also through this shorter piece. We'll talk more about "Dracula's Guest" in the Book 3 introduction, but know that this is a worthy addition to the canon and essentially serves as a prequel to "Dracula."

Preface

A few months before the lamented death of my husband—I might say even as the shadow of death was over him—he planned three series of short stories for publication, and the present volume is one of them. To his original list of stories in this book, I have added an hitherto unpublished episode from Dracula. It was originally excised owing to the length of the book, and may prove of interest to the many readers of what is considered my husband's most remarkable work. The other stories have already been published in English and American periodicals. Had my husband lived longer, he might have seen fit to revise this work, which is mainly from the earlier years of his strenuous life. But, as fate has entrusted to me the issuing of it, I consider it fitting and proper to let it go forth practically as it was left by him.

FLORENCE BRAM STOKER

To MY SON
First published 1914

Dracula's Guest

by Bram Stoker

by Bram Stoker

When we started for our drive the sun was shining brightly on Munich, and the air was full of the joyousness of early summer. Just as we were about to depart, Herr Delbrück (the maître d'hôtel of the Quatre Saisons, where I was staying) came down, bareheaded, to the carriage and, after wishing me a pleasant drive, said to the coachman, still holding his hand on the handle of the carriage door:

"Remember you are back by nightfall. The sky looks bright but there is a shiver in the north wind that says there may be a sudden storm. But I am sure you will not be late." Here he smiled, and added, "for you know what night it is."

Johann answered with an emphatic, "Ja, mein Herr," and, touching his hat, drove off quickly. When we had cleared the town, I said, after signalling to him to stop:

"Tell me, Johann, what is tonight?"

He crossed himself, as he answered laconically: "Walpurgis nacht." Then he took out his watch, a great, old-fashioned German silver thing as big as a turnip, and looked at it, with his eyebrows gathered together and a little impatient shrug of his shoulders. I realised that this was his way of respectfully protesting against the unnecessary delay, and sank back in the carriage, merely motioning him to proceed. He started off rapidly, as if to make up for lost time. Every now and then the horses seemed to throw up their heads and sniffed the air suspiciously. On such occasions I often looked round in alarm. The road was pretty bleak, for we were traversing a sort of high, wind-swept plateau. As we drove, I saw a road that looked but little used, and which seemed to dip through a little, winding valley. It looked so inviting that, even at the risk of offending him, I called Johann to stop—and when he had pulled up, I told him I would like to drive down that road. He made all sorts of excuses, and frequently crossed himself as he spoke. This somewhat piqued my curiosity, so I asked him various questions. He answered fencingly, and repeatedly looked at his watch in protest. Finally I said:

"Well, Johann, I want to go down this road. I shall not ask you to come unless you like; but tell me why you do not like to go, that is all I ask." For answer he seemed to throw himself off the box, so quickly did he reach the ground. Then he stretched out his hands appealingly to me, and implored me not to go. There was just enough of English mixed with the German for me to understand the drift of his talk. He seemed always just about to tell me something—the very idea of which evidently frightened him; but each time he pulled himself up, saying, as he crossed himself: "Walpurgis-Nacht!"

I tried to argue with him, but it was difficult to argue with a man when I did not know his language. The advantage certainly rested with him, for although he began to speak in English, of a very crude and broken kind, he always got excited and broke into his native tongue—and every time he did so, he looked at his watch. Then the horses became restless and sniffed the air. At this he grew very pale, and, looking around in a frightened way, he suddenly jumped forward, took them by the bridles and led them on some twenty feet. I followed, and asked why he had done this. For answer he crossed himself, pointed to the spot we had left and drew his carriage in the direction of the other road, indicating a cross, and said, first in

German, then in English: "Buried him—him what killed themselves."

I remembered the old custom of burying suicides at cross-roads: "Ah! I see, a suicide. How interesting!" But for the life of me I could not make out why the horses were frightened.

Whilst we were talking, we heard a sort of sound between a yelp and a bark. It was far away; but the horses got very restless, and it took Johann all his time to quiet them. He was pale, and said, "It sounds like a wolf—but yet there are no wolves here now."

"No?" I said, questioning him; "isn't it long since the wolves were so near the city?"

"Long, long," he answered, "in the spring and summer; but with the snow the wolves have been here not so long."

Whilst he was petting the horses and trying to quiet them, dark clouds drifted rapidly across the sky. The sunshine passed away, and a breath of cold wind seemed to drift past us. It was only a breath, however, and more in the nature of a warning than a fact, for the sun came out brightly again. Johann looked under his lifted hand at the horizon and said:

"The storm of snow, he comes before long time." Then he looked at his watch again, and, straightway holding his reins firmly—for the horses were still pawing the ground restlessly and shaking their heads—he climbed to his box as though the time had come for proceeding on our journey.

I felt a little obstinate and did not at once get into the carriage.

"Tell me," I said, "about this place where the road leads," and I pointed down.

Again he crossed himself and mumbled a prayer, before he answered, "It is unholy."

"What is unholy?" I enquired.

"The village."

"Then there is a village?"

"No, no. No one lives there hundreds of years." My curiosity was piqued, "But you said there was a village."

"There was."

"Where is it now?"

Whereupon he burst out into a long story in German and English, so mixed up that I could not quite understand exactly what he said, but roughly I gathered that long ago, hundreds of years, men had died there

and been buried in their graves; and sounds were heard under the clay, and when the graves were opened, men and women were found rosy with life, and their mouths red with blood. And so, in haste to save their lives (aye, and their souls! —and here he crossed himself) those who were left fled away to other places, where the living lived, and the dead were dead and not—not something. He was evidently afraid to speak the last words. As he proceeded with his narration, he grew more and more excited. It seemed as if his imagination had got hold of him, and he ended in a perfect paroxysm of fear—white-faced, perspiring, trembling and looking round him, as if expecting that some dreadful presence would manifest itself there in the bright sunshine on the open plain. Finally, in an agony of desperation, he cried:

"Walpurgis nacht!" and pointed to the carriage for me to get in. All my English blood rose at this, and, standing back, I said:

"You are afraid, Johann—you are afraid. Go home; I shall return alone; the walk will do me good." The carriage door was open. I took from the seat my oak walking-stick—which I always carry on my holiday excursions—and closed the door, pointing back to Munich, and said, "Go home, Johann— Walpurgis-nacht doesn't concern Englishmen."

The horses were now more restive than ever, and Johann was trying to hold them in, while excitedly imploring me not to do anything so foolish. I pitied the poor fellow, he was deeply in earnest; but all the same I could not help laughing. His English was quite gone now. In his anxiety he had forgotten that his only means of making me understand was to talk my language, so he jabbered away in his native German. It began to be a little tedious. After giving the direction, "Home!" I turned to go down the cross-road into the valley.

With a despairing gesture, Johann turned his horses towards Munich. I leaned on my stick and looked after him. He went slowly along the road for a while: then there came over the crest of the hill a man tall and thin. I could see so much in the distance. When he drew near the horses, they began to jump and kick about, then to scream with terror. Johann could not hold them in; they bolted down the road, running away madly. I watched them out of sight, then looked for the stranger, but I found that he, too, was gone.

With a light heart I turned down the side road through the deepening valley to which Johann had objected. There was not the slightest reason, that I could see, for his objection; and I daresay I tramped for a couple of hours without thinking of time or distance, and certainly without seeing a person or a house. So far as the place was concerned, it was desolation itself. But I did not notice this particularly till, on turning a bend in the road, I came upon a scattered fringe of wood; then I recognised that I had been impressed unconsciously by the desolation of the region through which I had passed.

I sat down to rest myself, and began to look around. It struck me that it was considerably colder than it had been at the commencement of my walk—a sort of sighing sound seemed to be around me, with, now and then, high overhead, a sort of muffled roar. Looking upwards I noticed that great thick clouds were drifting rapidly across the sky from North to South at a great height. There were signs of coming storm in some lofty stratum of the air. I was a little chilly, and, thinking that it was the sitting still after the exercise of walking, I resumed my journey.

The ground I passed over was now much more picturesque. There were no striking objects that the eye might single out; but in all there was a charm of beauty. I took little heed of time and it was only when the deepening twilight forced itself upon me that I began to think of how I should find my way home. The brightness of the day had gone. The air was cold, and the drifting of clouds high overhead was more marked. They were accompanied by a sort of far-away rushing sound, through which seemed to come at intervals that myste-rious cry which the driver had said came from a wolf. For a while I hesitated. I had said I would see the deserted village, so on I went, and presently came on a wide stretch of open coun-try, shut in by hills all around. Their sides were covered with trees which spread down to the plain, dotting, in clumps, the gentler slopes and hollows which showed here and there. I followed with my eye the winding of the road, and saw that it curved close to one of the densest of these clumps and was lost behind it.

As I looked there came a cold shiver in the air, and the snow began to fall. I thought of the miles and miles of bleak country I had passed, and then hurried on to seek the shelter of the wood in front. Darker and darker grew the sky, and faster and heavier fell the snow, till the earth before and around me was a glistening white carpet the further edge of which was lost in misty vagueness. The road was here but crude, and when on the level its boundaries were not so marked, as when it passed through the cuttings; and in a little while I found that I must have strayed from it, for I missed underfoot the hard surface, and my feet sank deeper in the grass and moss. Then the wind grew stronger and blew with ever increasing force, till I was fain to run before it. The air became icy-cold, and in spite of my exercise I began to suffer. The snow was now falling so thickly and whirling around me in such rapid eddies that I could hardly keep my eyes open. Every now and then the heavens were torn asunder by vivid lightning, and in the flashes I could see ahead of me a great mass of trees, chiefly yew and cypress all heavily coated with snow.

I was soon amongst the shelter of the trees, and there, in comparative silence, I could hear the rush of the wind high overhead. Presently the blackness of the storm had become merged in the darkness of the night. By-and-by the storm seemed to be passing away: it now only came in fierce puffs or blasts. At such moments the weird sound of the wolf appeared to be echoed by many similar sounds around me.

Now and again, through the black mass of drifting cloud,

came a straggling ray of moonlight, which lit up the expanse, and showed me that I was at the edge of a dense mass of cypress and yew trees. As the snow had ceased to fall, I walked out from the shelter and began to investigate more closely. It appeared to me that, amongst so many old foundations as I had passed, there might be still standing a house in which, though in ruins, I could find some sort of shelter for a while. As I skirted the edge of the copse, I found that a low wall encircled it, and following this I presently found an opening. Here the cypresses formed an alley leading up to a square mass of some kind of building. Just as I caught sight of this, however, the drifting clouds obscured the moon, and I passed up the path in darkness. The wind must have grown colder, for I felt myself shiver as I walked; but there was hope of shelter, and I groped my way blindly on.

I stopped, for there was a sudden stillness. The storm had passed; and, perhaps in sympathy with nature's silence, my heart seemed to cease to beat. But this was only momentarily; for suddenly the moonlight broke through the clouds, showing me that I was in a graveyard, and that the square object before me was a great massive tomb of marble, as white as the snow that lay on and all around it. With the moonlight there came a fierce sigh of the storm, which appeared to resume its course with a long, low howl, as of many dogs or wolves. I was awed and shocked, and felt the cold perceptibly grow upon me till it seemed to grip me by the heart. Then while the flood of moonlight still fell on the marble tomb, the storm gave further evidence of renewing, as though it was returning on its track. Impelled by some sort of fascination, I approached the sepulchre to see what it was, and why such a thing stood alone in such a place. I walked around it, and read, over the Doric door, in German:

COUNTESS DOLINGEN OF GRATZ
IN STYRIA
SOUGHT AND FOUND DEATH
1801

On the top of the tomb, seemingly driven through the solid marble—for the structure was composed of a few vast blocks of stone—was a great iron spike or stake. On going to the back I saw, graven in great Russian letters:

"The dead travel fast."

There was something so weird and uncanny about the whole thing that it gave me a turn and made me feel quite faint. I began to wish, for the first time, that I had taken Johann's advice. Here a thought struck me, which came under almost mysterious circumstances and with a terrible shock. This was Walpurgis Night!

Walpurgis Night, when, according to the belief of millions of people, the devil was abroad—when the graves were opened and the dead came forth and walked. When all evil things of earth and air and water held revel. This very place the driver had specially shunned. This was the depopulated village of centuries ago. This was where the suicide lay; and this was the place where I was alone—unmanned, shivering with cold in a shroud of snow with a wild storm gathering again upon me! It took all my philosophy, all the religion I had been taught, all my courage, not to collapse in a paroxysm of fright.

And now a perfect tornado burst upon me. The ground shook as though thousands of horses thundered across it; and this time the storm bore on its icy wings, not snow, but great hailstones which drove with such violence that they might have come from the thongs of Balearic slingers—hailstones that beat down leaf and branch and made the shelter of the cypresses of no more avail than though their stems were standing-corn. At the first I had rushed to the nearest tree; but I was soon fain to leave it and seek the only spot that seemed to afford refuge, the deep Doric doorway of the marble tomb. There, crouching against the massive bronze door, I gained a certain amount of protection from the beating of the hailstones, for now they only drove against me as they ricocheted from the ground and the side of the marble.

As I leaned against the door, it moved slightly and opened

inwards. The shelter of even a tomb was welcome in that piti-less tempest, and I was about to enter it when there came a flash of forked-lightning that lit up the whole expanse of the heavens. In the instant, as I am a living man, I saw, as my eyes were turned into the darkness of the tomb, a beautiful woman, with rounded cheeks and red lips, seemingly sleeping on a bier. As the thunder broke overhead, I was grasped as by the hand of a giant and hurled out into the storm. The whole thing was so sudden that, before I could realise the shock, moral as well as physical, I found the hailstones beating me down. At the same time I had a strange, dominating feeling that I was not alone. I looked towards the tomb. Just then there came another blinding flash, which seemed to strike the iron stake that surmounted the tomb and to pour through to the earth, blasting and crumbling the marble, as in a burst of flame. The dead woman rose for a moment of agony, while she was lapped in the flame, and her bitter scream of pain was drowned in the thundercrash. The last thing I heard was this mingling of dreadful sound, as again I was seized in the giant-grasp and dragged away, while the hailstones beat on me, and the air around seemed reverberant with the howling of wolves. The last sight that I remembered was a vague, white, moving mass, as if all the graves around me had sent out the phantoms of their sheeted-dead, and that they were closing in on me through the white cloudiness of the driving hail.

Gradually there came a sort of vague beginning of consciousness; then a sense of weariness that was dreadful. For a time I remembered nothing; but slowly my senses returned. My feet seemed positively racked with pain, yet I could not move them. They seemed to be numbed. There was an icy feeling at the back of my neck and all down my spine, and my ears, like my feet, were dead, yet in torment; but there was in my breast a sense of warmth which was, by comparison, deli-cious. It was as a nightmare—a physical nightmare, if one may use such an expression; for some heavy weight on my chest made it difficult for me to breathe.

This period of semi-lethargy seemed to remain a long time,

and as it faded away I must have slept or swooned. Then came a sort of loathing, like the first stage of sea-sickness, and a wild desire to be free from something—I knew not what. A vast stillness enveloped me, as though all the world were asleep or dead—only broken by the low panting as of some animal close to me. I felt a warm rasping at my throat, then came a consciousness of the awful truth, which chilled me to the heart and sent the blood surging up through my brain. Some great animal was lying on me and now licking my throat. I feared to stir, for some instinct of prudence bade me lie still; but the brute seemed to realise that there was now some change in me, for it raised its head. Through my eyelashes I saw above me the two great flaming eyes of a gigantic wolf. Its sharp white teeth gleamed in the gaping red mouth, and I could feel its hot breath fierce and acrid upon me.

For another spell of time I remembered no more. Then I became conscious of a low growl, followed by a yelp, renewed again and again. Then, seemingly very far away, I heard a "Holloa! holloa!" as of many voices calling in unison. Cautiously I raised my head and looked in the direction whence the sound came; but the cemetery blocked my view. The wolf still continued to yelp in a strange way, and a red glare began to move round the grove of cypresses, as though following the sound. As the voices drew closer, the wolf yelped faster and louder. I feared to make either sound or motion. Nearer came the red glow, over the white pall which stretched into the darkness around me. Then all at once from beyond the trees there came at a trot a troop of horsemen bearing torches. The wolf rose from my breast and made for the cemetery. I saw one of the horsemen (soldiers by their caps and their long military cloaks) raise his carbine and take aim. A companion knocked up his arm, and I heard the ball whizz over my head. He had evidently taken my body for that of the wolf. Another sighted the animal as it slunk away, and a shot followed. Then, at a gallop, the troop rode forward—some towards me, others following the wolf as it disappeared amongst the snow-clad cypresses.

As they drew nearer I tried to move, but was powerless, although I could see and hear all that went on around me. Two or three of the soldiers jumped from their horses and knelt beside me. One of them raised my head, and placed his hand over my heart.

"Good news, comrades!" he cried. "His heart still beats!"

Then some brandy was poured down my throat; it put vigour into me, and I was able to open my eyes fully and look around. Lights and shadows were moving among the trees, and I heard men call to one another. They drew together, uttering frightened exclamations; and the lights flashed as the others came pouring out of the cemetery pell-mell, like men possessed. When the further ones came close to us, those who were around me asked them eagerly:

"Well, have you found him?"

The reply rang out hurriedly:

"No! no! Come away quick—quick! This is no place to stay, and on this of all nights!"

"What was it?" was the question, asked in all manner of keys. The answer came variously and all indefinitely as though the men were moved by some common impulse to speak, yet were restrained by some common fear from giving their thoughts.

"It—it—indeed!" gibbered one, whose wits had plainly given out for the moment.

"A wolf—and yet not a wolf!" another put in shudderingly.

"No use trying for him without the sacred bullet," a third remarked in a more ordinary manner.

"Serve us right for coming out on this night! Truly we have earned our thousand marks!" were the ejaculations of a fourth.

"There was blood on the broken marble," another said after a pause—"the lightning never brought that there. And for him—is he safe? Look at his throat! See, comrades, the wolf has been lying on him and keeping his blood warm."

The officer looked at my throat and replied:

"He is all right; the skin is not pierced. What does it all

mean? We should never have found him but for the yelping of the wolf."

"What became of it?" asked the man who was holding up my head, and who seemed the least panic-stricken of the party, for his hands were steady and without tremor. On his sleeve was the chevron of a petty officer.

"It went to its home," answered the man, whose long face was pallid, and who actually shook with terror as he glanced around him fearfully. "There are graves enough there in which it may lie. Come, comrades—come quickly! Let us leave this cursed spot."

The officer raised me to a sitting posture, as he uttered a word of command; then several men placed me upon a horse. He sprang to the saddle behind me, took me in his arms, gave the word to advance; and, turning our faces away from the cypresses, we rode away in swift, military order.

As yet my tongue refused its office, and I was perforce silent. I must have fallen asleep; for the next thing I remembered was finding myself standing up, supported by a soldier on each side of me. It was almost broad daylight, and to the north a red streak of sunlight was reflected, like a path of blood, over the waste of snow. The officer was telling the men to say nothing of what they had seen, except that they found an English stranger, guarded by a large dog.

"Dog! that was no dog," cut in the man who had exhibited such fear. "I think I know a wolf when I see one."

The young officer answered calmly: "I said a dog."

"Dog!" reiterated the other ironically. It was evident that his courage was rising with the sun; and, pointing to me, he said, "Look at his throat. Is that the work of a dog, master?"

Instinctively I raised my hand to my throat, and as I touched it I cried out in pain. The men crowded round to look, some stooping down from their saddles; and again there came the calm voice of the young officer:

"A dog, as I said. If aught else were said we should only be laughed at."

I was then mounted behind a trooper, and we rode on into

the suburbs of Munich. Here we came across a stray carriage, into which I was lifted, and it was driven off to the Quatre Saisons—the young officer accompanying me, whilst a trooper followed with his horse, and the others rode off to their barracks.

When we arrived, Herr Delbrück rushed so quickly down the steps to meet me, that it was apparent he had been watching within. Taking me by both hands he solicitously led me in. The officer saluted me and was turning to withdraw, when I recognised his purpose, and insisted that he should come to my rooms. Over a glass of wine I warmly thanked him and his brave comrades for saving me. He replied simply that he was more than glad, and that Herr Delbrück had at the first taken steps to make all the searching party pleased; at which ambiguous utterance the maître d'hôtel smiled, while the officer pleaded duty and withdrew.

"But Herr Delbrück," I enquired, "how and why was it that the soldiers searched for me?"

He shrugged his shoulders, as if in depreciation of his own deed, as he replied:

"I was so fortunate as to obtain leave from the commander of the regiment in which I served, to ask for volunteers."

"But how did you know I was lost?" I asked.

"The driver came hither with the remains of his carriage, which had been upset when the horses ran away."

"But surely you would not send a search-party of soldiers merely on this account?"

"Oh, no!" he answered; "but even before the coachman arrived, I had this telegram from the Boyar whose guest you are," and he took from his pocket a telegram which he handed to me, and I read:

Bistritz. Be careful of my guest—his safety is most precious to me. Should aught happen to him, or if he be missed, spare nothing to find him and ensure his safety. He is English and therefore adventurous. There are often dangers from snow and wolves and night. Lose not a moment if you suspect harm to him. I answer your zeal with my fortune.—Dracula.

As I held the telegram in my hand, the room seemed to whirl around me; and, if the attentive maître d'hôtel had not caught me, I think I should have fallen. There was something so strange in all this, something so weird and impossible to imagine, that there grew on me a sense of my being in some way the sport of opposite forces—the mere vague idea of which seemed in a way to paralyse me. I was certainly under some form of mysterious protection. From a distant country had come, in the very nick of time, a message that took me out of the danger of the snow-sleep and the jaws of the wolf.

The End

A Fragment

by Lord Byron

Lord Byron, aka George Gordon Byron (1788-1824) is considered one of the greatest poets in history. Byron's contemporaries included fellow poet Percy Bysshe Shelley and Mary Wollstonecraft Shelley, the author of "Frankenstein." Appropriately enough, Byron's vampire story and "Frankenstein" were conceived around the same time. Both were the result of a ghost-story contest that Byron came up with. Needless to say, Mary Shelley's work was the best, but Byron's piece is a fascinating read. It's interesting to note, also, that this is an uncompleted fragment because Byron decided he didn't like writing about vampires.

A Fragment

by George Gordon Byron, 1788-1824

Published: 1916

In the year 17-, having for some time determined on a journey through countries not hitherto much frequented by travellers I set out, accompanied by a friend, whom I shall designate by the name of Augustus Darvell. He was a few years my elder, and a man of considerable fortune and ancient family — advantages which an extensive capacity prevented him alike from under-valuing or overrating. Some peculiar circumstances in his private history had rendered him to me an object of attention, of interest, and even of regard, which neither the reserve of his manners, nor occasional indications of an inquietude at times nearly approaching to alienation of mind, could extinguish.

I was yet young in life, which I had begun early; but my intimacy with him was of a recent date: we had been educated at the same schools and university; but his progress through these had preceded mine, and he had been deeply initiated into what is called the world, while I was yet in my noviciate. While thus engaged, I had heard much both of his past and present life; and although in these accounts there were many and irrec-oncileable contradictions, I could still gather from the whole that he was a being of no common order, and one who, what-ever pains he might take to avoid remark, would still be remarkable. I had cultivated his acquaintance subsequently, and endeavoured to obtain his friendship, but this last appeared to be unattainable; whatever affections he might have possessed seemed now, some to have been extinguished, and others to be concentred: that his feelings were acute, I had sufficient opportunities of observing; for, although he could control, he could not altogether disguise them: still he had a power of giving to one passion the appearance of another in such a manner that it was difficult to define the nature of what was working within him; and the expressions of his features would vary so rapidly, though slightly, that it was useless to trace them to their sources. It was evident that he was a prey to some cureless disquiet; but whether it arose from ambition, love, remorse, grief, from one or all of these, or merely from a morbid temperament akin to disease, I could not discover: there were circumstances alleged, which might have justified the application to each of these causes; but, as I have before said, these were so contradictory and contradicted, that none could be fixed upon with accuracy. Where there is mystery, it is generally supposed that there must also be evil: I know not how this may be, but in him there certainly was the one, though I could not ascertain the extent of the other — and felt loth, as far as regarded himself, to believe in its existence. My advances were received with sufficient coldness; but I was young, and not easily discouraged, and at length succeeded in obtaining, to a certain degree, that common-place intercourse and moderate confidence of common and every day concerns, created and cemented by similarity of pursuit and frequency of meeting, which is called intimacy, or friendship, according to the ideas of him who uses those words to express them.

Darvell had already travelled extensively; and to him I had applied for information with regard to the conduct of my intended journey. It was my secret wish that he might be prevailed on to accompany me: it was also a probable hope, founded upon the shadowy restlessness which I had observed in him, and to which the animation which he appeared to feel on such subjects, and his apparent indifference to all by which he was more immediately surrounded, gave fresh strength. This wish I first hinted, and then expressed: his answer, though I had partly expected it, gave me all the pleasure of surprise — he consented; and, after the requisite arrangements, we commenced our voyages. After journeying through various countries of the south of Europe, our attention was turned towards the East, according to our original destination; and it was in my progress through those regions that the incident occurred upon which will turn what I may have to relate.

The constitution of Darvell, which must from his appearance have been in early life more than usually robust, had been for some time gradually giving way, without the intervention of any apparent disease: he had neither cough nor hectic, yet he became daily more enfeebled: his habits were temperate, and he neither declined nor complained of fatigue, yet he was evidently wasting away: he became more and more silent and sleepless, and at length so seriously altered, that my alarm grew proportionate to what I conceived to be his danger.

We had determined, on our arrival at Smyrna, on an excursion to the ruins of Ephesus and Sardis, from which I endeavoured to dissuade him in his present state of indisposition — but in vain: there appeared to be an oppression on his mind, and a solemnity in his manner, which ill corresponded with his eagerness to proceed on what I regarded as a mere party of pleasure, little suited to a valetudinarian; but I opposed him no longer — and in a few days we set off together, accompanied only by a serrugee and a single janizary.

We had passed halfway towards the remains of Ephesus, leaving behind us the more fertile environs of Smyrna, and were entering upon that wild and tenantless track through the marshes and defiles which lead to the few huts yet lingering over the broken columns of Diana — the roofless walls of expelled Christianlty, and the still more recent but complete desolation of abandoned mosques — when the sudden and rapid illness of my companion obliged us to halt at a Turkish cemetery, the turbaned tombstones of which were the sole indication that human life had ever been a sojourner in this wilderness. The only caravansera we had seen was left some hours behind us, not a vestige of a town or even cottage was within sight or hope, and this "city of the dead" appeared to be the sole refuge for my unfortunate friend, who seemed on the verge of becoming the last of its inhabitants.

In this situation, I looked round for a place where he might most conveniently repose: — contrary to the usual aspect of Mohometan burial-grounds, the cypresses were in this few in number, and these thinly scattered over its extent: the tombstones were mostly fallen, and worn with age: — upon one of the most considerable of these, and beneath one of the most spreading trees, Darvell supported himself, in a half-reclining posture, with great difficulty. He asked for water. I had some doubts of our being able to find any, and prepared to go in search of it with hesitating despondency — but he desired me to remain; and turning to Suleiman, our janizary, who stood by us smoking with great tranquillity, he said, "Suleiman, verbana su," (i.e. bring some water,) and went on describing the spot where it was to be found with great minuteness, at a small well for camels, a few hundred yards to the right: the janizary obeyed. I said to Darvell, "How did you know this?" — He replied, "From our situation; you must perceive that this place was once inhabited, and could not have been so without springs: I have also been here before."

"You have been here before! — How came you never to mention this to me? and what could you be doing in a place where no one would remain a moment longer than they could help it?"

To this question I received no answer. In the mean time Suleiman returned with the water, leaving the serrugee and the horses at the fountain. The quenching of his thirst had the appearance of reviving him for a moment; and I conceived hopes of his being able to proceed, or at least to return, and I urged the attempt. He was silent — and appeared to be collecting his spirits for an effort to speak. He began.

"This is the end of my journey, and of my life — I came

here "to die: but I have a request to make, a command — for such my "last words must be — You will observe it?"

"Most certainly; but have better hopes."

"I have no hopes, nor wishes, but this — conceal my death from every human being."

"I hope there will be no occasion; that you will recover, and —"

"Peace! — it must be so: promise this."

"I do."

"Swear it, by all that" — He here dictated an oath of great solemnity.

"There is no occasion for this — I will observe your request; and to doubt me is —"

"It cannot be helped, — you must swear."

I took the oath: it appeared to relieve him. He removed a seal ring from his finger, on which were some Arabic characters, and presented it to me. He proceeded —

"On the ninth day of the month, at noon precisely (what month you please, but this must be the day), you must fling this ring into the salt springs which run into the Bay of Eleusis: the day after, at the same hour, you must repair to the ruins of the temple of Ceres, and wait one hour."

"Why?"

"You will see."

"The ninth day of the month, you say?"

"The ninth."

As I observed that the present was the ninth day of the month, his countenance changed, and he paused. As he sate, evidently becoming more feeble, a stork, with a snake in her beak, perched upon a tombstone near us; and, without devouring her prey, appeared to be stedfastly regarding us. I know not what impelled me to drive it away. but the attempt was useless; she made a few circles in the air, and returned exactly to the same spot. Darvell pointed to it, and smiled: he spoke — I know not whether to himself or to me — but the words were only, "'Tis well!"

"What is well? what do you mean?"

"No matter: you must bury me here this evening, and exactly where that bird is now perched. You know the rest of my injunctions."

He then proceeded to give me several directions as to the manner in which his death might be best concealed. After these were finished, he exclaimed, "You perceive that bird?"

"Certainly."

"And the serpent writhing in her beak?"

"Doubtless: there is nothing uncommon in it; it is her natural "prey. But it is odd that she does not devour it."

He smiled in a ghastly manner, and said, faintly, "It is not yet "time!" As he spoke, the stork flew away. My eyes followed it for a moment, it could hardly be longer than ten might be counted. I felt Darvell's weight, as it were, increase upon my shoulder, and, turning to look upon his face, perceived that he was dead!

I was shocked with the sudden certainty which could not be mistaken — his countenance in a few minutes became nearly black. I should have attributed so rapid a change to poison, had I not been aware that he had no opportunity of receiving it unperceived. The day was declining, the body was rapidly altering, and nothing remained but to fulfil his request. With the aid of Suleiman's ataghan and my own sabre, we scooped a shallow grave upon the spot which Darvell had indicated: the earth easily gave way, having already received some Mahometan tenant. We dug as deeply as the time permitted us, and throwing the dry earth upon all that remained of the singular being so lately departed, we cut a few sods of greener turf from the less withered soil around us, and laid them upon his sepulchre.

Between astonishment and grief, I was tearless.

The Unfinished End

THE VAMPYRE
BY JOHN WILLIAM POLIDORI

John William Polidori (1795-1821) was a British writer and physician. His vampire tale is considered one of the first, best entries in the vampire genre. Polidori's story is based on Lord Byron's vampire tale (which is included in this collection), and early additions even credited Byron as the author. Polidori's finished version, however, is decidedly his, and it is one of the early greats.

Vampyre

A Tale By John William Polidori

"I breathe freely in the neighbourhood of this lake; the ground upon which I tread has been subdued from the earliest ages; the principal objects which immediately strike my eye, bring to my recollection scenes, in which man acted the hero and was the chief object of interest. Not to look back to earlier times of battles and sieges, here is the bust of Rousseau—here is a house with an inscription denoting that the Genevan philosopher first drew breath under its roof. A little out of the town is Ferney, the residence of Voltaire; where that wonderful, though certainly in many respects contemptible, character, received, like the hermits of old, the visits of pilgrims, not only from his own nation, but from the farthest boundaries of Europe. Here too is Bonnet's abode, and, a few steps beyond, the house of that astonishing woman Madame de Stael: perhaps the first of her sex, who has really proved its often claimed equality with, the nobler man. We have before had women who have written interesting novels and poems, in which their tact at observing drawing-room characters has availed them; but never since the days of Heloise have those faculties which are peculiar to man, been developed as the possible inheritance of woman. Though even here, as in the case of Heloise, our sex have not been backward in alledging the existence of an Abeilard in the person of M. Schlegel as the inspirer of her works. But to proceed: upon the same side of the lake, Gibbon, Bonnivard, Bradshaw, and others mark, as it were, the stages for our progress; whilst upon the other side there is one house, built by Diodati, the friend of Milton, which has contained within its walls, for several months, that poet whom we have so often read together, and who—if human passions remain the same, and human feelings, like chords, on being swept by nature's impulses shall vibrate as before—will be placed by posterity in the first rank of our English Poets. You must have heard, or the Third Canto of Childe Harold will have informed you, that Lord Byron resided many months in this neighbourhood. I went with some friends a few days ago, after having seen Ferney, to view this mansion. I trod the floors with the same feelings of awe and respect as we did, together, those of Shakespeare's dwelling at Stratford. I sat down in a chair of the saloon, and satisfied myself that I was resting on what he had made his constant seat. I found a servant there who had lived with him; she, however, gave me but little information. She pointed out his bed-chamber upon the same level as the saloon and dining-room, and informed me that he retired to rest at three, got up at two, and employed himself a long time over his toilette; that he never went to sleep without a pair of pistols and a dagger by his side, and that he never ate animal food. He apparently spent some part of every day upon the lake in an English boat. There is a balcony from the saloon which looks upon the lake and the mountain Jura; and I imagine, that it must have been hence, he contemplated the storm so magnificently described in the Third Canto; for you have from here a most extensive view of all the points he has therein depicted. I can fancy him like the scathed pine, whilst all around was sunk to repose, still waking to observe, what gave but a weak image of the storms which had desolated his own breast.

The sky is changed!—and such a change; Oh, night!
And storm and darkness, ye are wond'rous strong,
Yet lovely in your strength, as is the light
Of a dark eye in woman! Far along
From peak to peak, the rattling crags among,
Leaps the lire thunder! Not from one lone cloud,
But every mountain now hath found a tongue,
And Jura answers thro' her misty shroud,
Back to the joyous Alps who call to her aloud!

And this is in the night:—Most glorious night!
Thou wer't not sent for slumber! let me be
A sharer in thy far and fierce delight,—
A portion of the tempest and of me!
How the lit lake shines a phosphoric sea,
And the big rain comet dancing to the earth!
And now again 'tis black,—and now the glee
Of the loud hills shakes with its mountain mirth,
As if they did rejoice o'er a young; earthquake's birth,

Now where the swift Rhine cleaves his way between
Heights which appear, as lovers who have parted
In haste, whose mining depths so intervene,
That they can meet no more, tho' broken hearted;
Tho' in their souls which thus each other thwarted,
Love was the very root of the fond rage
Which blighted their life's bloom, and then departed—
Itself expired, but leaving; them an age
Of years all winter—war within themselves to wage.

I went down to the little port, if I may use the expression, wherein his vessel used to lay, and conversed with the cottager, who had the care of it. You may smile, but I have my pleasure in thus helping my personification of the individual I admire, by attaining to the knowledge of those circumstances which were daily around him. I have made numerous enquiries in the town concerning him, but can learn nothing. He only went into society there once, when M. Pictet took him to the house of a lady to spend the evening. They say he is a very singular man, and seem to think him very uncivil. Amongst other things they relate, that having invited M. Pictet and Bonstetten to dinner, he went on the lake to Chillon, leaving a gentleman who travelled with him to receive them and make his apologies. Another evening, being invited to the house of Lady D—— H ——, he promised to attend, but upon approaching the windows of her ladyship's villa, and perceiving the room to be full of company, he set down his friend, desiring him to plead his excuse, and immediately returned home. This will serve as a contradiction to the report which you tell me is current in England, of his having been avoided by his countrymen on the continent. The case happens to be directly the reverse, as he has been generally sought by them, though on most occasions, apparently without success. It is said, indeed, that upon paying his first visit at Coppet, following the servant who had announced his name, he was surprised to meet a lady carried out fainting; but before he had been seated many minutes, the same lady, who had been so affected at the sound of his name, returned and conversed with him a considerable time—such is female curiosity and affectation! He visited Coppet frequently, and of course associated there with several of his countrymen, who evinced no reluctance to meet him whom his enemies alone would represent as an outcast.

Though I have been so unsuccessful in this town, I have been more fortunate in my enquiries elsewhere. There is a society three or four miles from Geneva, the centre of which is the Countess of Breuss, a Russian lady, well acquainted with the agrémens de la Société, and who has collected them round herself at her mansion. It was chiefly here, I find, that the gentleman who travelled with Lord Byron, as physician, sought for society. He used almost every day to cross the lake by himself, in one of their flat-bottomed boats, and return after passing the evening with his friends, about eleven or twelve at night, often whilst the storms were raging in the circling summits of the mountains around. As he became intimate, from long acquaintance, with several of the families in this neighbourhood, I have gathered from their accounts some excellent traits of his lordship's character, which I will relate to you at some future opportunity. I must, however, free him from one imputation attached to him—of having in his house two sisters as the partakers of his revels. This is, like many other charges which have been brought against his lordship, entirely destitute of truth. His only companion was the physician I have already mentioned. The report originated from the following circumstance: Mr. Percy Bysshe Shelly, a gentleman well known for extravagance of doctrine, and for his daring, in their profession, even to sign himself with the title of ATHeos in the Album at Chamouny, having taken a house below, in which he resided with Miss M. W. Godwin and Miss Clermont, (the daughters of the celebrated Mr. Godwin) they were frequently visitors at Diodati, and were often seen upon the lake with his Lordship, which gave rise to the report, the truth of which is here positively denied.

Among other things which the lady, from whom I procured these anecdotes, related to me, she mentioned the outline of a ghost story by Lord Byron. It appears that one evening Lord B., Mr. P. B. Shelly, the two ladies and the gentleman before alluded to, after having perused a German work, which was entitled Phantasmagoriana, began relating ghost stories; when his lordship having recited the beginning of Christabel, then unpublished, the whole took so strong a hold of Mr. Shelly's mind, that he suddenly started up and ran out of the room. The physician and Lord Byron followed, and discovered him leaning against a mantle-piece, with cold drops of perspiration trickling down his face. After having given him something to refresh him, upon enquiring into the cause of his alarm, they found that his wild imagination having pictured to him the bosom of one of the ladies with eyes (which was reported of a lady in the neighbourhood where he lived) he was obliged to leave the room in order to destroy the impression. It was afterwards proposed, in the course of conversation, that each of the company present should write a tale depending upon some supernatural agency, which was undertaken by Lord B., the physician, and Miss M. W. Godwin.[1] My friend, the lady above referred to, had in her possession the outline of each of these stories; I obtained them as a great favour, and herewith forward them to you, as I was assured you would feel as much curiosity as myself, to peruse the ebauches of so great a genius, and those immediately under his influence."

[1] Since published under the title of "Frankenstein; or, The Modern Prometheus."

Vampyre

Original Introduction

The superstition upon which this tale is founded is very general in the East. Among the Arabians it appears to be common: it did not, however, extend itself to the Greeks until after the establishment of Christianity; and it has only assumed its present form since the division of the Latin and Greek churches; at which time, the idea becoming prevalent, that a Latin body could not corrupt if buried in their territory, it gradually increased, and formed the subject of many wonderful stories, still extant, of the dead rising from their graves, and feeding upon the blood of the young and beautiful. In the West it spread, with some slight variation, all over Hungary, Poland, Austria, and Lorraine, where the belief existed, that vampyres nightly imbibed a certain portion of the blood of their victims, who became emaciated, lost their strength, and speedily died of consumptions; whilst these human blood-suckers fattened— and their veins became distended to such a state of repletion, as to cause the blood to flow from all the passages of their bodies, and even from the very pores of their skins.

In the London Journal, of March, 1732, is a curious, and, of course, credible account of a particular case of vampyrism, which is stated to have occurred at Madreyga, in Hungary. It appears, that upon an examination of the commander-in-chief and magistrates of the place, they positively and unanimously affirmed, that, about five years before, a certain Heyduke, named Arnold Paul, had been heard to say, that, at Cassovia, on the frontiers of the Turkish Servia, he had been tormented by a vampyre, but had found a way to rid himself of the evil, by eating some of the earth out of the vampyre's grave, and rubbing himself with his blood. This precaution, however, did not prevent him from becoming a vampyre[2] himself; for, about twenty or thirty days after his death and burial, many persons complained of having been tormented by him, and a deposition was made, that four persons had been deprived of life by his attacks. To prevent further mischief, the inhabitants having consulted their Hadagni,[3] took up the body, and found it (as is supposed to be usual in cases of vampyrism) fresh, and entirely free from corruption, and emitting at the mouth, nose, and ears, pure and florid blood. Proof having been thus obtained, they resorted to the accustomed remedy. A stake was driven entirely through the heart and body of Arnold Paul, at which he is reported to have cried out as dreadfully as if he had been alive. This done, they cut off his head, burned his body, and threw the ashes into his grave. The same measures were adopted with the corses of those persons who had previously died from vampyrism, lest they should, in their turn, become agents upon others who survived them.

[2] The universal belief is, that a person sucked by a vampyre becomes a vampyre himself, and sucks in his turn.

[3] Chief bailiff.

This monstrous rodomontade is here related, because it seems better adapted to illustrate the subject of the present observations than any other instance which could be adduced. In many parts of Greece it is considered as a sort of punishment after death, for some heinous crime committed whilst in existence, that the deceased is not only doomed to vampyrise, but compelled to confine his infernal visitations solely to those beings he loved most while upon earth—those to whom he was bound by ties of kindred and affection.—A supposition alluded to in the "Giaour."

But first on earth, as Vampyre sent,
Thy corse shall from its tomb be rent;
Then ghastly haunt the native place,
And suck the blood of all thy race;
There from thy daughter, sister, wife,
At midnight drain the stream of life;
Yet loathe the banquet which perforce
Must feed thy livid living corse,
Thy victims, ere they yet expire,
Shall know the demon for their sire;
As cursing thee, thou cursing them,
Thy flowers are withered on the stem.
But one that for thy crime must fall,
The youngest, best beloved of all,
Shall bless thee with a father's name—
That word shall wrap thy heart in flame!
Yet thou must end thy task and mark
Her cheek's last tinge—her eye's last spark,
And the last glassy glance must view
Which freezes o'er its lifeless blue;
Then with unhallowed hand shall tear
The tresses of her yellow hair,
Of which, in life a lock when shorn
Affection's fondest pledge was worn—
But now is borne away by thee
Memorial of thine agony!
Yet with thine own best blood shall drip;
Thy gnashing tooth, and haggard lip;
Then stalking to thy sullen grave,
Go—and with Gouls and Afrits rave,
Till these in horror shrink away
From spectre more accursed than they.

Mr. Southey has also introduced in his wild but beautiful poem of "Thalaba," the vampyre corse of the Arabian maid Oneiza, who is represented as having returned from the grave for the purpose of tormenting him she best loved whilst in existence. But this cannot be supposed to have resulted from the sinfulness of her life, she being pourtrayed throughout the whole of the tale as a complete type of purity and innocence.

The veracious Tournefort gives a long account in his travels of several astonishing cases of vampyrism, to which he pretends to have been an eyewitness; and Calmet, in his great work upon this subject, besides a variety of anecdotes, and traditionary narratives illustrative of its effects, has put forth some learned dissertations, tending to prove it to be a classical, as well as barbarian error.

Many curious and interesting notices on this singularly horrible superstition might be added; though the present may suffice for the limits of a note, necessarily devoted to explanation, and which may now be concluded by merely remarking, that though the term Vampyre is the one in most general acceptation, there are several others synonymous with it, made use of in various parts of the world: as Vroucolocha, Vardoulacha, Goul, Broucoloka, &c.

Vampyre

It happened that in the midst of the dissipations attendant upon a London winter, there appeared at the various parties of the leaders of the ton a nobleman, more remarkable for his singularities, than his rank. He gazed upon the mirth around him, as if he could not participate therein. Apparently, the light laughter of the fair only attracted his attention, that he might by a look quell it, and throw fear into those breasts where thoughtlessness reigned. Those who felt this sensation of awe, could not explain whence it arose: some attributed it to the dead grey eye, which, fixing upon the object's face, did not seem to penetrate, and at one glance to pierce through to the inward workings of the heart; but fell upon the cheek with a leaden ray that weighed upon the skin it could not pass. His peculiarities caused him to be invited to every house; all wished to see him, and those who had been accustomed to violent excitement, and now felt the weight of ennui, were pleased at having something in their presence capable of engaging their attention. In spite of the deadly hue of his face, which never gained a warmer tint, either from the blush of modesty, or from the strong emotion of passion, though its form and outline were beautiful, many of the female hunters after notoriety attempted to win his attentions, and gain, at least, some marks of what they might term affection: Lady Mercer, who had been the mockery of every monster shewn in drawing-rooms since her marriage, threw herself in his way, and did all but put on the dress of a mountebank, to attract his notice:—though in vain:—when she stood before him, though his eyes were apparently fixed upon her's, still it seemed as if they were unperceived;—even her unappalled impudence was baffled, and she left the field. But though the common adultress could not influence even the guidance of his eyes, it was not that the female sex was indifferent to him: yet such was the apparent caution with which he spoke to the virtuous wife and innocent daughter, that few knew he ever addressed himself to females. He had, however, the reputation of a winning tongue; and whether it was that it even overcame the dread of his singular character, or that they were moved by his apparent hatred of vice, he was as often among those females who form the boast of their sex from their domestic virtues, as among those who sully it by their vices.

About the same time, there came to London a young gentleman of the name of Aubrey: he was an orphan left with an only sister in the possession of great wealth, by parents who died while he was yet in childhood. Left also to himself by guardians, who thought it their duty merely to take care of his fortune, while they relinquished the more important charge of his mind to the care of mercenary subalterns, he cultivated more his imagination than his judgment. He had, hence, that high romantic feeling of honour and candour, which daily ruins so many milliners' apprentices. He believed all to sympathise with virtue, and thought that vice was thrown in by Providence merely for the picturesque effect of the scene, as we see in romances: he thought that the misery of a cottage merely consisted in the vesting of clothes, which were as warm, but which were better adapted to the painter's eye by their irregular folds and various coloured patches. He thought, in fine, that the dreams of poets were the realities of life. He was handsome, frank, and rich: for these reasons, upon his entering into the gay circles, many mothers surrounded him, striving which should describe with least truth their languishing or romping favourites: the daughters at the same time, by their brightening countenances when he approached, and by their sparkling eyes, when he opened his lips, soon led him into false notions of his talents and his merit. Attached as he was to the romance of his solitary hours, he was startled at finding, that, except in the tallow and wax candles that flickered, not from the presence of a ghost, but from want of snuffing, there was no foundation in real life for any of that congeries of pleasing pictures and descriptions contained in those volumes, from which he had formed his study. Finding, however, some compensation in his gratified vanity, he was about to relinquish his dreams, when the extraordinary being we have above described, crossed him in his career.

He watched him; and the very impossibility of forming an idea of the character of a man entirely absorbed in himself, who gave few other signs of his observation of external objects, than the tacit assent to their existence, implied by the avoidance of their contact: allowing his imagination to picture every thing that flattered its propensity to extravagant ideas, he soon formed this object into the hero of a romance, and determined to observe the offspring of his fancy, rather than the person before him. He became acquainted with him, paid him attentions, and so far advanced upon his notice, that his presence was always recognised. He gradually learnt that Lord Ruthven's affairs were embarrassed, and soon found, from the notes of preparation in —— Street, that he was about to travel. Desirous of gaining some information respecting this singular character, who, till now, had only whetted his curiosity, he hinted to his guardians, that it was time for him to perform the tour, which for many generations has been thought necessary to enable the young to take some rapid steps in the career of vice towards putting themselves upon an equality with the aged, and not allowing them to appear as if fallen from the skies, whenever scandalous intrigues are mentioned as the subjects of pleasantry or of praise, according to the degree of skill shewn in carrying them on. They consented: and Aubrey immediately mentioning his intentions to Lord Ruthven, was surprised to receive from him a proposal to join him. Flattered by such a mark of esteem from him, who, apparently, had nothing in common with other men, he gladly accepted it, and in a few days they had passed the circling waters.

Hitherto, Aubrey had had no opportunity of studying Lord Ruthven's character, and now he found, that, though many more of his actions were exposed to his view, the results offered different conclusions from the apparent motives to his conduct. His companion was profuse in his liberality;—the idle, the vagabond, and the beggar, received from his hand more than enough to relieve their immediate wants. But Aubrey could not avoid remarking, that it was not upon the virtuous, reduced to indigence by the misfortunes attendant even upon virtue, that he bestowed his alms;—these were sent from the door with hardly suppressed sneers; but when the profligate came to ask something, not to relieve his wants, but to allow him to wallow in his lust, or to sink him still deeper in his iniquity, he was sent away with rich charity. This was, however, attributed by him to the greater importunity of the vicious, which generally prevails over the retiring bashfulness of the virtuous indigent. There was one circumstance about the charity of his Lordship, which was still more impressed upon his mind: all those upon whom it was bestowed, inevitably found that there was a curse upon it, for they were all either led to the scaffold, or sunk to the lowest and the most abject misery. At Brussels and other towns through which they passed, Aubrey was surprized at the apparent eagerness with which his companion sought for the centres of all fashionable vice; there he entered into all the spirit of the faro table: he betted, and always gambled with success, except where the known sharper was his antagonist, and then he lost even more than he gained; but it was always with the same unchanging face, with which he generally watched the society around: it was not, however, so when he encountered the rash youthful novice, or the luckless father of a numerous family; then his very wish seemed fortune's law—this apparent abstractedness of mind was laid aside, and his eyes sparkled with more fire than that of the cat whilst dallying with the half-dead mouse. In every town, he left the formerly affluent youth, torn from the circle he adorned, cursing, in the solitude of a dungeon, the fate that had drawn him within the reach of this fiend; whilst many a father sat frantic, amidst the speaking looks of mute hungry children, without a single farthing of his late immense wealth, wherewith to buy even sufficient to satisfy their present craving. Yet he took no money from the gambling table; but immediately lost, to the ruiner of many, the last gilder he had just snatched from the convulsive grasp of the innocent: this might but be the result of a certain degree of knowledge, which was not, however, capable of combating the cunning of the more experienced. Aubrey often wished to represent this to his friend, and beg him to resign that charity and pleasure which proved the ruin of all, and did not tend to his own profit;—but he delayed it—for each day he hoped his friend would give him some opportunity of speaking frankly and openly to him; however, this never occurred. Lord Ruthven in his carriage, and amidst the various wild and rich scenes of nature, was always the same: his eye spoke less than his lip; and though Aubrey was near the object of his curiosity, he obtained no greater gratification from it than the constant excitement of vainly wishing to break that mystery, which to his exalted imagination began to assume the appearance of something supernatural.

They soon arrived at Rome, and Aubrey for a time lost sight of his companion; he left him in daily attendance upon the morning circle of an Italian countess, whilst he went in search of the memorials of another almost deserted city. Whilst he was thus engaged, letters arrived from England, which he opened with eager impatience; the first was from his sister, breathing nothing but affection; the others were from his guardians, the latter astonished him; if it had before entered into his imagination that there was an evil power resident in his companion, these seemed to give him sufficient reason for the belief. His guardians insisted upon his immediately leaving his friend, and urged, that his character was dreadfully vicious, for that the possession of irresistible powers of seduction, rendered his licentious habits more dangerous to society. It had been discovered, that his contempt for the adultress had not originated in hatred of her character; but that he had required, to enhance his gratification, that his victim, the partner of his guilt, should be hurled from the pinnacle of unsullied virtue, down to the lowest abyss of infamy and degradation: in fine, that all those females whom he had sought, apparently on account of their virtue, had, since his departure, thrown even the mask aside, and had not scrupled to expose the whole deformity of their vices to the public gaze.

Aubrey determined upon leaving one, whose character had not yet shown a single bright point on which to rest the eye. He resolved to invent some plausible pretext for abandoning him altogether, purposing, in the mean while, to watch him more closely, and to let no slight circumstances pass by unnoticed. He entered into the same circle, and soon perceived, that his Lordship was endeavouring to work upon the inexperience of the daughter of the lady whose house he chiefly frequented. In Italy, it is seldom that an unmarried female is met with in society; he was therefore obliged to carry on his plans in secret; but Aubrey's eye followed him in all his windings, and soon discovered that an assignation had been appointed, which would most likely end in the ruin of an innocent, though thoughtless girl. Losing no time, he entered the apartment of Lord Ruthven, and abruptly asked him his intentions with respect to the lady, informing him at the same time that he was aware of his being about to meet her that very night. Lord Ruthven answered, that his intentions were such as he supposed all would have upon such an occasion; and upon being pressed whether he intended to marry her, merely laughed. Aubrey retired; and, immediately writing a note, to say, that from that moment he must decline accompanying his Lordship in the remainder of their proposed tour, he ordered his servant to seek other apartments, and calling upon the mother of the lady, informed her of all he knew, not only with regard to her daughter, but also concerning the character of his Lordship. The assignation was prevented. Lord Ruthven next day merely sent his servant to notify his complete assent to a separation; but did not hint any suspicion of his plans having been foiled by Aubrey's interposition.

Having left Rome, Aubrey directed his steps towards Greece, and crossing the Peninsula, soon found himself at Athens. He then fixed his residence in the house of a Greek; and soon occupied himself in tracing the faded records of ancient glory upon monuments that apparently, ashamed of chronicling the deeds of freemen only before slaves, had hidden themselves beneath the sheltering soil or many coloured lichen. Under the same roof as himself, existed a being, so beautiful and delicate, that she might have formed the model for a painter wishing to pourtray on canvass the promised hope of the faithful in Mahomet's paradise, save that her eyes spoke too much mind for any one to think she could belong to those who had no souls. As she danced upon the plain, or tripped along the mountain's side, one would have thought the gazelle a poor type of her beauties; for who would have exchanged her eye, apparently the eye of animated nature, for that sleepy luxurious look of the animal suited but to the taste of an epicure. The light step of Ianthe often accompanied Aubrey in his search after antiquities, and often would the unconscious girl, engaged in the pursuit of a Kashmere butterfly, show the whole beauty of her form, floating as it were upon the wind, to the eager gaze of him, who forgot the letters he had just decyphered upon an almost effaced tablet, in the contemplation of her sylph-like figure. Often would her tresses falling, as she flitted around, exhibit in the sun's ray such delicately brilliant and swiftly fading hues, it might well excuse the forgetfulness of the antiquary, who let escape from his mind the very object he had before thought of vital importance to the proper interpretation of a passage in Pausanias. But why attempt to describe charms which all feel, but none can appreciate?—It was innocence, youth, and beauty, unaffected by crowded drawing-rooms and stifling balls. Whilst he drew those remains of which he wished to preserve a memorial for his future hours, she would stand by, and watch the magic effects of his pencil, in tracing the scenes of her native place; she would then describe to him the circling dance upon the open plain, would paint, to him in all the glowing colours of youthful memory, the marriage pomp she remembered viewing in her infancy; and then, turning to subjects that had evidently made a greater impression upon her mind, would tell him all the supernatural tales of her nurse. Her earnestness and apparent belief of what she narrated, excited the interest even of Aubrey; and often as she told him the tale of the living vampyre, who had passed years amidst his friends, and dearest ties, forced every year, by feeding upon the life of a lovely female to prolong his existence for the ensuing months, his blood would run cold, whilst he attempted to laugh her out of such idle and horrible fantasies; but Ianthe cited to him the names of old men, who had at last detected one living among themselves, after several of their near relatives and children had been found marked with the stamp of the fiend's appetite; and when she found him so incredulous, she begged of him to believe her, for it had been, remarked, that those who had dared to question their existence, always had some proof given, which obliged them, with grief and heart-breaking, to confess it was true. She detailed to him the tradi-tional appearance of these monsters, and his horror was increased, by hearing a pretty accurate description of Lord Ruthven; he, however, still persisted in persuading her, that there could be no truth in her fears, though at the same time he wondered at the many coincidences which had all tended to excite a belief in the supernatural power of Lord Ruthven.

Aubrey began to attach himself more and more to Ianthe; her innocence, so contrasted with all the affected virtues of the women among whom he had sought for his vision of romance, won his heart; and while he ridiculed the idea of a young man of English habits, marrying an uneducated Greek girl, still he found himself more and more attached to the almost fairy form before him. He would tear himself at times from her, and, forming a plan for some antiquarian research, he would depart, determined not to return until his object was attained; but he always found it impossible to fix his attention upon the ruins around him, whilst in his mind he retained an image that seemed alone the rightful possessor of his thoughts. Ianthe was unconscious of his love, and was ever the same frank infantile being he had first known. She always seemed to part from him with reluctance; but it was because she had no longer any one with whom she could visit her favourite haunts, whilst her guardian was occupied in sketching or uncovering some fragment which had yet escaped the destructive hand of time. She had appealed to her parents on the subject of Vampyres, and they both, with several present, affirmed their existence, pale with horror at the very name. Soon after, Aubrey determined to proceed upon one of his excursions, which was to detain him for a few hours; when they heard the name of the place, they all at once begged of him not to return at night, as he must necessarily pass through a wood, where no Greek would ever remain, after the day had closed, upon any consideration. They described it as the resort of the vampyres in their nocturnal orgies, and denounced the most heavy evils as impending upon him who dared to cross their path. Aubrey made light of their representations, and tried to laugh them out of the idea; but when he saw them shudder at his daring thus to mock a superior, infernal power, the very name of which apparently made their blood freeze, he was silent.

Next morning Aubrey set off upon his excursion unattended; he was surprised to observe the melancholy face of his host, and was concerned to find that his words, mocking the belief of those horrible fiends, had inspired them with such terror. When he was about to depart, Ianthe came to the side of his horse, and earnestly begged of him to return, ere night allowed the power of these beings to be put in action;—he promised. He was, however, so occupied in his research, that he did not perceive that day-light would soon end, and that in the horizon there was one of those specks which, in the warmer climates, so rapidly gather into a tremendous mass, and pour all their rage upon the devoted country.—He at last, however, mounted his horse, determined to make up by speed for his delay: but it was too late. Twilight, in these southern climates, is almost unknown; immediately the sun sets, night begins: and ere he had advanced far, the power of the storm was above—its echoing thunders had scarcely an interval of rest—its thick heavy rain forced its way through the canopying foliage, whilst the blue forked lightning seemed to fall and radiate at his very feet. Suddenly his horse took fright, and he was carried with dreadful rapidity through the entangled forest. The animal at last, through fatigue, stopped, and he found, by the glare of lightning, that he was in the neighbourhood of a hovel that hardly lifted itself up from the masses of dead leaves and brush-wood which surrounded it. Dismounting, he approached, hoping to find some one to guide him to the town, or at least trusting to obtain shelter from the pelting of the storm. As he approached, the thunders, for a moment silent, allowed him to hear the dreadful shrieks of a woman mingling with the stifled, exultant mockery of a laugh, continued in one almost unbroken sound;—he was startled: but, roused by the thunder which again rolled over his head, he, with a sudden effort, forced open the door of the hut. He found himself in utter darkness: the sound, however, guided him. He was apparently unperceived; for, though he called, still the sounds continued, and no notice was taken of him. He found himself in contact with some one, whom he immediately seized; when a voice cried, "Again baffled!" to which a loud laugh succeeded; and he felt himself grappled by one whose strength seemed superhu-man: determined to sell his life as dearly as he could, he strug-gled; but it was in vain: he was lifted from his feet and hurled with enormous force against the ground:—his enemy threw himself upon him, and kneeling upon his breast, had placed his hands upon his throat—when the glare of many torches pene-trating through the hole that gave light in the day, disturbed him;—he instantly rose, and, leaving his prey, rushed through the door, and in a moment the crashing of the branches, as he broke through the wood, was no longer heard. The storm was now still; and Aubrey, incapable of moving, was soon heard by those without. They entered; the light of their torches fell upon the mud walls, and the thatch loaded on every individual straw with heavy flakes of soot. At the desire of Aubrey they searched for her who had attracted him by her cries; he was again left in darkness; but what was his horror, when the light of the torches once more burst upon him, to perceive the airy form of his fair conductress brought in a lifeless corse. He shut his eyes, hoping that it was but a vision arising from his disturbed imagination; but he again saw the same form, when he unclosed them, stretched by his side. There was no colour upon her cheek, not even upon her lip; yet there was a stillness about her face that seemed almost as attaching as the life that once dwelt there:—upon her neck and breast was blood, and upon her throat were the marks of teeth having opened the vein:—to this the men pointed, crying, simultaneously struck with horror, "A Vampyre! a Vampyre!" A litter was quickly formed, and Aubrey was laid by the side of her who had lately been to him the object of so many bright and fairy visions, now fallen with the flower of life that had died within her. He knew not what his thoughts were—his mind was benumbed and seemed to shun reflection, and take refuge in vacancy—he held almost unconsciously in his hand a naked dagger of a particular construction, which had been found in the hut. They were soon met by different parties who had been engaged in the search of her whom a mother had missed. Their lamentable cries, as they approached the city, forewarned the parents of some dreadful catastrophe. —To describe their grief would be impossible; but when they ascertained the cause of their child's death, they looked at Aubrey, and pointed to the corse. They were inconsolable; both died broken-hearted.

Aubrey being put to bed was seized with a most violent fever, and was often delirious; in these intervals he would call upon Lord Ruthven and upon Ianthe—by some unaccountable combination he seemed to beg of his former companion to spare the being he loved. At other times he would imprecate maledictions upon his head, and curse him as her destroyer.

Lord Ruthven, chanced at this time to arrive at Athens, and, from whatever motive, upon hearing of the state of Aubrey, immediately placed himself in the same house, and became his constant attendant. When the latter recovered from his delirium, he was horrified and startled at the sight of him whose image he had now combined with that of a Vampyre; but Lord Ruthven, by his kind words, implying almost repentance for the fault that had caused their separation, and still more by the attention, anxiety, and care which he showed, soon reconciled him to his presence. His lordship seemed quite changed; he no longer appeared that apathetic being who had so astonished Aubrey; but as soon as his convalescence began to be rapid, he again gradually retired into the same state of mind, and Aubrey perceived no difference from the former man, except that at times he was surprised to meet his gaze fixed intently upon him, with a smile of malicious exultation playing upon his lips: he knew not why, but this smile haunted him. During the last stage of the invalid's recovery, Lord Ruthven was apparently engaged in watching the tideless waves raised by the cooling breeze, or in marking the progress of those orbs, circling, like our world, the moveless sun;—indeed, he appeared to wish to avoid the eyes of all.

Aubrey's mind, by this shock, was much weakened, and that elasticity of spirit which had once so distinguished him now seemed to have fled for ever. He was now as much a lover of solitude and silence as Lord Ruthven; but much as he wished for solitude, his mind could not find it in the neighbourhood of Athens; if he sought it amidst the ruins he had formerly frequented, Ianthe's form stood by his side—if he sought it in the woods, her light step would appear wandering amidst the underwood, in quest of the modest violet; then suddenly turning round, would show, to his wild imagination, her pale face and wounded throat, with a meek smile upon her lips. He determined to fly scenes, every feature of which created such bitter associations in his mind. He proposed to Lord Ruthven, to whom he held himself bound by the tender care he had taken of him during his illness, that they should visit those parts of Greece neither had yet seen. They travelled in every direction, and sought every spot to which a recollection could be attached: but though they thus hastened from place to place, yet they seemed not to heed what they gazed upon. They heard much of robbers, but they gradually began to slight these reports, which they imagined were only the invention of individuals, whose interest it was to excite the generosity of those whom they defended from pretended dangers. In consequence of thus neglecting the advice of the inhabitants, on one occasion they travelled with only a few guards, more to serve as guides than as a defence. Upon entering, however, a narrow defile, at the bottom of which was the bed of a torrent, with large masses of rock brought down from the neighbouring precipices, they had reason to repent their negligence; for scarcely were the whole of the party engaged in the narrow pass, when they were startled by the whistling of bullets close to their heads, and by the echoed report of several guns. In an instant their guards had left them, and, placing themselves behind rocks, had begun to fire in the direction whence the report came. Lord Ruthven and Aubrey, imitating their example, retired for a moment behind the sheltering turn of the defile: but ashamed of being thus detained by a foe, who with insulting shouts bade them advance, and being exposed to unresisting slaughter, if any of the robbers should climb above and take them in the rear, they determined at once to rush forward in search of the enemy. Hardly had they lost the shelter of the rock, when Lord Ruthven received a shot in the shoulder, which brought him to the ground. Aubrey hastened to his assistance; and, no longer heeding the contest or his own peril, was soon surprised by seeing the robbers' faces around him— his guards having, upon Lord Ruthven's being wounded, immediately thrown up their arms and surrendered.

By promises of great reward, Aubrey soon induced them to convey his wounded friend to a neighbouring cabin; and having agreed upon a ransom, he was no more disturbed by their presence—they being content merely to guard the entrance till their comrade should return with the promised sum, for which he had an order. Lord Ruthven's strength rapidly decreased; in two days mortification ensued, and death seemed advancing with hasty steps. His conduct and appearance had not changed; he seemed as unconscious of pain as he had been of the objects about him: but towards the close of the last evening, his mind became apparently uneasy, and his eye often fixed upon Aubrey, who was induced to offer his assistance with more than usual earnestness—"Assist me! you may save me—you may do more than that—I mean not my life, I heed the death of my existence as little as that of the passing day; but you may save my honour, your friend's honour."—"How? tell me how? I would do any thing," replied Aubrey.—"I need but little—my life ebbs apace—I cannot explain the whole—but if you would conceal all you know of me, my honour were free from stain in the world's mouth—and if my death were unknown for some time in England—I—I—but life."—"It shall not be known."—"Swear!" cried the dying man, raising himself with exultant violence, "Swear by all your soul reveres, by all your nature fears, swear that, for a year and a day you will not impart your knowledge of my crimes or death to any living being in any way, whatever may happen, or whatever you may see. "—His eyes seemed bursting from their sockets: "I swear!" said Aubrey; he sunk laughing upon his pillow, and breathed no more.

Aubrey retired to rest, but did not sleep; the many circumstances attending his acquaintance with this man rose upon his mind, and he knew not why; when he remembered his oath a cold shivering came over him, as if from the presentiment of something horrible awaiting him. Rising early in the morning, he was about to enter the hovel in which he had left the corpse, when a robber met him, and informed him that it was no longer there, having been conveyed by himself and comrades, upon his retiring, to the pinnacle of a neighbouring mount, according to a promise they had given his lordship, that it should be exposed to the first cold ray of the moon that rose after his death. Aubrey astonished, and taking several of the men, determined to go and bury it upon the spot where it lay.

But, when he had mounted to the summit he found no trace of either the corpse or the clothes, though the robbers swore they pointed out the identical rock on which they had laid the body. For a time his mind was bewildered in conjectures, but he at last returned, convinced that they had buried the corpse for the sake of the clothes.

Weary of a country in which he had met with such terrible misfortunes, and in which all apparently conspired to heighten that superstitious melancholy that had seized upon his mind, he resolved to leave it, and soon arrived at Smyrna. While waiting for a vessel to convey him to Otranto, or to Naples, he occupied himself in arranging those effects he had with him belonging to Lord Ruthven. Amongst other things there was a case containing several weapons of offence, more or less adapted to ensure the death of the victim. There were several daggers and ataghans. Whilst turning them over, and examining their curious forms, what was his surprise at finding a sheath apparently ornamented in the same style as the dagger discovered in the fatal hut—he shuddered—hastening to gain further proof, he found the weapon, and his horror may be imagined when he discovered that it fitted, though peculiarly shaped, the sheath he held in his hand. His eyes seemed to need no further certainty—they seemed gazing to be bound to the dagger; yet still he wished to disbelieve; but the particular form, the same varying tints upon the haft and sheath were alike in splendour on both, and left no room for doubt; there were also drops of blood on each.

He left Smyrna, and on his way home, at Rome, his first inquiries were concerning the lady he had attempted to snatch from Lord Ruthven's seductive arts. Her parents were in distress, their fortune ruined, and she had not been heard of since the departure of his lordship. Aubrey's mind became almost broken under so many repeated horrors; he was afraid that this lady had fallen a victim to the destroyer of Ianthe. He became morose and silent; and his only occupation consisted in urging the speed of the postilions, as if he were going to save the life of some one he held dear. He arrived at Calais; a breeze, which seemed obedient to his will, soon wafted him to the English shores; and he hastened to the mansion of his fathers, and there, for a moment, appeared to lose, in the embraces and caresses of his sister, all memory of the past. If she before, by her infantine caresses, had gained his affection, now that the woman began to appear, she was still more attaching as a companion.

Miss Aubrey had not that winning grace which gains the gaze and applause of the drawing-room assemblies. There was none of that light brilliancy which only exists in the heated atmosphere of a crowded apartment. Her blue eye was never lit up by the levity of the mind beneath. There was a melancholy charm about it which did not seem to arise from misfortune, but from some feeling within, that appeared to indicate a soul conscious of a brighter realm. Her step was not that light foot-ing, which strays where'er a butterfly or a colour may attract— it was sedate and pensive. When alone, her face was never brightened by the smile of joy; but when her brother breathed to her his affection, and would in her presence forget those griefs she knew destroyed his rest, who would have exchanged her smile for that of the voluptuary? It seemed as if those eyes, —that face were then playing in the light of their own native sphere. She was yet only eighteen, and had not been presented to the world, it having been thought by her guardians more fit that her presentation should be delayed until her brother's return from the continent, when he might be her protector. It was now, therefore, resolved that the next drawing-room, which was fast approaching, should be the epoch of her entry into the "busy scene." Aubrey would rather have remained in the mansion of his fathers, and fed upon the melancholy which overpowered him. He could not feel interest about the frivoli-ties of fashionable strangers, when his mind had been so torn by the events he had witnessed; but he determined to sacrifice his own comfort to the protection of his sister. They soon arrived in town, and prepared for the next day, which had been announced as a drawing-room.

The crowd was excessive—a drawing-room had not been

held for a long time, and all who were anxious to bask in the smile of royalty, hastened thither. Aubrey was there with his sister. While he was standing in a corner by himself, heedless of all around him, engaged in the remembrance that the first time he had seen Lord Ruthven was in that very place—he felt himself suddenly seized by the arm, and a voice he recognized too well, sounded in his ear—"Remember your oath." He had hardly courage to turn, fearful of seeing a spectre that would blast him, when he perceived, at a little distance, the same figure which had attracted his notice on this spot upon his first entry into society. He gazed till his limbs almost refusing to bear their weight, he was obliged to take the arm of a friend, and forcing a passage through the crowd, he threw himself into his carriage, and was driven home. He paced the room with hurried steps, and fixed his hands upon his head, as if he were afraid his thoughts were bursting from his brain. Lord Ruthven again before him—circumstances started up in dreadful array—the dagger—his oath.—He roused himself, he could not believe it possible—the dead rise again!—He thought his imagination had conjured up the image his mind was resting upon. It was impossible that it could be real—he determined, therefore, to go again into society; for though he attempted to ask concerning Lord Ruthven, the name hung upon his lips, and he could not succeed in gaining information. He went a few nights after with his sister to the assembly of a near relation. Leaving her under the protection of a matron, he retired into a recess, and there gave himself up to his own devouring thoughts. Perceiving, at last, that many were leaving, he roused himself, and entering another room, found his sister surrounded by several, apparently in earnest conversation; he attempted to pass and get near her, when one, whom he requested to move, turned round, and revealed to him those features he most abhorred. He sprang forward, seized his sister's arm, and, with hurried step, forced her towards the street: at the door he found himself impeded by the crowd of servants who were waiting for their lords; and while he was engaged in passing them, he again heard that voice whisper close to him—"Remember your oath!"—He did not dare to turn, but, hurrying his sister, soon reached home.

Aubrey became almost distracted. If before his mind had been absorbed by one subject, how much more completely was it engrossed, now that the certainty of the monster's living again pressed upon his thoughts. His sister's attentions were now unheeded, and it was in vain that she intreated him to explain to her what had caused his abrupt conduct. He only uttered a few words, and those terrified her. The more he thought, the more he was bewildered. His oath startled him;—was he then to allow this monster to roam, bearing ruin upon his breath, amidst all he held dear, and not avert its progress? His very sister might have been touched by him. But even if he were to break his oath, and disclose his suspicions, who would believe him? He thought of employing his own hand to free the world from such a wretch; but death, he remembered, had been already mocked. For days he remained in this state; shut up in his room, he saw no one, and ate only when his sister came, who, with eyes streaming with tears, besought him, for her sake, to support nature. At last, no longer capable of bearing stillness and solitude, he left his house, roamed from street to street, anxious to fly that image which haunted him. His dress became neglected, and he wandered, as often exposed to the noon-day sun as to the midnight damps. He was no longer to be recognized; at first he returned with the evening to the house; but at last he laid him down to rest wherever fatigue overtook him. His sister, anxious for his safety, employed people to follow him; but they were soon distanced by him who fled from a pursuer swifter than any—from thought. His conduct, however, suddenly changed. Struck with the idea that he left by his absence the whole of his friends, with a fiend amongst them, of whose presence they were unconscious, he determined to enter again into society, and watch him closely, anxious to forewarn, in spite of his oath, all whom Lord Ruthven approached with intimacy. But when he entered into a room, his haggard and suspicious looks were so striking, his inward shudderings so visible, that his sister was at last obliged to beg of him to abstain from seeking, for her sake, a society which affected him so strongly. When, however, remonstrance proved unavailing, the guardians thought proper to interpose, and, fearing that his mind was becoming alienated, they thought it high time to resume again that trust which had been before imposed upon them by Aubrey's parents.

Desirous of saving him from the injuries and sufferings he had daily encountered in his wanderings, and of preventing him from exposing to the general eye those marks of what they considered folly, they engaged a physician to reside in the house, and take constant care of him. He hardly appeared to notice it, so completely was his mind absorbed by one terrible subject. His incoherence became at last so great, that he was confined to his chamber. There he would often lie for days, incapable of being roused. He had become emaciated, his eyes had attained a glassy lustre;—the only sign of affection and recollection remaining displayed itself upon the entry of his sister; then he would sometimes start, and, seizing her hands, with looks that severely afflicted her, he would desire her not to touch him. "Oh, do not touch him—if your love for me is aught, do not go near him!" When, however, she inquired to whom he referred, his only answer was, "True! true!" and again he sank into a state, whence not even she could rouse him. This lasted many months: gradually, however, as the year was passing, his incoherences became less frequent, and his mind threw off a portion of its gloom, whilst his guardians observed, that several times in the day he would count upon his fingers a definite number, and then smile.

The time had nearly elapsed, when, upon the last day of the year, one of his guardians entering his room, began to converse with his physician upon the melancholy circumstance of Aubrey's being in so awful a situation, when his sister was going next day to be married. Instantly Aubrey's attention was attracted; he asked anxiously to whom. Glad of this mark of returning intellect, of which they feared he had been deprived, they mentioned the name of the Earl of Marsden. Thinking this was a young Earl whom he had met with in society, Aubrey seemed pleased, and astonished them still more by his expressing his intention to be present at the nuptials, and desiring to see his sister. They answered not, but in a few minutes his sister was with him. He was apparently again capable of being affected by the influence of her lovely smile; for he pressed her to his breast, and kissed her cheek, wet with tears, flowing at the thought of her brother's being once more alive to the feelings of affection. He began to speak with all his wonted warmth, and to congratulate her upon her marriage with a person so distinguished for rank and every accomplishment; when he suddenly perceived a locket upon her breast; opening it, what was his surprise at beholding the features of the monster who had so long influenced his life. He seized the portrait in a paroxysm of rage, and trampled it under foot. Upon her asking him why he thus destroyed the resemblance of her future husband, he looked as if he did not understand her —then seizing her hands, and gazing on her with a frantic expression of countenance, he bade her swear that she would never wed this monster, for he—— But he could not advance —it seemed as if that voice again bade him remember his oath —he turned suddenly round, thinking Lord Ruthven was near him but saw no one. In the meantime the guardians and physician, who had heard the whole, and thought this was but a return of his disorder, entered, and forcing him from Miss Aubrey, desired her to leave him. He fell upon his knees to them, he implored, he begged of them to delay but for one day. They, attributing this to the insanity they imagined had taken possession of his mind, endeavoured to pacify him, and retired.

Lord Ruthven had called the morning after the drawing-room, and had been refused with every one else. When he heard of Aubrey's ill health, he readily understood himself to be the cause of it; but when he learned that he was deemed insane, his exultation and pleasure could hardly be concealed from those among whom he had gained this information. He hastened to the house of his former companion, and, by constant attendance, and the pretence of great affection for the brother and interest in his fate, he gradually won the ear of

Miss Aubrey. Who could resist his power? His tongue had dangers and toils to recount—could speak of himself as of an individual having no sympathy with any being on the crowded earth, save with her to whom he addressed himself;—could tell how, since he knew her, his existence, had begun to seem worthy of preservation, if it were merely that he might listen to her soothing accents;—in fine, he knew so well how to use the serpent's art, or such was the will of fate, that he gained her affections. The title of the elder branch falling at length to him, he obtained an important embassy, which served as an excuse for hastening the marriage, (in spite of her brother's deranged state,) which was to take place the very day before his departure for the continent.

Aubrey, when he was left by the physician and his guardians, attempted to bribe the servants, but in vain. He asked for pen and paper; it was given him; he wrote a letter to his sister, conjuring her, as she valued her own happiness, her own honour, and the honour of those now in the grave, who once held her in their arms as their hope and the hope of their house, to delay but for a few hours that marriage, on which he denounced the most heavy curses. The servants promised they would deliver it; but giving it to the physician, he thought it better not to harass any more the mind of Miss Aubrey by, what he considered, the ravings of a maniac. Night passed on without rest to the busy inmates of the house; and Aubrey heard, with a horror that may more easily be conceived than described, the notes of busy preparation. Morning came, and the sound of carriages broke upon his ear. Aubrey grew almost frantic. The curiosity of the servants at last overcame their vigilance, they gradually stole away, leaving him in the custody of an helpless old woman. He seized the opportunity, with one bound was out of the room, and in a moment found himself in the apartment where all were nearly assembled. Lord Ruthven was the first to perceive him: he immediately approached, and, taking his arm by force, hurried him from the room, speechless with rage. When on the staircase, Lord Ruthven whispered in his ear—"Remember your oath, and know, if not my bride to day, your sister is dishonoured. Women are frail!" So saying, he pushed him towards his attendants, who, roused by the old woman, had come in search of him. Aubrey could no longer support himself; his rage not finding vent, had broken a blood-vessel, and he was conveyed to bed. This was not mentioned to his sister, who was not present when he entered, as the physician was afraid of agitating her. The marriage was solemnized, and the bride and bridegroom left London.

Aubrey's weakness increased; the effusion of blood produced symptoms of the near approach of death. He desired his sister's guardians might be called, and when the midnight hour had struck, he related composedly what the reader has perused—he died immediately after.

The guardians hastened to protect Miss Aubrey; but when they arrived, it was too late. Lord Ruthven had disappeared, and Aubrey's sister had glutted the thirst of a VAMPYRE!

EXTRACT OF A LETTER, CONTAINING AN ACCOUNT OF LORD BYRON'S RESIDENCE

In The
Island Of Mitylene.

"The world was all before him, where to choose his place of rest, and Providence his guide."

IN Sailing through the Grecian Archipelago, on board one of his Majesty's vessels, in the year 1812, we put into the harbour of Mitylene, in the island of that name. The beauty of this place, and the certain supply of cattle and vegetables always to be had there, induce many British vessels to visit it—both men of war and merchantmen; and though it lies rather out of the track for ships bound to Smyrna, its bounties amply repay for the deviation of a voyage. We landed; as usual, at the bottom of the bay, and whilst the men were employed in watering, and the purser bargaining for cattle with the natives, the clergyman and myself took a ramble to the cave called Homer's School, and other places, where we had been before. On the brow of Mount Ida (a small monticule so named) we met with and engaged a young Greek as our guide, who told us he had come from Scio with an English lord, who left the island four days previous to our arrival in his felucca. "He engaged me as a pilot," said the Greek, "and would have taken me with him; but I did not choose to quit Mitylene, where I am likely to get married. He was an odd, but a very good man. The cottage over the hill, facing the river, belongs to him, and he has left an old man in charge of it: he gave Dominick, the wine-trader, six hundred zechines for it, (about L250 English currency,) and has resided there about fourteen months, though not constantly; for he sails in his felucca very often to the different islands."

This account excited our curiosity very much, and we lost no time in hastening to the house where our countryman had resided. We were kindly received by an old man, who conducted us over the mansion. It consisted of four apartments on the ground-floor—an entrance hall, a drawing-room, a sitting parlour, and a bed-room, with a spacious closet annexed. They were all simply decorated: plain green-stained walls, marble tables on either side, a large myrtle in the centre, and a small fountain beneath, which could be made to play through the branches by moving a spring fixed in the side of a small bronze Venus in a leaning posture; a large couch or sofa completed the furniture. In the hall stood half a dozen English cane chairs, and an empty book-case: there were no mirrors, nor a single painting. The bedchamber had merely a large mattress spread on the floor, with two stuffed cotton quilts and a pillow—the common bed throughout Greece. In the sitting-room we observed a marble recess, formerly, the old man told us, filled with books and papers, which were then in a large seaman's chest in the closet: it was open, but we did not think ourselves justified in examining the contents. On the tablet of the recess lay Voltaire's, Shakspeare's, Boileau's, and Rousseau's works complete; Volney's Ruins of Empires; Zimmerman, in the German language; Klopstock's Messiah; Kotzebue's novels; Schiller's play of the Robbers; Milton's Paradise Lost, an

Italian edition, printed at Parma in 1810; several small pamphlets from the Greek press at Constantinople, much torn, but no English book of any description. Most of these books were filled with marginal notes, written with a pencil, in Italian and Latin. The Messiah was literally scribbled all over, and marked with slips of paper, on which also were remarks.

The old man said: "The lord had been reading these books the evening before he sailed, and forgot to place them with the others; but," said he, "there they must lie until his return; for he is so particular, that were I to move one thing without orders, he would frown upon me for a week together; he is otherways very good. I once did him a service; and I have the produce of this farm for the trouble of taking care of it, except twenty zechines which I pay to an aged Armenian who resides in a small cottage in the wood, and whom the lord brought here from Adrianople; I don't know for what reason."

The appearance of the house externally was pleasing. The portico in front was fifty paces long and fourteen broad, and the fluted marble pillars with black plinths and fret-work cornices, (as it is now customary in Grecian architecture,) were considerably higher than the roof. The roof, surrounded by a light stone balustrade, was covered by a fine Turkey carpet, beneath an awning of strong coarse linen. Most of the house-tops are thus furnished, as upon them the Greeks pass their evenings in smoking, drinking light wines, such as "lachryma christi," eating fruit, and enjoying the evening breeze.

On the left hand as we entered the house, a small streamlet glided away, grapes, oranges and limes were clustering together on its borders, and under the shade of two large myrtle bushes, a marble seat with an ornamental wooden back was placed, on which we were told, the lord passed many of his evenings and nights till twelve o'clock, reading, writing, and talking to himself. "I suppose," said the old man, "praying" for he was very devout, "and always attended our church twice a week, besides Sundays."

The view from this seat was what may be termed "a bird's-eye view." A line of rich vineyards led the eye to Mount Calcla, covered with olive and myrtle trees in bloom, and on the summit of which an ancient Greek temple appeared in majestic decay. A small stream issuing from the ruins descended in broken cascades, until it was lost in the woods near the mountain's base. The sea smooth as glass, and an horizon unshadowed by a single cloud, terminates the view in front; and a little on the left, through a vista of lofty chesnut and palm-trees, several small islands were distinctly observed, studding the light blue wave with spots of emerald green. I seldom enjoyed a view more than I did this; but our enquiries were fruitless as to the name of the person who had resided in this romantic solitude: none knew his name but Dominick, his banker, who had gone to Candia. "The Armenian," said our conductor, "could tell, but I am sure he will not,"—"And cannot you tell, old friend?" said I—"If I can," said he, "I dare not." We had not time to visit the Armenian, but on our return to the town we learnt several particulars of the isolated lord. He had portioned eight young girls when he was last upon the island, and even danced with them at the nuptial feast. He gave a cow to one man, horses to others, and cotton and silk to the girls who live by weaving these articles. He also bought a new boat for a fisherman who had lost his own in a gale, and he often gave Greek Testaments to the poor children. In short, he appeared to us, from all we collected, to have been a very eccentric and benevolent character. One circumstance we learnt, which our old friend at the cottage thought proper not to disclose. He had a most beautiful daughter, with whom the lord was often seen walking on the sea-shore, and he had bought her a piano-forte, and taught her himself the use of it.

Such was the information with which we departed from the peaceful isle of Mitylene; our imaginations all on the rack, guessing who this rambler in Greece could be. He had money it was evident: he had philanthropy of disposition, and all those eccentricities which mark peculiar genius. Arrived at Palermo, all our doubts were dispelled. Falling in company with Mr. FOSTER, the architect, a pupil of WYATT'S, who had been travelling in Egypt and Greece, "The individual," said he, "about whom you are so anxious, is Lord Byron; I met him in my travels on the island of Tenedos, and I also visited him at Mitylene." We had never then heard of his lordship's fame, as we had been some years from home; but "Childe Harolde" being put into our hands we recognized the recluse of Calcla in every page. Deeply did we regret not having been more curious in our researches at the cottage, but we consoled ourselves with the idea of returning to Mitylene on some future day; but to me that day will never return. I make this statement, believing it not quite uninteresting, and in justice to his lordship's good name, which has been grossly slandered. He has been described as of an unfeeling disposition, averse to associating with human nature, or contributing in any way to sooth its sorrows, or add to its pleasures. The fact is directly the reverse, as may be plainly gathered from these little anecdotes. All the finer feelings of the heart, so elegantly depicted in his lordship's poems, seem to have their seat in his bosom. Tenderness, sympathy, and charity appear to guide all his actions: and his courting the repose of solitude is an additional reason for marking him as a being on whose heart Religion hath set her seal, and over whose head Benevolence hath thrown her mantle. No man can read the preceding pleasing "traits" without feeling proud of him as a countryman. With respect to his loves or pleasures, I do not assume a right to give an opinion. Reports are ever to be received with caution, particularly when directed against man's moral integrity; and he who dares justify himself before that awful tribunal where all must appear, alone may censure the errors of a fellow-mortal. Lord Byron's character is worthy of his genius. To do good in secret, and shun the world's applause, is the surest testimony of a virtuous heart and self-approving conscience.

The End
Gillet, Printer, Crown-court, Fleet-street.

Although not mentioned on the cover, the following story was published in this October 1936 issue of Weird Tales Magazine.

Doom of the House of Duryea

by Earl Peirce

Earl Peirce Jr. (1917-1983) was an American writer who history has largely forgotten. (And yes, we're sure he spelled his last name that way.) But one story that is sure to live on is his vampire tale "Doom of the House of Durea." According to the blog "Tellers of Weird Tales," Peirce's story first was published in "Weird Tales" magazine in 1936. The story takes place in Maine, which is territory Stephen King would eventually claim, of course. But Peirce's tale came first and is a fun read.

Doom of the House of Duryea

By EARL PEIRCE, JR.

ONE

Arthur Duryea, a young, handsome man, came to meet his father for the first time in twenty years. As he strode into the hotel lobby—long strides which had the spring of elastic in them—idle eyes lifted to appraise him, for he was an impressive figure, somehow grim with exaltation.

The desk clerk looked up with his habitual smile of expectation; how-do-you-do-Mr.-so-and-so, and his fingers strayed to the green fountain pen which stood in a holder on the desk.

Arthur Duryea cleared his throat, but still his voice was clogged and unsteady. To the clerk he said:

"I'm looking for my father, Doctor Henry Duryea. I understand he is registered here. He has recently arrived from Paris."

The clerk lowered his glance to a list of names. "Doctor Duryea is in suite 600, sixth floor." He looked up, his eyebrows arched questioningly. "Are you staying too, sir, Mr. Duryea?"

Arthur took the pen and scribbled his name rapidly. Without a further word, neglecting even to get his key and own room number, he turned and walked to the elevators. Not until he reached his father's suite on the sixth floor did he make an audible noise, and this was a mere sigh which fell from his lips like a prayer.

The man who opened the door was unusually tall, his slender frame clothed in tight-fitting black. He hardly dared to smile. His clean-shaven face was pale, an almost livid whiteness against the sparkle in his eyes. His jaw had a bluish luster.

"Arthur!" The word was scarcely a whisper. It seemed choked up quietly, as if it had been repeated time and again on his thin lips.

Arthur Duryea felt the kindliness of those eyes go through him, and then he was in his father's embrace.

Later, when these two grown men had regained their outer calm, they closed the door and went into the drawing-room. The elder Duryea held out a humidor of fine cigars, and his hand shook so hard when he held the match that his son was forced to cup his own hands about the flame. They both had tears in their eyes, but their eyes were smiling.

Henry Duryea placed a hand on his son's shoulder. "This is the happiest day of my life," he said. "You can never know how much I have longed for this moment."

Arthur, looking into that glance, realized, with growing pride, that he had loved his father all his life, despite any of those things which had been cursed against him. He sat down on the edge of a chair.

"I—I don't know how to act," he confessed. "You surprize me, Dad. You're so different from what I had expected."

A cloud came over Doctor Duryea's features. "What *did* you expect, Arthur?" he demanded quickly. "An evil eye? A shaven head and knotted jowls?"

"Please, Dad—no!" Arthur's words clipped short. "I don't think I ever really visualized you. I knew you would be a splendid man. But I thought you'd look older, more like a man who has really suffered."

"I have suffered, more than I can ever describe. But seeing you again, and the prospect of spending the rest of my life with you, has more than compensated for my sorrows. Even during the twenty years we were apart I found an ironic joy in learning of your progress in college, and in your American game of football."

"Then you've been following my work?"

"Yes, Arthur; I've received monthly reports ever since you left me. From my study in Paris I've been really close to you, working out your problems as if they were my own. And now that the twenty years are completed, the ban which kept us apart is lifted for ever. From now on, son, we shall be the closest of companions—unless your Aunt Cecilia has succeeded in her terrible mission."

<hr>

The mention of that name caused an unfamiliar chill to come between the two men. It stood for something, in each of them, which gnawed their minds like a malignancy. But to the younger Duryea, in his intense effort to forget the awful past, her name as well as her madness must be forgotten.

He had no wish to carry on this subject of conversation, for it betrayed an internal weakness which he hated. With forced determination, and a ludicrous lift of his eyebrows, he said,

"Cecilia is dead, and her silly superstition is dead also. From now on, Dad, we're going to enjoy life as we should. Bygones are really bygones in this case."

Doctor Duryea closed his eyes slowly, as though an exquisite pain had gone through him.

"Then you have no indignation?" he questioned. "You have none of your aunt's hatred?"

"Indignation? Hatred?" Arthur laughed aloud. "Ever since I was twelve years old I have disbelieved Cecilia's stories. I have known that those horrible things were impossible, that they belonged to the ancient category of mythology and tradition. How, then, can I be indignant, and how can I hate you? How can I do anything but recognize Cecilia for what she was—a mean, frustrated woman, cursed with an insane grudge against you and your family? I tell you, Dad, that nothing she has ever said can possibly come between us again."

Henry Duryea nodded his head. His lips were tight together, and the muscles in his throat held back a cry. In that same soft tone of defense he spoke further, doubting words.

"Are you so sure of your subconscious mind, Arthur? Can you be so certain that you are free from all suspicion, however vague? Is there not a lingering premonition—a premonition which warns of peril?"

"No, Dad—no!" Arthur shot to his feet. "I don't believe it. I've never believed it. I know, as any sane man would know, that you are neither a vampire nor a murderer. You know it, too; and Cecilia knew it, only she was mad.

"That family rot is dispelled, Father. This is a civilized century. Belief in vampirism is sheer lunacy. Wh-why, it's too absurd even to think about!"

"You have the enthusiasm of youth," said his father, in a rather tired voice. "But have you not heard the legend?"

Arthur stepped back instinctively. He moistened his lips, for their dryness might crack them. "The—legend?"

He said the word in a curious hush of awed softness, as he had heard his Aunt Cecilia say it many times before.

"That awful legend that you——"

"That I *eat* my children?"

"Oh, God, Father!" Arthur went to his knees as a cry burst through his lips. "Dad, that—that's ghastly! We must forget Cecilia's ravings."

"You are affected, then?" asked Doctor Duryea bitterly.

"Affected? Certainly I'm affected, but only as I should be at such an accusation. Cecilia was mad, I tell you. Those books she showed me years ago, and those folk-tales of vampires and ghouls—they burned into my infantile mind like acid. They haunted me day and night in my youth, and caused me to hate you worse than death itself.

"But in Heaven's name, Father, I've outgrown those things as I have outgrown my clothes. I'm a man now; do you understand that? A man, with a man's sense of logic."

"Yes, I understand." Henry Duryea threw his cigar into the fireplace, and placed a hand on his son's shoulder.

"We shall forget Cecilia," he said. "As I told you in my letter, I have rented a lodge in Maine where we can go to be alone for the rest of the summer. We'll get in some fishing and hiking and perhaps some hunting. But first, Arthur, I must be sure in my own mind that you are sure in yours. I must be sure you won't bar your door against me at night, and sleep with a loaded revolver at your elbow. I must be sure that you're not afraid of going up there alone with me, and dying——"

His voice ended abruptly, as if an age-long dread had taken hold of it. His son's face was waxen, with sweat standing out like pearls on his brow. He said nothing, but his eyes were filled with questions which his lips could not put into words. His own hand touched his father's, and tightened over it.

Henry Duryea drew his hand away.

"I'm sorry," he said, and his eyes looked straight over Arthur's lowered head. "This thing must be thrashed out now. I believe you when you say that you discredit Cecilia's stories, but for a sake greater than sanity I must tell you the truth behind the legend—and believe me, Arthur; there is a truth!"

He climbed to his feet and walked to the window which looked out over the street below. For a moment he gazed into space, silent. Then he turned and looked down at his son.

"You have heard only your aunt's version of the legend, Arthur. Doubtless it was warped into a thing far more hideous than it actually was—if that is possible! Doubtless she spoke to you of the Inquisitorial stake in Carcassonne where one of my ancestors perished. Also she may have mentioned that book, *Vampyrs*, which a former Duryea is supposed to have written. Then certainly she told you about your two younger brothers —my own poor, motherless children—who were sucked bloodless in their cradles...."

Arthur Duryea passed a hand across his aching eyes. Those words, so often repeated by that witch of an aunt, stirred up the same visions which had made his childhood nights sleepless with terror. He could hardly bear to hear them again—and from the very man to whom they were accredited.

"Listen, Arthur," the elder Duryea went on quickly, his voice low with the pain it gave him. "You must know that true basis to your aunt's hatred. You must know of that curse—that curse of vampirism which is supposed to have followed the Duryeas through five centuries of French history, but which we can dispel as pure superstition, so often connected with ancient families. But I must tell you that this part of the legend is true:

"Your two young brothers actually died in their cradles, bloodless. And I stood trial in France for their murder, and my name was smirched throughout all of Europe with such an inhuman damnation that it drove your aunt and you to America, and has left me childless, hated, and ostracized from society the world over.

"I must tell you that on that terrible night in Duryea Castle I had been working late on historic volumes of Crespet and Prinn, and on that loathsome tome, *Vampyrs*. I must tell you of the soreness that was in my throat and of the heaviness of the blood which coursed through my veins.... And of that *presence*, which was neither man nor animal, but which I knew was some place near me, yet neither within the castle nor outside of it, and which was closer to me than my heart and more terrible to me than the touch of the grave....

"I was at the desk in my library, my head swimming in a delirium which left me senseless until dawn. There were nightmares that frightened me—frightened *me*, Arthur, a grown man who had dissected countless cadavers in morgues and medical schools. I know that my tongue was swollen in my mouth and that brine moistened my lips, and that a rottenness pervaded my body like a fever.

"I can make no recollection of sanity or of consciousness. That night remains vivid, unforgettable, yet somehow completely in shadows. When I had fallen asleep—if in God's name it *was* sleep—I was slumped across my desk. But when I awoke in the morning I was lying face down on my couch. So you see, Arthur, I *had* moved during that night, *and I had never known it!*

"What I'd done and where I'd gone during those dark hours will always remain an impenetrable mystery. But I do know this. On the morrow I was torn from my sleep by the shrieks of maids and butlers, and by that mad wailing of your aunt. I stumbled through the open door of my study, and in the nursery I saw those two babies there—lifeless, white and dry like mummies, and with twin holes in their necks that were caked black with their own blood....

"Oh, I don't blame you for your incredulousness, Arthur. I cannot believe it yet myself, nor shall I ever believe it. The belief of it would drive me to suicide; and still the doubting of it drives me mad with horror.

"All of France was doubtful, and even the savants who defended my name at the trial found that they could not explain it nor disbelieve it. The case was quieted by the Repub-lic, for it might have shaken science to its very foundation and split the pedestals of religion and logic. I was released from the charge of murder; but the actual murder has hung about me like a stench.

"The coroners who examined those tiny cadavers found them both dry of all their blood, but could find no blood on the floor of the nursery nor in the cradles. Something from hell stalked the halls of Duryea that night—and I should blow my brains out if I dared to think deeply of who that was. You, too, my son, would have been dead and bloodless if you hadn't been sleeping in a separate room with your door barred on the inside.

"You were a timid child, Arthur. You were only seven years old, but you were filled with the folk-lore of those mad Lombards and the decadent poetry of your aunt. On that same night, while I was some place between heaven and hell, you, also, heard the padded footsteps on the stone corridor and heard the tugging at your door handle, for in the morning you complained of a chill and of terrible nightmares which frightened you in your sleep.... I only thank God that your door was barred!"

Henry Duryea's voice choked into a sob which brought the stinging tears back into his eyes. He paused to wipe his face, and to dig his fingers into his palm.

"You understand, Arthur, that for twenty years, under my sworn oath at the Palace of Justice, I could neither see you nor write to you. Twenty years, my son, while all of that time you had grown to hate me and to spit at my name. Not until your aunt's death have you called yourself a Duryea.... And now you come to me at my bidding, and say you love me as a son should love his father.

"Perhaps it is God's forgiveness for everything. Now, at last, we shall be together, and that terrible, unexplainable past will be buried for ever...."

He put his handkerchief back into his pocket and walked slowly to his son. He dropped to one knee, and his hands gripped Arthur's arms.

"My son, I can say no more to you. I have told you the truth as I alone know it. I may be, by all accounts, some ghoulish creation of Satan on earth. I may be a child-killer, a vampire, some morbidly diseased specimen of *vrykolakas*—things which science cannot explain.

"Perhaps the dreaded legend of the Duryeas is true. Autiel Duryea was convicted of murdering his brother in that same monstrous fashion in the year 1576, and he died in flames at the stake. François Duryea, in 1802, blew his head apart with a blunderbuss on the morning after his youngest son was found dead, apparently from anemia. And there are others, of whom I cannot bear to speak, that would chill your soul if you were to hear them.

"So you see, Arthur, there is a hellish tradition behind our family. There is a heritage which no sane God would ever have allowed. The future of the Duryeas lies in you, for you are the last of the race. I pray with all of my heart that providence will permit you to live your full share of years, and to leave other Duryeas behind you. And so if ever again I feel that presence as I did in Duryea Castle, I am going to die as François Duryea died, over a hundred years ago...."

He stood up, and his son stood up at his side.

"If you are willing to forget, Arthur, we shall go up to that lodge in Maine. There is a life we've never known awaiting us. We must find that life, and we must find the happiness which a curious fate snatched from us on those Lombard sourlands, twenty years ago...."

TWO

Henry Duryea's tall stature, coupled with a slenderness of frame and a sleekness of muscle, gave him an appearance that was unusually *gaunt*. His son couldn't help but think of that word as he sat on the rustic porch of the lodge, watching his father sunning himself at the lake's edge.

Henry Duryea had a kindliness in his face, at times an almost sublime kindliness which great prophets often possess. But when his face was partly in shadows, particularly about his brow, there was a frightening tone which came into his features; for it was a tone of farness, of mysticism and conjuration. Somehow, in the late evenings, he assumed the unapproachable mantle of a dreamer and sat silently before the fire, his mind ever off in unknown places.

In that little lodge there was no electricity, and the glow of the oil lamps played curious tricks with the human expression which frequently resulted in something unhuman. It may have been the dusk of night, the flickering of the lamps, but Arthur Duryea had certainly noticed how his father's eyes had sunken further into his head, and how his cheeks were tighter, and the outline of his teeth pressed into the skin about his lips.

It was nearing sundown on the second day of their stay at Timber Lake. Six miles away the dirt road wound on toward Houlton, near the Canadian border. So it was lonely there, on a solitary little lake hemmed in closely with dark evergreens and a sky which drooped low over dusty-summited mountains.

Within the lodge was a homy fireplace, and a glossy elk's-head which peered out above the mantel. There were guns and fishing-tackle on the walls, shelves of reliable American fiction —Mark Twain, Melville, Stockton, and a well-worn edition of Bret Harte.

A fully supplied kitchen and a wood stove furnished them with hearty meals which were welcome after a whole day's tramp in the woods. On that evening Henry Duryea prepared a select French stew out of every available vegetable, and a can of soup. They ate well, then stretched out before the fire for a smoke. They were outlining a trip to the Orient together, when the back door blew open with a terrific bang, and a wind swept into the lodge with a coldness which chilled them both.

"A storm," Henry Duryea said, rising to his feet. "Sometimes they have them up here, and they're pretty bad. The roof might leak over your bedroom. Perhaps you'd like to sleep down here with me." His fingers strayed playfully over his son's head as he went out into the kitchen to bar the swinging door.

Arthur's room was upstairs, next to a spare room filled with extra furniture. He'd chosen it because he liked the altitude, and because the only other bedroom was occupied....

He went upstairs swiftly and silently. His roof didn't leak; it was absurd even to think it might. It had been his father again, suggesting that they sleep together. He had done it before, in a jesting, whispering way—as if to challenge them both if they *dared* to sleep together.

Arthur came back downstairs dressed in his bath-robe and slippers. He stood on the fifth stair, rubbing a two-day's growth of beard. "I think I'll shave tonight," he said to his father. "May I use your razor?"

Henry Duryea, draped in a black raincoat and with his face haloed in the brim of a rain-hat, looked up from the hall. A frown glided obscurely from his features. "Not at all, son. Sleeping upstairs?"

Arthur nodded, and quickly said, "Are you—going out?"

"Yes, I'm going to tie the boats up tighter. I'm afraid the lake will rough it up a bit."

Duryea jerked back the door and stepped outside. The door slammed shut, and his footsteps sounded on the wood flooring of the porch.

Arthur came slowly down the remaining steps. He saw his father's figure pass across the dark rectangle of a window, saw the flash of lightning that suddenly printed his grim silhouette against the glass.

He sighed deeply, a sigh which burned in his throat; for his throat was sore and aching. Then he went into the bedroom, found the razor lying in plain view on a birch table-top.

As he reached for it, his glance fell upon his father's open Gladstone bag which rested at the foot of the bed. There was a book resting there, half hidden by a gray flannel shirt. It was a narrow, yellow-bound book, oddly out of place.

Frowning, he bent down and lifted it from the bag. It was surprizingly heavy in his hands, and he noticed a faintly sickening odor of decay which drifted from it like a perfume. The title of the volume had been thumbed away into an indecipherable blur of gold letters. But pasted across the front cover was a white strip of paper, on which was typewritten the word—INFANTIPHAGI.

He flipped back the cover and ran his eyes over the title-page. The book was printed in French—an early French—yet to him wholly comprehensible. The publication date was 1580, in Caen.

Breathlessly he turned back a second page, saw a chapter headed, *Vampires*.

He slumped to one elbow across the bed. His eyes were four inches from those mildewed pages, his nostrils reeked with the stench of them.

He skipped long paragraphs of pedantic jargon on theology, he scanned brief accounts of strange, blood-eating monsters, *vrykolakes*, and leprechauns. He read of Jeanne d'Arc, of Ludvig Prinn, and muttered aloud the Latin snatches from *Episcopi*.

He passed pages in quick succession, his fingers shaking with the fear of it and his eyes hanging heavily in their sockets. He saw vague reference to "Enoch," and saw the terrible drawings by an ancient Dominican of Rome....

Paragraph after paragraph he read: the horror-striking testimony of Nider's *Ant-Hill*, the testimony of people who died shrieking at the stake; the recitals of grave-tenders, of jurists and hang-men. Then unexpectedly, among all of this monumental vestige, there appeared before his eyes the name of—

Autiel Duryea; and he stopped reading as though invisibly struck.

Thunder clapped near the lodge and rattled the window-panes. The deep rolling of bursting clouds echoed over the valley. But he heard none of it. His eyes were on those two short sentences which his father—someone—had underlined with dark red crayon.

... The execution, four years ago, of Autiel Duryea does not end the Duryea controversy. Time alone can decide whether the Demon has claimed that family from its beginning to its end....

Arthur read on about the trial of Autiel Duryea before Veniti, the Carcassonnean Inquisitor-General; read, with mounting horror, the evidence which had sent that far-gone Duryea to the pillar—the evidence of a bloodless corpse who had been Autiel Duryea's young brother.

Unmindful now of the tremendous storm which had centered over Timber Lake, unheeding the clatter of windows and the swish of pines on the roof—even of his father who worked down at the lake's edge in a drenching rain—Arthur fastened his glance to the blurred print of those pages, sinking deeper and deeper into the garbled legends of a dark age....

On the last page of the chapter he again saw the name of his ancestor, Autiel Duryea. He traced a shaking finger over the narrow lines of words, and when he finished reading them he rolled sideways on the bed, and from his lips came a sobbing, mumbling prayer.

"God, oh God in Heaven protect me...."

For he had read:

As in the case of Autiel Duryea we observe that this specimen of *vrykolakas* preys only upon the blood in its own family. It possesses none of the characteristics of the undead vampire, being usually a living male person of otherwise normal appearances, unsuspecting its inherent demonism.

But this *vrykolakas* cannot act according to its demoniacal possession unless it is in the presence of a second member of the same family, who acts as a medium between the man and its demon. This medium has none of the traits of the vampire, but it senses the being of this creature (when the metamorphosis is about to occur) by reason of intense pains in the head and throat. Both the vampire and the medium undergo similar reactions, involving nausea, nocturnal visions, and physical disquietude.

When these two outcasts are within a certain distance of each other, the coalescence of inherent demonism is completed, and the vampire is subject to its attacks, demanding blood for its sustenance. No member of the family is safe at these times, for the *vrykolakas*, acting in its true agency on earth, will unerringly seek out the blood. In rare cases, where other victims are unavailable, *the vampire will even take the blood from the very medium which made it possible.*

This vampire is born into certain aged families, and naught but death can destroy it. It is not conscious of its blood-madness, and acts only in a psychic state. The medium, also, is unaware of its terrible rôle; and when these two are together, despite any lapse of years, the fusion of inheritance is so violent that no power known on earth can turn it back.

THREE

The lodge door slammed shut with a sudden, interrupting bang. The lock grated, and Henry Duryea's footsteps sounded on the planked floor.

Arthur shook himself from the bed. He had only time to fling that haunting book into the Gladstone bag before he sensed his father standing in the doorway.

"You—you're not shaving, Arthur." Duryea's words, spliced hesitantly, were toneless. He glanced from the table-top to the Gladstone, and to his son. He said nothing for a moment, his glance inscrutable. Then,

"It's blowing up quite a storm outside."

Arthur swallowed the first words which had come into his throat, nodded quickly. "Yes, isn't it? Quite a storm." He met his father's gaze, his face burning. "I—I don't think I'll shave, Dad. My head aches."

Duryea came swiftly into the room and pinned Arthur's arms in his grasp. "What do you mean—your head aches? How? Does your throat——"

"No!" Arthur jerked himself away. He laughed. "It's that French stew of yours! It's hit me in the stomach!" He stepped past his father and started up the stairs.

"The stew?" Duryea pivoted on his heel. "Possibly. I think I feel it myself."

Arthur stopped, his face suddenly white. "You—too?"

The words were hardly audible. Their glances met—clashed like dueling-swords.

For ten seconds neither of them said a word or moved a muscle: Arthur, from the stairs, looking down; his father below, gazing up at him. In Henry Duryea the blood drained slowly from his face and left a purple etching across the bridge of his nose and above his eyes. He looked like a death's-head.

Arthur winced at the sight and twisted his eyes away. He turned to go up the remaining stairs.

"Son!"

He stopped again; his hand tightened on the banister.

"Yes, Dad?"

Duryea put his foot on the first stair, "I want you to lock your door tonight. The wind would keep it banging!"

"Yes," breathed Arthur, and pushed up the stairs to his room.

Doctor Duryea's hollow footsteps sounded in steady, unhesitant beats across the floor of Timber Lake Lodge. Sometimes they stopped, and the crackling hiss of a sulfur match took their place, then perhaps a distended sigh, and, again, footsteps....

Arthur crouched at the open door of his room. His head was cocked for those noises from below. In his hands was a double-barrel shotgun of violent gage.

... thud ... thud ... thud....

Then a pause, the clinking of a glass and the gurgling of liquid. The sigh, the tread of his feet over the floor....

"He's thirsty," Arthur thought—*Thirsty!*

Outside, the storm had grown into fury. Lightning zigzagged between the mountains, filling the valley with weird phosphorescence. Thunder, like drums, rolled incessantly.

Within the lodge the heat of the fireplace piled the atmosphere thick with stagnation. All the doors and windows were locked shut, the oil-lamps glowed weakly—a pale, anemic light.

Henry Duryea walked to the foot of the stairs and stood looking up.

Arthur sensed his movements and ducked back into his room, the gun gripped in his shaking fingers.

Then Henry Duryea's footstep sounded on the first stair.

Arthur slumped to one knee. He buckled a fist against his teeth as a prayer tumbled through them.

Duryea climbed a second step ... and another ... and still one more. On the fourth stair he stopped.

"Arthur!" His voice cut into the silence like the crack of a whip. "Arthur! Will you come down here?"

"Yes, Dad." Bedraggled, his body hanging like cloth, young Duryea took five steps to the landing.

"We can't be zanies!" cried Henry Duryea. "My soul is sick with dread. Tomorrow we're going back to New York. I'm going to get the first boat to open sea.... Please come down here." He turned about and descended the stairs to his room.

Arthur choked back the words which had lumped in his mouth. Half dazed, he followed....

In the bedroom he saw his father stretched face-up along the bed. He saw a pile of rope at his father's feet.

"Tie me to the bedposts, Arthur," came the command. "Tie both my hands and both my feet."

Arthur stood gaping.

"Do as I tell you!"

"Dad, what hor——"

"Don't be a fool! You read that book! You know what relation you are to me! I'd always hoped it was Cecilia, but now I know it's you. I should have known it on that night twenty years ago when you complained of a headache and nightmares.... Quickly, my head rocks with pain. *Tie me!*"

Speechless, his own pain piercing him with agony, Arthur fell to that grisly task. Both hands he tied—and both feet ... tied them so firmly to the iron posts that his father could not lift himself an inch off the bed.

Then he blew out the lamps, and without a further glance at that Prometheus, he reascended the stairs to his room, and slammed and locked his door behind him.

He looked once at the breech of his gun, and set it against a chair by his bed. He flung off his robe and slippers, and within five minutes he was senseless in slumber.

"He lay like a waxen figure tied to his bed."

The tragedy at Timber Lake was discovered accidentally three days later. A party of fishermen, upon finding the two bodies, notified state authorities, and an investigation was directly under way.

Arthur Duryea had undoubtedly met death at his own hands. The condition of his wounds, and the manner with which he held the lethal weapon, at once foreclosed the suspicion of any foul play.

But the death of Doctor Henry Duryea confronted the police with an inexplicable mystery; for his trussed-up body, unscathed except for two jagged holes over the jugular vein, *had been drained of all its blood.*

The autopsy protocol of Henry Duryea laid death to "undetermined causes," and it was not until the yellow tabloids commenced an investigation into the Duryea family history that the incredible and fantastic explanations were offered to the public.

Obviously such talk was held in popular contempt; yet in view of the controversial war which followed, the authorities considered it expedient to consign both Duryeas to the crematory....

The End

Clarimonde

by Théophile Gautier

Théophile Gautier (1811-1872) was a French writer who is largely unknown today, but according to historians, his influence can be felt in such literary giants as Balzac, T.S. Eliot, Marcel Proust, and Oscar Wilde, among others. Gautier was no stranger to "weird" stories, as he wrote about mummies, devils, and a vampire in "Clarimonde," which is also known as "La Morte amoureuse" ("The Dead Woman in Love"). This tale has a touch of the forbidden in other ways, too, in that it involves a priest who falls in love.

Clarimonde

by Théophile Gautier

Translated By Lafcadio Hearn

Text from 1908 Edition

Brother, you ask me if I have ever loved. Yes. My story is a strange and terrible one; and though I am sixty-six years of age, I scarcely dare even now to disturb the ashes of that memory. To you I can refuse nothing; but I should not relate such a tale to any less experienced mind. So strange were the circumstances of my story, that I can scarcely believe myself to have ever actually been a party to them. For more than three years I remained the victim of a most singular and diabolical illusion. Poor country priest though I was, I led every night in a dream —would to God it had been all a dream!—a most worldly life, a damning life, a life of Sardanapalus. One single look too freely cast upon a woman well-nigh caused me to lose my soul; but finally by the grace of God and the assistance of my patron saint, I succeeded in casting out the evil spirit that possessed me. My daily life was long interwoven with a nocturnal life of a totally different character. By day I was a priest of the Lord, occupied with prayer and sacred things; by night, from the instant that I closed my eyes I became a young nobleman, a fine connoisseur in women, dogs, and horses; gambling, drinking, and blaspheming; and when I awoke at early daybreak, it seemed to me, on the other hand, that I had been sleeping, and had only dreamed that I was a priest. Of this somnambulistic life there now remains to me only the recollection of certain scenes and words which I cannot banish from my memory; but although I never actually left the walls of my presbytery, one would think to hear me speak that I were a man who, weary of all worldly pleasures, had become a religious, seeking to end a tempestuous life in the service of God, rather than a humble seminarist who has grown old in this obscure curacy, situated in the depths of the woods and even isolated from the life of the century.

Yes, I have loved as none in the world ever loved—with an insensate and furious passion—so violent that I am astonished it did not cause my heart to burst asunder. Ah, what nights—what nights!

From my earliest childhood I had felt a vocation to the priesthood, so that all my studies were directed with that idea in view. Up to the age of twenty-four my life had been only a prolonged novitiate. Having completed my course of theology I successively received all the minor orders, and my superiors judged me worthy, despite my youth, to pass the last awful degree. My ordination was fixed for Easter week.

I had never gone into the world. My world was confined by the walls of the college and the seminary. I knew in a vague sort of a way that there was something called Woman, but I never permitted my thoughts to dwell on such a subject, and I lived in a state of perfect innocence. Twice a year only I saw my infirm and aged mother, and in those visits were comprised my sole relations with the outer world.

I regretted nothing; I felt not the least hesitation at taking the last irrevocable step; I was filled with joy and impatience. Never did a betrothed lover count the slow hours with more feverish ardour; I slept only to dream that I was saying mass; I believed there could be nothing in the world more delightful than to be a priest; I would have refused to be a king or a poet in preference. My ambition could conceive of no loftier aim.

I tell you this in order to show you that what happened to me could not have happened in the natural order of things, and to enable you to understand that I was the victim of an inexplicable fascination.

At last the great day came. I walked to the church with a step so light that I fancied myself sustained in air, or that I had wings upon my shoulders. I believed myself an angel, and wondered at the sombre and thoughtful faces of my companions, for there were several of us. I had passed all the night in prayer, and was in a condition wellnigh bordering on ecstasy. The bishop, a venerable old man, seemed to me God the Father leaning over His Eternity, and I beheld Heaven through the vault of the temple.

You well know the details of that ceremony—the benediction, the communion under both forms, the anointing of the palms of the hands with the Oil of Catechumens, and then the holy sacrifice offered in concert with the bishop.

Ah, truly spake Job when he declared that the imprudent man is one who hath not made a covenant with his eyes! I accidentally lifted my head, which until then I had kept down, and beheld before me, so close that it seemed that I could have touched her—although she was actually a considerable distance from me and on the further side of the sanctuary railing—a young woman of extraordinary beauty, and attired with royal magnificence. It seemed as though scales had suddenly fallen from my eyes. I felt like a blind man who unexpectedly recovers his sight. The bishop, so radiantly glorious but an instant before, suddenly vanished away, the tapers paled upon their golden candlesticks like stars in the dawn, and a vast darkness seemed to fill the whole church. The charming creature appeared in bright relief against the background of that darkness, like some angelic revelation. She seemed herself radiant, and radiating light rather than receiving it.

I lowered my eyelids, firmly resolved not to again open them, that I might not be influenced by external objects, for distraction had gradually taken possession of me until I hardly knew what I was doing.

In another minute, nevertheless, I reopened my eyes, for through my eyelashes I still beheld her, all sparkling with prismatic colours, and surrounded with such a penumbra as one beholds in gazing at the sun.

Oh, how beautiful she was! The greatest painters, who followed ideal beauty into heaven itself, and thence brought back to earth the true portrait of the Madonna, never in their delineations even approached that wildly beautiful reality which I saw before me. Neither the verses of the poet nor the palette of the artist could convey any conception of her. She was rather tall, with a form and bearing of a goddess. Her hair, of a soft blonde hue, was parted in the midst and flowed back over her temples in two rivers of rippling gold; she seemed a diademed queen. Her forehead, bluish-white in its transparency, extended its calm breadth above the arches of her eyebrows, which by a strange singularity were almost black, and admirably relieved the effect of sea-green eyes of unsustainable vivacity and brilliancy. What eyes! With a single flash they could have decided a man's destiny. They had a life, a limpidity, an ardour, a humid light which I have never seen in human eyes; they shot forth rays like arrows, which I could distinctly *see* enter my heart. I know not if the fire which illumined them came from heaven or from hell, but assuredly it came from one or the other. That woman was either an angel or a demon, perhaps both. Assuredly she never sprang from the flank of Eve, our common mother. Teeth of the most lustrous pearl gleamed in her ruddy smile, and at every inflection of her lips little dimples appeared in the satiny rose of her adorable cheeks. There was a delicacy and pride in the regal outline of her nostrils bespeaking noble blood. Agate gleams played over the smooth lustrous skin of her half-bare shoulders, and strings of great blonde pearls—almost equal to her neck in beauty of colour—descended upon her bosom. From time to time she elevated her head with the undulating grace of a startled serpent or peacock, thereby imparting a quivering motion to the high lace ruff which surrounded it like a silver trellis-work.

She wore a robe of orange-red velvet, and from her wide ermine-lined sleeves there peeped forth patrician hands of infinite delicacy, and so ideally transparent that, like the fingers of Aurora, they permitted the light to shine through them.

All these details I can recollect at this moment as plainly as though they were of yesterday, for notwithstanding I was greatly troubled at the time, nothing escaped me; the faintest touch of shading, the little dark speck at the point of the chin, the imperceptible down at the corners of the lips, the velvety floss upon the brow, the quivering shadows of the eyelashes upon the cheeks—I could notice everything with astonishing lucidity of perception.

And gazing I felt opening within me gates that had until then remained closed; vents long obstructed became all clear, permitting glimpses of unfamiliar perspectives within; life suddenly made itself visible to me under a totally novel aspect. I felt as though I had just been born into a new world and a new order of things. A frightful anguish commenced to torture my heart as with red-hot pincers. Every successive minute seemed to me at once but a second and yet a century. Meanwhile the ceremony was proceeding, and I shortly found myself transported far from that world of which my newly born desires were furiously besieging the entrance. Nevertheless I answered 'Yes' when I wished to say 'No,' though all within me protested against the violence done to my soul by my tongue. Some occult power seemed to force the words from my throat against my will. Thus it is, perhaps, that so many young girls walk to the altar firmly resolved to refuse in a startling manner the husband imposed upon them, and that yet not one ever fulfils her intention. Thus it is, doubtless, that so many poor novices take the veil, though they have resolved to tear it into shreds at the moment when called upon to utter the vows. One dares not thus cause so great a scandal to all present, nor deceive the expectation of so many people. All those eyes, all those wills seem to weigh down upon you like a cope of lead, and, moreover, measures have been so well taken, everything has been so thoroughly arranged beforehand and after a fashion so evidently irrevocable, that the will yields to the weight of circumstances and utterly breaks down.

As the ceremony proceeded the features of the fair unknown changed their expression. Her look had at first been one of caressing tenderness; it changed to an air of disdain and of mortification, as though at not having been able to make itself understood.

With an effort of will sufficient to have uprooted a mountain, I strove to cry out that I would not be a priest, but I could not speak; my tongue seemed nailed to my palate, and I found it impossible to express my will by the least syllable of negation. Though fully awake, I felt like one under the influence of a nightmare, who vainly strives to shriek out the one word upon which life depends.

She seemed conscious of the martyrdom I was undergoing, and, as though to encourage me, she gave me a look replete with divinest promise. Her eyes were a poem; their every glance was a song.

She said to me:

'If thou wilt be mine, I shall make thee happier than God Himself in His paradise. The angels themselves will be jealous of thee. Tear off that funeral shroud in which thou art about to wrap thyself. I am Beauty, I am Youth, I am Life. Come to me! Together we shall be Love. Can Jehovah offer thee aught in exchange? Our lives will flow on like a dream, in one eternal kiss.

'Fling forth the wine of that chalice, and thou art free. I will conduct thee to the Unknown Isles. Thou shalt sleep in my bosom upon a bed of massy gold under a silver pavilion, for I love thee and would take thee away from thy God, before whom so many noble hearts pour forth floods of love which never reach even the steps of His throne!'

These words seemed to float to my ears in a rhythm of infinite sweetness, for her look was actually sonorous, and the utterances of her eyes were reechoed in the depths of my heart as though living lips had breathed them into my life. I felt myself willing to renounce God, and yet my tongue mechanically fulfilled all the formalities of the ceremony. The fair one gave me another look, so beseeching, so despairing that keen blades seemed to pierce my heart, and I felt my bosom transfixed by more swords than those of Our Lady of Sorrows.

All was consummated; I had become a priest.

Never was deeper anguish painted on human face than

upon hers. The maiden who beholds her affianced lover suddenly fall dead at her side, the mother bending over the empty cradle of her child, Eve seated at the threshold of the gate of Paradise, the miser who finds a stone substituted for his stolen treasure, the poet who accidentally permits the only manuscript of his finest work to fall into the fire, could not wear a look so despairing, so inconsolable. All the blood had abandoned her charming face, leaving it whiter than marble; her beautiful arms hung lifelessly on either side of her body as though their muscles had suddenly relaxed, and she sought the support of a pillar, for her yielding limbs almost betrayed her. As for myself, I staggered toward the door of the church, livid as death, my forehead bathed with a sweat bloodier than that of Calvary; I felt as though I were being strangled; the vault seemed to have flattened down upon my shoulders, and it seemed to me that my head alone sustained the whole weight of the dome.

As I was about to cross the threshold a hand suddenly caught mine—a woman's hand! I had never till then touched the hand of any woman. It was cold as a serpent's skin, and yet its impress remained upon my wrist, burnt there as though branded by a glowing iron. It was she. 'Unhappy man! Unhappy man! What hast thou done?' she exclaimed in a low voice, and immediately disappeared in the crowd.

The aged bishop passed by. He cast a severe and scrutinising look upon me. My face presented the wildest aspect imaginable: I blushed and turned pale alternately; dazzling lights flashed before my eyes. A companion took pity on me. He seized my arm and led me out. I could not possibly have found my way back to the seminary unassisted. At the corner of a street, while the young priest's attention was momentarily turned in another direction, a negro page, fantastically garbed, approached me, and without pausing on his way slipped into my hand a little pocket-book with gold-embroidered corners, at the same time giving me a sign to hide it. I concealed it in my sleeve, and there kept it until I found myself alone in my cell. Then I opened the clasp. There were only two leaves within, bearing the words, 'Clarimonde. At the Concini Palace.' So little acquainted was I at that time with the things of this world that I had never heard of Clarimonde, celebrated as she was, and I had no idea as to where the Concini Palace was situated. I hazarded a thousand conjectures, each more extravagant than the last; but, in truth, I cared little whether she were a great lady or a courtesan, so that I could but see her once more.

My love, although the growth of a single hour, had taken imperishable root. I did not even dream of attempting to tear it up, so fully was I convinced such a thing would be impossible. That woman had completely taken possession of me. One look from her had sufficed to change my very nature. She had breathed her will into my life, and I no longer lived in myself, but in her and for her. I gave myself up to a thousand extravagancies. I kissed the place upon my hand which she had touched, and I repeated her name over and over again for hours in succession. I only needed to close my eyes in order to see her distinctly as though she were actually present; and I reiterated to myself the words she had uttered in my ear at the church porch: 'Unhappy man! Unhappy man! What hast thou done?' I comprehended at last the full horror of my situation, and the funereal and awful restraints of the state into which I had just entered became clearly revealed to me. To be a priest!—that is, to be chaste, to never love, to observe no distinction of sex or age, to turn from the sight of all beauty, to put out one's own eyes, to hide for ever crouching in the chill shadows of some church or cloister, to visit none but the dying, to watch by unknown corpses, and ever bear about with one the black soutane as a garb of mourning for oneself, so that your very dress might serve as a pall for your coffin.

And I felt life rising within me like a subterranean lake, expanding and overflowing; my blood leaped fiercely through my arteries; my long-restrained youth suddenly burst into active being, like the aloe which blooms but once in a hundred years, and then bursts into blossom with a clap of thunder.

What could I do in order to see Clarimonde once more? I had no pretext to offer for desiring to leave the seminary, not knowing any person in the city. I would not even be able to remain there but a short time, and was only waiting my assignment to the curacy which I must thereafter occupy. I tried to remove the bars of the window; but it was at a fearful height from the ground, and I found that as I had no ladder it would be useless to think of escaping thus. And, furthermore, I could descend thence only by night in any event, and afterward how should I be able to find my way through the inextricable labyrinth of streets? All these difficulties, which to many would have appeared altogether insignificant, were gigantic to me, a poor seminarist who had fallen in love only the day before for the first time, without experience, without money, without attire.

'Ah!' cried I to myself in my blindness, 'were I not a priest I could have seen her every day; I might have been her lover, her spouse. Instead of being wrapped in this dismal shroud of mine I would have had garments of silk and velvet, golden chains, a sword, and fair plumes like other handsome young cavaliers. My hair, instead of being dishonoured by the tonsure, would flow down upon my neck in waving curls;

I would have a fine waxed moustache; I would be a gallant.'

But one hour passed before an altar, a few hastily articulated words, had for ever cut me off from the number of the living, and I had myself sealed down the stone of my own tomb; I had with my own hand bolted the gate of my prison! I went to the window. The sky was beautifully blue; the trees had donned their spring robes; nature seemed to be making parade of an ironical joy. The *Place* was filled with people, some going, others coming; young beaux and young beauties were sauntering in couples toward the groves and gardens; merry youths passed by, cheerily trolling refrains of drinking-songs—it was all a picture of vivacity, life, animation, gaiety, which formed a bitter contrast with my mourning and my solitude. On the steps of the gate sat a young mother playing with her child. She kissed its little rosy mouth still impearled with drops of milk, and performed, in order to amuse it, a thousand divine little puerilities such as only mothers know how to invent. The father standing at a little distance smiled gently upon the charming group, and with folded arms seemed to hug his joy to his heart. I could not endure that spectacle. I closed the window with violence, and flung myself on my bed, my heart filled with frightful hate and jealousy, and gnawed my fingers and my bedcovers like a tiger that has passed ten days without food.

I know not how long I remained in this condition, but at last, while writhing on the bed in a fit of spasmodic fury, I suddenly perceived the Abbé Sérapion, who was standing erect in the centre of the room, watching me attentively. Filled with shame of myself, I let my head fall upon my breast and covered my face with my hands.

'Romuald, my friend, something very extraordinary is transpiring within you,' observed Sérapion, after a few moments' silence; 'your conduct is altogether inexplicable. You—always so quiet, so pious, so gentle—you to rage in your cell like a wild beast! Take heed, brother—do not listen to the suggestions of the devil The Evil Spirit, furious that you have consecrated yourself for ever to the Lord, is prowling around you like a ravening wolf and making a last effort to obtain possession of you. Instead of allowing yourself to be conquered, my dear Romuald, make to yourself a cuirass of prayers, a buckler of mortifications, and combat the enemy like a valiant man; you will then assuredly overcome him. Virtue must be proved by temptation, and gold comes forth purer from the hands of the assayer. Fear not. Never allow yourself to become discouraged. The most watchful and steadfast souls are at moments liable to such temptation. Pray, fast, meditate, and the Evil Spirit will depart from you.'

The words of the Abbé Sérapion restored me to myself, and I became a little more calm. 'I came,' he continued, 'to tell you that you have been appointed to the curacy of C———. The priest who had charge of it has just died, and Monseigneur the Bishop has ordered me to have you installed there at once. Be ready, therefore, to start to-morrow.' I responded with an inclination of the head, and the Abbé retired. I opened my missal and commenced reading some prayers, but the letters became confused and blurred under my eyes, the thread of the ideas entangled itself hopelessly in my brain, and the volume at last fell from my hands without my being aware of it.

To leave to-morrow without having been able to see her again, to add yet another barrier to the many already interposed between us, to lose for ever all hope of being able to meet her, except, indeed, through a miracle! Even to write to her, alas! would be impossible, for by whom could I dispatch my letter? With my sacred character of priest, to whom could I dare unbosom myself, in whom could I confide? I became a prey to the bitterest anxiety.

Then suddenly recurred to me the words of the Abbé Séra-pion regarding the artifices of the devil; and the strange character of the adventure, the supernatural beauty of Clarimonde, the phosphoric light of her eyes, the burning imprint of her hand, the agony into which she had thrown me, the sudden change wrought within me when all my piety vanished in a single instant—these and other things clearly testified to the work of the Evil One, and perhaps that satiny hand was but the glove which concealed his claws. Filled with terror at these fancies, I again picked up the missal which had slipped from my knees and fallen upon the floor, and once more gave myself up to prayer.

Next morning Sérapion came to take me away. Two mules freighted with our miserable valises awaited us at the gate. He mounted one, and I the other as well as I knew how.

As we passed along the streets of the city, I gazed attentively at all the windows and balconies in the hope of seeing Clarimonde, but it was yet early in the morning, and the city had hardly opened its eyes. Mine sought to penetrate the blinds and window-curtains of all the palaces before which we were passing. Sérapion doubtless attributed this curiosity to my admiration of the architecture, for he slackened the pace of his animal in order to give me time to look around me. At last we passed the city gates and commenced to mount the hill beyond. When we arrived at its summit I turned to take a last look at the place where Clarimonde dwelt. The shadow of a great cloud hung over all the city; the contrasting colours of its blue and red roofs were lost in the uniform half-tint, through which here and there floated upward, like white flakes of foam, the smoke of freshly kindled fires. By a singular optical effect one edifice, which surpassed in height all the neighbouring buildings that were still dimly veiled by the vapours, towered up, fair and lustrous with the gilding of a solitary beam of sunlight—although actually more than a league away it seemed quite near. The smallest details of its architecture were plainly distinguishable—the turrets, the platforms, the window-casements, and even the swallow-tailed weather-vanes.

'What is that palace I see over there, all lighted up by the sun?' I asked Sérapion. He shaded his eyes with his hand, and having looked in the direction indicated, replied: 'It is the ancient palace which the Prince Concini has given to the courtesan Clarimonde. Awful things are done there!'

At that instant, I know not yet whether it was a reality or an illusion, I fancied I saw gliding along the terrace a shapely white figure, which gleamed for a moment in passing and as quickly vanished. It was Clarimonde.

Oh, did she know that at that very hour, all feverish and restless—from the height of the rugged road which separated me from her, and which, alas! I could never more descend—I was directing my eyes upon the palace where she dwelt, and which a mocking beam of sunlight seemed to bring nigh to me, as though inviting me to enter therein as its lord? Undoubtedly she must have known it, for her soul was too sympathetically united with mine not to have felt its least emotional thrill, and that subtle sympathy it must have been which prompted her to climb—although clad only in her nightdress—to the summit of the terrace, amid the icy dews of the morning.

The shadow gained the palace, and the scene became to the eye only a motionless ocean of roofs and gables, amid which one mountainous undulation was distinctly visible. Sérapion urged his mule forward, my own at once followed at the same gait, and a sharp angle in the road at last hid the city of S ——— for ever from my eyes, as I was destined never to return thither. At the close of a weary three-days' journey through dismal country fields, we caught sight of the cock upon the steeple of the church which I was to take charge of, peeping above the trees, and after having followed some winding roads fringed with thatched cottages and little gardens, we found ourselves in front of the façade, which certainly possessed few features of magnificence. A porch ornamented with some mouldings, and two or three pillars rudely hewn from sandstone; a tiled roof with counterforts of the same sandstone as the pillars—that was all. To the left lay the cemetery, overgrown with high weeds, and having a great iron cross rising up in its centre; to the right stood the presbytery under the shadow of the church. It was a house of the most extreme simplicity and frigid cleanliness. We entered the enclosure. A few chickens were picking up some oats scattered upon the ground; accustomed, seemingly, to the black habit of ecclesiastics, they showed no fear of our presence and scarcely troubled themselves to get out of our way. A hoarse, wheezy barking fell upon our ears, and we saw an aged dog running toward us.

It was my predecessor's dog. He had dull bleared eyes, grizzled hair, and every mark of the greatest age to which a dog can possibly attain. I patted him gently, and he proceeded at once to march along beside me with an air of satisfaction unspeakable. A very old woman, who had been the housekeeper of the former curé, also came to meet us, and after having invited me into a little back parlour, asked whether I intended to retain her. I replied that I would take care of her, and the dog, and the chickens, and all the furniture her master had bequeathed her at his death. At this she became fairly transported with joy, and the Abbé Sérapion at once paid her the price which she asked for her little property.

As soon as my installation was over, the Abbé Sérapion returned to the seminary. I was, therefore, left alone, with no one but myself to look to for aid or counsel. The thought of Clarimonde again began to haunt me, and in spite of all my endeavours to banish it, I always found it present in my meditations. One evening, while promenading in my little garden along the walks bordered with box-plants, I fancied that I saw through the elm-trees the figure of a woman, who followed my every movement, and that I beheld two sea-green eyes gleaming through the foliage; but it was only an illusion, and on going round to the other side of the garden, I could find nothing except a footprint on the sanded walk—a footprint so small that it seemed to have been made by the foot of a child. The garden was enclosed by very high walls. I searched every nook and corner of it, but could discover no one there. I have never succeeded in fully accounting for this circumstance, which, after all, was nothing compared with the strange things which happened to me afterward.

For a whole year I lived thus, filling all the duties of my calling with the most scrupulous exactitude, praying and fasting, exhorting and lending ghostly aid to the sick, and bestowing alms even to the extent of frequently depriving myself of the very necessaries of life. But I felt a great aridness within me, and the sources of grace seemed closed against me. I never found that happiness which should spring from the fulfilment of a holy mission; my thoughts were far away, and the words of Clarimonde were ever upon my lips like an involuntary refrain. Oh, brother, meditate well on this! Through having but once lifted my eyes to look upon a woman, through one fault apparently so venial, I have for years remained a victim to the most miserable agonies, and the happiness of my life has been destroyed for ever.

I will not longer dwell upon those defeats, or on those inward victories invariably followed by yet more terrible falls, but will at once proceed to the facts of my story. One night my door-bell was long and violently rung. The aged housekeeper arose and opened to the stranger, and the figure of a man, whose complexion was deeply bronzed, and who was richly clad in a foreign costume, with a poniard at his girdle, appeared under the rays of Barbara's lantern. Her first impulse was one of terror, but the stranger reassured her, and stated that he desired to see me at once on matters relating to my holy calling. Barbara invited him upstairs, where I was on the point of retiring.

The stranger told me that his mistress, a very noble lady, was lying at the point of death, and desired to see a priest. I replied that I was prepared to follow him, took with me the sacred articles necessary for extreme unction, and descended in all haste. Two horses black as the night itself stood without the gate, pawing the ground with impatience, and veiling their chests with long streams of smoky vapour exhaled from their nostrils. He held the stirrup and aided me to mount upon one; then, merely laying his hand upon the pommel of the saddle, he vaulted on the other, pressed the animal's sides with his knees, and loosened rein. The horse bounded forward with the velocity of an arrow. Mine, of which the stranger held the bridle, also started off at a swift gallop, keeping up with his companion. We devoured the road. The ground flowed backward beneath us in a long streaked line of pale gray, and the black silhouettes of the trees seemed fleeing by us on either side like an army in rout. We passed through a forest so profoundly gloomy that I felt my flesh creep in the chill darkness with superstitious fear. The showers of bright sparks which flew from the stony road under the ironshod feet of our horses remained glowing in our wake like a fiery trail; and had any one at that hour of the night beheld us both—my guide and myself —he must have taken us for two spectres riding upon nightmares. Witch-fires ever and anon flitted across the road before us, and the night-birds shrieked fearsomely in the depth of the woods beyond, where we beheld at intervals glow the phosphorescent eyes of wild cats. The manes of the horses became more and more dishevelled, the sweat streamed over their flanks, and their breath came through their nostrils hard and fast. But when he found them slacking pace, the guide reanimated them by uttering a strange, gutteral, unearthly cry, and the gallop recommenced with fury. At last the whirlwind race ceased; a huge black mass pierced through with many bright points of light suddenly rose before us, the hoofs of our horses echoed louder upon a strong wooden drawbridge, and we rode under a great vaulted archway which darkly yawned between two enormous towers. Some great excitement evidently reigned in the castle. Servants with torches were crossing the courtyard in every direction, and above lights were ascending and descending from landing to landing. I obtained a confused glimpse of vast masses of architecture—columns, arcades, flights of steps, stairways—a royal voluptuousness and elfin magnificence of construction worthy of fairyland. A negro page—the same who had before brought me the tablet from Clarimonde, and whom I instantly recognised—approached to aid me in dismounting, and the major-domo, attired in black velvet with a gold chain about his neck, advanced to meet me, supporting himself upon an ivory cane. Large tears were falling from his eyes and streaming over his cheeks and white beard. 'Too late!' he cried, sorrowfully shaking his venerable head. 'Too late, sir priest! But if you have not been able to save the soul, come at least to watch by the poor body.'

He took my arm and conducted me to the death-chamber. I wept not less bitterly than he, for I had learned that the dead one was none other than that Clarimonde whom I had so deeply and so wildly loved. A *prie-dieu* stood at the foot of the bed; a bluish flame flickering in a bronze patern filled all the room with a wan, deceptive light, here and there bringing out in the darkness at intervals some projection of furniture or cornice.

In a chiselled urn upon the table there was a faded white rose, whose leaves—excepting one that still held—had all fallen, like odorous tears, to the foot of the vase. A broken black mask, a fan, and disguises of every variety, which were lying on the armchairs, bore witness that death had entered suddenly and unannounced into that sumptuous dwelling. Without daring to cast my eyes upon the bed, I knelt down and commenced to repeat the Psalms for the Dead, with exceeding fervour, thanking God that He had placed the tomb between me and the memory of this woman, so that I might thereafter be able to utter her name in my prayers as a name for ever sanctified by death. But my fervour gradually weakened, and I fell insensibly into a reverie. That chamber bore no semblance to a chamber of death. In lieu of the fetid and cadaverous odours which I had been accustomed to breathe during such funereal vigils, a languorous vapour of Oriental perfume—I know not what amorous odour of woman—softly floated through the tepid air. That pale light seemed rather a twilight gloom contrived for voluptuous pleasure, than a substitute for the yellow-flickering watch-tapers which shine by the side of corpses. I thought upon the strange destiny which enabled me to meet Clarimonde again at the very moment when she was lost to me for ever, and a sigh of regretful anguish escaped from my breast. Then it seemed to me that some one behind me had also sighed, and I turned round to look. It was only an echo. But in that moment my eyes fell upon the bed of death which they had till then avoided. The red damask curtains, decorated with large flowers worked in embroidery and looped up with gold bullion, permitted me to behold the fair dead, lying at full length, with hands joined upon her bosom. She was covered with a linen wrapping of dazzling whiteness, which formed a strong contrast with the gloomy purple of the hangings, and was of so fine a texture that it concealed nothing of her body's charming form, and allowed the eye to follow those beautiful outlines—undulating like the neck of a swan—which even death had not robbed of their supple grace. She seemed an alabaster statue executed by some skilful sculptor to place upon the tomb of a queen, or rather, perhaps, like a slumbering maiden over whom the silent snow had woven a spotless veil.

I could no longer maintain my constrained attitude of prayer. The air of the alcove intoxicated me, that febrile perfume of half-faded roses penetrated my very brain, and I commenced to pace restlessly up and down the chamber, pausing at each turn before the bier to contemplate the graceful corpse lying beneath the transparency of its shroud. Wild fancies came thronging to my brain. I thought to myself that she might not, perhaps, be really dead; that she might only have feigned death for the purpose of bringing me to her castle, and then declaring her love. At one time I even thought I saw her foot move under the whiteness of the coverings, and slightly disarrange the long straight folds of the winding-sheet.

And then I asked myself: 'Is this indeed Clarimonde? What proof have I that it is she? Might not that black page have passed into the service of some other lady? Surely, I must be going mad to torture and afflict myself thus!' But my heart answered with a fierce throbbing: 'It is she; it is she indeed!' I approached the bed again, and fixed my eyes with redoubled attention upon the object of my incertitude. Ah, must I confess it? That exquisite perfection of bodily form, although purified and made sacred by the shadow of death, affected me more voluptuously than it should have done; and that repose so closely resembled slumber that one might well have mistaken it for such. I forgot that I had come there to perform a funeral ceremony; I fancied myself a young bridegroom entering the chamber of the bride, who all modestly hides her fair face, and through coyness seeks to keep herself wholly veiled. Heartbroken with grief, yet wild with hope, shuddering at once with fear and pleasure, I bent over her and grasped the corner of the sheet. I lifted it back, holding my breath all the while through fear of waking her. My arteries throbbed with such violence that I felt them hiss through my temples, and the sweat poured from my forehead in streams, as though I had lifted a mighty slab of marble. There, indeed, lay Clarimonde, even as I had seen her at the church on the day of my ordination. She was not less charming than then. With her, death seemed but a last coquetry. The pallor of her cheeks, the less brilliant carnation of her lips,

her long eyelashes lowered and relieving their dark fringe against that white skin, lent her an unspeakably seductive aspect of melancholy chastity and mental suffering; her long loose hair, still intertwined with some little blue flowers, made a shining pillow for her head, and veiled the nudity of her shoulders with its thick ringlets; her beautiful hands, purer, more diaphanous, than the Host, were crossed on her bosom in an attitude of pious rest and silent prayer, which served to counteract all that might have proven otherwise too alluring— even after death—in the exquisite roundness and ivory polish of her bare arms from which the pearl bracelets had not yet been removed. I remained long in mute contemplation, and the more I gazed, the less could I persuade myself that life had really abandoned that beautiful body for ever. I do not know whether it was an illusion or a reflection of the lamplight, but it seemed to me that the blood was again commencing to circulate under that lifeless pallor, although she remained all motionless. I laid my hand lightly on her arm; it was cold, but not colder than her hand on the day when it touched mine at the portals of the church. I resumed my position, bending my face above her, and bathing her cheek with the warm dew of my tears. Ah, what bitter feelings of despair and helplessness,

what agonies unutterable did I endure in that long watch! Vainly did I wish that I could have gathered all my life into one mass that I might give it all to her, and breathe into her chill remains the flame which devoured me. The night advanced, and feeling the moment of eternal separation approach, I could not deny myself the last sad sweet pleasure of imprinting a kiss upon the dead lips of her who had been my only love.... Oh, miracle! A faint breath mingled itself with my breath, and the mouth of Clarimonde responded to the passionate pressure of mine. Her eyes unclosed, and lighted up with something of their former brilliancy; she uttered a long sigh, and uncrossing her arms, passed them around my neck with a look of ineffable delight. 'Ah, it is thou, Romuald!' she murmured in a voice languishingly sweet as the last vibrations of a harp. 'What ailed thee, dearest? I waited so long for thee that I am dead; but we are now betrothed: I can see thee and visit thee. Adieu, Romuald, adieu! I love thee. That is all I wished to tell thee, and I give thee back the life which thy kiss for a moment recalled. We shall soon meet again.'

Her head fell back, but her arms yet encircled me, as though to retain me still. A furious whirlwind suddenly burst in the window, and entered the chamber. The last remaining leaf of the white rose for a moment palpitated at the extremity of the stalk like a butterfly's wing, then it detached itself and flew forth through the open casement, bearing with it the soul of Clarimonde. The lamp was extinguished, and I fell insensible upon the bosom of the beautiful dead.

When I came to myself again I was lying on the bed in my little room at the presbytery, and the old dog of the former curé was licking my hand, which had been hanging down outside of the covers. Barbara, all trembling with age and anxiety, was busying herself about the room, opening and shutting drawers, and emptying powders into glasses. On seeing me open my eyes, the old woman uttered a cry of joy, the dog yelped and wagged his tail, but I was still so weak that I could not speak a single word or make the slightest motion. Afterward I learned that I had lain thus for three days, giving no evidence of life beyond the faintest respiration. Those three days do not reckon in my life, nor could I ever imagine whither my spirit had departed during those three days; I have no recollection of aught relating to them. Barbara told me that the same coppery-complexioned man who came to seek me on the night of my departure from the presbytery had brought me back the next morning in a close litter, and departed immediately afterward. When I became able to collect my scattered thoughts, I reviewed within my mind all the circumstances of that fateful night. At first I thought I had been the victim of some magical illusion, but ere long the recollection of other circumstances, real and palpable in themselves, came to forbid that supposition. I could not believe that I had been dreaming, since Barbara as well as myself had seen the strange man with his two black horses, and described with exactness every detail of his figure and apparel. Nevertheless it appeared that none knew of any castle in the neighbourhood answering to the description of that in which I had again found Clarimonde.

One morning I found the Abbé Sérapion in my room. Barbara had advised him that I was ill, and he had come with all speed to see me. Although this haste on his part testified to an affectionate interest in me, yet his visit did not cause me the pleasure which it should have done. The Abbé Sérapion had something penetrating and inquisitorial in his gaze which made me feel very ill at ease. His presence filled me with embarrassment and a sense of guilt. At the first glance he divined my interior trouble, and I hated him for his clairvoyance.

While he inquired after my health in hypocritically honeyed accents, he constantly kept his two great yellow lion-eyes fixed upon me, and plunged his look into my soul like a sounding-lead. Then he asked me how I directed my parish, if I was happy in it, how I passed the leisure hours allowed me in the intervals of pastoral duty, whether I had become acquainted with many of the inhabitants of the place, what was my favourite reading, and a thousand other such questions. I answered these inquiries as briefly as possible, and he, without ever waiting for my answers, passed rapidly from one subject of query to another. That conversation had evidently no connection with what he actually wished to say. At last, without any premonition, but as though repeating a piece of news which he had recalled on the instant, and feared might otherwise be forgotten subsequently, he suddenly said, in a clear vibrant voice, which rang in my ears like the trumpets of the Last Judgment:

'The great courtesan Clarimonde died a few days ago, at the close of an orgie which lasted eight days and eight nights. It was something infernally splendid. The abominations of the banquets of Belshazzar and Cleopatra were re-enacted there. Good God, what age are we living in? The guests were served by swarthy slaves who spoke an unknown tongue, and who seemed to me to be veritable demons. The livery of the very least among them would have served for the gala-dress of an emperor. There have always been very strange stories told of this Clarimonde, and all her lovers came to a violent or miserable end. They used to say that she was a ghoul, a female vampire; but I believe she was none other than Beelzebub himself.'

He ceased to speak, and commenced to regard me more attentively than ever, as though to observe the effect of his words on me. I could not refrain from starting when I heard him utter the name of Clarimonde, and this news of her death, in addition to the pain it caused me by reason of its coincidence with the nocturnal scenes I had witnessed, filled me with an agony and terror which my face betrayed, despite my utmost endeavours to appear composed. Sérapion fixed an anxious and severe look upon me, and then observed: 'My son, I must warn you that you are standing with foot raised upon the brink of an abyss; take heed lest you fall therein. Satan's claws are long, and tombs are not always true to their trust. The tombstone of Clarimonde should be sealed down with a triple seal, for, if report be true, it is not the first time she has died. May God watch over you, Romuald!'

And with these words the Abbé walked slowly to the door. I did not see him again at that time, for he left for S——— almost immediately.

I became completely restored to health and resumed my accustomed duties. The memory of Clarimonde and the words of the old Abbé were constantly in my mind; nevertheless no extraordinary event had occurred to verify the funereal predictions of Sérapion, and I had commenced to believe that his fears and my own terrors were over-exaggerated, when one night I had a strange dream. I had hardly fallen asleep when I heard my bed-curtains drawn apart, as their rings slided back upon the curtain rod with a sharp sound. I rose up quickly upon my elbow, and beheld the shadow of a woman standing erect before me. I recognised Clarimonde immediately. She bore in her hand a little lamp, shaped like those which are placed in tombs, and its light lent her fingers a rosy transparency, which extended itself by lessening degrees even to the opaque and milky whiteness of her bare arm. Her only garment was the linen winding-sheet which had shrouded her when lying upon the bed of death. She sought to gather its folds over her bosom as though ashamed of being so scantily clad, but her little hand was not equal to the task. She was so white that the colour of the drapery blended with that of her flesh under the pallid rays of the lamp. Enveloped with this subtle tissue which betrayed all the contour of her body, she seemed rather the marble statue of some fair antique bather than a woman endowed with life. But dead or living, statue or woman, shadow or body, her beauty was still the same, only that the green light of her eyes was less brilliant, and her mouth, once so warmly crimson, was only tinted with a faint tender rosiness, like that of her cheeks. The little blue flowers which I had noticed entwined in her hair were withered and dry, and had lost nearly all their leaves, but this did not prevent her from being charming—so charming that, notwithstanding the strange character of the adventure, and the unexplainable manner in which she had entered my room, I felt not even for a moment the least fear.

She placed the lamp on the table and seated herself at the foot of my bed; then bending toward me, she said, in that voice at once silvery clear and yet velvety in its sweet softness, such as I never heard from any lips save hers:

'I have kept thee long in waiting, dear Romuald, and it must have seemed to thee that I had forgotten thee. But I come from afar off, very far off, and from a land whence no other has ever yet returned. There is neither sun nor moon in that land whence I come: all is but space and shadow; there is neither road nor pathway: no earth for the foot, no air for the wing; and nevertheless behold me here, for Love is stronger than Death and must conquer him in the end. Oh what sad faces and fearful things I have seen on my way hither! What diffi-culty my soul, returned to earth through the power of will alone, has had in finding its body and reinstating itself therein! What terrible efforts I had to make ere I could lift the ponderous slab with which they had covered me! See, the palms of my poor hands are all bruised! Kiss them, sweet love, that they may be healed!' She laid the cold palms of her hands upon ray mouth, one after the other. I kissed them, indeed, many times, and she the while watched me with a smile of ineffable affection.

I confess to my shame that I had entirely forgotten the advice of the Abbé Sérapion and the sacred office wherewith I had been invested. I had fallen without resistance, and at the first assault. I had not even made the least effort to repel the tempter. The fresh coolness of Clarimonde's skin penetrated my own, and I felt voluptuous tremors pass over my whole body. Poor child! in spite of all I saw afterward, I can hardly yet believe she was a demon; at least she had no appearance of being such, and never did Satan so skilfully conceal his claws and horns. She had drawn her feet up beneath her, and squatted down on the edge of the couch in an attitude full of negligent coquetry. From time to time she passed her little hand through my hair and twisted it into curls, as though trying how a new style of wearing it would become my face. I abandoned myself to her hands with the most guilty pleasure, while she accompanied her gentle play with the prettiest prattle. The most remarkable fact was that I felt no astonishment whatever at so extraordinary ah adventure, and as in dreams one finds no difficulty in accepting the most fantastic events as simple facts, so all these circumstances seemed to me perfectly natural in themselves.

'I loved thee long ere I saw thee, dear Romuald, and sought thee everywhere. Thou wast my dream, and I first saw thee in the church at the fatal moment. I said at once, "It is he!" I gave thee a look into which I threw all the love I ever had, all the love I now have, all the love I shall ever have for thee—a look that would have damned a cardinal or brought a king to his knees at my feet in view of all his court. Thou remainedst unmoved, preferring thy God to me!

'Ah, how jealous I am of that God whom thou didst love and still lovest more than me!

'Woe is me, unhappy one that I am! I can never have thy heart all to myself, I whom thou didst recall to life with a kiss—dead Clarimonde, who for thy sake bursts asunder the gates of the tomb, and comes to consecrate to thee a life which she has resumed only to make thee happy!'

All her words were accompanied with the most impassioned caresses, which bewildered my sense and my reason to such an extent, that I did not fear to utter a frightful blasphemy for the sake of consoling her, and to declare that I loved her as much as God.

Her eyes rekindled and shone like chrysoprases. 'In truth? —in very truth?—as much as God!' she cried, flinging her beautiful arms around me. 'Since it is so, thou wilt come with me; thou wilt follow me whithersoever I desire. Thou wilt cast away thy ugly black habit. Thou shalt be the proudest and most envied of cavaliers; thou shalt be my lover! To be the acknowledged lover of Clarimonde, who has refused even a Pope! That will be something to feel proud of. Ah, the fair, unspeakably happy existence, the beautiful golden life we shall live together! And when shall we depart, my fair sir?'

'To-morrow! To-morrow!' I cried in my delirium.

'To-morrow, then, so let it be!' she answered. 'In the meanwhile I shall have opportunity to change my toilet, for this is a little too light and in nowise suited for a voyage. I must also forthwith notify all my friends who believe me dead, and mourn for me as deeply as they are capable of doing. The money, the dresses, the carriages—all will be ready. I shall call for thee at this same hour. Adieu, dear heart!' And she lightly touched my forehead with her lips. The lamp went out, the curtains closed again, and all became dark; a leaden, dreamless sleep fell on me and held me unconscious until the morning following.

I awoke later than usual, and the recollection of this singular adventure troubled me during the whole day. I finally persuaded myself that it was a mere vapour of my heated imagination. Nevertheless its sensations had been so vivid that it was difficult to persuade myself that they were not real, and it was not without some presentiment of what was going to happen that I got into bed at last, after having prayed God to drive far from me all thoughts of evil, and to protect the chastity of my slumber.

I soon fell into a deep sleep, and my dream was continued. The curtains again parted, and I beheld Clarimonde, not as on the former occasion, pale in her pale winding-sheet, with the violets of death upon her cheeks, but gay, sprightly, jaunty, in a superb travelling-dress of green velvet, trimmed with gold lace, and looped up on either side to allow a glimpse of satin petticoat.

Her blond hair escaped in thick ringlets from beneath a broad black felt hat, decorated with white feathers whimsically twisted into various shapes. In one hand she held a little riding-whip terminated by a golden whistle. She tapped me lightly with it, and exclaimed: 'Well, my fine sleeper, is this the way you make your preparations? I thought I would find you up and dressed. Arise quickly, we have no time to lose.'

I leaped out of bed at once.

'Come, dress yourself, and let us go,' she continued, pointing to a little package she had brought with her. 'The horses are becoming impatient of delay and champing their bits at the door. We ought to have been by this time at least ten leagues distant from here.'

I dressed myself hurriedly, and she handed me the articles of apparel herself one by one, bursting into laughter from time to time at my awkwardness, as she explained to me the use of a garment when I had made a mistake. She hurriedly arranged my hair, and this done, held up before me a little pocket-mirror of Venetian crystal, rimmed with silver filigree-work, and play-fully asked: 'How dost find thyself now? Wilt engage me for thy valet de chambre?'

I was no longer the same person, and I could not even recognise myself. I resembled my former self no more than a finished statue resembles a block of stone. My old face seemed but a coarse daub of the one reflected in the mirror. I was handsome, and my vanity was sensibly tickled by the metamorphosis.

That elegant apparel, that richly embroidered vest had made of me a totally different personage, and I marvelled at the power of transformation owned by a few yards of cloth cut after a certain pattern. The spirit of my costume penetrated my very skin and within ten minutes more I had become something of a coxcomb.

In order to feel more at ease in my new attire, I took several turns up and down the room. Clarimonde watched me with an air of maternal pleasure, and appeared well satisfied with her work. 'Come, enough of this child's play! Let us start, Romuald, dear. We have far to go, and we may not get there in time.' She took my hand and led me forth. All the doors opened before her at a touch, and we passed by the dog without awaking him.

At the gate we found Margheritone waiting, the same swarthy groom who had once before been my-escort. He held the bridles of three horses, all black like those which bore us to the castle—one for me, one for him, one for Clarimonde. Those horses must have been Spanish genets born of mares fecundated by a zephyr, for they were fleet as the wind itself, and the moon, which had just risen at our departure to light us on the way, rolled over the sky like a wheel detached from her own chariot. We beheld her on the right leaping from tree to tree, and putting herself out of breath in the effort to keep up with us. Soon we came upon a level plain where, hard by a clump of trees, a carriage with four vigorous horses awaited us. We entered it, and the postillions urged their animals into a mad gallop. I had one arm around Clarimonde's waist, and one of her hands clasped in mine; her head leaned upon my shoulder, and I felt her bosom, half bare, lightly pressing against my arm. I had never known such intense happiness. In that hour I had forgotten everything, and I no more remembered having ever been a priest than I remembered what I had been doing in my mother's womb, so great was the fascination which the evil spirit exerted upon me. From that night my nature seemed in some sort to have become halved, and there were two men within me, neither of whom knew the other. At one moment I believed myself a priest who dreamed nightly that he was a gentleman, at another that I was a gentleman who dreamed he was a priest. I could no longer distinguish the dream from the reality, nor could I discover where the reality began or where ended the dream. The exquisite young lord and libertine railed at the priest, the priest loathed the dissolute habits of the young lord. Two spirals entangled and confounded the one with the other, yet never touching, would afford a fair representation of this bicephalic life which I lived. Despite the strange character of my condition, I do not believe that I ever inclined, even for a moment, to madness. I always retained with extreme vividness all the perceptions of my two lives. Only there was one absurd fact which I could not explain to myself—namely, that the consciousness of the same individuality existed in two men so opposite in character. It was an anomaly for which I could not account—whether I believed myself to be the curé of the little village of C———, o *Il Signor Romualdo*, the titled lover of Clarimonde.

Be that as it may, I lived, at least I believed that I lived, in Venice. I have never been able to discover rightly how much of illusion and how much of reality there was in this fantastic adventure. We dwelt in a great palace on the Canaleio, filled with frescoes and statues, and containing two Titians in the noblest style of the great master, which were hung in Clarimonde's chamber. It was a palace well worthy of a king.

We had each our gondola, our *barcarolli* in family livery, our music hall, and our special poet. Clarimonde always lived upon a magnificent scale; there was something of Cleopatra in her nature. As for me, I had the retinue of a prince's son, and I was regarded with as much reverential respect as though I had been of the family of one of the twelve Apostles or the four Evangelists of the Most Serene Republic. I would not have turned aside to allow even the Doge to pass, and I do not believe that since Satan fell from heaven, any creature was ever prouder or more insolent than I. I went to the Ridotto, and played with a luck which seemed absolutely infernal. I received the best of all society—the sons of ruined families, women of the theatre, shrewd knaves, parasites, hectoring swashbucklers. But notwithstanding the dissipation of such a life, I always remained faithful to Clarimonde. I loved her wildly. She would have excited satiety itself, and chained inconstancy. To have Clarimonde was to have twenty mistresses; ay, to possess all women: so mobile, so varied of aspect, so fresh in new charms was she all in herself—a very chameleon of a woman, in sooth. She made you commit with her the infidelity you would have committed with another, by donning to perfection the character, the attraction, the style of beauty of the woman who appeared to please you. She returned my love a hundred-fold, and it was in vain that the young patricians and even the Ancients of the Council of Ten made her the most magnificent proposals. A Foscari even went so far as to offer to espouse her. She rejected all his overtures. Of gold she had enough. She wished no longer for anything but love—a love youthful, pure, evoked by herself, and which should be a first and last passion. I would have been perfectly happy but for a cursed nightmare which recurred every night, and in which I believed myself to be a poor village curé, practising mortification and penance for my excesses during the day. Reassured by my constant association with her, I never thought further of the strange manner in which I had become acquainted with Clarimonde. But the words of the Abbé Sérapion concerning her recurred often to my memory, and never ceased to cause me uneasiness.

For some time the health of Clarimonde had not been so good as usual; her complexion grew paler day by day. The physicians who were summoned could not comprehend the nature of her malady and knew not how to treat it. They all prescribed some insignificant remedies, and never called a second time. Her paleness, nevertheless, visibly increased, and she became colder and colder, until she seemed almost as white and dead as upon that memorable night in the unknown castle. I grieved with anguish unspeakable to behold her thus slowly perishing; and she, touched by my agony, smiled upon me sweetly and sadly with the fateful smile of those who feel that they must die.

One morning I was seated at her bedside, and breakfasting from a little table placed close at hand, so that I might not be obliged to leave her for a single instant. In the act of cutting some fruit I accidentally inflicted rather a deep gash on my finger. The blood immediately gushed forth in a little purple jet, and a few drops spurted upon Clarimonde. Her eyes flashed,

her face suddenly assumed an expression of savage and ferocious joy such as I had never before observed in her. She leaped out of her bed with animal agility—the agility, as it were, of an ape or a cat—and sprang upon my wound, which she commenced to suck with an air of unutterable pleasure. She swallowed the blood in little mouthfuls, slowly and carefully, like a connoisseur tasting a wine from Xeres or Syracuse. Gradually her eyelids half closed, and the pupils of her green eyes became oblong instead of round. From time to time she paused in order to kiss my hand, then she would recommence to press her lips to the lips of the wound in order to coax forth a few more ruddy drops. When she found that the blood would no longer come, she arose with eyes liquid and brilliant, rosier than a May dawn; her face full and fresh, her hand warm and moist—in fine, more beautiful than ever, and in the most perfect health.

'I shall not die! I shall not die!' she cried, clinging to my neck, half mad with joy. 'I can love thee yet for a long time. My life is thine, and all that is of me comes from thee. A few drops of thy rich and noble blood, more precious and more potent than all the elixirs of the earth, have given me back life.'

This scene long haunted my memory, and inspired me with strange doubts in regard to Clarimonde; and the same evening, when slumber had transported me to my presbytery, I beheld the Abbé Sérapion, graver and more anxious of aspect than ever. He gazed attentively at me, and sorrowfully exclaimed: 'Not content with losing your soul, you now desire also to lose your body. Wretched young man, into how terrible a plight have you fallen!' The tone in which he uttered these words powerfully affected me, but in spite of its vividness even that impression was soon dissipated, and a thousand other cares erased it from my mind. At last one evening, while looking into a mirror whose traitorous position she had not taken into account, I saw Clarimonde in the act of emptying a powder into the cup of spiced wine which she had long been in the habit of preparing after our repasts. I took the cup, feigned to carry it to my lips, and then placed it on the nearest article of furniture as though intending to finish it at my leisure. Taking advantage of a moment when the fair one's back was turned, I threw the contents under the table, after which I retired to my chamber and went to bed, fully resolved not to sleep, but to watch and discover what should come of all this mystery. I did not have to wait long, Clarimonde entered in her nightdress,

and having removed her apparel, crept into bed and lay down beside me. When she felt assured that I was asleep, she bared my arm, and drawing a gold pin from her hair, commenced to murmur in a low voice:

'One drop, only one drop! One ruby at the end of my needle.... Since thou lovest me yet, I must not die!... Ah, poor love! His beautiful blood, so brightly purple, I must drink it. Sleep, my only treasure! Sleep, my god, my child! I will do thee no harm; I will only take of thy life what I must to keep my own from being for ever extinguished. But that I love thee so much, I could well resolve to have other lovers whose veins I could drain; but since I have known thee all other men have become hateful to me.... Ah, the beautiful arm! How round it is! How white it is! How shall I ever dare to prick this pretty blue vein!' And while thus murmuring to herself she wept, and I felt her tears raining on my arm as she clasped it with her hands. At last she took the resolve, slightly punctured me with her pin, and commenced to suck up the blood which oozed from the place. Although she swallowed only a few drops, the fear of weakening me soon seized her, and she carefully tied a little band around my arm, afterward rubbing the wound with an unguent which immediately cicatrised it. Further doubts were impossible. The Abbé Sérapion was right. Notwithstanding this positive knowledge, however, I could not cease to love Clarimonde, and I would gladly of my own accord have given her all the blood she required to sustain her factitious life. Moreover, I felt but little fear of her. The woman seemed to plead with me for the vampire, and what I had already heard and seen sufficed to reassure me completely. In those days I had plenteous veins, which would not have been so easily exhausted as at present; and I would not have thought of bargaining for my blood, drop by drop. I would rather have opened myself the veins of my arm and said to her: 'Drink, and may my love infiltrate itself throughout thy body together with my blood!' I carefully avoided ever making the least reference to the narcotic drink she had prepared for me, or to the incident of the pin, and we lived in the most perfect harmony.

Yet my priestly scruples commenced to torment me more than ever, and I was at a loss to imagine what new penance I could invent in order to mortify and subdue my flesh. Although these visions were involuntary, and though I did not actually participate in anything relating to them, I could not dare to touch the body of Christ with hands so impure and a mind defiled by such debauches whether real or imaginary. In the effort to avoid falling under the influence of these wearisome hallucinations, I strove to prevent myself from being overcome by sleep. I held my eyelids open with my fingers, and stood for hours together leaning upright against the wall, fighting sleep with all my might; but the dust of drowsiness invariably gathered upon my eyes at last, and finding all resistance useless, I would have to let my arms fall in the extremity of despairing weariness, and the current of slumber would again bear me away to the perfidious shores. Sérapion addressed me with the most vehement exhortations, severely reproaching me for my softness and want of fervour. Finally, one day when I was more wretched than usual, he said to me: 'There is but one way by which you can obtain relief from this continual torment, and though it is an extreme measure it must be made use of; violent diseases require violent remedies. I know where Clarimonde is buried. It is necessary that we shall disinter her remains, and that you shall behold in how pitiable a state the object of your love is. Then you will no longer be tempted to lose your soul for the sake of an unclean corpse devoured by worms, and ready to crumble into dust. That will assuredly restore you to yourself.'

For my part, I was so tired of this double life that I at once consented, desiring to ascertain beyond a doubt whether a priest or a gentleman had been the victim of delusion. I had become fully resolved either to kill one of the two men within me for the benefit of the other, or else to kill both, for so terrible an existence could not last long and be endured. The Abbé Sérapion provided himself with a mattock, a lever, and a lantern, and at midnight we wended our way to the cemetery of ———, the location and place of which were perfectly familiar to him. After having directed the rays of the dark lantern upon the inscriptions of several tombs, we came at last upon a great slab, half concealed by huge weeds and devoured by mosses and parasitic plants, whereupon we deciphered the opening lines of the epitaph:

> **_Here lies Clarimonde,_**
> **_who was the most beautiful in the world_**
> **_during her lifetime._**

'It is here without a doubt,' muttered Sérapion, and placing his lantern on the ground, he forced the point of the lever under the edge of the stone and commenced to raise it. The stone yielded, and he proceeded to work with the mattock. Darker and more silent than the night itself, I stood by and watched him do it, while he, bending over his dismal toil, streamed with sweat, panted, and his hard-coming breath seemed to have the harsh tone of a death rattle. It was a weird scene, and had any persons from without beheld us, they would assuredly have taken us rather for profane wretches and shroud-stealers than for priests of God. There was something grim and fierce in Sérapion's zeal which lent him the air of a demon rather than of an apostle or an angel, and his great aquiline face, with all its stern features, brought out in strong relief by the lantern-light, had something fearsome in it which enhanced the unpleasant fancy. I felt an icy sweat come out upon my forehead in huge beads, and my hair stood up with a hideous fear. Within the depths of my own heart I felt that the act of the austere Sérapion was an abominable sacrilege; and I could have prayed that a triangle of fire would issue from the entrails of the dark clouds, heavily rolling above us, to reduce him to cinders. The owls which had been nestling in the cypress-trees, startled by the gleam of the lantern, flew against it from time to time, striking their dusty wings against its panes, and uttering plaintive cries of lamentation; wild foxes yelped in the far darkness, and a thousand sinister noises detached themselves from the silence.

At last Séra-pion's mattock struck the coffin itself, making its planks re-echo with a deep sonorous sound, with that terrible sound nothingness utters when stricken. He wrenched apart and tore up the lid, and I beheld Clarimonde, pallid as a figure of marble, with hands joined; her white winding-sheet made but one fold from her head to her feet. A little crimson drop sparkled like a speck of dew at one corner of her colourless mouth. Sérapion, at this spectacle, burst into fury: 'Ah, thou art here, demon! Impure courtesan! Drinker of blood and gold! 'And he flung holy water upon the corpse and the coffin, over which he traced the sign of the cross with his sprinkler. Poor Clarimonde had no sooner been touched by the blessed spray than her beautiful body crumbled into dust, and became only a shapeless and frightful mass of cinders and half-calcined bones.

'Behold your mistress, my Lord Romuald!' cried the inexorable priest, as he pointed to these sad remains. 'Will you be easily tempted after this to promenade on the Lido or at Fusina with your beauty?' I covered my face with my hands, a vast ruin had taken place within me. I returned to my presbytery, and the noble Lord Romuald, the lover of Clarimonde, separated himself from the poor priest with whom he had kept such strange company so long. But once only, the following night, I saw Clarimonde. She said to me, as she had said the first time at the portals of the church: 'Unhappy man! Unhappy man! What hast thou done? Wherefore have hearkened to that imbecile priest? Wert thou not happy? And what harm had I ever done thee that thou shouldst violate my poor tomb, and lay bare the miseries of my nothingness? All communication between our souls and our bodies is henceforth for ever broken. Adieu! Thou wilt yet regret me!' She vanished in air as smoke, and I never saw her more.

Alas! she spoke truly indeed. I have regretted her more than once, and I regret her still. My soul's peace has been very dearly bought. The love of God was not too much to replace such a love as hers. And this, brother, is the story of my youth. Never gaze upon a woman, and walk abroad only with eyes ever fixed upon the ground; for however chaste and watchful one may be, the error of a single moment is enough to make one lose eternity.

The End

THE TRUE STORY OF A VAMPIRE

BY ERIC STENBOCK

Eric Stenbock (1860-1895) was an English and Swedish writer who died tragically young. In his short life, Stenbock - a count - left several memorable works, including a Faust story and "The True Story of a Vampire." His vampire tale can be read as a "gay" vampire story, much like the work by Karl Heinrich Ulrichs, which is also in this collection. According to some sources, Stenbock's story was admired by the great H.P. Lovecraft.

The True Story of A Vampire

by Eric Stenbock

Vampire stories are generally located in Styria; mine is also. Styria is by no means the romantic kind of place described by those who have certainly never been there. It is a flat, uninteresting country, only celebrated for its turkeys, its capons, and the stupidity of its inhabitants. Vampires generally arrive at night, in carriages drawn by two black horses.

Our Vampire arrived by the commonplace means of the railway train, and in the afternoon.

You must think I am joking, or perhaps that by the word "Vampire" I mean a financial vampire.

No, I am quite serious. The Vampire of whom I am speaking, who laid waste our hearth and home, was a real vampire.

Vampires are generally described as dark, sinister-looking, and singularly handsome. Our Vampire was, on the contrary, rather fair, and certainly was not at first sight sinister-looking, and though decidedly attractive in appearance, not what one would call singularly handsome.

Yes, he desolated our home, killed my brother—the one object of my adoration—also my dear father. Yet, at the same time, I must say that I myself came under the spell of his fascination, and, in spite of all, have no ill-will towards him now.

Doubtless you have read in the papers passim of "the Baroness and her beasts." It is to tell how I came to spend most of my useless wealth on an asylum for stray animals that I am writing this.

I am old now; what happened then was when I was a little girl of about thirteen. I will begin by describing our household. We were Poles: our name was Wronski: we lived in Styria, where we had a castle. Our household was very limited. It consisted, with the exclusion of domestics, of only my father, our governess—a worthy Belgian named Mademoiselle Vonnaert—my brother, and myself. Let me begin with my father: he was old and both my brother and I were children of his old age. Of my mother I remember nothing: she died in giving birth to my brother, who was only one year, or not as much, younger than in self. Our father was studious, continually occupied in reading books, chiefly on recondite subjects and in all kinds of unknown languages.

He had a long white beard, and wore habitually a black velvet skull-cap.

How kind he was to us! It was more than I could tell. Still it was not I who was the favourite.

His whole heart went out to Gabriel—Gabryel as we spelt it in Polish. He was always called by the Russian abbreviation Gavril—I mean, of course, my brother, who had a resemblance to the only portrait of my mother, a slight chalk sketch which hung in my father's study. But I was by no means jealous: my brother was and has been the only love of my life. It is for his sake that I am now keeping in Westbourne Park a home for stray cats and dogs.

I was at that time, as I said before, a little girl; my name was Carmela. My long tangled hair was always all over the place, and never would combed straight. I was not pretty—at least, looking at a photograph of me at that time. I do not think I could describe myself as such. Yet at the same time, when I look at the photograph, I think my expression may have been pleasing to some people: irregular features, large mouth, and large wild eyes.

I was by way of being naughty—not so naughty Gabriel in the opinion of Mlle Vonnaert. Mlle Vonnaert. I may intercalate, was a wholly excellent person, middle-aged, who really did speak good French, although she was a Belgian, and could also make herself understood in German, which, as you may or may not know, is the current language of Styria.

I find it difficult to describe my brother Gabriel; there was something about him strange and superhuman, or perhaps I should rather say praeterhuman, something between the animal and the divine. Perhaps the Greek idea of the Faun might illustrate what I mean: but that will not do either. He had large, wild, gazelle-like eyes: his hair, like mine, was in a perpetual tangle—that point he had in common with me, and indeed, as I afterwards heard, our mother having been of gipsy race, it will account for much of the innate wildness there was in our natures. I was wild enough, but Gabriel was much wilder. Nothing would induce him to put on shoes and stockings, except on Sundays—when he also allowed his hair to be combed, but only by me. How shall I describe the grace of that lovely mouth, shaped verily "en arc d'amour." I always think of the text in the Psalm, "Grace is shed forth on thy lips, therefore has God blessed thee eternally"—-lips that seemed to exhale the very breath of life. Then that beautiful, lithe, living, elastic form!

He could run faster than any deer: spring like a squirrel to the topmost branch of a tree: he might have stood for the sign and symbol of vitality itself. But seldom could he be induced by Mlle Vonnaert to learn lessons; but when he did so, he learnt with extraordinary quickness. He would play upon every conceivable instrument, holding a violin here, there, and everywhere except the right place: manufacturing instruments for himself out of reeds—even sticks. Mlle Vonnaert made futile efforts to induce him to learn to play the piano. I suppose he was what was called spoilt, though merely in the superficial sense of the word. Our father allowed him to indulge in every caprice.

One of his peculiarities, when quite a little child, was horror at the sight of meat. Nothing on earth would induce him to taste it. Another thing which was particularly remarkable about him was his extraordinary power over animals. Everything seemed to come tame to his hand. Birds would sit on his shoulder. Then sometimes Mlle Vonnaert and I would lose him in the woods—-he would suddenly dart away. Then we would find him singing softly or whistling to himself, with all manner of woodland creatures around him—hedgehogs, little foxes, wild rabbits, marmots, squirrels, and such like. He would frequently bring these things home with him and insist on keeping them. This strange menagerie was the terror of poor Mlle Vonnaert's heart. He chose to live in a little room at the top of a turret; but which, instead of going upstairs, he chose to reach by means of a very tall chestnut-tree, through the window. But in contradiction of all his, it was his custom to serve every Sunday Mass in the parish church, with hair nicely combed and with white surplice and red cassock. He looked as demure and tamed as possible. Then came the element of the divine. What an expression of ecstasy there was in those glorious eyes!

Thus far I have not been speaking about the Vampire. However, let me begin with my narrative at last. One day my father had to go to the neighbouring town—as he frequently had. This time he returned accompanied by a guest. The gentleman, he said, had missed his train, through the late arrival of another at our station, which was a junction, and he would therefore, as trains were not frequent in our parts, have had to wait there all night. He had joined in conversation with my father in the too-late-arriving train from the town: and had consequently accepted my father's invitation to stay the night at our house. But of course, you know, in those out-of-the-way parts we are almost patriarchal in our hospitality.

He was announced under the name of Count Vardalek— the name being Hungarian. But he spoke German well enough: not with the monotonous accentuation of Hungarians, but rather, if anything, with a slight Slavonic intonation. His voice was peculiarly soft and insinuating. We soon afterwards found that he could talk Polish, and Mlle Vonnaert vouched for his good French.

Indeed he seemed to know all languages. But let me give my first impressions. He was rather tall with fair wavy hair, rather long, which accentuated a certain effeminacy about his smooth face.

His figure had something—I cannot say what—serpentine about it. The features were refined; and he had long, slender, subtle, magnetic-looking hands, a somewhat long sinuous nose, a graceful mouth, and an attractive smile, which belied the intense sadness of the expression of the eyes. When he arrived his eyes were half closed—indeed they were habitually so—so that I could not decide their colour. He looked worn and wearied. I could not possibly guess his age.

Suddenly Gabriel burst into the room: a yellow butterfly was clinging to his hair. He was carrying in his arms a little squirrel. Of course he was barelegged as usual. The stranger looked up at his approach; then I noticed his eves. They were green: they seemed to dilate and grow larger. Gabriel stood stock-still, with a startled look, like that of a bird fascinated by a serpent.

But nevertheless he held out his hand to the newcomer Vardalek, taking his hand—I don't know why I noticed this trivial thing—pressed the pulse with his forefinger. Suddenly Gabriel darted from the room and rushed upstairs, going to his turret-room this time by the staircase instead of the tree. I was in terror what the Count might think of him. Great was my relief when he came down in his velvet Sunday suit, and shoes and stockings. I combed his hair, and set him generally right.

When the stranger came down to dinner his appearance had somewhat altered; he looked much younger. There was an elasticity of the skin, combined with a delicate complexion, rarely to be found in a man. Before, he had struck me as being very pale.

Well, at dinner we were all charmed with him, especially my father. He seemed to be thoroughly acquainted with all my father's particular hobbies. Once, when my father was relating some of his military experiences, he said something about a drummer-boy who was wounded in battle. His eyes opened completely again and dilated: this time with a particularly disagreeable expression, dull and dead, yet at the same time animated by some horrible excitement. But this was only momentary.

The chief subject of his conversation with my father was about certain curious mystical books which my father had just lately picked up, and which he could not make out, but Vardalek seemed completely to understand. At dessert-time my father asked him if he were in a great hurry to reach his destination: if not, would he not stay with us a little while: though our place was out of the way, he would find much that would interest him in his library.

He answered, "I am in no hurry. I have no particular reason for going to that place at all, and if I can be of service to you in deciphering these books, I shall be only too glad." He added with a smile which was bitter, very very bitter: "You see I am a cosmopolitan, a wanderer on the face of the earth."

After dinner my father asked him if he played the piano. He said, "Yes, I can a little," and he sat down at the piano. Then he played a Hungarian csardas—wild, rhapsodic, wonderful.

That is the music which makes men mad. He went on in the same strain.

Gabriel stood stock-still by the piano, his eyes dilated and fixed, his form quivering. At last he said very slowly, at one particular motive—for want of a better word you may call it the relâche of a csardas, by which I mean that point where the original quasi-slow movement begins again—-"Yes, I think I could play that."

Then he quickly fetched his fiddle and self-made xylophone, and did, actually alternating the instruments, render the same very well indeed.

Vardalek looked at him, and said in a very sad voice, "Poor child! you have the soul of music within you."

I could not understand why he should seem to commiserate instead of congratulate Gabriel on what certainly showed an extraordinary talent.

Gabriel was shy even as the wild animals who were tame to him. Never before had he taken to a stranger. Indeed, as a rule, if any stranger came to the house by any chance, he would hide himself, and I had to bring him up his food to the turret chamber. You may imagine what was my surprise when I saw him walking about hand in hand with Vardalek the next morning, in the garden, talking lively with him, and showing his collection of pet animals, which he had gathered from the woods, and for which we had had to fit up a regular zoological gardens. He seemed utterly under the domination of Vardalek. What surprised us was (for otherwise we liked the stranger, especially for being kind to him) that he seemed, though not noticeably at first—except perhaps to me, who noticed everything with regard to him—to be gradually losing his general health and vitality. He did not become pale as yet; but there was a certain languor about his movements which certainly there was by no means before.

My father got more and more devoted to Count Vardalek. He helped him in his studies: and my father would hardly allow him to go away, which he did sometimes—to Trieste, he said: he always came back, bringing us presents of strange Oriental jewellery or textures.

I knew all kinds of people came to Trieste, Orientals included. Still, there was a strangeness and magnificence about these things which I was sure even then could not possibly have come from such a place as Trieste, memorable to me chiefly for its necktie shops.

When Vardalek was away, Gabriel was continually asking for him and talking about him. Then at the same time he seemed to regain his old vitality and spirits. Vardalek always returned looking much older, wan, and weary. Gabriel would rush to meet him, and kiss him on the mouth. Then he gave a slight shiver: and after a little while began to look quite young again.

Things continued like this for some time. My father would not hear of Vardalek's going away permanently. He came to be an inmate of our house. I indeed, and Mlle Vonnaert also, could not help noticing what a difference there was altogether about Gabriel. But my father seemed totally blind to it.

One night I had gone downstairs to fetch something which I had left in the drawing-room. As I was going up again I passed Vardalek's room. He was playing on a piano, which had been specially put there for him, one of Chopin's nocturnes, very beautifully: I stopped, leaning on the banisters to listen.

Something white appeared on the dark staircase. We believed in ghosts in our part. I was transfixed with terror, and clung to the ballisters. What was my astonishment to see Gabriel walking slowly down the staircase, his eyes fixed as though in a trance! This terrified me even more than a ghost would. Could I believe my senses? Could that be Gabriel?

I simply could not move. Gabriel, clad in his long white night-shirt, came downstairs and opened the door. He left it open. Vardalek still continued playing, but talked as he played.

He said—this time speaking in Polish—Nie umiem wyrazic jak ciechi kocham—"My darling, I fain would spare thee: but thy life is my life, and I must live, I who would rather die. Will God not have any mercy on me? Oh! Oh! life; oh, the torture of life!" Here he struck one agonized and strange chord, then continued playing softly, "O, Gabriel, my beloved! my life, yes life—oh, why life? I am sure this is but a little that I demand of thee. Sorely thy superabundance of life can spare little to one who is already dead. No, stay," he said now almost harshly, "what must be, must be!"

Gabriel stood there quite still, with the same fixed vacant expression, in the room. He was evidently walking in his sleep. Vardalek played on: then said, "Ah!" with a sign of terrible agony. Then very gently, "Go now, Gabriel; it is enough." And Gabriel went out of the room and ascended the staircase at the same slow pace, with the same unconscious stare. Vardalek struck the piano, and although he did not play loudly, it seemed as though the strings would break. You never heard music so strange and so heart-rending!

I only know I was found by Mlle Vonnaert in the morning, in an unconscious state, at the foot of the stairs. Was it a dream after all? I am sure now that it was not. I thought then it might be, and said nothing to anyone about it. Indeed, what could I say?

Well, to let me cut a long story short, Gabriel, who had never known a moment's sickness in his life, grew ill: and we had to send to Gratz for a doctor, who could give no explanation of Gabriel's strange illness. Gradual wasting away, he said: absolutely no organic complaint. What could this mean?

My father at last became conscious of the fact that Gabriel was ill. His anxiety was fearful. The last trace of grey faded from his hair, and it became quite white. We sent to Vienna for doctors.

But all with the same result.

Gabriel was generally unconscious, and when conscious, only seemed to recognize Vardalek, who sat continually by his bedside, nursing him with the utmost tenderness.

One day I was alone in the room: and Vardalek cried suddenly, almost fiercely, "Send for a priest at once, at once," he repeated. "It is now almost too late!"

Gabriel stretched out his arms spasmodically, and put them round Vardalek's neck. This was the only movement he had made, for some time. Vardalek bent down and kissed him on the lips.

I rushed downstairs: and the priest was sent for. When I came back Vardalek was not there. The priest administered extreme unction. I think Gabriel was already dead, although we did not think so at the time.

Vardalek had utterly disappeared; and when we looked for him he was nowhere to be found; nor have I seen or heard of him since.

My father died very soon afterwards: suddenly aged, and bent down with grief. And so the whole of the Wronski property came into my sole possession. And here I am, an old woman, generally laughed at for keeping, in memory of Gabriel, an asylum for stray animals—and—-people do not, as a rule, believe in Vampires!

The End

Manor

by Karl Heinrich Ulrichs

Karl Heinrich Ulrichs (1825-1895) was a German writer whose legacy includes being a pioneer in campaigning for gay rights. In fact, today he's largely overlooked for his literary contributions, but we do have stories like "Manor" that live on. "Manor" could be regarded as a forerunner of "sexy" vampire stories, and it also can easily be read as a "gay" vampire story. It's about a boy whose best friend dies but visits him at night to suck his blood.

The present short novella **Manor** by K. H. Ulrichs was published as Wegwalt Edition No. 3 at the end of January 1914 in 1,200 copies. Of these, 200 copies were printed as a special edition on Japan paper and hand-numbered for the benefit of book enthusiasts. The production was carried out by the fine printing house Emil Nagel Nachf. in Berlin SW 68, Lindenstr. 105. The publishing was handled by the Wegwalt Workshop Wilhelmshagen.

Manor

By Karl Heinrich Ulrichs

I.

In the midst of the northern ocean lies a group of 35 islands, lonely and deserted, equally distant from Scotland, Iceland, and Norway, called the Faroes; barren, rocky, veiled in clouds, filled with the melancholy cries of fluttering gulls and kittiwakes, surrounded by crashing waves, almost always shrouded in mist. In summer, mountain peaks rise 1,800 and 2,000 feet above the sea; rugged cliffs; gloomy gorges; pine forests; thousands of springs, often cascading noisily and frothily from great heights, leaping from boulder to boulder. The shores are deeply indented with bays and fjords, almost everywhere inaccessible, bordered by high cliffs. The sea around is full of reefs, sometimes completely blocked, disturbed by whirlpools, and swept by wild currents. Only 17 of the islands are inhabited. Strömö and Wagö are separated only by a narrow sound, swimmable, though it takes a bold swimmer. Many place names recall a time when no churches stood on the Faroes, and the old faith had not yet been driven out, such as Thorshavn on the coast of Strömö, meaning "Strom Island."

In those days, a fisherman from Strömö rowed out to the open sea with his 15-year-old son. A storm arose; the boat capsized; the waves threw the son onto the cliffs of Wagö. A young sailor on Wagö saw this. He leaped into the waves, swam between the cliffs, seized the drifting body, and pulled him to shore. He sat with him on a boulder, cradling the half-frozen boy in his arms on his knees. Then the boy opened his eyes.

Sailor: "What's your name?"

Boy: "Har; I'm from Strömö."

The sailor rowed him back across the sound to Strömö, bringing him to Lära, his mother. Gratefully, the boy embraced his rescuer's neck at parting. The father's body was washed ashore by the waves. The sailor, named Manor, was an orphan, four years older than Har. He had grown fond of him and longed to see him again. He rowed to Strömö now and then, or swam the lukewarm waves when summer came, in the evenings after the day's work was done. Har went to the shore, climbed a cliff, and waved his cloth when he saw Manor's boat approaching from afar. They would spend an hour or two together. They rowed out on calm seas and sang sailor songs. Or they stripped, dove into the waves, swam to the nearby sandbank opposite, where seals fled from sunning themselves on the sand. Or they walked into the dark-green forest of tall pines, whose rustling treetops spoke the language of Thor, or sat under the branches of an old beech tree on a stone. They chatted, made plans. If a ship ever came to hunt whales, they would both go. When they sat on the stone, Manor would put his arm around Har's shoulders and call him "Min Jong" (my boy), and Har felt no greater comfort than when Manor held him so. If it was late when Manor arrived, he would quietly approach the lilac bush that shaded Har's window and tap on the panes. Har would wake and steal out to him, feeling so happy to be with Manor.

II.

Then a Danish three-master anchored in Wagö's safe bay, seeking sailors for a two-month whaling voyage. Manor went aboard. The captain immediately took on the slender, youthful lad. Har wanted to join as a cabin boy, but Lära wailed, "You're my only child! The sea took your father. Will you leave me?" Har stayed. Manor went. The ship raised anchor.

Two months passed. It was already growing wintry again. Har climbed the cliff, looked out to sea, and one morning saw the ship approaching, joyfully waving his cloth. But it was stormy; the surf was high. The ship steered toward Wagö's bay but couldn't reach it, driven instead into Strömö's dangerous reefs, where it ran aground before Har's eyes. He saw the shipwrecked men battling the waves. He spotted one among them, who with a strong arm grabbed a plank but was soon sucked down with it into the whirlpool of the surf. Har recognized him. It was Manor.

The tide washed many bodies ashore. They spread straw on the beach and laid them out, body by body. Har helped, examining the fallen. Then they brought Manor's body and laid it on the straw. There he lay before him with wet hair dripping seawater, eyes closed, cold, with pale lips and ashen cheeks drained of blood, slender in form, still beautiful even in death. "So, Manor, this is how I must see you again!" Har cried, throwing himself sobbing over the beloved body, savoring one last moment of embrace.

They brought the bodies across the sound and buried them that same day in Wagö's sand dunes.

III.

That evening, Har sat in the hut, gloomy and silent. Lära tried to comfort him, but he wanted no comfort; he cursed the gods. He went to bed but couldn't sleep. Near midnight, he fell into a half-slumber.

A noise woke him. He looked up. It came from outside the

window. The lilac bush's branches bent, and its dry leaves rustled. The window opened; a figure climbed in. Ha! He knew the figure! Despite the darkness, he recognized it at once! It approached slowly, lay down beside him in bed; he trembled but didn't resist. It stroked his cheeks, but with a cold hand, oh, so cold, so cold! A feverish chill ran through him. It kissed his warm, full lips with icy ones. He felt the figure's wet clothes; wet hair fell over his forehead. Horror gripped him, but it was mixed with bliss. The figure sighed, as if to say:

"My longing drove me to you! I find no rest in the grave!"

He dared not speak, hardly dared to breathe. Then the figure rose, sighing as if to say:

"Now I must go back!" It climbed the windowsill and left as it had come.

"Manor was here," Har whispered to himself.

That same night, a fisherman from Strömö was out in the sound with his boat. The sea glowed. Shimmering sparks dripped from his oars. Just before midnight, he heard a strange rushing. He saw something shoot through the glowing waves, something he couldn't make out, moving with the speed of a large fish, heading toward Strömö. It wasn't a fish, that much he could tell in the dark.

The next night, Manor came again, as cold as before but more insistent. He embraced Har with icy arms, kissed his cheek and lips, rested his head on the boy's soft chest. Har trembled. His heart began to pound at this intimate embrace. Manor laid his head right over the beating heart. His lips sought the gentle swell above it, moved by its pulsing. There he began to suck, eagerly, thirstily, like an infant at its mother's breast. But after a few moments, he stopped, rose, and left. Har felt as though a sucking creature had fed on him.

That night, too, the fisherman was out in the sound. At the same hour as before, it came rushing again, this time passing close by. In the pale moonlight, he saw it was a swimming man, lying on his right side as sailors sometimes swim, but clad in a shroud. The swimmer seemed not to notice him, though his face was turned toward him, eyes closed. The sight was so strange that the fisherman pulled in his nets and rowed away.

Manor returned the following nights, sometimes embracing Har in his sleep, for Har occasionally slept until Manor came. He awoke in his arms. Each time, the lips sought the soft rise above his heart. By day, Har sometimes noticed a faint drop of blood pearling from his left nipple. He wiped it with his shirt, or a drop had already soaked into it. Only on the full moon's night did Manor not come.

It is an old belief that a dead person is often filled with such longing for a loved one left behind that they leave their grave at night to visit them. Urda grants some a brief half-life at midnight, endowing them with strange powers from beyond the grave. This happens especially with young people cut down in their prime. The visitor is consumed with a great need for blood and warmth, craving the fresh blood of the living and, like a lover, their embraces. But they also impart great longing, often causing intense torment.

So it was here. Har suffered all day, wasting away. Yet he awaited the night with impatience, yearning for the blissful shivers of the midnight embrace.

IV.

About twelve days passed.

Lära: "You're so pale, so wan. What's wrong, Har?"

He: "Nothing, Mother."

She: "You're so quiet."

He sighed.

In the village's last hut lived a wise woman who knew many secrets. The worried mother went to her. The wise woman cast rune sticks.

Wise Woman: "The dead visit him."

Lära: "The dead?"

Wise Woman: "Yes, at night. One will die from it if the visits aren't stopped in time, before it's too late."

Dismayed, Lära returned home.

She: "Is it true, Har? Do the dead visit you?"

He looked down. "Manor was here," he said softly, collapsing into her arms, weeping.

She: "May the gods be merciful to you!"

He: "The gods? Pah! What are the gods to me now? When he clung to that plank, oh woe, oh woe! That was the time for mercy if they'd willed it. But they let him sink without pity. How I loved him!"

She noticed the bloodstains on his shirt. She went to the village elders. They rowed to Wagö with mother and son, taking the wise woman along. To the Wagö folk, they said:

"Your graves don't hold. One leaves his grave every night, comes to us, and feeds on this boy's blood."

The Wagö folk: "Then we'll bind him fast."

They took a pine stake, man-length and thicker than an arm, hewed it square with an axe, and sharpened a foot-long point at the end. They went to the dunes; one carried the stake, another a heavy axe. They opened Manor's grave. There he lay, calm and still, in his shroud.

First Wagö Man: "Look! He lies just as we left him."

Wise Woman: "Because he returns to his position each time."

Second Wagö Man: "His face looks almost fresher than before."

Wise Woman: "No wonder. Har's face is all the paler for it."

Har climbed down and threw himself once more over the beloved body.

"Manor! Manor!" he cried in anguished tones. "They'll stake you! Manor, awake! Open your eyes! Your Har calls you!"

But he didn't open his eyes. Motionless, he lay under Har's embrace, as he had twelve days before on the straw by the shore.

Har wouldn't let go. They tore him away. They placed the stake's point on Manor's chest. Har groaned, turning away, and fell into his mother's arms, hiding his face on her shoulder.

"Mother!" he cried, "why have you done this to me!"

He heard the axe's flat back strike the stake, the stake groan. A heavy blow; another, and half a dozen more.

First Wagö Man: "Now he's bound fast!"

Second: "He'll not come back now."

They carried Har away, half-fainting. "Now he'll leave you in peace, my dear child," Lära said when they were back in their hut.

Sorrowful, he went to bed. "Now he'll come no more," he said mournfully to himself. Tired and weak, he tossed restlessly on his pallet. The minutes crawled; the hours dragged. Midnight came, and still no sleep had touched his eyes.

Hark! What was that? In the lilac tree... But no, it was impossible. Yet—again, as before, the branches rustled. The window opened. Manor was there again. He sighed deeply. A great, square wound gaped in his chest, piercing through to his back. He lay beside Har, embraced him, and sucked—more eagerly, more thirstily than ever.

But that night, Lära kept watch nearby, listening, trembling. Early in the morning, she came to Har's bed.

She: "My poor child! He came again."

He: "Yes, Mother, he was with me again."

The bed was stained with corpse-blood that had dripped from the great wound.

V.

Hours later, a boat rowed back across the sound, without Har. They went to the dunes again and opened the grave. The square stake still stood in the crypt, but no longer in Manor's chest. He lay twisted beside it, the stake preventing him from lying straight.

Wise Woman: "He freed himself. The stake is the same thickness top and bottom."

First Wagö Man: "He wound himself upward along it."

Second: "It must have taken inhuman effort."

On the wise woman's advice, they hewed a stronger stake, twice as thick at the top as at the bottom, like a nail with a head. They pulled out the old stake and drove the new one through him.

"There! Now he's nailed fast," said the axeman, giving the stake's head a final blow.

Second Wagö Man: "Let him twist and turn, he won't free himself from that."

Lära returned to Har and told him what had happened. "Now it's over," he said to himself as he went to bed. Sleepless, he lay there. Midnight came. All was still. No rustling came from the lilac's branches outside the window. No swimmer startled the fisherman, slicing through the sound's waves with closed eyes by night.

Lära: "Now you're free of him. He tormented you so."

He: "Oh, Mother, Mother! He didn't torment me!"

He wasted away in vain longing. "Mother," he said, "it's over for me." He grew weaker, unable to rise from bed.

She: "You're so tired, so weak, my dear son!"

He: "He's pulling me down to him."

One morning, she sat by his bed as he slept. A month had passed since the shipwreck. It was still early. She wept. Then he opened his eyes.

"Mother," he said faintly, "I must die."

She: "Oh no, my child! You're too young to die!"

He: "Yes, yes! He was with me again. We spoke together. We sat on the stone under the old beech in the forest as before; he put his arm around my neck again and called me 'Min Jong.' Tonight, he'll come again to take me. He promised. I can't bear it without him."

She bent over him, her tears falling freely onto his bed. "My poor child!" she said, placing her hand on his forehead.

When night fell, she lit a lamp and kept watch by his bed. Silently, he lay there, not sleeping, staring quietly ahead.

He: "Mother!"

She: "What is it, my good son?"

He: "Bury me with him! Yes? And pull that dreadful stake from his chest!"

She promised with a clasp of hands and a kiss.

He: "Oh, it must be so sweet to lie with him in the grave!"

Midnight approached. Suddenly, his face lit up. He raised his head slightly, as if listening. With shining eyes, he looked toward the window and the lilac's branches.

"Look, Mother, there he comes!"

Those were his last words. His eyes broke.

He sank back into the pillows and passed away.

And they did as he had asked.

The End

FOR THE BLOOD IS LIFE

BY F. MARION CRAWFORD

F. Marion Crawford (1854-1909) was an American writer who touched on many subjects (he is said to have written one of the first books about the Mafia), including weird, fantastic stories such as "For the Blood is Life." Crawford isn't very well-known these days, but he had an influence on early writers such as M. R. James, who also is featured in this collection. This story is a gothic horror tale of a man controlled by a vampire.

For the
Blood is Life
by F. Marion Crawford

We had dined at sunset on the broad roof of the old tower, because it was cooler there during the great heat of summer. Besides, the little kitchen was built at one corner of the great square platform, which made it more convenient than if the dishes had to be carried down the steep stone steps broken in places and everywhere worn with age. The tower was one of those built all down the west coast of Calabria by the Emperor Charles V early in the sixteenth century, to keep off the Barbary pirates, when the unbelievers were allied with Francis I against the Emperor and the Church. They have gone to ruin, a few still stand intact, and mine is one of the largest. How it came into my possession ten years ago, and why I spend a part of each year in it, are matters which do not concern this tale. The tower stands in one of the loneliest spots in Southern Italy, at the extremity of a curving, rocky promontory, which forms a small but safe natural harbour at the southern extremity of the Gulf of Policastro, and just north of Cape Scalea, the birthplace of Judas Iscariot, according to the old local legend. The tower stands alone on this hooked spur of the rock, and there is not a house to be seen within three miles of it. When I go there I take a couple of sailors, one of whom is a fair cook, and when I am away it is in charge of a gnome-like little being who was once a miner and who attached himself to me long ago.

My friend, who sometimes visits me in my summer solitude, is an artist by profession, a Scandinavian by birth, and a cosmopolitan by force of circumstances.

We had dined at sunset; the sunset glow had reddened and faded again, and the evening purple steeped the vast chain of the mountains that embrace the deep gulf to eastward and rear themselves higher and higher towards the south. It was hot, and we sat at the landward corner of the platform, waiting for the night breeze to come down from the lower hills. The colour sank out of the air, there was a little interval of deep-grey twilight, and a lamp sent a yellow streak from the open door of the kitchen, where the men were getting their supper.

Then the moon rose suddenly above the crest of the promontory, flooding the platform and lighting up every little spur of rock and knoll of grass below us, down to the edge of the motionless water. My friend lighted his pipe and sat looking at a spot on the hillside. I knew that he was looking at it, and for a long time past I had wondered whether he would ever see anything there that would fix his attention. I knew that spot well. It was clear that he was interested at last, though it was a long time before he spoke. Like most painters, he trusts to his own eyesight, as a lion trusts his strength and a stag his speed, and he is always disturbed when he cannot reconcile what he sees with what he believes that he ought to see.

"It's strange," he said. "Do you see that little mound just on this side of the boulder?"

"Yes," I said, and I guessed what was coming.

"It looks like a grave," observed Holger.

"Very true. It does look like a grave."

"Yes," continued my friend, his eyes still fixed on the spot. "But the strange thing is that I see the body lying on the top of it. Of course," continued Holger, turning his head on one side as artists do, "it must be an effect of light. In the first place, it is not a grave at all. Secondly, if it were, the body would be inside and not outside. Therefor, it's an effect of the moonlight. Don't you see it?"

"Perfectly; I always see it on moonlight nights."

"It doesn't seem it interest you much," said Holger.

"On the contrary, it does interest me, though I am used to it. You're not so far wrong, either. The mound is really a grave."

"Nonsense!" cried Holger incredulously. "I suppose you'll tell me that what I see lying on it is really a corpse!"

"No," I answered, "it's not. I know, because I have taken the trouble to go down and see."

"Then what is it?" asked Holger.

"It's nothing."

"You mean that it's an effect of light, I suppose?"

"Perhaps it is. But the inexplicable part of the matter is that it makes no difference whether the moon is rising or setting, or waxing or waning. If there's any moonlight at all, from east or west or overhead, so long as it shines on the grave you can see the outline of the body on top."

Holger stirred up his pipe with the point of his knife, and then used his finger for a stopper. When the tobacco burned well, he rose from his chair.

"If you don't mind," he said, "I'll go down and take a look at it."

He left me, crossed the roof, and disappeared down the dark steps. I did not move, but sat looking down until he came out of the tower below. I heard him humming an old Danish song as he crossed the open space in the bright moonlight, going straight to the mysterious mound. When he was ten paces from it, Holger stopped short, made two steps forward, and then three or four backward, and then stopped again. I know what that meant. He had reached the spot where the Thing ceased to be visible—where, as he would have said, the effect of light changed.

Then he went on till he reached the mound and stood upon it. I could see the Thing still, but it was no longer lying down; it was on its knees now, winding its white arms round Holger's body and looking up into his face. A cool breeze stirred my hair at that moment, as the night wind began to come down from the hills, but it felt like a breath from another world.

The Thing seemed to be trying to climb to its feet helping itself up by Holger's body while he stood upright, quite unconcious of it and apparently looking toward the tower, which is very picturesque when the moonlight falls upon it on that side.

"Come along!" I shouted. "Don't stay there all night!"

It seemed to me that he moved reluctantly as he stepped from the mound, or else with difficulty. That was it. The Thing's arms were still round his waist, but its feet could not leave the grave. As he came slowly forward it was drawn and lengthened like a wreath of mist, thin and white, till I saw distinctly that Holger shook himself, as a man does who feels a chill. At the same instant a little wail of pain came to me on the breeze—it might have been the cry of the small owl that lives amongst the rocks—and the misty presence floated swiftly back from Holger's advancing figure and lay once more at its length upon the mound.

Again I felt the cool breeze in my hair, and this time an icy thrill of dread ran down my spine. I remembered very well that I had once gone down there alone in the moonlight; that presently, being near, I had seen nothing; that, like Holger, I had gone and had stood upon the mound; and I remembered how when I came back, sure that there was nothing there, I had felt the sudden conviction that there was something after all if I would only look back, a temptation I had resisted as unworthy of a man of sense, until, to get rid of it, I had shaken myself just as Holger did.

And now I knew that those white, misty arms had been round me, too; I knew it in a flash, and I shuddered as I remembered that I had heard the night owl then, too. But it had not been the night owl. It was the cry of the Thing.

I refilled my pipe and poured out a cup of strong southern wine; in less than a minute Holger was seated beside me again.

"Of course there's nothing there," he said, "but it's creepy, all the same. Do you know, when I was coming back I was so sure that there was something behind me that I wanted to turn around and look? It was an effort not to."

He laughed a little, knocked the ashes out of his pipe, and poured himself out some wine. For a while neither of us spoke, and the moon rose higher and we both looked at the Thing that lay on the mound.

"You might make a story about that," said Holger after a long time.

"There is one," I answered. "If you're not sleepy, I'll tell it to you."

"Go ahead," said Holger, who likes stories.

Old Aderio was dying up there in the village beyond the hill. You remember him, I have no doubt. They say that he made his money by selling sham jewelry in South America, and escaped with his gains when he was found out.. Like all those fellows, if they bring anything back with them, he at once set to work to enlarge his house, and as there are no masons here, he sent all the way to Paola for two workmen. They were a rough-looking pair of scoundrels—a Neapolitan who had lost one eye and a Sicilian with an old scar half an inch deep across his left cheek. I often saw them, for on Sundays they used to come down here and fish off the rocks. When Alario caught the fever that killed him the masons were still at work. As he had agreed that part of their pay should be their board and lodging, he made them sleep in the house. His wife was dead, and he had an only son called Angelo, who was a much better sort than himself. Angelo was to marry the daughter of the richest man in the village, and, strange to say, though the marriage was arranged by their parents, the young people were said to be in love with eachother.

For that matter, the whole village was in love with Angelo, and among the rest a wild, good-looking creature called Cristina, who was more like a gipsy than any girl I ever saw about here. She had very red lips and very black eyes, she was built like a greyhound, and had the tongue of the devil. But Angelo did not care a straw for her. He was rather a simple-minded fellow, quite different from his old scoundrel of a father, and under what I should call normal circumstances I really believe that he would never have looked at any girl except the nice plump little creature, with a fat dowry, whom his father meant him to marry. But things turned up which were neither normal nor natural.

On the other hand, a very handsome young shepherd from the hills above Maratea was in love with Cristina, who seems to have been quite indifferent to him. Cristina had no regular means of subsistence, but she was a good girl and willing to do any work or go on errands to any distance for the sake of a loaf of bread or a mess of beans, and permission to sleep under cover. She was especially glad when she could get something to do about the house of Angelo's father. There is no doctor in the village, and when the neighbours saw that old Alario was dying they sent Cristina to Scalea to fetch one. That was late in the afternoon, and if they had waited so long it was because the dying miser refused to allow any such extravagance while he was able to speak. But while Cristina was gone matters grew rapidly worse, the priest was brough tothe bedside, and when he had done what he could he gave it as his opinion to the bystanders that the old man was dead, and left the house.

You know these people. They have a physical horror of death. Until the priest spoke, the room had been full of people. The words were hardly out of his mouth before it was empty. It was night now. They hurried down the dark steps and out into the street.

Angelo, as I have said, was away, Cristina had not come back—the simple woman-servant who had nursed the sick man fled with the rest, and the body was left alone in the flickering light of the earthen oil lamp.

Five minutes later two men looked in cautiously and crept forward toward the bed. They were the one-eyed Neapolitan mason and his Sicilian companion. They knew what they wanted. In a moment they had dragged from under the bed a small but heavy iron-bound box, and long before anyone thought of coming back to the dead man they had left the house and the village under cover of darkness. It was easy enough, for Alario's house is the last toward the gorge which leads down here, and the thieves merely went out by the back door, got over the stone wall, and had nothing to risk after that except that possibility of meeting some belated countryman, which was very small indeed, since few of the people use that path. They had a mattock and shovel, and they made their way without accident.

I am telling you this story as it must have happened, for, of course, there were no witnesses to this part of it. The men brought the box down by the gorge, intending to bury it on the beach in the wet sand, where it would have been much safer. But the paper would have rotted if they had been obliged to leave it there long, so they dug their hole down there, close to that boulder. Yes, just where the mound is now.

Cristina did not find the doctor in Scalea, for he had been sent for from a place up the valley, half-way to San Domenico. If she had found him we would have come on his mule by the upper road, which is smoother but much longer. But Cristina took the short cut by the rocks, which passes about fifty feet above the mound, and goes round that corner. The men were digging when she passed, and she heard them at work. It would not hav been like her to go by without finding out what the noise was, for she was never afraid of anything in her life, and, besides, the fishermen sometimes come ashore here at night to get a stone for an anchor or to gather sticks to make a little fire. The night was dark and Cristina probably came close to the two men before she could see what they were doing. She knew them, of course, and they knew her, and understood instantly that they were in her power. There was only one thing to be done for their safety, and they did it. They knocked her on the head, they dug the hole deep, and they buried her quickly with the iron-bound chest. They must have understood that their only chance of escaping suspicion lay in getting back to the village before their absence was noticed, for they returned immediately, and were found half and hour later gossiping quietly with the man who was making Alario's coffin. He was a crony of theirs, and had been working at the repairs in the old man's house. So far as I have been able to make out, the only persons who were supposed to know where Alario kept his treasure were Angelo and the one woman-servant I have mentioned. Angelo was away; it was the woman who discovered the theft.

It was easy enough to understand why no one else knew where the money was. The old man kept his door locked and the key in his pocket when he was out, and did not let the woman enter to clean the place unless he was there himself. The whole village knew that he had money somewhere, however, and the masons had probably discovered the whereabouts of the chest by climbing in at the window in his absence. If the old man had not been delirious until he lost conciousness he would have been in frightful agony of mind for his riches. The faithful woman-servant forgot their existence only for a few moments when she fled with the rest, overcome by the horror of death. Twenty minutes had not passed before she returned with the two hideous old hags who are always called in to prepare the dead for burial. Even then she had not at first the courage to go near the bed with them, but she made a pretence of dropping something, went down on her knees as if to find it, and looked under the bedstead. The walls of the room were newly whitewashed down to the floor and she saw at a glance that the chest was gone. It had been there in the afternoon, it had therefore been stolen in the short interval since she had left the room.

There are no carabineers stationed in the village; there is not so much as a municipal watchman, for there is no municipality. There never was such a place, I believe. Scalea is supposed to look after it in some mysterious way, and it takes a couple of hours to get anybody from there. As the old woman had lived in the village all her life, it did not even occur to her to apply to any civil authority for help. She simply set up a howl and ran through the village in the dark, screaming out that her dead master's house had been robbed. Many of the people looked out, but at first no one seemed inclined to help her. Most of them, judging her by themselves, whispered to each other that she had probably stolen the money herself. The first man to move was the father of the girl whom Angelo was to marry; having collected his household, all of whom felt a personal interest in the wealth which was to have come into the family, he declared it to be his opinion that the chest had been stolen by the two journeymen masons who lodged in the house. He headed a search for them, which naturally began in Alario's house and ended in the carpenter's workshop, where the thieves were found discussing a measure of wine with the carpenter over the half-finished coffin, by the light of one earthen lamp filled with oil and tallow. The search-party at once accused the delinquents of the crime, and threatened to lock them up in the cellar till the carabineers could be fetched from Scalea. The two men looked at each other for one moment, and then without the slightest hesitation they put out the single light, seized the unfinished coffin between them, and using it as a sort of battering ram, dashed upon their assailants in the dark. In a few moments they were beyond pursuit.

That is the end of the first part of the story. The tresure had disappeared, and as no trace of it could be found the people supposed that the thieves had succeeded in carrying it off. The old man was buried, and when Angelo came back at last he had to borrow money to pay for the miserable funeral, and had some difficulty in doing so. He hardly needed to be told that in losing his inheritance he had lost his bride. In this part of the world marriages are made on strictly business principles, and if the promised cash is not forthcoming on the appointed day, the bride or the bridegroom whose parents have failed to produce it may as well take themselves off, for there will be no wedding. Poor Angelo knew that well enough. His father had been possessed of hardly any land, and now that the hard cash which he had brought from South America was gone, there was nothing left but debts for the building materials that were to have been used for enlarging and improving the old house. Angelo was beggared, and the nice plump little creature who was to have been his, turned up her nose at him in the most approved fashion. As for Cristina, it was several days before she was missed, for no one remembered that she had been sent to Scalea for the doctor, who had never come. She often disappeared in the same way for days together, when she could find a little work here and there at the distant farms among the hills. But when she did not come back at all, people began to wonder, and at last made up their minds that she had connived with the masons and had escaped with them.

I paused and emptied my glass.

"That sort of thing could not happen anywhere else," observed Holger, filling his everlasting pipe again. "It is wonderful what a natural charm there is about murder and sudden death in a romantic country like this. Deeds that would be simply brutal and disgusting anywhere else become dramatic and mysterious because this is Italy, and we are living in a genuine tower of Charles V built against Barbary pirates."

"There's something in that," I admitted. Holger is the most romantic man in the world inside of himself, but he always thinks it necessary to explain why he feels anything.

"I suppose the found the poor girl's body with the box," he said presently.

"As it seems to interest you," I answered, "I'll tell you the rest of the story."

The mood had risen by this time; the outline of the Thing on the mound was clearer to our eyes than before.

The village very soon settled down to its small dull life. No one missed old Alario, who had been away so much on his voyages to South America that he had never been a familiar figure in his native place. Angelo lived in the half-finished house, and because he had no money to pay the old woman-servant, she would not stay with him, but once in a long time she would come and wash a shirt for him for old acquaintance' sake. Besides the house, he had inherited a small patch of ground at some distance from the village; he tried to cultivate it, but he had no heart in the work, for he knew he could neer pay the taxes on it and on the house, which would certainly be confiscated by the Government, or seized for the debt of the building material, which the man who had supplied it refused to take back.

Angelo was very unhappy. So long as his father had been alive and rich, every girl in the village had been in love with him; but that was all changed now. It had been pleasant to be admired and courted, and invited to drink wine by fathers who had girls to marry. It was hard to be stared at coldly, and sometimes laughed at because he had been robbed of his inheritance. He cooked his miserable meals for himself, and from being sad became melancholy and morose.

At twilight, when the day's work was done, instead of hanging about in the open space before the church with young fellows of his own age, he took to wandering in lonely places on the outskirts of the village till it was quite dark. Then he slunk home and went to bed to save the expense of a light. But in those lonely twilight hours he began to have strange waking dreams. He was not always alone, for often when he sat on the stump of a tree, where the narrow path turns down the gorge, he was sure that a woman came up noiselessly over the rough stones, as if her feet were bare; and she stood under a clump of chestnut trees only half a dozen yards down the path, and beckoned to him without speaking. Though she was in the shadow he knew that her lips were red, and that when they parted a little and smiled at him she showed two small sharp teeth. He knew this at first rather than saw it, and he knew that it was Cristina, and that she was dead. Yet he was not afraid; he only wondered whether it was a dream, for he thought that if he had been awake he should have been frightened.

Besides, the dead woman had red lips, and that could only happen in a dream. Whenever he went near the gorget after sunset she was already there waiting for him, or else she very soon appeared, and he began to be sure of her blood-red mouth, but now each feature grew distinct, and the pale face looked at him with deep and hungry eyes.

It was the eyes that grew dim. Little by little he came to know that someday the dream would not end when he turned away to go home, but would lead him down the gorge out of which the vision rose. She was nearer now when she beckoned to him. Her cheeks were not livid like those of the dead, but pale with starvation, with the furious and unappeased physical hunger of her eyes that devoured him. They feasted on his soul and cast a spell over him, and at last they were close to his own and held him. He could not tell whether her breath was as hot as fire, or as cold as ice; he could not tell whether her red lips burned his or froze them, or whether her five fingers on his wrists seared scorching scars or bit his flesh like frost; he could not tell whether he was awake or asleep, whether she was alive or dead, but he knew that she loved him, she alone of all creatures, earthly or unearthly, and her spell had power over him.

When the moon rose high that night the shadow of that Thing was not alone down there upon the mound.

Angelo awoke in the cool dawn, drenched with dew and chilled through flesh, and blood, and bone. He opened his eyes to the faint grey light, and saw the stars were still shining overhead. He was very weak, and his heart was beating so slowly that he was almost like a man fainting. Slowly he turned his head on the mound, as on a pillow, but the other face was not there. Fear seized him suddenly, a fear unspeakable and unknown; he sprang to his feet and fled up the gorge, and he never looked behind him until he reached the door of the house on the outskirts of the village. Drearily he went to his work that day, and wearily the hours dragged themselves after the sun, till at last it touched the sea and sank, and the great sharp hills above Maratea turned purple against the dove-coloured eastern sky.

Angelo shouldered his heavy hoe and left the field. He felt less tired now than in the morning when he had begun to work, but he promised himself that he would go home without lingering by the gorge, and eat the best supper he could get himself, and sleep all night in his bed like a Christian man. Not again would he be tempted down the narrow way by a shadow with red lips and icy breath; not again would he dream that dream of terror and delight. He was near the village now; it was half an hour since the sun had set, and the cracked church bell sent little discordant echoes across the rocks and ravines to tell all good people that the day was done. Angelo stood still a moment where the path forked, where it led toward the village on the left, and down to the gorge on the right, where a clump of chestnut trees overhung the narrow way. He stood still a minute, lifting his battered hat from his head and gazing at the fast-fading sea westward, and his lips moved as he silently repeated the familiar evening prayer. His lips moved, but the words that followed them in his brain lost their meaning and turned into others, and ended in a name that he spoke aloud— Cristina! With the name, the tension of his will relaxed suddenly, reality went out and the dream took him again, and bore him on swiftly and surely like a man walking in his sleep, down, down, by the steep path in the gathering darkness. And as she glided beside him, Cristina whispered strange, sweet things in his ear, which somehow, if he had been awake, he knew that he could not quite have understood; but now they were the most wonderful words he had ever heard in his life. And she kissed him also, but not upon his mouth. He felt her sharp kisses upon his white throat, and he knew that her lips were red. So the wild dream sped on through twilight and darkness and moonrise, and all the glory of the summer's night. But in the chilly dawn he lay as one half dead upon the mound down there, recalling and not recalling, drained of his blood, yet strangely longing to give those red lips more. Then came the fear, the awful nameless panic, the mortal horror that guards the confines of the world we see not, neither know of as we know of other things, but which we feel when its icy chill freezes our bones and stirs our hair with the touch of a ghostly hand. Once more Angelo sprang from the mound and fled up the gorge in the breaking day, but his step was less sure this time, and he panted for breath as he ran; and when he came to the bright spring of water that rises half way up the hillside, he dropped upon his knees and hands and plunged his whole face in and drank as he had never drunk before—for it was the thirst of the wounded man who has lain bleeding all night upon the battle-field.

She had him fast now, and he could not escape her, but would come to her every evening at dusk until she had drained him of his last drop of blood. It was in vain that when the day was done he tried to take another turning and to go home by a path that did not lead near the gorge. It was in vain that he made promises to himself each morning at dawn when he climbed the lonely way up from the shore to the village. It was all in vain, for when the sun sank burning into the sea, and the coolness of the evening stole out as from a hiding-place to delight the weary world, his feet turned toward the old way, and she was waiting for him in the shadow under the chestnut trees; and then all happened as before, and she fell to kissing his white throat even as she flitted lightly down the way, winding one arm about him. And as his blood failed, she grew more hungry and more thirsty every day, and every day when he awoke in the early dawn it was harder to rouse himself to the effort of climbing the steep path to the village; and when he went to his work his feet dragged painfully, and there was hardly strength in his arms to wield the heavy hoe. He scarcely spoke to anyone now, but the people said he was "consuming himself" for love of the girl he was to have married when he lost his inheritance; and they laughed heartily at the thought, for this is not a very romantic country. At this time Antonio, the man who stays here to look after the tower, returned from a visit to his people, who live near Salerno. He had been away all the time since before Alario's death and knew nothing of what had happened. He has told me that he came back late in the afternoon and shut himself up in the tower to eat and sleep, for he was very tired. It was past midnight when he awoke, and when he looked out toward the mound, and he saw something, and he did not sleep again that night. When he went out again in the morning it was broad daylight, and there was nothing to be seen on the mound but loose stones and driven sand. Yet he did not go very near it; he went straight up the path to the village and directly to the house of the old priest.

"I have seen an evil thing this night," he said; "I have seen how the dead drink the blood of the living. And the blood is the life."

"Tell me what you have seen," said the priest in reply.

Antonio told him everything he had seen.

"You must bring your book and your holy water to-night," he added. "I will be here before sunset to go down with you, and if it pleases your reverence to sup with me while we wait, I will make ready."

"I will come," the priest answered, "for I have read in old books of these strange beings which are neither quick nor dead, and which lie ever fresh in their graves, stealing out in the dusk to taste life and blood."

Antonio cannot read, but he was glad to see that the priest understood the business; for, of course, the books must have been instructed him as to the best means of quieting the half-living Thing for ever.

So Antonio went away to his work, which consists largely in sitting on the shady side of the tower, when he is not perched upon a rock with a fishing-line catching nothing. But on that day he went twice to look at the mound in the bright sunlight, and he searched round and round it for some hole through which the being might get in and out; but he found none. When the sun began to sink and the air was cooler in the shadows, he went up to fetch the old priest, carrying a little wicker basket with him; and in this they placed a bottle of holy water, and the basin, and sprinkler, and the stole which the priest would need; and they came down and waited in the door of the tower till it should be dark. But while the light still lingered very grey and faint, they saw something moving, just there, two figures, a man's that walked, and a woman's that flitted beside him, and while her head lay on his shoulder she kissed his throat. The priest has told me that, too, and that his teeth chattered and he grasped Antonio's arm. The vision passed and disappeared into the shadow. Then Antonio got the leathern flask of strong liquor, which he kept for great occasions, and poured such a draught as made the old man feel almost young again; and gave the priest his stole to put on and the holy water to carry, and they went out together toward the spot where the work was to be done. Antonio says that in spite of the rum his own knees shook together, and the priest stumbled over his Latin. For when they were yet a few yards from the mound the flickering light of the lantern fell upon Angelo's white face, unconscious as if in sleep, and on his upturned throat, over which a very thin red line of blood trickled down into his collar; and the flickering light of the lantern played upon another face that looked up from the feast, upon two deep, dead eyes that saw in spite of death—upon parted lips, redder than life itself—upon two gleaming teeth on which glistened a rosy drop. Then the priest, good old man, shut his eyes tight and showered holy water before him, and his cracked voice rose almost to a scream; and then Antonio, who is no coward after all, raised his pick in one hand and the lantern in the other, as he sprang forward, not knowing what the end should be; and then he swears that he heard a woman's cry, and the Thing was gone, and Angelo lay alone on the mound unconscious, with the red line on his throat and the beads of deathly sweat on his cold forehead. They lifted him, half-dead as he was, and laid him on the ground close by; then Antonio went to work, and the priest helped him, thought he was old and could not do much; and they dug deep, and at last Antonio, standing in the grave, stooped down with his lantern to see what he might see.

His hair used to be dark brown, with grizzled streaks about the temples; in less than a month from that day he was as grey as a badger. He was a miner when he was young, and most of these fellows have seen ugly sights now and then, when accidents have happened, but he had never seen what he saw that night—that Thing which is neither alive nor dead, that Thing that will abide neither above ground nor in the grave. Antonio had brought something with him which the priest had not noticed—a sharp stake shaped from a piece of tough old driftwood. He had it with him now, and he had his heavy pick, and he had taken the lantern down into the grave. I don't think any power on earth could make him speak of what happened then, and the old priest was too frightened to look in. He says he heard Antonio breathing like a wild beast, and moving as if he were fighting with something almost as strong as himself; and he heard an evil sound also, with blows, as of something violently driven through flesh and bone; and then, the most awful sound of all—a woman's shriek, the unearthly scream of a woman neither dead nor alive, but buried deep for many days. And he, the poor old priest, could only rock himself as he knelt there in the sand, crying aloud his prayers and exorcisms to drown these dreadful sounds. Then suddenly a small iron-bound chest was thrown up and rolled over against the old man's knee, and in a moment more Antonio was beside him, his face as white as tallow in the flickering light of the lantern, shoveling the sand and pebbles into the grave with furious haste, and looking over the edge till the pit was half full; and the priest said that there was much fresh blood on Antonio's hands and on his clothes.

I had come to the end of my story. Holger finished his wine and leaned back in his chair.

"So Angelo got his own again." he said. "Did he marry the prim and plump young person to whom he had been betrothed?"

"No; he had been badly frightened. He went to South America, and has not been heard of since."

"And that poor thing's body is there still, I suppose," said Holger. "Is it quite dead yet, I wonder?"

I wonder, too. But whether it be dead or alive, I should hardly care to see it, even in broad daylight. Antonio is as grey as a badger, and he has never been quite the same man since that night.

The End

**The following Story was published in this March 1951
issue of Weird Tales.**

EACH MAN KILLS

BY VICTORIA GLAD

It's difficult to find information about Victoria Glad, but we do know that her short story "Each Man Kills" was a vampire story published by "Weird Tales" magazine in 1951. The story concerns a man who is in love with a woman who travels to Transylvania, and he loses contact with her, so he tries to track her down. The story appears to be an homage to "Dracula" and is a fun entry by a woman into a genre dominated by men (in the early years - today that's no longer the case).

"... to live you must feed on the living"

Each Man Kills

by Victoria Glad

Original art by Pulp Artist Vincent Napoli

Now that it's all over, it seems like a bad dream. But when I look at Maria's picture on my desk, I realize it couldn't have been a dream. Actually, it was only six months ago that I sat at this same desk, looking at her picture, wondering what could have happened to her. It had been six weeks since there had been any word from her, and she had promised to write as soon as she arrived in Europe. Considering that my future rested in her small hands, I had every right to be apprehensive.

We had grown up together, had lost our folks within a few years of each other and had been fond of each other the way kids are apt to be. Then the change came: It seemed I loved her, and she was still just "fond" of me. During our early college days I sort of let things ride, but once we went on to graduate school, I began to crowd her.

The next thing I knew, she had signed up with a student tour destined for Central Europe, and told me she would give me my answer when she returned. I had to be content with that, but couldn't help worrying. Maria was a strange girl—withdrawn, dreamy and soft-hearted. Knowing the section she was going to, I was inclined to be uneasy, since it is the realm of gypsies, fortune tellers and the like. It is also the birthplace of many strange legends, and Maria claimed to be strongly psychic. As a matter of fact, she had foretold one or two things which were probably coincidental, like the death of our parents, and which even made an impression on me—and you'd hardly call me a "believer."

This so-called talent of hers led her into trouble on more than one occasion. I remember in her senior year at college she fell under the spell of a short, fat, greasy spook-reader with a strictly phony accent and all but gave her eye teeth away, until I realized something was amiss, got to the bottom of it, and dispatched friend spook-reader *pronto*. If she should meet some unscrupulous person now, with no one around to get her out of the scrape—but I didn't want to think of that. I was sure this time everything would be all right.

When she didn't write at first, I let it go that she was busy. Finally, six weeks' silent treatment aroused my curiosity. It also aroused my nasty temper, and the next thing I knew I was on a plane bound for the Continent. Within two hours after landing, I found her at a little inn in Transylvania, a quaint little place that looked as if it were made of gingerbread, and was surrounded by the huge, craggy Transylvania Mountain range. I also found Tod Hunter.

"What's wrong, Maria? Why didn't you write?" I asked.

Her usually gay, shining brown eyes flashed angrily. "Why couldn't you leave me alone? I told you not to come after me. I came here so I could think this out. For God's sake, Bill, can't you see I wanted to think? To be by myself?"

"But you promised to write," I persisted, wondering at this change in her, this impatience. Wondered, too, at her wraithlike slimness. She'd always been curved in the right places.

"Maria has been studying much too diligently," Tod said slowly. "She's always tired lately. She hasn't been too well, either. Her throat bothers her."

I wanted to punch his head in. For some reason I didn't like him. Not because I sensed his rivalry; I was above that. God knows I wanted her to be happy, above everything. It was just something about him that irritated me. An attitude. Not supercilious; I could have coped with that. Rather, it was a calm imperturbability that seemed to speak his faith in his eventual success, regardless of any effort on my part.

I don't know how to fight that sort of strategy. I look like I am: blunt and obvious. Suddenly I didn't care if he was there.

"Maria. Ria, darling. This guy's no good for you, can't you see that? What do you know about him?"

She looked at me, her eyes surprised and a little hurt. Then she looked at him, seemed to be looking *through* him and into herself, if you know what I mean. A slow flush spread from the base of her throat, that thin, almost transparent throat.

"All I have to know," she said softly. "I love him."

She looked out the window. "I'm going up into *Konigstein*

Mountain, to a small sanitarium for my health shortly; the doctor has told me I must go away, and Tod has suggested this place. There Tod and I shall be married."

I knew then how it felt to be on the receiving end of a monkey-punch. That she had come to this decision because of my objections, I had not the slightest doubt. She was going to marry someone about whom she knew absolutely nothing. She was much more ill than she knew. Hunter was undoubtedly after her money; she was considerably well-off. Obviously she was once more being influenced in the wrong direction.

"I won't let you!" I warned. "Give it some more time, if for nothing else, then for old times' sake."

"How about me, Morris?" Tod interrupted. "You haven't asked me my feelings on the subject. I happen to love Maria dearly. Have I no say just because you're a childhood friend of hers?"

"Childhood friend! I was her whole family for years before she ever heard of you! I'll see you in hell before I let her marry you!" I shouted. Looking back, I'm sure that had he said anything else, I would have killed him, if Ria hadn't come between us.

"That's enough, Bill Morris! I've heard all I want to from you. I'm twenty-three, and if I choose to marry Tod, I'll do so and there's nothing you can do about it. Now, please go."

"Okay, Ria," I said, "if that's the way you want it. But I'm not through. If you won't protect yourself, I'll do it for you. I'd like to know more about the mysterious Mr. Tod Hunter, American, and I do wish, for your own sake, you'd do the same. I wouldn't care if you married King Tut, so long as you knew all about him. People just don't marry strangers; not if they're smart. For God's sake, ask him about himself!"

"All right, Bill," she replied, smiling patiently. "I'll ask him. Now, do stop being childish."

"Okay, darling," I said sheepishly. "But do me one more favor. Don't marry him until I get back. Only a little while; give me a week. Just wait a little longer."

As I closed the door, I could still feel his smile, mocking—yet a little sad.

But Maria didn't wait. I was gone a week. I had walked my legs off trying to track down the elusive Mister Hunter and discovered exactly—nothing. All his landlady could tell me was that he was an American who had come to this climate for his health, and that he slept late mornings. I was licked and I knew it. If I had been a pup, I would have fitted my tail neatly between my legs and made for home. But I wasn't a pup, so I headed straight for Ria's flat to face the music.

They were waiting for me, she and Tod. When I saw her, I wished I were dead.

She lay in Tod's arms, her body a mere whisper of a body. White and cold she was, like frozen milk on a cold winter's day. They were both dead.

You know how it is when at a wake someone views the deceased and says kindly, "She's beautiful," and "she" isn't beautiful at all; just a made-up, lifeless handful of clay. Dead as dead, and frightening. Well, it wasn't that way this time. Their fair skins were faintly pink-tinted and their blonde heads, hers ashen and his a reddish cast, gleamed brightly. And they sat so close in the sofa before the fire, his head resting in the hollow of her throat. They looked—peaceful; no line marred their faces. I almost fancied I saw them breathe. And on her third finger, left hand, was the ring—a thin, platinum band. He had won, and in winning somehow he had lost. How they had died and why they found each other and death at the same time, I would probably never know. I only knew one thing: I had to get away from there—quickly. I almost ran the distance to my flat. Stumbled into the place and poured a triple Scotch which I could scarcely hold. The Scotch seared my throat and tasted bitter; someone must have poured salt in it. Then I realized that it was tears—my tears. I, Bill Morris, who hadn't cried since my fifth birthday—I was sobbing like a baby.

I didn't call the police. That would mean I would have to go back and watch them cover that lovely body, carry it away and submit it to untold indignities in order to ascertain the cause of death. The cleaning girl would find them in the morning and would notify the police.

But it wasn't so simple as that. In the morning I found I couldn't shake off the guilt which possessed me. Even two bottles of Scotch hadn't helped me to forget. I was dead drunk and cold sober at the same time.

I phoned Ria's landlady and told her I had failed to reach the Hunters by phone, that I was sure something was amiss. Would she please go to their flat and see if anything was wrong.

She was amused. "Really, Mr. Morris, you must be mistaken. Miss Maria went out just an hour ago with her new husband. Surely you are jesting. Why she has never looked better. So happy. They have left for *Konigstein*. They have also left you a note.

I told her I would be right over, and hopped a cab. I began to think I was losing my mind. I had seen them both—dead. The landlady had seen them this morning—*alive!*"

When I arrived, the landlady looked at me for a long moment, taking in my rough, dark-blue complexion, unpressed clothes, red-rimmed eyes, then wagged a finger playfully.

"You are playing a joke, no? A wedding joke, maybe. Here, too, we haze newlyweds. But of course I understood. Who could help loving Miss Maria? Be of good heart, young man. For you there will be another, some day. But I talk too much. Here is your letter."

I went where I would be undisturbed, to the reading room of the library on the same street as my flat. To the musty, oblong, dimly lit room whose threshold sunshine and fresh air dared not cross. Without the saving warmth of sunlight or the fresh, clean relief of sweet-smelling air, I read. Read, inhaling the pungent, sour smell of the Scotch I had consumed during the long, sleepless night. Read, and then doubted that I had read at all—but the blue ink on the white paper forced me to acknowledge its actuality. It had been written by Hunter, in a neat, scholar's script.

Dear Morris: (It began)

Why should I not have wanted Maria? You did; others doubtless did. Why then should she not be mine? There are many things worse than being married to me; she might have married a man who beat her!

With her I have known the two happiest days of my life. I want no more than that. I have no right to ask for more. Have we, any of us, a right to endless bliss on this earth? Hardly.

You thought of her welfare above all; for that I owe you some explanation. You must be patient, you must believe, and in the end, you must do as I ask. You must.

You wanted to know about me—of my life before Maria. Before Maria? It seems strange to think about it. There is no life without Maria. Still, there was a time when for me she didn't exist. I have been constantly going forward to the day when I would meet her, yet there was a time when I didn't know where I would find her, or even what her name would be!

It was chance that brought us together. For me, good chance; for you, possibly ill chance; for Maria? Only she can say. Some three years ago I was studying in England under a Rhodes Scholarship. The future held great things for me. I was a Yank like yourself, and damn proud of it. Life in England seemed strange and slow and sometimes utterly dismal under Austerity. Then, little by little I slipped into their slower ways, growing to love the people for their spunk, and finally coming to feel I was one of them, so to speak.

I have said everything slowed down: I was wrong. Studying intensified for me. The folklore of the British Isles intrigued me. I delved into the Black Welsh tales, the mischievous fancies of the Irish, the English legends of the prowling werewolf. For me it was a relief from polit-

ical science, which suddenly palled and which smacked of treason in the light of current events. My extracurricular research consumed the better part of my evenings. My books were and always have been a part of me, and as was to be expected, I overdid it. I studied too hard with too little let-up. Sometimes it seemed to me there was more truth to what I read than myth. It became somewhat of an obsession. Suddenly, one night, everything blacked out.

I came to in a sanatorium. I didn't know how I got there, and when they explained it to me, I laughed. I thought they were joking. When I tried to get up, to walk, I collapsed. Then I knew how bad it had been. I knew, too, I would have to go slowly.

It was there I met Eve. She was beautiful. Not like Maria, who is like a fragile, fair, spun-sugar angel. Eve was more earthy, with skin like ivory, creamy and rich and pale. Her blue-black hair she wore long and gathered in the back. She looked about twenty-five, but a streak of pure white ran back from each of her temples. She was the most striking woman I have ever met. I had never known anyone like her, nor have I since I saw her last.

You know how it is: the air of mystery about a woman makes a man like a kid again. She reminded me of a sleek, black cat, with her large, hazel eyes. I bumped into her one day on the verandah, and spent every day with her after that.

The doctors wanted me to take exercise—short walks and the like, and Eve went with me, struggling to keep up with me. The slightest effort tired her. She suffered from a rather nasty case of anemia. She seldom smiled; the effort was probably too much for her. I saw her really smile only once.

We had been on one of our short hikes in the woods close by the grounds. She stumbled over a twig or a branch, I'm not sure which. Suddenly she was in my arms. Have you ever held a cloud in your arms, Morris? So light she was, although she was almost as tall as I. Warm and pulsating. Her eyes held mine; it was almost uncanny. I have never been affected like that by a woman. Then I was kissing her; then a sharp sting, and I winced. There was the warm, salt taste of blood on my lips. I never knew how it happened. But she was smiling, her full mouth parted in the strangest smile I have ever seen. And those small white teeth gleamed; and in her eyes, which were all black pupils now, with the iris quite hidden, was desire—or something beyond desire. I couldn't define it then; now, I think I can. Her small, pink tongue darted over her lips, tasting, seeming to savor.

I was frightened, for some indefinable reason. I wanted to get away from her, from the woods, from myself. I grasped her arm roughly and we started back for the grounds. We never mentioned the episode again, but we neither of us ever forgot. She intrigued me now, more than ever. The doctors were able to satisfy my curiosity somewhat. They told me she had been a patient for some four years. Some days she was better, some days worse. She needed rest—much rest. Most days she slept past noon with their approval. Some days there was a faint flush beneath that ivory skin; other days it was pale and cool.

Just when we became lovers, I scarcely remember. Things were happening so fast I could barely keep pace with them. There was a magnetism about Eve which compelled. I couldn't have resisted if I'd wanted to—and I didn't.

I began to have long periods of lassitude, times when I would black out and remember nothing afterwards. And the dreams began. I would dream I was stroking a large, velvety-black cat, a cat with shining yellow eyes that looked at me as if they knew my every thought. I would stroke it continuously and it would nip me play-

fully. Then, one night the dream intensified: I was playing with the creature, caressing it gently, when of a sudden its lips drew back in a snarl, and without warning it sprang at my throat and buried its fangs deep! I thought I could feel life being drawn from me; I screamed.

The doctors told me afterwards that I was semi-conscious for days; that I had to be restrained.

When I was well again, Eve came to see me. She was gentle—soothing. She held me close to her and oh! it was good to be alive and to belong to someone.

I remember to this day what she wore. Black velvet lounging slacks, a low-necked amber satin blouse, caught at the "V" by a curiously wrought antique silver pin. It was round, about four inches in diameter. In its center was the carved figure of a serpent coiled to strike. Its eyes were deep amber topazes and its darting tongue was raised and set with a blood-red ruby.

"What an unusual pin, Eve," I said "I've never seen it before, have I?"

"No," she replied. "It belongs to the deep, dark, seldom discussed skeleton in the Orcaczy closet, Tod. You see, my great-great grandmother was quite a wicked lady, to hear tell. Went in for Witches' masses and the like. They say she poisoned her husband, a rather elderly and very childish man, for her lover, whom she subsequently married. Together they did away with relatives who stood in the way of their accumulating more money. This pin was the instrument of death."

Her slim fingers pressed the ruby tongue and the pin opened, revealing a space large enough to secrete powder.

"It's like those employed by the infamous Borgias, as you can see," she continued, shrugging. "Perhaps it was fate then, that her devoted new husband tired of her once her fortune was assured him, took a young mistress for himself, and disposed of the unfortunate wife, using her own pin to perpetrate her murder. She was excommuni-

cated by her church, too, which must have made it most unpleasant for her, poor old dear." The slim shoulders straightened. "But let's not discuss such unpleasant things, my dear. The important thing now is for you to get well quickly. I've missed you terribly, you know."

It was then I asked her to marry me. I knew I didn't really love her, but there seemed nothing to prevent our marriage. And she had gotten under my skin. It was as elemental as that. She said she thought we should wait until I fully recovered.

"Don't say any more, darling," she said. "Rest your poor, sore throat."

She bent over me solicitously and I reached up to stroke that smooth black hair. It had a familiar feel to it that I couldn't quite place. Of course I had stroked it hundreds of times before, but it wasn't that. Then she looked straight at me, those large, glowing hazel eyes boring into mine, and I knew. Knew and disbelieved at the same time. I froze where I lay, paralyzed by my fear; unable to make a sound.

"So you know," she whispered. "It is well. I have marked you for my own these many months. Now that you know, you will not fight. You know what I am, or at least you can guess. This pin you admired so—it was mine three hundred years ago and it will always be mine!"

Her lips were on mine. She had never kissed me like this. It was like the touch of hot ice, freezing, then searing. Unendurable. I lay inert; I couldn't have moved if I wanted to. I could scarcely breathe. Then I felt the blood within me pounding, pulsing, beginning to answer in spite of myself. I tasted once more the warm, salty fluid on my lips. Eve's body was liquid in my arms; warm, heady, narcotizing. Once again I felt the agonizing, dagger sharp pain in my throat and—darkness.

Have you ever wakened to a bright, sunny afternoon and heard yourself pronounced dead? They spoke *in low, hushed tones. How unfortunate. Young fellow only thirty, dying so far away from his homeland. No family. Good thing he was well-set in life. This sudden anemia was most extraordinary; fellow showed no signs of it previously. All he had really needed was rest. If he had recovered, that lovely Eve Orcaczy might have made both their lives happier, richer. Sad ending to what might have been an idyll. Good of her to claim the body. She said she was going to inter it in the family vault in* Konigstein Mountain *in Tran-sylvania.*

I heard them distinctly. I wanted to shout that I wasn't dead; I wanted to wake up from this horrible nightmare. I was as alive as they. I knew I had to get out of there, some way; to get away from Eve, whom I now feared. They left to make arrangements.

The lassitude crept through me without warning; I dozed in spite of myself. And I dreamed again. I was a cat running, leaping through windows, loping over the countryside, stopping for no one. I panted with my exer-tions. Towns and cities flew by; I had to get someplace and quickly. Then the dream ended.

"Tod," she said, "Get up, my dear." I heard Her and I hated Her. Hated Her while I was drawn to Her. There was a white mist before my eyes. I reached up to brush it away. It was not a mist; it was a cloth. I shivered.

"I must wake up," I whispered hoarsely, "I must! I'm going mad!"

There was a creaking sound and daylight descended upon me. When I saw where I was, I covered my face with my hands and sobbed. I tried to pray, but the words froze on my lips. I was sitting in a coffin in a mausoleum! I had been buried alive!

"What am I?" I shrieked. "Where am I and what have You done? I'm out of my mind; stark, staring mad!"

Eve's lips parted, showing the even white teeth—those slightly pointed teeth.

"You're quite sane, my dear," She said calmly. "You are now one of us; a revenant, even as I, and to live you must feed on the living."

"It's not true!" I shouted. "This is all a crazy nightmare, part of my illness! You're not real! Nothing is real!"

"I'm quite real, Tod. To be trite, I am what I am, and have accepted it calmly, as you shall in time. I have told you of my life. You have been a student of legends. Legends are often—more often than you think—reality. When one has been murdered, if one has lived a so-called wicked life, he is doomed to walk the earth battening on the living. My fate was sealed as I lay in my coffin. But that wasn't enough. As I lay there, my pet cat, Suma, slunk into the room and leapt over me. That was a double insurance of my life after death. Those whom I mark for my own must, too, live on. Accept it, my dear. You have no other choice."

"No!" I cried. "I'm an American! Things like this don't happen to us! It's only in stories, and then to foreigners!"

She chuckled drily. "I'm afraid these things do happen, and in this case, you're it, my dear. Make the best of it."

But I wouldn't; I refused to—for a while. I would not feast on the blood of the living. Something within me fought. For a time.

Then, the awful hunger began. The tearing pangs of hunger that ordinary food wouldn't arrest. I fought it as long as I could. I lost.

First it was small animals; animals that I loved. It was my life or theirs. Then there was a little girl; a dear little creature who might have been my child under different circumstances.

After the episode of the little girl, Eve left me. She

had no further use for me; she had wanted the child, too, and I had got it. I was now competition to be shunned. I was alone once again alone and thoroughly miserable. I couldn't understand myself, my motives, so how could I expect someone else to understand?

I only knew what I was; nor could I rationalize on why I had become this way. I could only presume it had happened to others equally as innocent as myself of wrong-doing. In the daytime, when I was like others, I reproached myself; goodness knows I loathed myself and what I had to do in order to "live." I wished I might really die, for I was tired—so frightfully tired and sick of it all. But I knew of no way to accomplish this, so I had to bear it all, fasting until my voracious, disgusting appetites got the better of me.

I decided there must be some information on my kind, particularly in this area where vampire legends are rife, so I took to haunting reading rooms. It was there I met Maria. She told me, after we knew each other better, that she was doing graduate work in regional superstitions and had decided that her thesis would treat of the history of vampirism. She found it terribly amusing, but at the same time frightening: Didn't I? I fear I saw nothing laughable about it, but I held my peace. Why, I could have done a thesis for her that would have driven some mild-mannered prof completely out of his mind! I kept my knowledge to myself, though; I didn't want to scare Maria.

She was like a flash of sunshine in a darkened room. She made each day worth living. For the first time the hunger pangs ceased. Ceased for one week, then two. I was certain I was cured. Perhaps, I thought, the whole thing was just a dream and I am finally awake.

I felt then I had the right to tell her of my love. She looked infinitely sad. She wasn't certain, she said. She knew she was awfully fond of me, but she was confused. She had just come away from the States, trying to make up her mind about someone dear, whom she didn't want to hurt, and she wanted a breather. I said I would wait up to and through eternity, if she wished.

Things, went along peacefully then. We would walk for hours together, walk in complete silence and understanding. My strength seemed to be returning more day by day. We went far afield in search of material for her thesis. She would track down the most minute speck of hearsay, to get authenticity.

One day, in our wanderings, I thoughtlessly let myself be led too near my resting place. One of the locals mentioned a "place of horror" nearby and Maria wanted to investigate. I had no choice. We poked amid the still fustiness of the deserted mausoleum I knew so well. She thought it odd that the door was unlocked. I said, yes, wasn't it. Then she saw the box, that gleaming copper box which Eve had so thoughtfully provided. She stroked it gently, commenting on its beauty, and before I could prevent it or divert her attention, she had lifted the heavy lid exposing the disarranged shroud, the remains of one or two hapless small creatures, the horrible blood-stained satin lining. She screamed and dropped the lid, somehow pinching her finger. She hopped on one foot, as one usually does to fight down sudden pain. Then she was clinging to me, thoroughly frightened.

"What does it mean, Tod?"

I quieted her with the usual platitudes. Then I was kissing that poor, red little finger. Without warning to myself or her, I nipped it affectionately. A warm glow spread through me; there was a taste more delightful than fine old brandy, or vintage wine, and I knew irrevocably that I was not cured; no, nor ever should be! And I knew, too, that I wanted Maria—not just as a man longs for the woman he loves—but to drink of the fountain of her life, that warm, intoxicating fountain, greedily, joyously. She never knew what went through my mind at that moment. If I could have killed myself then,

I would have, and with no compunction. But there is more to killing a revenant than that. The Church knows the procedure. I hurried Maria home as fast as I could and told her I had to go away for a week on business. She believed me and said she would miss me. But I didn't go away. That night I fought a losing battle with myself, and then and every night thereafter, I returned to her, partook of her and slunk away, loathing myself. I knew that I must soon kill the one being I loved above all others, kill, too, her immortal soul, and there was nothing I could do to prevent it.

She began to fade visibly. When I "returned" in a week, she was so ill that a few steps tired her. Her appetite all but vanished. She seemed genuinely glad to see me. She was beset by nightmares, she said. Could I help her get some rest? I took her to a physician who sagely prescribed a change in climate, rest and a diet rich in blood and iron, gave her a prescription for sedatives, and called it a day.

You know how she looked when you saw her. The day was approaching when she would have no more blood, when life as you know it would stop and she would become like me. Somehow I couldn't take her with me without some warning, but I didn't know how to do it. You see, since I was an innocent victim myself. I could speak, could warn my intended victim, because although my soul had all but died, there was still a spark that evil hadn't touched. I knew she would think it a joke if I told her about myself without warning.

Then, happily for me, you came along. I knew you would sense something amiss and I didn't care. I was almost certain of her love, and I decided to seize the few minutes left me and devil take the hindmost! When you told her to confront me, you gave me the happiest days of my life. For this I thank you sincerely. For what I have done and will ask you to do, forgive me!

Maria asked me directly, as you had known she

would. I replied frankly, sparing her nothing. I told her that the fact that this life had been wished on me, as it were, gave me some rights, and that I could tell her how to rid herself of me, if she wished. Then she turned to me, her large, lovely eyes thoughtful.

"Tod, dearest," she said softly, "I must die some day, really die, so what difference does it make when? I only know that I love you. Why wait until I'm decrepit and alone, with only a few memories to look back on? Why not now, with you, where life doesn't really stop? With all I've read about this, don't you think I could free myself if I wished?"

I still wonder if she really believed me. We were married three days later. I never told her what her life with me would be like—that one day I would desert her, fearing and hating her rivalry for the very source of my life, and the ghastly chain would continue. I couldn't. I loved her so, Morris, can you understand that? I couldn't betray her then and I can't now.

On the second night of our marriage, she died as you know it, in my arms. I don't think she knows it yet. But it won't be long until she does discover it. We were quite alive when you found us; she was in an hypnotic state induced by her condition. She heard and saw nothing. But I knew. And I must keep my faith. I must, and you are the only one who can help me.

If you will show this to a priest, he will gladly accompany you to the place in Konigstein, where we rest during the morning in a new "bed" I had specially constructed for us. I couldn't bring Maria to that other bed of corruption. A map of how to get there is enclosed. There you will perform the ancient, effective rites, and you will lay us to rest together, as we wish. That is all I ask....

When I had finished reading I stared at nothing, trying to force myself to think. This was "all" he asked. In substance, he wished me to murder the girl I loved. I could refuse; I could

ignore his request. I could even doubt the verity of his state-
ments. He might be a madman. But I didn't doubt. I believed
every word, and I knew I would do as he asked.

That she had gone willingly I didn't doubt. I no longer
hated him so much; rather I pitied him, the hapless victim of a
horrible chain of circumstance.

———

I found the priest, a venerable, gentle soul, after much
searching. The younger men had looked at me searchingly,
laughed and told me to read the Good Book for consolation,
and to lay off the bottle. Father Kalman was understanding,
with the wisdom of the very old.

"Yes, my son," he said, "I will go. Many might doubt, but I
believe. Lucifer roams the earth in many guises and must be
recognized and exorcised."

It was five o'clock in the morning when we approached the
mausoleum. The Good Father explained that the "creatures of
darkness" had to be back in their resting places before the cock
crew. At night they drew sustenance; during the morning they
slept.

There was a gleaming copper casket. Tod had not lied. We
approached it warily. In it was nothing but grisly remains,
bloodstains and dust. We drew back, fearful. Then we saw the
other, newer casket in richest mahogany, almost twice the
width of the copper box: *Their bridal bed!*

They lay together, his arm about her. She wore a gown of
palest blue, but oh, that mockery of a gown! Stained it was
with fresh blood which had seeped onto it from him. Obviously she had not taken to prowling yet. His mouth was dark,
rich with blood, slightly open in a half-smile. His hand pressed
her fair head close to his chest. She lay trustingly within the
circle of his arm, like a small child. The priest crossed himself.
The bodies twitched slightly.

"You know what you must do," Father Kalman whispered.

I nodded, the pit of my stomach churning madly. I

couldn't do it! Not Maria, the lovely. But I knew I would; I had to. She must not wake again to see that blood-stained gown or to wonder at her husband's gory lips. She should know rest, eternal rest.

Father Kalman circled the box several times, ringing his small bell, and at one point laid a crucifix upon each of their chests. Their faces writhed and I felt my skin creep.

Then, chanting in a low, firm voice, the priest gave me the signal. Together we drove two long stakes, dipped first in Holy Water, home, piercing their hearts simultaneously.

The bodies leapt forward in the box, straining against the stake, and a horrible, drawn-out wail shattered the stillness of the tomb. The priest dropped to his knees and I clapped my hands over my ears, but the dreadful shriek penetrated. My stomach turned over and I retched. The Good Father followed suit. We were no supermen and our bodies and our very souls revolted against this monstrous thing.

"Let us finish, my son," the priest said slowly, after a time, his face the color of ashes. "We must bury these dead, that they may sleep in consecrated ground."

I couldn't. I had to see her again before it was done. She lay, small and fragile as ever, her face calm, only there was no trace of life now. She was still and white, as only the dead—the truly dead—are. Tod's arm was flung across her chest, as if to protect her. I made myself move the arm, resting her head upon his shoulder, where it belonged. Then, as I looked, there was just Maria. Tod was gone and only a handful of dust lay piled up around the stake. It was enough. I slammed the lid shut.

Looking back now, I can see it was all for the best. Ria was different—apart from other women. A dreamer, a mystic, too easily influenced by the bizarre and un-normal. I, on the other hand, am practical almost to a fault. Had she married me I might have crushed in her the very thing that drew me to her. In time she might have grown to hate me.

Hunter, on the other hand, was a student. Introspective, given to romanticizing. Susceptible to suggestion. Had I been confronted with an Eve, I should have run like hell. To him, though, she was cloaked in mystery; hence, more desirable. What better choice for him ultimately than Ria? That Ria had to die to achieve her happiness is of no real importance. Life is a transitory thing anyway.

Sometimes, though, when I look at Ria's picture, it's hard to be practical. She was everything I shall ever want.

I had never been to Europe before the summer of 1947. I went to find Maria, to marry her. Instead, I found and murdered her, and I will never go back again.

The End

Count Magnus

by M.R. James

M.R. James (1862-1936) is considered one of the greatest ghost story writers ever, and his influence can still be felt on modern writers; Stephen King himself cites James as an influence. While James, who was born in England, was known for his ghost stories, he was a respected scholar as well. In "Count Magnus," James created a character who isn't explicitly a vampire but who qualifies in most respects. Some consider it more in keeping with his ghost stories, but the similarities to stories like "Dracula" are fascinating and well worth examining.

Count Magnus

by M.R. James

By what means the papers out of which I have made a connected story came into my hands is the last point which the reader will learn from these pages. But it is necessary to prefix to my extracts from them a statement of the form in which I possess them.

They consist, then, partly of a series of collections for a book of travels, such a volume as was a common product of the forties and fifties. Horace Marryat's *Journal of a Residence in Jutland and the Danish Isles* is a fair specimen of the class to which I allude. These books usually treated of some unfamiliar district on the Continent. They were illustrated with woodcuts or steel plates. They gave details of hotel accommodation, and of means of communication, such as we now expect to find in any well-regulated guide-book, and they dealt largely in reported conversations with intelligent foreigners, racy innkeepers and garrulous peasants. In a word, they were chatty.

Begun with the idea of furnishing material for such a book, my papers as they progressed assumed the character of a record of one single personal experience, and this record was continued up to the very eve, almost, of its termination.

The writer was a Mr. Wraxall. For my knowledge of him I

have to depend entirely on the evidence his writings afford, and from these I deduce that he was a man past middle age, possessed of some private means, and very much alone in the world. He had, it seems, no settled abode in England, but was a denizen of hotels and boarding-houses. It is probable that he entertained the idea of settling down at some future time which never came; and I think it also likely that the Pantechnicon fire in the early seventies must have destroyed a great deal that would have thrown light on his antecedents, for he refers once or twice to property of his that was warehoused at that establishment.

It is further apparent that Mr. Wraxall had published a book, and that it treated of a holiday he had once taken in Brittany. More than this I cannot say about his work, because a diligent search in bibliographical works has convinced me that it must have appeared either anonymously or under a pseudonym.

As to his character, it is not difficult to form some superficial opinion. He must have been an intelligent and cultivated man. It seems that he was near being a Fellow of his college at Oxford—Brasenose, as I judge from the Calendar. His besetting fault was pretty clearly that of over-inquisitiveness, possibly a good fault in a traveller, certainly a fault for which this traveller paid dearly enough in the end.

On what proved to be his last expedition, he was plotting another book. Scandinavia, a region not widely known to Englishmen forty years ago, had struck him as an interesting field. He must have lighted on some old books of Swedish history or memoirs, and the idea had struck him that there was room for a book descriptive of travel in Sweden, interspersed with episodes from the history of some of the great Swedish families. He procured letters of introduction, therefore, to some persons of quality in Sweden, and set out thither in the early summer of 1863.

Of his travels in the North there is no need to speak, nor of his residence of some weeks in Stockholm. I need only mention that some *savant* resident there put him on the track of an important collection of family papers belonging to the propri-etors of an ancient manor-house in Vestergothland, and obtained for him permission to examine them.

The manor-house, or *herrgård*, in question is to be called Råbäck (pronounced something like Roebeck), though that is not its name. It is one of the best buildings of its kind in all the country, and the picture of it in Dahlenberg's *Suecia antiqua et moderna*, engraved in 1694, shows it very much as the tourist may see it to-day. It was built soon after 1600, and is, roughly speaking, very much like an English house of that period in respect of material—red-brick with stone facings—and style. The man who built it was a scion of the great house of De la Gardie, and his descendants possess it still. De la Gardie is the name by which I will designate them when mention of them becomes necessary.

They received Mr. Wraxall with great kindness and cour-tesy, and pressed him to stay in the house as long as his researches lasted. But, preferring to be independent, and mistrusting his powers of conversing in Swedish, he settled himself at the village inn, which turned out quite sufficiently comfortable, at any rate during the summer months. This arrangement would entail a short walk daily to and from the manor-house of something under a mile. The house itself stood in a park, and was protected—we should say grown up—with large old timber. Near it you found the walled garden, and then entered a close wood fringing one of the small lakes with which the whole country is pitted. Then came the wall of the demesne, and you climbed a steep knoll—a knob of rock lightly covered with soil—and on the top of this stood the church, fenced in with tall dark trees. It was a curious building to English eyes. The nave and aisles were low, and filled with pews and galleries. In the western gallery stood the handsome old organ, gaily painted, and with silver pipes. The ceiling was flat, and had been adorned by a seventeenth-century artist with a strange and hideous "Last Judgment," full of lurid flames, falling cities, burning ships, crying souls, and brown and smiling demons. Handsome brass coronæ hung from the roof;

the pulpit was like a doll's-house, covered with little painted wooden cherubs and saints; a stand with three hour-glasses was hinged to the preacher's desk. Such sights as these may be seen in many a church in Sweden now, but what distinguished this one was an addition to the original building. At the eastern end of the north aisle the builder of the manor-house had erected a mausoleum for himself and his family. It was a largish eight-sided building, lighted by a series of oval windows, and it had a domed roof, topped by a kind of pumpkin-shaped object rising into a spire, a form in which Swedish architects greatly delighted. The roof was of copper externally, and was painted black, while the walls, in common with those of the church, were staringly white. To this mausoleum there was no access from the church. It had a portal and steps of its own on the northern side.

Past the churchyard the path to the village goes, and not more than three or four minutes bring you to the inn door.

On the first day of his stay at Råbäck Mr. Wraxall found the church door open, and made those notes of the interior which I have epitomized. Into the mausoleum, however, he could not make his way. He could by looking through the keyhole just descry that there were fine marble effigies and sarcophagi of copper, and a wealth of armorial ornament, which made him very anxious to spend some time in investigation.

The papers he had come to examine at the manor-house proved to be of just the kind he wanted for his book. There were family correspondence, journals, and account-books of the earliest owners of the estate, very carefully kept and clearly written, full of amusing and picturesque detail. The first De la Gardie appeared in them as a strong and capable man. Shortly after the building of the mansion there had been a period of distress in the district, and the peasants had risen and attacked several châteaux and done some damage. The owner of Råbäck took a leading part in suppressing the trouble, and there was reference to executions of ringleaders and severe punishments inflicted with no sparing hand.

The portrait of this Magnus de la Gardie was one of the best in the house, and Mr. Wraxall studied it with no little interest after his day's work. He gives no detailed description of it, but I gather that the face impressed him rather by its power than by its beauty or goodness; in fact, he writes that Count Magnus was an almost phenomenally ugly man.

On this day Mr. Wraxall took his supper with the family, and walked back in the late but still bright evening.

"I must remember," he writes, "to ask the sexton if he can let me into the mausoleum at the church. He evidently has access to it himself, for I saw him to-night standing on the steps, and, as I thought, locking or unlocking the door."

I find that early on the following day Mr. Wraxall had some conversation with his landlord. His setting it down at such length as he does surprised me at first; but I soon realized that the papers I was reading were, at least in their beginning, the materials for the book he was meditating, and that it was to have been one of those quasi-journalistic productions which admit of the introduction of an admixture of conversational matter.

His object, he says, was to find out whether any traditions of Count Magnus de la Gardie lingered on in the scenes of that gentleman's activity, and whether the popular estimate of him were favourable or not. He found that the Count was decidedly not a favourite. If his tenants came late to their work on the days which they owed to him as Lord of the Manor, they were set on the wooden horse, or flogged and branded in the manor-house yard. One or two cases there were of men who had occupied lands which encroached on the lord's domain, and whose houses had been mysteriously burnt on a winter's night, with the whole family inside. But what seemed to dwell on the innkeeper's mind most—for he returned to the subject more than once—was that the Count had been on the Black Pilgrimage, and had brought something or someone back with him.

You will naturally inquire, as Mr. Wraxall did, what the Black Pilgrimage may have been. But your curiosity on the point must remain unsatisfied for the time being, just as his did. The landlord was evidently unwilling to give a full answer, or indeed any answer, on the point, and, being called out for a moment, trotted off with obvious alacrity, only putting his head in at the door a few minutes afterwards to say that he was called away to Skara, and should not be back till evening.

So Mr. Wraxall had to go unsatisfied to his day's work at the manor-house. The papers on which he was just then engaged soon put his thoughts into another channel, for he had to occupy himself with glancing over the correspondence between Sophia Albertina in Stockholm and her married cousin Ulrica Leonora at Råbäck in the years 1705-1710. The letters were of exceptional interest from the light they threw upon the culture of that period in Sweden, as anyone can testify who has read the full edition of them in the publications of the Swedish Historical Manuscripts Commission.

In the afternoon he had done with these, and after returning the boxes in which they were kept to their places on the shelf, he proceeded, very naturally, to take down some of the volumes nearest to them, in order to determine which of them had best be his principal subject of investigation next day. The shelf he had hit upon was occupied mostly by a collection of account-books in the writing of the first Count Magnus. But one among them was not an account-book, but a book of alchemical and other tracts in another sixteenth-century hand. Not being very familiar with alchemical litera-ture, Mr. Wraxall spends much space which he might have spared in setting out the names and beginnings of the various treatises: The book of the Phœnix, book of the Thirty Words, book of the Toad, book of Miriam, Turba philosophorum, and so forth; and then he announces with a good deal of circumstance his delight at finding, on a leaf originally left blank near the middle of the book, some writing of Count Magnus himself headed "Liber nigræ peregrinationis." It is true that only a few lines were written, but there was quite enough to show that the landlord had that morning been referring to a belief at least as old as the time of Count

Magnus, and probably shared by him. This is the English of what was written:

"If any man desires to obtain a long life, if he would obtain a faithful messenger and see the blood of his enemies, it is necessary that he should first go into the city of Chorazin, and there salute the prince...." Here there was an erasure of one word, not very thoroughly done, so that Mr. Wraxall felt pretty sure that he was right in reading it as *aëris* ("of the air"). But there was no more of the text copied, only a line in Latin: "Quære reliqua hujus materiei inter secretiora" (See the rest of this matter among the more private things).

It could not be denied that this threw a rather lurid light upon the tastes and beliefs of the Count; but to Mr. Wraxall, separated from him by nearly three centuries, the thought that he might have added to his general forcefulness alchemy, and to alchemy something like magic, only made him a more picturesque figure; and when, after a rather prolonged contemplation of his picture in the hall, Mr. Wraxall set out on his homeward way, his mind was full of the thought of Count Magnus. He had no eyes for his surroundings, no perception of the evening scents of the woods or the evening light on the lake; and when all of a sudden he pulled up short, he was astonished to find himself already at the gate of the churchyard, and within a few minutes of his dinner. His eyes fell on the mausoleum.

"Ah," he said, "Count Magnus, there you are. I should dearly like to see you."

"Like many solitary men," he writes, "I have a habit of talking to myself aloud; and, unlike some of the Greek and Latin particles, I do not expect an answer. Certainly, and perhaps fortunately in this case, there was neither voice nor any that regarded: only the woman who, I suppose, was cleaning up the church, dropped some metallic object on the floor, whose clang startled me. Count Magnus, I think, sleeps sound enough."

That same evening the landlord of the inn, who had heard Mr. Wraxall say that he wished to see the clerk or deacon (as he would be called in Sweden) of the parish, introduced him to that official in the inn parlour. A visit to the De la Gardie tomb-house was soon arranged for the next day, and a little general conversation ensued.

Mr. Wraxall, remembering that one function of Scandinavian deacons is to teach candidates for Confirmation, thought he would refresh his own memory on a Biblical point.

"Can you tell me," he said, "anything about Chorazin?"

The deacon seemed startled, but readily reminded him how that village had once been denounced.

"To be sure," said Mr. Wraxall; "it is, I suppose, quite a ruin now?"

"So I expect," replied the deacon. "I have heard some of our old priests say that Antichrist is to be born there; and there are tales——"

"Ah! what tales are those?" Mr. Wraxall put in.

"Tales, I was going to say, which I have forgotten," said the deacon; and soon after that he said good night.

The landlord was now alone, and at Mr. Wraxall's mercy; and that inquirer was not inclined to spare him.

"Herr Nielsen," he said, "I have found out something about the Black Pilgrimage. You may as well tell me what you know. What did the Count bring back with him?"

Swedes are habitually slow, perhaps, in answering, or perhaps the landlord was an exception. I am not sure; but Mr. Wraxall notes that the landlord spent at least one minute in looking at him before he said anything at all. Then he came close up to his guest, and with a good deal of effort he spoke:

"Mr. Wraxall, I can tell you this one little tale, and no more —not any more. You must not ask anything when I have done. In my grandfather's time—that is, ninety-two years ago—there were two men who said: 'The Count is dead; we do not care for him. We will go to-night and have a free hunt in his wood'— the long wood on the hill that you have seen behind Råbäck. Well, those that heard them say this, they said: 'No, do not go; we are sure you will meet with persons walking who should not be walking. They should be resting, not walking.' These men laughed. There were no forest-men to keep the wood, because no one wished to hunt there. The family were not here at the house. These men could do what they wished.

"Very well, they go to the wood that night. My grandfather was sitting here in this room. It was the summer, and a light night. With the window open, he could see out to the wood, and hear.

"So he sat there, and two or three men with him, and they listened. At first they hear nothing at all; then they hear someone—you know how far away it is—they hear someone scream, just as if the most inside part of his soul was twisted out of him. All of them in the room caught hold of each other, and they sat so for three-quarters of an hour. Then they hear someone else, only about three hundred ells off. They hear him laugh out loud: it was not one of those two men that laughed, and, indeed, they have all of them said that it was not any man at all. After that they hear a great door shut.

"Then, when it was just light with the sun, they all went to the priest. They said to him:

"'Father, put on your gown and your ruff, and come to bury these men, Anders Bjornsen and Hans Thorbjorn.'

"You understand that they were sure these men were dead. So they went to the wood—my grandfather never forgot this. He said they were all like so many dead men themselves. The priest, too, he was in a white fear. He said when they came to him:

"'I heard one cry in the night, and I heard one laugh afterwards. If I cannot forget that, I shall not be able to sleep again.'

"So they went to the wood, and they found these men on the edge of the wood. Hans Thorbjorn was standing with his back against a tree, and all the time he was pushing with his hands—pushing something away from him which was not there. So he was not dead. And they led him away, and took him to the house at Nykjoping, and he died before the winter; but he went on pushing with his hands. Also Anders Bjornsen was there; but he was dead. And I tell you this about Anders Bjornsen, that he was once a beautiful man, but now his face was not there, because the flesh of it was sucked away off the bones. You understand that? My grandfather did not forget that. And they laid him on the bier which they brought, and they put a cloth over his head, and the priest walked before; and they began to sing the psalm for the dead as well as they could. So, as they were singing the end of the first verse, one fell down, who was carrying the head of the bier, and the others looked back, and they saw that the cloth had fallen off, and the eyes of Anders Bjornsen were looking up, because there was nothing to close over them. And this they could not bear. Therefore the priest laid the cloth upon him, and sent for a spade, and they buried him in that place."

The next day Mr. Wraxall records that the deacon called for him soon after his breakfast, and took him to the church and mausoleum. He noticed that the key of the latter was hung on a nail just by the pulpit, and it occurred to him that, as the church door seemed to be left unlocked as a rule, it would not be difficult for him to pay a second and more private visit to the monuments if there proved to be more of interest among them than could be digested at first. The building, when he entered it, he found not unimposing. The monuments, mostly large erections of the seventeenth and eighteenth centuries, were dignified if luxuriant, and the epitaphs and heraldry were copious. The central space of the domed room was occupied by three copper sarcophagi, covered with finely-engraved ornament. Two of them had, as is commonly the case in Denmark and Sweden, a large metal crucifix on the lid. The third, that of Count Magnus, as it appeared, had, instead of that, a full-length effigy engraved upon it, and round the edge were several bands of similar ornament representing various scenes. One was a battle, with cannon belching out smoke, and walled towns, and troops of pikemen. Another showed an execution. In a third, among trees, was a man running at full speed, with flying hair and outstretched hands. After him followed a strange form; it would be hard to say whether the artist had intended it for a man, and was unable to give the requisite similitude, or whether it was intentionally made as monstrous as it looked. In view of the skill with which the rest of the drawing was done, Mr. Wraxall felt inclined to adopt the latter idea. The figure was unduly short, and was for the most part muffled in a hooded garment which swept the ground. The only part of the form which projected from that shelter was not shaped like any hand or arm. Mr. Wraxall compares it to the tentacle of a devil-fish, and continues: "On seeing this, I said to myself, 'This, then, which is evidently an allegorical representation of some kind—a fiend pursuing a hunted soul—may be the origin of the story of Count Magnus and his mysterious companion. Let us see how the huntsman is pictured: doubtless it will be a demon blowing his horn.'" But, as it turned out, there was no such sensational figure, only the semblance of a cloaked man on a hillock, who stood leaning on a stick, and watching the hunt with an interest which the engraver had tried to express in his attitude.

Mr. Wraxall noted the finely-worked and massive steel padlocks—three in number—which secured the sarcophagus. One of them, he saw, was detached, and lay on the pavement. And then, unwilling to delay the deacon longer or to waste his own working-time, he made his way onward to the manor-house.

"It is curious," he notes, "how on retracing a familiar path one's thoughts engross one to the absolute exclusion of surrounding objects. To-night, for the second time, I had entirely failed to notice where I was going (I had planned a private visit to the tomb-house to copy the epitaphs), when I suddenly, as it were, awoke to consciousness, and found myself (as before) turning in at the churchyard gate, and, I believe, singing or chanting some such words as, 'Are you awake, Count Magnus? Are you asleep, Count Magnus?' and then something more which I have failed to recollect. It seemed to me that I must have been behaving in this nonsensical way for some time."

He found the key of the mausoleum where he had expected to find it, and copied the greater part of what he wanted; in fact, he stayed until the light began to fail him.

"I must have been wrong," he writes, "in saying that one of the padlocks of my Count's sarcophagus was unfastened; I see to-night that two are loose. I picked both up, and laid them carefully on the window-ledge, after trying unsuccessfully to close them. The remaining one is still firm, and, though I take it to be a spring lock, I cannot guess how it is opened. Had I succeeded in undoing it, I am almost afraid I should have taken the liberty of opening the sarcophagus. It is strange, the interest I feel in the personality of this, I fear, somewhat ferocious and grim old noble."

The day following was, as it turned out, the last of Mr. Wraxall's stay at Råbäck. He received letters connected with certain investments which made it desirable that he should return to England; his work among the papers was practically done, and travelling was slow. He decided, therefore, to make his farewells, put some finishing touches to his notes, and be off.

These finishing touches and farewells, as it turned out, took more time than he had expected. The hospitable family insisted on his staying to dine with them—they dined at three —and it was verging on half-past six before he was outside the iron gates of Råbäck. He dwelt on every step of his walk by the lake, determined to saturate himself, now that he trod it for the last time, in the sentiment of the place and hour. And when he reached the summit of the churchyard knoll, he lingered for many minutes, gazing at the limitless prospect of woods near and distant, all dark beneath a sky of liquid green. When at last he turned to go, the thought struck him that surely he must bid farewell to Count Magnus as well as the rest of the De la Gardies. The church was but twenty yards away, and he knew where the key of the mausoleum hung. It was not long before he was standing over the great copper coffin, and, as usual, talking to himself aloud. "You may have been a bit of a rascal in your time, Magnus," he was saying, "but for all that I should like to see you, or, rather——"

"Just at that instant," he says, "I felt a blow on my foot. Hastily enough I drew it back, and something fell on the pavement with a clash. It was the third, the last of the three padlocks which had fastened the sarcophagus. I stooped to pick it up, and—Heaven is my witness that I am writing only the bare truth—before I had raised myself there was a sound of metal hinges creaking, and I distinctly saw the lid shifting upwards. I may have behaved like a coward, but I could not for my life stay for one moment. I was outside that dreadful building in less time than I can write—almost as quickly as I could have said—the words; and what frightens me yet more, I could not turn the key in the lock. As I sit here in my room noting these facts, I ask myself (it was not twenty minutes ago) whether that noise of creaking metal continued, and I cannot tell whether it did or not. I only know that there was something more than I have written that alarmed me, but whether it was sound or sight I am not able to remember. What is this that I have done?"

Poor Mr. Wraxall! He set out on his journey to England on the next day, as he had planned, and he reached England in safety; and yet, as I gather from his changed hand and inconsequent jottings, a broken man. One of several small notebooks that have come to me with his papers gives, not a key to, but a kind of inkling of, his experiences. Much of his journey was made by canal-boat, and I find not less than six painful attempts to enumerate and describe his fellow-passengers. The entries are of this kind:

"24. Pastor of village in Skåne. Usual black coat and soft black hat.

"25. Commercial traveller from Stockholm going to Troll-hättan. Black cloak, brown hat.

"26. Man in long black cloak, broad-leafed hat, very old-fashioned."

This entry is lined out, and a note added: "Perhaps identical with No. 13. Have not yet seen his face." On referring to No. 13, I find that he is a Roman priest in a cassock.

The net result of the reckoning is always the same. Twenty-eight people appear in the enumeration, one being always a man in a long black cloak and broad hat, and the other a "short figure in dark cloak and hood." On the other hand, it is always noted that only twenty-six passengers appear at meals, and that the man in the cloak is perhaps absent, and the short figure is certainly absent.

On reaching England, it appears that Mr. Wraxall landed at Harwich, and that he resolved at once to put himself out of the reach of some person or persons whom he never specifies, but whom he had evidently come to regard as his pursuers. Accordingly he took a vehicle—it was a closed fly—not trusting the railway, and drove across country to the village of Belchamp St. Paul. It was about nine o'clock on a moonlight August night when he neared the place. He was sitting forward, and looking out of the window at the fields and thickets—there was little else to be seen—racing past him. Suddenly he came to a cross-road. At the corner two figures were standing motionless; both were in dark cloaks; the taller one wore a hat, the shorter a hood. He had no time to see their faces, nor did they make any motion that he could discern. Yet the horse shied violently and broke into a gallop, and Mr. Wraxall sank back into his seat in something like desperation. He had seen them before.

Arrived at Belchamp St. Paul, he was fortunate enough to find a decent furnished lodging, and for the next twenty-four hours he lived, comparatively speaking, in peace. His last notes were written on this day. They are too disjointed and ejaculatory to be given here in full, but the substance of them is clear enough. He is expecting a visit from his pursuers—how or when he knows not—and his constant cry is "What has he done?" and "Is there no hope?" Doctors, he knows, would call him mad, policemen would laugh at him. The parson is away. What can he do but lock his door and cry to God?

People still remembered last year at Belchamp St. Paul how a strange gentleman came one evening in August years back; and how the next morning but one he was found dead, and there was an inquest; and the jury that viewed the body fainted, seven of 'em did, and none of 'em wouldn't speak to what they see, and the verdict was visitation of God; and how the people as kep' the 'ouse moved out that same week, and went away from that part. But they do not, I think, know that any glimmer of light has ever been thrown, or could be thrown, on the mystery. It so happened that last year the little house came into my hands as part of a legacy. It had stood empty since 1863, and there seemed no prospect of letting it; so I had it pulled down, and the papers of which I have given you an abstract were found in a forgotten cupboard under the window in the best bedroom.

The End

THE CRIMSON WEAVER

BY R. MURRAY GILCHRIST

R. Murray Gilchrist was an English author active in the late 1800s. He wrote more than 20 novels, many short stories, and several other works. This classic tale can be read as a vampire story but isn't as explicit as some others in this collection. Our vampire here is the Crimson Weaver, who dines on blood and appears to be a god-like creature.

The Crimson Weaver

by R. Murray Gilchrist

My master and I had wandered from our track and lost ourselves on the side of a great "edge." It was a two-days journey from the Valley of the Willow Brakes, and we had roamed aimlessly; eating at hollow-echoing inns where grey-haired hostesses ministered, and sleeping side by side through the dewless midsummer nights on beds of fresh-gathered heather.

Beyond a single-arched wall-less bridge that crossed a brown stream whose waters leaped straight from the upland, we reached the Domain of the Crimson Weaver. No sooner had we reached the keystone when a beldam, wrinkled as a walnut and bald as an egg, crept from a cabin of turf and osier and held out her hands in warning.

"Enter not the Domain of the Crimson Weaver!" she shrieked. "One I loved entered.—I am here to warn men. Behold, I was beautiful once!"

She tore her ragged smock apart and discovered the foulness of her bosom, where the heart pulsed behind a curtain of livid skin. My Master drew money from his wallet and scattered it on the ground.

"She is mad," he said. "The evil she hints cannot exist. There is no fiend."

So we passed on, but the bridge-keeper took no heed of the coins. For awhile we heard her bellowed sighs issuing from the openings of her den.

Strangely enough, the tenour of our talk changed from the moment that we left the bridge. He had been telling me of the Platonists, but when our feet pressed the sun-dried grass I was impelled to question him of love. It was the first time I had thought of the matter.

"How does passion first touch a man's life?" I asked, laying my hand on his arm.

His ruddy colour faded, he smiled wryly.

"You divine what passes in my brain," he replied. "I also had begun to meditate. . . . . But I may not tell you. . . . . In my boyhood—I was scarce older than you at the time—I loved the true paragon. 'Twere sacrilege to speak of the birth of passion. Let it suffice that ere I tasted of wedlock the woman died, and her death sealed for ever the door of that chamber of my heart. . . . . Yet, if one might see therein, there is an altar crowned with ever-burning tapers and with wreaths of unwithering asphodels."

By this time we had reached the skirt of a yew-forest, traversed in every direction by narrow paths. The air was moist and heavy, but ever and anon a light wind touched the tree-tops and bowed them, so that the pollen sank in golden veils to the ground.

Everywhere we saw half-ruined fountains, satyrs vomiting senilely, nymphs emptying wine upon the lambent flames of dying phœnixes, creatures that were neither satyrs nor nymphs, nor gryphins, but grotesque adminglings of all, slain by one another, with water gushing from wounds in belly and thigh.

At length the path we had chosen terminated beside an oval mere that was surrounded by a colonnade of moss-grown arches. Huge pike quivered on the muddy bed, crayfish moved sluggishly amongst the weeds.

There was an island in the middle, where a leaden Diana,

more compassionate than a crocodile, caressed Actæon s horns ere delivering him to his hounds. The huntress head and shoulders were white with the excrement of a crowd of culvers that moved as if entangled in a snare.

Northwards an avenue rose for the space of a mile, to fall abruptly before an azure sky. For many years the yew-mast on the pathway had been undisturbed by human foot; it was covered with a crust of greenish lichen.

My Master pressed my fingers. "There is some evil in the air of this place," he said. "I am strong, but you—you may not endure. We will return."

"'Tis an enchanted country," I made answer, feverishly. "At the end of yonder avenue stands the palace of the sleeping maiden who awaits the kiss. Nay, since we have pierced the country thus far, let us not draw back. You are strong, Master —no evil can touch us."

So we fared to the place where the avenue sank, and then our eyes fell on the wondrous sight of a palace, lying in a concave pleasaunce, all treeless, but so bestarred with fainting flowers, that neither blade of grass nor grain of earth was visible.

Then came a rustling of wings above our heads, and looking skywards I saw flying towards the house a flock of culvers like unto those that had drawn themselves over Diana s head. The hindmost bird dropped its neck, and behold it gazed upon us with the face of a mannikin!

"They are charmed birds, made thus by the whim of the Princess," I said.

As the birds passed through the portals of a columbary that crowned a western tower, their white wings beat against a silver bell that glistened there, and the whole valley was filled with music.

My Master trembled and crossed himself. "In the name of our Mother," he exclaimed, "let us return. I dare not trust your life here."

But a great door in front of the palace swung open, and a woman with a swaying walk came out to the terrace. She wore a robe of crimson worn into tatters at skirt-hem and shoulders. She had been forewarned of our presence, for her face turned instantly in our direction. She smiled subtly, and her smile died away into a most tempting sadness.

She caught up such remnants of her skirt as trailed behind, and strutted about with the gait of a peacock. As the sun touched the glossy fabric I saw eyes inwrought in deeper hue.

My Master still trembled, but he did not move, for the gaze of the woman was fixed upon him. His brows twisted and his white hair rose and stood erect, as if he viewed some unspeakable horror.

Stooping, with sidelong motions of the head, she approached; bringing with her the smell of such an incense as when amidst Eastern herbs burns the corse. . . . . She was perfect of feature as the Diana, but her skin was deathly white and her lips fretted with pain.

She took no heed of me, but knelt at my Master's feet—a Magdalene before an impregnable priest.

"Prince and Lord, Tower of Chastity, hear!" she murmured. "For lack of love I perish. See my robe in tatters!"

He strove to avert his face, but his eyes still dwelt upon her. She half rose and shook nut-brown tresses over his knees.

Youth came back in a flood to my Master. His shrivelled skin filled out; the dying sunlight turned to gold the whiteness of his hair. He would have raised her had I not caught his hands. The anguish of foreboding made me cry:

"One forces roughly the door of your heart s chamber. The wreaths wither, the tapers bend and fall."

He grew old again. The Crimson Weaver turned to me.

"O marplot!" she said laughingly, "think not to vanquish me with folly. I am too powerful. Once that a man enter my domain he is mine."

But I drew my Master away.

"Tis I who am strong," I whispered. "We will go hence at once. Surely we may find our way back to the bridge. The journey is easy."

The woman, seeing that the remembrance of an old love

was strong within him, sighed heavily, and returned to the palace. As she reached the doorway the valves opened, and I saw in a distant chamber beyond the hall an ivory loom with a golden stool.

My Master and I walked again on the track we had made in the yew-mast. But twilight was falling, and ere we could reach the pool of Diana all was in utter darkness; so at the foot of a tree, where no anthill rose, we lay down and slept.

Dreams came to me—gorgeous visions from the romances of eld. Everywhere I sought vainly for a beloved. There was the Castle of the Ebony Dwarf, where a young queen reposed in the innermost casket of the seventh crystal cabinet; there was the Chamber of Gloom, where Lenore danced, and where I groped for ages around columns of living flesh; there was the White Minaret, where twenty-one princesses poised themselves on balls of burnished bronze; there was Melisandra's arbour, where the sacred toads crawled over the enchanted cloak.

Unrest fretted me: I woke in spiritual pain. Dawn was breaking—a bright yellow dawn, and the glades were full of vapours.

I turned to the place where my Master had lain. He was not there. I felt with my hands over his bed: it was key-cold. Terror of my loneliness overcame me, and I sat with covered face.

On the ground near my feet lay a broken riband, whereon was strung a heart of chrysolite. It enclosed a knot of ash-coloured hair—hair of the girl my Master had loved.

The mists gathered together and passed sunwards in one long many-cornered veil. When the last shred had been drawn into the great light, I gazed along the avenue, and saw the topmost bartizan of the Crimson Weaver's palace.

It was midday ere I dared start on my search. The culvers beat about my head. I walked in pain, as though giant spiders had woven about my body.

On the terrace strange beasts—dogs and pigs with human limbs,—tore ravenously at something that lay beside the balustrade. At sight of me they paused and lifted their snouts and bayed. Awhile afterwards the culvers rang the silver bell, and the monsters dispersed hurriedly amongst the drooping blossoms of the pleasaunce, and where they had swarmed I saw naught but a steaming sanguine pool.

I approached the house and the door fell open, admitting me to a chamber adorned with embellishments beyond the witchery of art. There I lifted my voice and cried eagerly: "My Master, my Master, where is my Master?" The alcoves sent out a babble of echoes, blended together like a harp-cord on a dulcimer: "My Master, my Master, where is my Master? For the love of Christ, where is my Master?" The echo replied only, "Where is my Master?"

Above, swung a globe of topaz, where a hundred suns gambolled. From its centre a convoluted horn, held by a crimson cord, sank lower and lower. It stayed before my lips and I blew therein, and heard the sweet voices of youth chant with one accord.

"Fall open, oh doors: fall open and show the way to the princess!"

Ere the last of the echoes had died a vista opened, and at the end of an alabaster gallery I saw the Crimson Weaver at her loom. She had doffed her tattered robe for one new and lustrous as freshly drawn blood. And marvellous as her beauty had seemed before, its wonder was now increased a hundredfold.

She came towards me with the same stately walk, but there was now a lightness in her demeanour that suggested the growth of wings.

Within arm's length she curtseyed, and curtseying showed me the firmness of her shoulders, the fulness of her breast. The sight brought no pleasure: my cracking tongue appealed in agony:

"My Master, where is my Master?"

She smiled happily. "Nay, do not trouble. He is not here. His soul talks with the culvers in the cote. He has forgotten you. In the night we supped, and I gave him of Nepenthe."

"Where is my Master? Yesterday he told me of the shrine in his heart—of ever-fresh flowers—of a love dead yet living."

Her eyebrows curved mirthfully.

"Tis foolish boys talk," she said. "If you sought till the end of time you would never find him—unless I chose. Yet—if you buy of me—myself to name the price."

I looked around hopelessly at the unimaginable riches of her home. All that I have is this Manor of the Willow Brakes— a moorish park, an ancient house where the thatch gapes and the casements swing loose.

"My possessions are pitiable," I said, "but they are all yours. I give all to save him."

"Fool, fool!" she cried. "I have no need of gear. If I but raise my hand, all the riches of the world fall to me. Tis not what I wish for."

Into her eyes came such a glitter as the moon makes on the moist skin of a sleeping snake. The firmness of her lips relaxed; they grew child-like in their softness. The atmosphere became almost tangible: I could scarce breathe.

"What is it? All that I can do, if it be no sin."

"Come with me to my loom," she said, "and if you do the thing I desire you shall see him. There is no evil in't—in past times kings have sighed for the same."

So I followed slowly to the loom, before which she had seated herself, and watched her deftly passing crimson thread over crimson thread.

She was silent for a space, and in that space her beauty fascinated me, so that I was no longer master of myself.

"What you wish for I will give, even if it be life."

The loom ceased. "A kiss of the mouth, and you shall see him who passed in the night."

She clasped her arms about my neck and pressed my lips. For one moment heaven and earth ceased to be; but there was one paradise, where we were sole governours. . . . .

Then she moved back and drew aside the web and shoved me the head of my Master, and the bleeding heart whence a crimson cord unravelled into many threads.

"I wear men's lives," the woman said. "Life is necessary to me, or even I—who have existed from the beginning—must die. But yesterday I feared the end, and he came. His soul is not dead—'tis truth that it plays with my culvers."

I fell back.

"Another kiss," she said. "Unless I wish, there is no escape for you. Yet you may return to your home, though my power over you shall never wane. Once more—lip to lip."

I crouched against the wall like a terrified dog. She grew angry; her eyes darted fire.

"A kiss," she cried, "for the penalty!"

My poor Master;s head, ugly and cadaverous, glared from the loom. I could not move.

The Crimson Weaver lifted her skirt, uncovering feet shapen as those of a vulture. I fell prostrate. With her claws she fumbled about the flesh of my breast. Moving away she bade me pass from her sight. . . . .

So, half-dead, I lie here at the Manor of the Willow Brakes, watching hour by hour the bloody clew ever unwinding from my heart and passing over the western hills to the Palace of the Siren.

The End

WAKE NOT THE DEAD

by Ernst Raupach

Ernst Raupach (1784-1852) was a German writer, mostly of plays, but he also penned the early vampire story "Wake Not the Dead." It was published in 1823 and is considered one of the first vampire stories written down. It also was said to be the inspiration for Edgar Allan Poe's story "Ligeia," though there is no definitive proof of that. Regardless, "Wake Not the Dead" is an important and fascinating story and stands up well.

Wake Not the Dead

by Ernst Raupach

"Wilt thou for ever sleep? Wilt thou never more awake, my beloved, but henceforth repose for ever from thy short pilgrimage on earth? O yet once again return! and bring back with thee the vivifying dawn of hope to one whose existence hath, since thy departure, been obscured by the dunnest shades. What! dumb? for ever dumb? Thy friend lamenteth, and thou heedest him not? He sheds bitter, scalding tears, and thou reposest unregarding his affliction? He is in despair, and thou no longer openest thy arms to him as an asylum from his grief? Say then, doth the paly shroud become thee better than the bridal veil? Is the chamber of the grave a warmer bed than the couch of love? Is the spectre death more welcome to thy arms than thy enamoured consort? Oh! return, my beloved, return once again to this anxious disconsolate bosom."

Such were the lamentations which Walter poured forth for his Brunhilda, the partner of his youthful passionate love; thus did he bewail over her grave at the midnight hour, what time the spirit that presides in the troublous atmosphere, sends his legions of monsters through mid-air; so that their shadows, as they flit beneath the moon and across the earth, dart as wild, agitating thoughts that chase each other o'er the sinner's bosom:—thus did he lament under the tall linden trees by her grave, while his head reclined on the cold stone.

Walter was a powerful lord in Burgundy, who, in his earliest youth, had been smitten with the charms of the fair Brunhilda, a beauty far surpassing in loveliness all her rivals; for her tresses, dark as the raven face of night, streaming over her shoulders, set off to the utmost advantage the beaming lustre of her slender form, and the rich dye of a cheek whose tint was deep and brilliant as that of the western heaven; her eyes did not resemble those burning orbs whose pale glow gems the vault of night, and whose immeasurable distance fills the soul with deep thoughts of eternity, but rather as the sober beams which cheer this nether world, and which, while they enlighten, kindle the sons of earth to joy and love. Brunhilda became the wife of Walter, and both being equally enamoured and devoted, they abandoned themselves to the enjoyment of a passion that rendered them reckless of aught besides, while it lulled them in a fascinating dream. Their sole apprehension was lest aught should awaken them from a delirium which they prayed might continue for ever. Yet how vain is the wish that would arrest the decrees of destiny! as well might it seek to divert the circling planets from their eternal course. Short was the duration of this phrenzied passion; not that it gradually decayed and subsided into apathy, but death snatched away his blooming victim, and left Walter to a widowed couch. Impetuous, however, as was his first burst of grief, he was not inconsolable, for ere long another bride became the partner of the youthful nobleman.

Swanhilda also was beautiful; although nature had formed her charms on a very different model from those of Brunhilda. Her golden locks waved bright as the beams of morn: only when excited by some emotion of her soul did a rosy hue tinge the lily paleness of her cheek: her limbs were proportioned in the nicest symmetry, yet did they not possess that luxuriant fullness of animal life: her eye beamed eloquently, but it was with the milder radiance of a star, tranquillizing to tenderness rather than exciting to warmth. Thus formed, it was not possible that she should steep him in his former delirium, although she rendered happy his waking hours—tranquil and serious, yet cheerful, studying in all things her husband's pleasure, she restored order and comfort in his family, where her presence shed a general influence all around. Her mild benevolence tended to restrain the fiery, impetuous disposition of Walter: while at the same time her prudence recalled him in some degree from his vain, turbulent wishes, and his aspirings after unattainable enjoyments, to the duties and pleasures of actual life. Swanhilda bore her husband two children, a son and a daughter; the latter was mild and patient as her mother, well contented with her solitary sports, and even in these recreations displayed the serious turn of her character. The boy possessed his father's fiery, restless disposition, tempered, however, with the solidity of his mother. Attached by his offspring more tenderly towards their mother, Walter now lived for several years very happily: his thoughts would frequently, indeed, recur to Brunhilda, but without their former violence, merely as we dwell upon the memory of a friend of our earlier days, borne from us on the rapid current of time to a region where we know that he is happy.

But clouds dissolve into air, flowers fade, the sands of the hourglass run impeceptibly away, and even so, do human feelings dissolve, fade, and pass away, and with them too, human happiness. Walter's inconstant breast again sighed for the ecstatic dreams of those days which he had spent with his equally romantic, enamoured Brunhilda—again did she present herself to his ardent fancy in all the glow of her bridal charms, and he began to draw a parallel between the past and the present; nor did imagination, as it is wont, fail to array the former in her brightest hues, while it proportionably obscured the latter; so that he pictured to himself, the one much more rich in enjoyment, and the other, much less so than they really were. This change in her husband did not escape Swanhilda; whereupon, redoubling her attentions towards him, and her cares towards their children, she expected, by this means, to reunite the knot that was slackened; yet the more she endeavoured to regain his affections, the colder did he grow,—the more intolerable did her caresses seem, and the more continually did the image of Brunhilda haunt his thoughts. The children, whose endearments were now become indispensable to him, alone stood between the parents as genii eager to affect a reconciliation; and, beloved by them both, formed a uniting link between them. Yet, as evil can be plucked from the heart of man, only ere its root has yet struck deep, its fangs being afterwards too firm to be eradicated; so was Walter's diseased fancy too far affected to have its disorder stopped, for, in a short time, it completely tyrannized over him. Frequently of a night, instead of retiring to his consort's chamber, he repaired to Brunhilda's grave, where he murmured forth his discontent, saying: "Wilt thou sleep for ever?"

One night as he was reclining on the turf, indulging in his wonted sorrow, a sorcerer from the neighbouring mountains, entered into this field of death for the purpose of gathering, for his mystic spells, such herbs as grow only from the earth wherein the dead repose, and which, as if the last production of mortality, are gifted with a powerful and supernatural influence. The sorcerer perceived the mourner, and approached the spot where he was lying.

"Wherefore, fond wretch, dost thou grieve thus, for what is now a hideous mass of mortality—mere bones, and nerves, and veins? Nations have fallen unlamented; even worlds themselves, long ere this globe of ours was created, have mouldered into nothing; nor hath any one wept over them; why then should'st thou indulge this vain affliction for a child of the dust—a being as frail as thyself, and like thee the creature but of a moment?"

Walter raised himself up:—"Let yon worlds that shine in the firmament" replied he, "lament for each other as they perish. It is true, that I who am myself clay, lament for my fellow-clay: yet is this clay impregnated with a fire,—with an essence, that none of the elements of creation possess—with love: and this divine passion, I felt for her who now sleepeth beneath this sod."

"Will thy complaints awaken her: or could they do so,

would she not soon upbraid thee for having disturbed that repose in which she is now hushed?"

"Avaunt, cold-hearted being: thou knowest not what is love. Oh! that my tears could wash away the earthy covering that conceals her from these eyes;—that my groan of anguish could rouse her from her slumber of death!—No, she would not again seek her earthy couch."

"Insensate that thou art, and couldst thou endure to gaze without shuddering on one disgorged from the jaws of the grave? Art thou too thyself the same from whom she parted; or hath time passed o'er thy brow and left no traces there? Would not thy love rather be converted into hate and disgust?"

"Say rather that the stars would leave yon firmament, that the sun will henceforth refuse to shed his beams through the heavens. Oh! that she stood once more before me;—that once again she reposed on this bosom!—how quickly should we then forget that death or time had ever stepped between us."

"Delusion! mere delusion of the brain, from heated blood, like to that which arises from the fumes of wine. It is not my wish to tempt thee;—to restore to thee thy dead; else wouldst thou soon feel that I have spoken truth."

"How! restore her to me," exclaimed Walter casting himself at the sorcerer's feet. "Oh! if thou art indeed able to effect that, grant it to my earnest supplication; if one throb of human feeling vibrates in thy bosom, let my tears prevail with thee; restore to me my beloved; so shalt thou hereafter bless the deed, and see that it was a good work."

"A good work! a blessed deed!"—returned the sorcerer with a smile of scorn; "for me there exists nor good nor evil; since my will is always the same. Ye alone know evil, who will that which ye would not. It is indeed in my power to restore her to thee: yet, bethink thee well, whether it will prove thy weal. Consider too, how deep the abyss between life and death; across this, my power can build a bridge, but it can never fill up the frightful chasm."

Walter would have spoken, and have sought to prevail on this powerful being by fresh entreaties, but the latter prevented him, saying: "Peace! bethink thee well! and return hither to me tomorrow at midnight. Yet once more do I warn thee, 'Wake not the dead.'"

Having uttered these words, the mysterious being disappeared. Intoxicated with fresh hope, Walter found no sleep on his couch; for fancy, prodigal of her richest stores, expanded before him the glittering web of futurity; and his eye, moistened with the dew of rapture, glanced from one vision of happiness to another. During the next day he wandered through the woods, lest wonted objects by recalling the memory of later and less happier times, might disturb the blissful idea. that he should again behold her—again fold her in his arms, gaze on her beaming brow by day, repose on her bosom at night: and, as this sole idea filled his imagination, how was it possible that the least doubt should arise; or that the warning of the mysterious old man should recur to his thoughts?

No sooner did the midnight hour approach, than he hastened before the grave-field where the sorcerer was already standing by that of Brunhilda. "Hast thou maturely considered?" inquired he.

"Oh! restore to me the object of my ardent passion," exclaimed Walter with impetuous eagerness. "Delay not thy generous action, lest I die even this night, consumed with disappointed desire; and behold her face no more."

"Well then," answered the old man, "return hither again tomorrow at the same hour. But once more do I give thee this friendly warning, 'Wake not the dead.'"

All in the despair of impatience, Walter would have prostrated himself at his feet, and supplicated him to fulfil at once a desire now increased to agony; but the sorcerer had already disappeared. Pouring forth his lamentations more wildly and impetuously than ever, he lay upon the grave of his adored one, until the grey dawn streaked the east. During the day, which seemed to him longer than any he had ever experienced, he wandered to and fro, restless and impatient, seemingly without any object, and deeply buried in his own reflections, inquest as the murderer who meditates his first deed of blood: and the stars of evening found him once more at the appointed spot. At midnight the sorcerer was there also.

"Hast thou yet maturely deliberated?" inquired he, "as on the preceding night?"

"Oh what should I deliberate?" returned Walter impatiently. "I need not to deliberate; what I demand of thee, is that which thou hast promised me—that which will prove my bliss. Or dost thou but mock me? if so, hence from my sight, lest I be tempted to lay my hand on thee."

"Once more do I warn thee." answered the old man with undisturbed composure, "'Wake not the dead'—let her rest."

"Aye, but not in the cold grave: she shall rather rest on this bosom which burns with eagerness to clasp her."

"Reflect, thou mayst not quit her until death, even though aversion and horror should seize thy heart. There would then remain only one horrible means."

"Dotard!" cried Walter, interrupting him, "how may I hate that which I love with such intensity of passion? how should I abhor that for which my every drop of blood is boiling?"

"Then be it even as thou wishest," answered the sorcerer; "step back."

The old man now drew a circle round the grave, all the while muttering words of enchantment. Immediately the storm began to howl among the tops of the trees; owls flapped their wings, and uttered their low voice of omen; the stars hid their mild, beaming aspect, that they might not behold so unholy and impious a spectacle; the stone then rolled from the grave with a hollow sound, leaving a free passage for the inhabitant of that dreadful tenement. The sorcerer scattered into the yawning earth, roots and herbs of most magic power, and of most penetrating odour, so that the worms crawling forth from the earth congregated together, and raised themselves in a fiery column over the grave: while rushing wind burst from the earth, scattering the mould before it, until at length the coffin lay uncovered. The moonbeams fell on it, and the lid burst open with a tremendous sound. Upon this the sorcerer poured upon it some blood from out of a human skull, exclaiming at the same time, "Drink, sleeper, of this warm stream, that thy heart may again beat within thy bosom." And, after a short pause, shedding on her some other mystic liquid, he cried aloud with the voice of one inspired: "Yes, thy heart beats once more with the flood of life: thine eye is again opened to sight. Arise, therefore, from the tomb."

As an island suddenly springs forth from the dark waves of the ocean, raised upwards from the deep by the force of subterraneous fires, so did Brunhilda start from her earthy couch, borne forward by some invisible power. Taking her by the hand, the sorcerer led her towards Walter, who stood at some little distance, rooted to the ground with amazement.

"Receive again," said he, "the object of thy passionate sighs: mayest thou never more require my aid; should that, however, happen, so wilt thou find me, during the full of the moon, upon the mountains in that spot and where the three roads meet."

Instantly did Walter recognize in the form that stood before him, her whom he so ardently loved; and a sudden glow shot through his frame at finding her thus restored to him: yet the night-frost had chilled his limbs and palsied his tongue. For a while he gazed upon her without either motion or speech, and during this pause, all was again become hushed and serene; and the stars shone brightly in the clear heavens.

"Walter!" exclaimed the figure; and at once the well-known sound, thrilling to his heart, broke the spell by which he was bound.

"Is it reality? Is it truth?" cried he, "or a cheating delusion?"

"No, it is no imposture; I am really living:—conduct me quickly to thy castle in the mountains."

Walter looked around: the old man had disappeared, but he perceived close by his side, a coal-black steed of fiery eye, ready equipped to conduct him thence; and on his back lay all proper attire for Brunhilda, who lost no time in arraying herself. This being done, she cried; "Haste, let us away ere the dawn breaks, for my eye is yet too weak to endure the light of day." Fully recovered from his stupor, Walter leaped into his saddle, and catching up, with a mingled feeling of delight and awe, the beloved being thus mysteriously restored from the power of the grave, he spurred on across the wild, towards the mountains, as furiously as if pursued by the shadows of the dead, hastening to recover from him their sister.

The castle to which Walter conducted his Brunhilda, was situated on a rock between other rocks rising up above it. Here they arrived, unseen by any save one aged domestic, on whom Walter imposed secrecy by the severest threats.

"Here will we tarry," said Brunhilda, "until I can endure the light, and until thou canst look upon me without trembling as if struck with a cold chill." They accordingly continued to make that place their abode: yet no one knew that Brunhilda existed, save only that aged attendant, who provided their meals. During seven entire days they had no light except that of tapers: during the next seven, the light was admitted through the lofty casements only while the rising or setting-sun faintly illumined the mountain-tops, the valley being still enveloped in shade.

Seldom did Walter quit Brunhilda's side: a nameless spell seemed to attach him to her; even the shudder which he felt in her presence, and which would not permit him to touch her, was not unmixed with pleasure, like that thrilling awful emotion felt when strains of sacred music float under the vault of some temple; he rather sought, therefore, than avoided this feeling. Often too as he had indulged in calling to mind the beauties of Brunhilda, she had never appeared so fair, so fascinating, so admirable when depicted by his imagination, as when now beheld in reality. Never till now had her voice sounded with such tones of sweetness; never before did her language possess such eloquence as it now did, when she conversed with him on the subject of the past. And this was the magic fairy-land towards which her words constantly conducted him. Ever did she dwell upon the days of their first love, those hours of delight which they had participated together when the one derived all enjoyment from the other:

and so rapturous, so enchanting, so full of life did she recall to
his imagination that blissful season, that he even doubted
whether he had ever experienced with her so much felicity, or
had been so truly happy. And, while she thus vividly portrayed
their hours of past delight, she delineated in still more glowing,
more enchanting colours, those hours of approaching bliss
which now awaited them, richer in enjoyment than any
preceding ones. In this manner did she charm her attentive
auditor with enrapturing hopes for the future, and lull him
into dreams of more than mortal ecstasy; so that while he
listened to her siren strain, he entirely forgot how little blissful
was the latter period of their union, when he had often sighed
at her imperiousness, and at her harshness both to himself and
all his household. Yet even had he recalled this to mind would it
have disturbed him in his present delirious trance? Had she not
now left behind in the grave all the frailty of mortality? Was
not her whole being refined and purified by that long sleep in
which neither passion nor sin had approached her even in
dreams? How different now was the subject of her discourse!
Only when speaking of her affection for him, did she betray
anything of earthly feeling: at other times, she uniformly dwelt
upon themes relating to the invisible and future world; when
in descanting and declaring the mysteries of eternity, a stream
of prophetic eloquence would burst from her lips.

In this manner had twice seven days elapsed, and, for the
first time, Walter beheld the being now dearer to him than ever,
in the full light of day. Every trace of the grave had disappeared
from her countenance; a roseate tinge like the ruddy streaks of
dawn again beamed on her pallid cheek; the faint, mouldering
taint of the grave was changed into a delightful violet scent; the
only sign of earth that never disappeared. He no longer felt
either apprehension or awe, as he gazed upon her in the sunny
light of day: it was not until now, that he seemed to have recovered her completely; and, glowing with all his former passion
towards her, he would have pressed her to his bosom, but she
gently repulsed him, saying:—"Not yet—spare your caresses
until the moon has again filled her horn."

Spite of his impatience, Walter was obliged to await the lapse of another period of seven days: but, on the night when the moon was arrived at the full, he hastened to Brunhilda, whom he found more lovely than she had ever appeared before. Fearing no obstacles to his transports, he embraced with all the fervour of a deeply enamoured and successful lover. Brunhilda, however, still refused to yield to his passion. "What!" exclaimed she, "is it fitting that I who have been purified by death from the frailty of mortality, should become thy concubine, while a mere daughter of the earth bears the title of thy wife: never shall it be. No, it must be within the walls of thy palace, within that chamber where I once reigned as queen, that thou obtainest the end of thy wishes,—and of mine also," added she, imprinting a glowing kiss on the lips, and immediately disappeared.

Heated with passion, and determined to sacrifice everything to the accomplishment of his desires, Walter hastily quitted the apartment, and shortly after the castle itself. He travelled over mountain and across heath, with the rapidity of a storm, so that the turf was flung up by his horse's hoofs; nor once stopped until he arrived home.

Here, however, neither the affectionate caresses of Swanhilda, or those of his children could touch his heart, or induce him to restrain his furious desires. Alas! is the impetuous torrent to be checked in its devastating course by the beauteous flowers over which it rushes, when they exclaim:—"Destroyer, commiserate our helpless innocence and beauty, nor lay us waste?"—the stream sweeps over them unregarding, and a single moment annihilates the pride of a whole summer.

Shortly afterwards did Walter begin to hint to Swanhilda that they were ill-suited to each other; that he was anxious to taste that wild, tumultuous life, so well according with the spirit of his sex, while she, on the contrary, was satisfied with the monotonous circle of household enjoyments:—that he was eager for whatever promised novelty, while she felt most attached to what was familiarized to her by habit: and lastly, that her cold disposition, bordering upon indifference, but ill assorted with his ardent temperament: it was therefore more prudent that they should seek apart from each other that happiness which they could not find together. A sigh, and a brief acquiescence in his wishes was all the reply that Swanhilda made: and, on the following morning, upon his presenting her with a paper of separation, informing her that she was at liberty to return home to her father, she received it most submissively: yet, ere she departed, she gave him the following warning: "Too well do I conjecture to whom I am indebted for this our separation. Often have I seen thee at Brunhilda's grave, and beheld thee there even on that night when the face of the heavens was suddenly enveloped in a veil of clouds. Hast thou rashly dared to tear aside the awful veil that separates the mortality that dreams, from that which dreameth not? Oh! then woe to thee, thou wretched man, for thou hast attached to thyself that which will prove thy destruction."

She ceased: nor did Walter attempt any reply, for the similar admonition uttered by the sorcerer flashed upon his mind, all obscured as it was by passion, just as the lightning glares momentarily through the gloom of night without dispersing the obscurity.

Swanhilda then departed, in order to pronounce to her children, a bitter farewell, for they, according to national custom, belonged to the father; and, having bathed them in her tears, and consecrated them with the holy water of maternal love, she quitted her husband's residence, and departed to the home of her father's.

Thus was the kind and benevolent Swanhilda driven an exile from those halls where she had presided with grace;—from halls which were now newly decorated to receive another mistress. The day at length arrived on which Walter, for the second time, conducted Brunhilda home as a newly made bride. And he caused it to be reported among his domestics that his new consort had gained his affections by her extraordinary likeness to Brunhilda, their former mistress. How ineffably happy did he deem himself as he conducted his beloved once more into the chamber which had often witnessed their former joys, and which was now newly gilded and adorned in a most costly style: among the other decorations were figures of angels scattering roses, which served to support the purple draperies whose ample folds o'ershadowed the nuptial couch. With what impatience did he await the hour that was to put him in possession of those beauties for which he had already paid so high a price, but, whose enjoyment was to cost him most dearly yet! Unfortunate Walter! revelling in bliss, thou beholdest not the abyss that yawns beneath thy feet, intoxicated with the luscious perfume of the flower thou hast plucked, thou little deemest how deadly is the venom with which it is fraught, although, for a short season, its potent fragrance bestows new energy on all thy feelings.

Happy, however, as Walter was now, his household were far from being equally so. The strange resemblance between their new lady and the deceased Brunhilda filled them with a secret dismay,—an undefinable horror; for there was not a single difference of feature, of tone of voice, or of gesture. To add too to these mysterious circumstances, her female attendants discovered a particular mark on her back, exactly like one which Brunhilda had. A report was now soon circulated, that their lady was no other than Brunhilda herself, who had been recalled to life by the power of necromancy. How truly horrible was the idea of living under the same roof with one who had been an inhabitant of the tomb, and of being obliged to attend upon her, and acknowledge her as mistress! There was also in Brunhilda much to increase this aversion, and favour their superstition: no ornaments of gold ever decked her person; all that others were wont to wear of this metal, she had formed of silver: no richly coloured and sparkling jewels glittered upon her; pearls alone, lent their pale lustre to adorn her bosom. Most carefully did she always avoid the cheerful light of the sun, and was wont to spend the brightest days in the most retired and gloomy apartments: only during the twilight of the commencing or declining day did she ever walk abroad, but her favourite hour was when the phantom light of the moon bestowed on all objects a shadowy appearance and a sombre hue; always too at the crowing of the cock an involuntary shudder was observed to seize her limbs. Imperious as before her death, she quickly imposed her iron yoke on every one around her, while she seemed even far more terrible than ever, since a dread of some supernatural power attached to her, appalled all who approached her. A malignant withering glance seemed to shoot from her eye on the unhappy object of her wrath, as if it would annihilate its victim. In short, those halls which, in the time of Swanhilda were the residence of cheerfulness and mirth, now resembled an extensive desert tomb. With fear imprinted on their pale countenances, the domestics glided through the apartments of the castle; and in this abode of terror, the crowing of the cock caused the living to tremble, as if they were the spirits of the departed; for the sound always reminded them of their mysterious mistress. There was no one but who shuddered at meeting her in a lonely place, in the dusk of evening, or by the light of the moon, a circumstance that was deemed to be ominous of some evil: so great was the apprehension of her female attendants, they pined in continual disquietude, and, by degrees, all quitted her. In the course of time even others of the domestics fled, for an insupportal horror had seized them.

The art of the sorcerer had indeed bestowed upon Brunhilda an artificial life, and due nourishment had continued to support the restored body: yet this body was not able of itself to keep up the genial glow of vitality, and to nourish the flame whence springs all the affections and passions, whether of love or hate; for death had for ever destroyed and withered it: all that Brunhilda now possessed was a chilled existence, colder than that of the snake. It was nevertheless necessary that she should love, and return with equal ardour the warm caresses of her spell-enthralled husband, to whose passion alone she was indebted for her renewed existence. It was necessary that a magic draught should animate the dull current in her veins and awaken her to the glow of life and the flame of love—a potion of abomination—one not even to be named without a curse— human blood, imbibed whilst yet warm, from the veins of youth. This was the hellish drink for which she thirsted: possessing no sympathy with the purer feelings of humanity; deriving no enjoyment from aught that interests in life and occupies its varied hours; her existence was a mere blank, unless when in the arms of her paramour husband, and therefore was it that she craved incessantly after the horrible draught. It was even with the utmost effort that she could forbear sucking even the blood of Walter himself, reclined beside her. Whenever she beheld some innocent child whose lovely face denoted the exuberance of infantine health and vigour, she would entice it by soothing words and fond caresses into her most secret apartment, where, lulling it to sleep in her arms, she would suck form its bosom the war, purple tide of life. Nor were youths of either sex safe from her horrid attack: having first breathed upon her unhappy victim, who never failed immediately to sink into a lengthened sleep, she would then in a similar manner drain his veins of the vital juice. Thus children, youths, and maidens quickly faded away, as flowers gnawn by the cankering worm: the fullness of their limbs disappeared; a sallow line succeeded to the rosy freshness of their cheeks, the liquid lustre of the eye was deadened, even as the sparkling stream when arrested by the touch of frost; and their locks became thin and grey, as if already ravaged by the storm of life. Parents beheld with horror this desolating pestilence devouring their offspring; nor could simple or charm, potion or amulet avail aught against it. The grave swallowed up one after the other; or did the miserable victim survive, he became cadaverous and wrinkled even in the very morn of existence. Parents observed with horror this devastating pestilence snatch away their offspring—a pestilence which, nor herb however potent, nor charm, nor holy taper, nor exorcism could avert. They either beheld their children sink one after the other into the grave, or their youthful forms, withered by the unholy, vampire embrace of Brunhilda, assume the decrepitude of sudden age.

At length strange surmises and reports began to prevail; it was whispered that Brunhilda herself was the cause of all these horrors; although no one could pretend to tell in what manner she destroyed her victims, since no marks of violence were discernible. Yet when young children confessed that she had frequently lulled them asleep in her arms, and elder ones said that a sudden slumber had come upon them whenever she began to converse with them, suspicion became converted into certainty, and those whose offspring had hitherto escaped unharmed, quitted their hearths and home—all their little possessions—the dwellings of their fathers and the inheritance of their children, in order to rescue from so horrible a fate those who were dearer to their simple affections than aught else the world could give.

Thus daily did the castle assume a more desolate appearance; daily did its environs become more deserted; none but a few aged decrepit old women and grey-headed menials were to be seen remaining of the once numerous retinue. Such will in the latter days of the earth be the last generation of mortals, when childbearing shall have ceased, when youth shall no more be seen, nor any arise to replace those who shall await their fate in silence.

Walter alone noticed not, or heeded not, the desolation around him; he apprehended not death, lapped as he was in a glowing elysium of love. Far more happy than formerly did he now seem in the possession of Brunhilda. All those caprices and frowns which had been wont to overcloud their former union had now entirely disappeared. She even seemed to doat on him with a warmth of passion that she had never exhibited even during the happy season of bridal love; for the flame of that youthful blood, of which she drained the veins of others, rioted in her own. At night, as soon as he closed his eyes, she would breathe on him till he sank into delicious dreams, from which he awoke only to experience more rapturous enjoyments. By day she would continually discourse with him on the bliss experienced by happy spirits beyond the grave, assuring him that, as his affection had recalled her from the tomb, they were now irrevocably united. Thus fascinated by a continual spell, it was not possible that he should perceive what was taking place around him. Brunhilda, however, foresaw with savage grief that the source of her youthful ardour was daily decreasing, for, in a short time, there remained nothing gifted with youth, save Walter and his children, and these latter she resolved should be her next victims.

On her first return to the castle, she had felt an aversion towards the offspring of another, and therefore abandoned them entirely to the attendants appointed by Swanhilda. Now, however, she began to pay considerable attention to them, and caused them to be frequently admitted into her presence. The aged nurses were filled with dread at perceiving these marks of regard from her towards their young charges, yet dared they not to oppose the will of their terrible and imperious mistress. Soon did Brunhilda gain the affection of the children, who were too unsuspecting of guile to apprehend any danger from her; on the contrary, her caresses won them completely to her. Instead of ever checking their mirthful gambols, she would rather instruct them in new sports: often too did she recite to them tales of such strange and wild interest as to exceed all the stories of their nurses. Were they wearied either with play or with listening to her narratives, she would take them on her knees and lull them to slumber. Then did visions of the most surpassing magnificence attend their dreams: they would fancy themselves in some garden where flowers of every hue rose in rows one above the other, from the humble violet to the tall sunflower, forming a parti-coloured broidery of every hue, sloping upwards towards the golden clouds where little angels whose wings sparkled with azure and gold descended to bring them delicious cakes or splendid jewels; or sung to them soothing melodious hymns. So delightful did these dream in short time become to the children that they longered for nothing so eagerly as to slumber on Brunhilda's lap, for never did they else enjoy such visions of heavenly forms. They were they most anxious for that which was to prove their destruction:—yet do we not all aspire after that which conducts us to the grave—after the enjoyment of life? These innocents stretched out their arms to approaching death because it assumed the mask of pleasure; for, which they were lapped in these ecstatic slumbers, Brunhilda sucked the life-stream from their bosoms. On waking, indeed, they felt themselves faint and exhausted, yet did no pain nor any mark betray the cause. Shortly, however, did their strength entirely fail, even as the summer brook is gradually dried up: their sports became less and less noisy; their loud, frolicsome laughter was converted into a faint smile; the full tones of their voices died away into a mere whisper. Their attendants were filled with horror and despair; too well did they conjecture the horrible truth, yet dared not to impart their suspicions to Walter, who was so devotedly attached to his horrible partner. Death had already smote his prey: the children were but the mere shadows of their former selves, and even this shadow quickly disappeared.

The anguished father deeply bemoaned their loss, for, notwithstanding his apparent neglect, he was strongly attached to them, nor until he had experienced their loss was he aware that his love was so great. His affliction could not fail to excite the displeasure of Brunhilda: "Why dost thou lament so fond-ly," said she, "for these little ones? What satisfaction could such unformed beings yield to thee unless thou wert still attached to their mother? Thy heart then is still hers? Or dost thou now regret her and them because thou art satiated with my fondness and weary of my endearments? Had these young ones grown up, would they not have attached thee, thy spirit and thy affections more closely to this earth of clay—to this dust and have alienated thee from that sphere to which I, who have already passed the grave, endeavour to raise thee? Say is thy spirit so heavy, or thy love so weak, or thy faith so hollow, that the hope of being mine for ever is unable to touch thee?" Thus did Brunhilda express her indignation at her consort's grief, and forbade him her presence. The fear of offending her beyond forgiveness and his anxiety to appease her soon dried up his tears; and he again abandoned himself to his fatal passion, until approaching destruction at length awakened him from his delusion.

Neither maiden, nor youth, was any longer to be seen, either within the dreary walls of the castle, or the adjoining territory:—all had disappeared; for those whom the grave had not swallowed up had fled from the region of death. Who, therefore, now remained to quench the horrible thirst of the female vampire save Walter himself? and his death she dared to contemplate unmoved; for that divine sentiment that unites two beings in one joy and one sorrow was unknown to her bosom. Was he in his tomb, so was she free to search out other victims and glut herself with destruction, until she herself should, at the last day, be consumed with the earth itself, such is the fatal law to which the dead are subject when awoke by the arts of necromancy from the sleep of the grave.

She now began to fix her blood-thirsty lips on Walter's breast, when cast into a profound sleep by the odour of her violet breath he reclined beside her quite unconscious of his impending fate: yet soon did his vital powers begin to decay; and many a grey hair peeped through his raven locks. With his strength, his passion also declined; and he now frequently left her in order to pass the whole day in the sports of the chase, hoping thereby to regain his wonted vigour. As he was reposing one day in a wood beneath the shade of an oak, he perceived, on the summit of a tree, a bird of strange appearance, and quite unknown to him; but, before he could take aim at it with his bow, it flew away into the clouds; at the same time letting fall a rose-coloured root which dropped at Walter's feet, who immediately took it up and, although he was well acquainted with almost every plant, he could not remember to have seen any at all resembling this. Its delightfully odoriferous scent induced him to try its flavour, but ten times more bitter than wormwood it was even as gall in his mouth; upon which, impatient of the disappointment, he flung it away with violence. Had he, however, been aware of its miraculous quality and that it acted as a counter charm against the opiate perfume of Brunhilda's breath, he would have blessed it in spite of its bitterness: thus do mortals often blindly cast away in displeasure the unsavoury remedy that would otherwise work their weal.

When Walter returned home in the evening and laid him down to repose as usual by Brunhilda's side, the magic power of her breath produced no effect upon him; and for the first time during many months did he close his eyes in a natural slumber. Yet hardly had he fallen asleep, ere a pungent smarting pain disturbed him from his dreams; and. opening his eyes, he discerned, by the gloomy rays of a lamp, that glimmered in the apartment what for some moments transfixed him quite aghast, for it was Brunhilda, drawing with her lips, the warm blood from his bosom. The wild cry of horror which at length escaped him, terrified Brunhilda, whose mouth was besmeared with the warm blood. "Monster!" exclaimed he, springing from the couch, "is it thus that you love me?"

"Aye, even as the dead love," replied she, with a malignant coldness.

"Creature of blood!" continued Walter, "the delusion which has so long blinded me is at an end: thou are the fiend who hast destroyed my children—who hast murdered the offspring of my vassels." Raising herself upwards and, at the same time, casting on him a glance that froze him to the spot with dread, she replied. "It is not I who have murdered them; —I was obliged to pamper myself with warm youthful blood, in order that I might satisfy thy furious desires—thou art the murderer!"—These dreadful words summoned, before Walter's terrified conscience, the threatening shades of all those who had thus perished; while despair choked his voice.

"Why," continued she, in a tone that increased his horror, "why dost thou make mouths at me like a puppet? Thou who hadst the courage to love the dead—to take into thy bed, one who had been sleeping in the grave, the bed-fellow of the worm —who hast clasped in thy lustful arms, the the corruption of the tomb—dost thou, unhallowed as thou art, now raise this hideous cry for the sacrifice of a few lives?—They are but leaves swept from their branches by a storm.—Come, chase these idiot fancies, and taste the bliss thou hast so dearly purchased." So saying, she extended her arms towards him; but this motion served only to increase his terror, and exclaiming: "Accursed Being,"—he rushed out of the apartment.

All the horrors of a guilty, upbraiding conscience became

his companions, now that he was awakened from the delirium of his unholy pleasures. Frequently did he curse his own obstinate blindness, for having given no heed to the hints and admonitions of his children's nurses, but treating them as vile calumnies. But his sorrow was now too late, for, although repentance may gain pardon for the sinner, it cannot alter the immutable decrees of fate—it cannot recall the murdered from the tomb. No sooner did the first break of dawn appear, than he set out for his lonely castle in the mountains, determined no longer to abide under the same roof with so terrific a being; yet vain was his flight, for, on waking the following morning, he perceived himself in Brunhilda's arms, and quite entangled in her long raven tresses, which seemed to involve him, and bind him in the fetters of his fate; the powerful fascination of her breath held him still more captivated, so that, forgetting all that had passed, he returned her caresses, until awakening as if from a dream he recoiled in unmixed horror from her embrace. During the day he wandered through the solitary wilds of the mountains, as a culprit seeking an asylum from his pursuers; and, at night, retired to the shelter of a cave; fearing less to couch himself within such a dreary place, than to expose himself to the horror of again meeting Brunhilda; but alas! it was in vain that he endeavoured to flee her. Again, when he awoke, he found her the partner of his miserable bed. Nay, had he sought the centre of the earth as his hiding place; had he even imbedded himself beneath rocks, or formed his chamber in the recesses of the ocean, still had he found her his constant companion; for, by calling her again into existence, he had rendered himself inseparably hers; so fatal were the links that united them.

Struggling with the madness that was beginning to seize him, and brooding incessantly on the ghastly visions that presented themselves to his horror-stricken mind, he lay motionless in the gloomiest recesses of the woods, even from the rise of sun till the shades of eve. But, no sooner was the light of day extinguished in the west, and the woods buried in impenetrable darkness, than the apprehension of resigning himself to sleep drove him forth among the mountains. The storm played wildly with the fantastic clouds, and with the rattling leaves, as they were caught up into the air, as if some dread spirit was sporting with these images of transitoriness and decay: it roared among the summits of the oaks as if uttering a voice of fury, while its hollow sound rebounding among the distant hills, seemed as the moans of a departing sinner, or as the faint cry of some wretch expiring under the murderer's hand: the owl too, uttered its ghastly cry as if fore-boding the wreck of nature. Walter's hair flew disorderly in the wind, like black snakes wreathing around his temples and shoulders; while each sense was awake to catch fresh horror. In the clouds he seemed to behold the forms of the murdered; in the howling wind to hear their laments and groans; in the chilling blast itself he felt the dire kiss of Brunhilda; in the cry of the screeching bird he heard her voice; in the mouldering leaves he scented the charnel-bed out of which he had awakened her. "Murderer of thy own offspring," exclaimed he in a voice making night, and the conflict of the element still more hideous, "paramour of a blood-thirsty vampire, reveller with the corruption of the tomb!" while in his despair he rent the wild locks from his head. Just then the full moon darted from beneath the bursting clouds; and the sight recalled to his remembrance the advice of the sorcerer, when he trembled at the first apparition of Brunhilda rising from her sleep of death; —namely, to seek him at the season of the full moon in the mountains, where three roads met. Scarcely had this gleam of hope broke in on his bewildered mind than he flew to the appointed spot.

On his arrival, Walter found the old man seated there upon a stone as calmly as though it had been a bright sunny day and completely regardless of the uproar around. "Art thou come then?" exclaimed he to the breathless wretch, who, flinging himself at his feet, cried in a tone of anguish:—"Oh save me— succour me—rescue me from the monster that scattereth death and desolation around her.

"Wherefore a mysterious warning? why didst thou not

rather disclose to me at once all the horrors that awaited my sacrilegious profanation of the grave?"

"And wherefore a mysterious warning? why didst thou not perceivest how wholesome was the advice—'Wake not the dead.'

"Wert thou able to listen to another voice than that of thy impetuous passions? Did not thy eager impatience shut my mouth at the very moment I would have cautioned thee?"

"True, true:—thy reproof is just: but what does it avail now;—I need the promptest aid."

"Well," replied the old man, "there remains even yet a means of rescuing thyself, but it is fraught with horror and demands all thy resolution."

"Utter it then, utter it; for what can be more appalling, more hideous than the misery I now endure?"

"Know then," continued the sorcerer, "that only on the night of the new moon does she sleep the sleep of mortals; and then all the supernaturural power which she inherits from the grave totally fails her. 'Tis then that thou must murder her."

"How! murder her!" echoed Walter.

"Aye," returned the old man calmly, "pierce her bosom with a sharpened dagger, which I will furnish thee with; at the same time renounce her memory for ever, swearing never to think of her intentionally, and that, if thou dost involuntarily, thou wilt repeat the curse."

"Most horrible! yet what can be more horrible than she herself is?—I'll do it."

"Keep then this resolution until the next new moon."

"What, must I wait until then?" cried Walter, "alas ere then, either her savage thirst for blood will have forced me into the night of the tomb, or horror will have driven me into the night of madness."

"Nay," replied the sorcerer, "that I can prevent;" and, so saying, he conducted him to a cavern further among the mountains. "Abide here twice seven days," said he; "so long can I protect thee against her deadly caresses. Here wilt thou find all due provision for thy wants; but take heed that nothing tempt thee to quit this place. Farewell, when the moon renews itself, then do I repair hither again." So saying, the sorcerer drew a magic circle around the cave, and then immediately disappeared.

Twice seven days did Walter continue in this solitude, where his companions were his own terrifying thoughts, and his bitter repentance. The present was all desolation and dread; the future presented the image of a horrible deed which he must perforce commit; while the past was empoisoned by the memory of his guilt. Did he think on his former happy union with Brunhilda, her horrible image presented itself to his imagination with her lips defiled with dropping blood: or, did he call to mind the peaceful days he had passed with Swanhilda, he beheld her sorrowful spirit with the shadows of her murdered children. Such were the horrors that attended him by day: those of night were still more dreadful, for then he beheld Brunhilda herself, who, wandering round the magic circle which she could not pass, called upon his name till the cavern reechoed the horrible sound. "Walter, my beloved," cried she, "wherefore dost thou avoid me? art thou not mine? for ever mine—mine here, and mine hereafter? And dost thou seek to murder me?—ah! commit not a deed which hurls us both to perdition—thyself as well as me." In this manner did the horrible visitant torment him each night, and, even when she departed, robbed him of all repose.

The night of the new moon at length arrived, dark as the deed it was doomed to bring forth. The sorcerer entered the cavern; "Come," said he to Walter, "let us depart hence, the hour is now arrived:" and he forthwith conducted him in silence from the cave to a coal-black steed, the sight of which recalled to Walter's remembrance the fatal night. He then related to the old man Brunhilda's nocturnal visits and anxiously inquired whether her apprehensions of eternal perdition would be fulfilled or not. "Mortal eye," exclaimed the sorcerer, "may not pierce the dark secrets of another world, or penetrate the deep abyss that separates earth from heaven." Walter hesitated to mount the steed. "Be resolute," exclaimed his companion, "but this once is it granted to thee to make the trial, and, should thou fail now, nought can rescue thee from her power."

"What can be more horrible than she herself?—I am determined:" and he leaped on the horse, the sorcerer mounting also behind him.

Carried with a rapidity equal to that of the storm that sweeps across the plain they in brief space arrived at Walter's castle. All the doors flew open at the bidding of his companion, and they speedily reached Brunhilda's chamber, and stood beside her couch. Reclining in a tranquil slumber; she reposed in all her native loveliness, every trace of horror had disappeared from her countenance; she looked so pure, meek and innocent that all the sweet hours of their endearments rushed to Walter's memory, like interceding angels pleading in her behalf. His unnerved hand could not take the dagger which the sorcerer presented to him. "The blow must be struck even now:" said the latter, "shouldst thou delay but an hour, she will lie at daybreak on thy bosom, sucking the warm life drops from thy heart."

"Horrible! most horrible!" faltered the trembling Walter, and turning away his face, he thrust the dagger into her bosom, exclaiming—"I curse thee for ever!—and the cold blood gushed upon his hand. Opening her eyes once more, she cast a look of ghastly horror on her husband, and, in a hollow dying accent said—"Thou too art doomed to perdition."

"Lay now thy hand upon her corpse," said the sorcerer, "and swear the oath."—Walter did as commanded, saying, "Never will I think of her with love, never recall her to mind intentionally, and, should her image recur to my mind involuntarily, so will I exclaim to it: be thou accursed."

"Thou hast now done everything," returned the sorcerer; —"restore her therefore to the earth, from which thou didst so foolishly recall her; and be sure to recollect thy oath: for, shouldst thou forget it but once, she would return, and thou wouldst be inevitably lost. Adieu—we see each other no more." Having uttered these words he quitted the apartment, and

Walter also fled from this abode of horror, having first given direction that the corpse should be speedily interred.

Again did the terrific Brunhilda repose within her grave; but her image continually haunted Walter's imagination, so that his existence was one continued martyrdom, in which he continually struggled, to dismiss from his recollection the hideous phantoms of the past; yet, the stronger his effort to banish them, so much the more frequently and the more vividly did they return; as the night-wanderer, who is enticed by a fire-wisp into quagmire or bog, sinks the deeper into his damp grave the more he struggles to escape. His imagination seemed incapable of admitting any other image than that of Brunhilda: now he fancied he beheld her expiring, the blood streaming from her beautiful bosom: at others he saw the lovely bride of his youth, who reproached him with having disturbed the slumbers of the tomb; and to both he was compelled to utter the dreadful words, "I curse thee for ever." The terrible imprecation was constantly passing his lips; yet was he in incessant terror lest he should forget it, or dream of her without being able to repeat it, and then, on awaking, find himself in her arms. Else would he recall her expiring words, and, appalled at their terrific import, imagine that the doom of his perdition was irrecoverably passed. Whence should he fly from himself? or how erase from his brain these images and forms of horror? In the din of combat, in the tumult of war and its incessant pour of victory to defeat; from the cry of anguish to the exultation of victory—in these he hoped to find at least the relief of distraction: but here too he was disappointed. The giant fang of apprehension now seized him who had never before known fear; each drop of blood that sprayed upon him seemed the cold blood that had gushed from Brunhilda's wound; each dying wretch that fell beside him looked like her, when expiring, she exclaimed,—"Thou too art doomed to perdition"; so that the aspect of death seemed more full of dread to him than aught beside, and this unconquerable terror compelled him to abandon the battle-field. At length, after many a weary and fruitless wandering, he returned to his castle. Here all was deserted and silent, as if the sword, or a still more deadly pestilence had laid everything waste: for the few inhabitants that still remained, and even those servants who had once shewn themselves the most attached, now fled from him, as though he had been branded with the mark of Cain. With horror he perceived that, by uniting himself as he had done with the dead, he had cut himself off from the living, who refused to hold any intercourse with him. Often, when he stood on the battlements of his castle, and looked down upon desolate fields, he compared their present solitude with the lively activity they were wont to exhibit, under the strict but benevolent discipline of Swanhilda. He now felt that she alone could reconcile him to life, but durst he hope that one, whom he so deeply aggrieved, could pardon him, and receive him again? Impatience at length got the better of fear; he sought Swanhilda, and, with the deepest contrition, acknowledged his complicated guilt; embracing her knees as he beseeched her to pardon him, and to return to his desolate castle, in order that it might again become the abode of contentment and peace. The pale form which she beheld at her feet, the shadow of the lately blooming youth, touched Swanhilda. "The folly," said she gently, "though it has caused me much sorrow, has never excited my resentment or my anger. But say, where are my children?" To this dreadful interrogation the agonized father could for a while frame no reply: at length he was obliged to confess the dreadful truth. "Then we are sundered for ever," returned Swanhilda; nor could all his tears or supplications prevail upon her to revoke the sentence she had given.

Stripped of his last earthly hope, bereft of his last consolation, and thereby rendered as poor as mortal can possibly be on this side of the grave. Walter returned homewards; when, as he was riding through the forest in the neighbourhood of his castle, absorbed in his gloomy meditations, the sudden sound of a horn roused him from his reverie. Shortly after he saw appear a female figure clad in black, and mounted on a steed of the same colour: her attire was like that of a huntress, but, instead of a falcon, she bore a raven in her hand; and she was attended by a gay troop of cavaliers and dames. The first salutations bring passed, he found that she was proceeding the same road as himself; and, when she found that Walter's castle was close at hand, she requested that he would lodge her for that night, the evening being far advanced. Most willingly did he comply with this request, since the appearance of the beautiful stranger had struck him greatly; so wonderfully did she resemble Swanhilda, except that her locks were brown, and her eye dark and full of fire. With a sumptous banquet did he entertain his guests, whose mirth and songs enlivened the lately silent halls. Three days did this revelry continue, and so exhilarating did it prove to Walter that he seemed to have forgotten his sorrows and his fears; nor could he prevail upon himself to dismiss his visitors, dreading lest, on their departure, the castle would seem a hundred times more desolate than before hand his grief be proportionally increased. At his earnest request, the stranger consented to stay seven, and again another seven days. Without being requested, she took upon herself the superintendence of the household, which she regulated as discreetly and cheerfully as Swanhilda had been wont to do, so that the castle, which had so lately been the abode of melancholy and horror, became the residence of pleasure and festivity, and Walter's grief disappeared altogether in the midst of so much gaiety. Daily did his attachment to the fair unknown increase; he even made her his confidant; and, one evening as they were walking together apart from any of her train, he related to her his melancholy and frightful history. "My dear friend," returned she, as soon as he he had finished his tale, "it ill beseems a man of thy discretion to afflict thyself on account of all this. Thou hast awakened the dead from the sleep of the grave and afterwards found,"—"what might have been anticipated, that the dead possess no sympathy with life. What then? thou wilt not commit this error a second time."

"Thou hast however murdered the being whom thou hadst thus recalled again to existence—but it was only in appearance, for thou couldst not deprive that of life which properly had none. Thou hast, too, lost a wife and two children: but at thy years such a loss is most easily repaired. There are beauties who will gladly share thy couch, and make thee again a father. But thou dreadst the reckoning of hereafter:—go, open the graves and ask the sleepers there whether that hereafter disturbs them." In such manner would she frequently exhort and cheer him, so that, in a short time, his melancholy entirely disappeared. He now ventured to declare to the unknown the passion with which she had inspired him, nor did she refuse him her hand. Within seven days afterwards the nuptials were celebrated, and the very foundations of the castle seemed to rock from the wild tumultuous uproar of unrestrained riot. The wine streamed in abundance; the goblets circled incessantly; intemperance reached its utmost bounds, while shouts of laughter almost resembling madness burst from the numerous train belonging to the unknown. At length Walter, heated with wine and love, conducted his bride into the nuptial chamber: but, oh! horror! scarcely had he clasped her in his arms ere she transformed herself into a monstrous serpent, which entwining him in its horrid folds, crushed him to death. Flames crackled on every side of the apartment; in a few minutes after, the whole castle was enveloped in a blaze that consumed it entirely: while, as the walls fell in with a tremendous crash, a voice exclaimed aloud—"Wake not the dead!"

The End

THE BLACK VAMPYRE

BY URIAH DERICK D'ARCY

"Uriah Derick D'Arcy" was a pen name, and his true identity has been lost to time. There is speculation he was actually Robert C. Sands or Richard Varick Dey, but there is no consensus. Whatever the case, "The Black Vampyre" is notable for a variety of reasons. First, some believe it's the first vampire story by an American. That, too, is disputed, but we know for sure this is the first black vampire story. It also happens to have comedic aspects and could be considered the first of that sub-genre.

The Black Vampyre
by Uriah Derick D'Arcy

So have I seen, upon another shore,
Another Lion give a grievous roar;
And the last Lion thought the first—A BOAR!
Bombast. Furios.

TO THE
AUTHOR OF "WALL-STREET."

MY DEAR SIR,

CHARMED with the success of your anomalous drama, which, without aspiring even to the character of nonsense, has already seen three editions, I have been myself induced to venture on publishing; with the sanguine hope of also scraping together a few shillings, in these hard times. Permit me to inscribe this tale to you, with a fellow- feeling for your lack of genius; and a fervent hope, that our names may be encircled by the same evergreen in the temple of the Muses; and that we may long flourish together, on the same pedestal, embellishing and elevating the literature of the Auction Room.

I remain,
My dear Sir,
Your affectionate Friend,
And obedient Servant,
THE AUTHOR.

Introduction

IF any person should have patience to read the following narrative, and can discover the Author's drift, it is more than he can do himself. If it be thought exquisite nonsense, it is more than the writer dares hope: and if it be pronounced simple, stupid, and unadulterated absurdity, his own private opinion will perfectly coincide with that of the public. He began to write without any fable, and before he had found any had spun out the thread of his ideas.

This tangled skein of absurdities is now exposed to criticism, from the laudable motive of showing, of how much nonsense an individual may be delivered, in the short space of two afternoons; without any excuse but idleness, or any object but amusement.

The prominent descriptions, which it is here attempted to ridicule, are fresh in the memory of all who have read the "White Vampyre;" and to those who have not, the Superstition must be so familiar, that it is unnecessary to make useless extracts.

That the Author may not, however, be misunderstood, it may be necessary to state, that in the speech of the Vampyre, he

had no design of descending to that meanest of all intellectual
exercises, a travestie on authors who are justly admired: but
meant, if any thing, simply to show how passages, which were
fine in their original use, when garbelled by the ignorant and
tasteless, become a melancholy rhapsody of nonsense.

"But first on earth, as Vampyre sent,
Thy corse shall from its tomb be rent;
Then ghastly haunt thy native place,
And suck the blood of all thy race;
There from thy *daughter, sister, wife,*
At midnight drain the stream of life;
Yet loathe the banquet, which perforce
Must feed thy livid living corse.
Thy victims, ere they yet expire,
Shall know the demon for their sire;
As cursing thee, thou cursing them,
Thy flowers are withered on the stem.
But one that for *thy crime* must fall,
The youngest, best beloved of all,
Shall bless thee with a *father's* name—
That word shall wrap thy heart in flame!
Yet thou must end thy task and mark
Her cheek's last tinge—her eye's last spark,
And the last glassy glance must view
Which freezes o'er its lifeless blue;
Then with unhallowed hand shall tear
The tresses of her yellow hair,
Of which, in life a lock when shorn
Affection's fondest pledge was worn—
But now is borne away by thee
Memorial of thine agony!
Yet with thine own best blood shall drip
Thy gnashing tooth, and haggard lip;
Then stalking to thy sullen grave,
Go—and with Gouls and Afrits rave,

Till these in horror shrink away
From spectre more accursed than they."

-BYRON.

The Black Vampyre

Mr. ANTHONY GIBBONS was a gentleman of African extraction. His ancestors emigrated from the eastern coast of GUINEA, in a French ship, and were sold in ST. DOMINGO remarkably cheap; as they were reduced to mere skeletons by the yaws on the passage; and all died shortly after their arrival, except one small negro, of a very slender constitution, and fit for no work whatever. The gentleman who purchased him, charitably knocked out his brains; and the body was thrown into the ocean. The tide returning in the night, it was washed upon the sands; and the moon then shining bright, the gentleman was taking a walk to enjoy the coolness of the evening; judge of his surprise, when the little corpse got up, and complaining of a pain in its bowels, begged for some bread and butter!

The PLANTER supposing his business to have been but half done, kicked him back in the water. The element seemed very familiar to him; and he swam back with much grace and agility; parting the sparkling waves with his jet black members, polished like ebony, but reflecting no single beam of light. His complexion was a dead black;—his eyes a pure white;—the iris was flame colour;—and the pupils of a clear, moonshiny lustre;

—but so peculiarly constructed, that, though prominent, they seemed to look into his own head. His hair was neither curled nor straight; but feathery, like the plumage of a crow. Having paddled again on shore, he came crawling crab fashion, to the feet of Mr. PERSONNE. The latter gentleman, in considerable alarm, (not knowing whether it was Satan, Obi, or some other worthy, with whom he had to deal,) mustered up sufficient resolution, to tie a large stone round the boy's middle: then, with a main exertion of strength, he hurled him into the sparkling ocean. He fell where the reflection of the moon was brightest, and sunk like lead; but immediately rose again like cork, perpendicularly, with the stone under his arm while the radiant lustre of the planet retreated from his dark figure, exhibiting in its most striking contrast its utter blackness!

In this predicament, he came buoyant to land; surrounded, as he "seemed, by a sphere of magic lustre. He now walked up to the Frenchman, with his arms a-kimbo, and looking remarkably fierce. Mr. PERSONNE'S particular hairs stood up on end, but being ashamed that a little negro of ten years old, should put him in bodily fear, he knocked him down. The Guinea-man rose again, without bending a joint; as fast as Mr. PERSONNE could upset him, he recovered his altitude; just like one of those small toys, fabricated from pith, tipt with lead, called witches and hobgoblins by the rising generation!

The PLANTER, in utter amazement and despair, took hold of the child by both his extremities; and pressing him to the earth, set down upon him! Then, halloing for his attendants, he ordered a tremendous fire to be kindled on the sand!! This was accordingly done. The GAUL congratulated himself on his perseverance and sagacity; and as he had never heard of ignaqueous animals, was confident that though the water fiend was so expert in his own element, he could not stand the fiery ordeal. The boy, meanwhile, lay perfectly passive, as if he had been a mere log; but presently, when the pile was all in a light blaze, with a sudden expansion, like that of a compressed Indian Rubber, he popped Mr. PERSONNE up into the air many yards, and he alighted head-foremost into the fire, where he had intended to have dedicated the sable brat, with his nine lives, to Moloch!!!

Whatever the negro was, it is notorious that Mr. PERSONNE was no salamander. He was rescued from the pyre, which, like Hercules, he had, (though unwittingly,) erected for himself; looking like a squizzed cat, and having apparently no life left in his body. The attention of the domestics was drawn entirely to their master; who soon betrayed signs of animation, though he exhibited a most awful spectacle: being one continual sore and blister. "His whole body was one wound," as Virgil or some other poet has hyperbolically expressed himself.

Mr. PERSONNE, when he perfectly recovered his senses, found himself in his own bed, wrapt in greasy sheets, and smarting as if in a Cayenne bath. He called for a glass of brandy,—his dear wife EUPHEMIA,—and his infant son, who had not yet been christened. His lady, with streaming eyes, presented herself before him; and, after tenderly inquiring into the state of his health, told him, (with a voice interrupted with sobs and hiccups,) that when she went in the morning to see her baby, whom she had left in the cradle, there was nothing to be seen, but the skin, hair, and nails!!! She declared that there never was such another object; except, indeed, the exsiccation in Scudder's Museum!

On the receipt of this horrid intelligence, Mr. PERSONNE was seized with a violent spasmodic affection; and shortly after expired, muttering something about sacre, and the Guinea-negro!

The amiable, but unfortunate Euphemia, was thrown into several hysterical convulsions; as well she might be, poor woman! when her husband had been made a holocaust, and served up like a broiled and peppered chicken, to feed the grim maw of death; and her interesting infant, the first pledge of her pure and perfect love, had been precociously sucked, like an unripe orange, and nothing left but its beautiful and tender skin. The disconsolate widow caused her husband to be embalmed; and he was buried amid the lamentations and tears of all the funeral; much regretted by all who had the honour of his acquaintance, particularly by his negroes; who could not soon forget him; as he had left too many sincere marks of his regard upon their backs, to be ever obliterated from their recollections.

Time, as all the Greek tragedians, Solomon, and others have remarked, is a benevolent deity. Mrs. PERSONNE'S grief yielded to the soothing hand of the consoling power; and her bloom and spirits returned with more lustre and elasticity than they had before exhibited: as the rose, that had drooped in the fury of the passing storm, erects its blushing honours, and shows more beautiful and vivid tints, when the squall is over!

Many years after these occurrences took place, while EUPHEMIA was in second mourning for her third husband, she was indulging in the luxury of solitary grief; and reading Burton's Anatomy of Melancholy, and The Melancholy Poems of Dr. Farmer, in an orangerie. The refreshing breezes from the ocean, which now tempered the sultry heats of the declining day,—the soft perfume of the opening blossoms;—and the mellow tints of the evening sky, shedding that holy light, so dear to sensitive hearts, diffused a calm over her soul, wrapt in the contemplation of departed days. While lost in this pensive reverie, she perceived two strangers approaching her, in the extremity of the long vista of the grove. One of them was a coloured gentleman, of remarkable height, and deep jetty blackness; a perfect model of the CONGO Apollo. He was drest in the rich garb of a Moorish Prince; and led by the hand a pale European boy, in an Asiatic dress; whose languid countenance, slender form and tristful gait, were strongly contrasted with the portly appearance and majestic step of his conductor!

They both saluted the lovely widow, and after an interchange of compliments, accepted her polite invitation to set down, and take tea with her in the bower. She learned from the elder stranger, that he had brought out a cargo of slaves, whom his subjects had lately taken prisoners in war; and whom he had resolved to dispose of himself; as he was desirous of seeing the world. His Page, he said, was an orphan, left by a slave merchant in Africa. The manners and conversation of the PRINCE had an irresistible charm. The regal port was manifest in his gigantic and well proportioned frame; and majesty was conspicuous on his brow, without its diadem. The turban and crescent had never graced a nobler front; but the winning condescension of his tones and language, while they could not banish the feeling of the presence of royalty, removed every restraint incident to that consciousness. He criticised the works, which EUPHEMIA had been perusing, with masterly precision; and displayed more knowledge than even the accomplished ideologist of Lady Morgan; with infinitely more discretion and good sense.

It is remarked by the Abbe Reynal, that there is a peculiar elegance and beauty in the complexion of the Africans, (when the eyes and nose are accustomed to their hue and odour.) This truth was realized by EUPHEMIA, as she gazed on the open visage of her illustrious guest. She thought surely that in him Nature might stand up and say "This was a man!" And certainly it is only the weakness and imperfection of our human senses, which, penetrating no further than the surface, is for ever deceived by superficial shadows. The empyrean is always blue, whatever vapours may float in our contracted atmosphere. And if we gaze on the rows of skulls, which festoon and garnish Surgeon's Hall, we can apply no standard, to determine their relative beauty. They are all equally ugly; and the block of Helen might be mistaken for that of Medusa. Shakspeare, true to nature, has also remarked, "Black men are pearls in beauteous ladies' eyes." The beauty then, the royalty, gentility, and various accomplishments of the BAMBUCK monarch, made captive the too sensible heart of the French widow. She forgot her ogles, graces, and even her loquacity; rooted to her seat, and fixed in immoveable contemplation of the AFRICAN'S face. What peculiar feature or lineament attracted her attention, she knew not: his eyes, though bright, did not sparkle; and the iris, though of a more vivid red than the roseate line in the rainbow, emitted no scintillations. In fact, his whole countenance seemed to look, and to perambulate her own.

The conversation gradually assumed a more empassioned and amorous complexion; and the little page, (who, though meagre and emaciated, evidently showed that he was no gump for his years,) taking certain broad hints, cast a mournful and intelligent look on the widow, said he would fetch a short walk in the plantation, and left the orangerie.

The PRINCE then spreading his glittering sash upon the grass, went down on his knees upon it; and broke out into the most ardent exclamations, of love and admiration; and professions of constant attachment. He said that the flat-nosed beauties of Zara; the scarred, squab figures of the golden coast; the well proportioned Zilias, Calypsos, and Zamas on the banks of the Niger; and even the great Hottentot Venus herself, had never for a moment made the least impression on his heart! His passion was a mystery to himself; its origin secret as the sources of the Nile ; but full and impetuous as its ample channel, when replenished from the celestial fountains of ABYSSINIA; while if Mrs. DUBOIS would shine upon its waves, its enlivened currents would fertilize his vast dominions, in the luxuriant realms of central Africa; making them to fructify yet more abundantly, with burning gold, and radiant diamonds!!!

What female heart could resist such pleadings, and the compliment implied in such a preference? When ZEMBO (the page) returned, the parties had agreed to be privately united on the same evening. The ceremony was accordingly performed, on the spot, by the family chaplain of Mrs. DUBOIS: not without many remonstrances on his part, as to the impropriety of marrying a negro. The PRINCE did not see to resent the affront; which, by the by, he had no right to do; as the priest got nothing for the job. ZEMBO, too, was extremely restless; till Mrs. DUBOIS gave him some sweet meats, which seemed to quiet his conscience; after which he took some stiff punch, and fell asleep!

About midnight, the PRINCE came to him; and, shaking him by the ears, bad him rise and follow him. His bride was hanging on his arm, in an enchanting dishabille; and did not seem to be in perfect possession of her right senses. ZEMBO mournfully followed the new married pair.

They went silently out of the back door, with cautious steps, and proceeded through the orangerie. No breath of wind was stirring. The moon was on the zenith, surrounded by a pale halo of ghostly lustre. When they had crossed the plantation, they came to a place of sepulture; where the dark cypresses, and lugubrious mahogany, admitted but sparse and glimmering streaks of funereal light; which, falling on the rank foliage, the white monuments and broken ground beneath, presented a thousand dusky shapes, flitting in the dim uncertainty dear to superstition

Vague terrors seized on the mind of the bride; and she began very naturally to inquire, what was the use of getting out of a comfortable bed, and trailing through the heavy dew, in her undress, to such an unusual spot for midnight recreation.

They now stood near the spot, where her three husbands, several children, and the skin, hair and nails of her first baby, were deposited in a row. At the foot of a tamarind, lay her third son; whose christian name was SPOONER, and who died, according to the tombstone, in a fit of intoxication, aged seven years and six months. On him she had bestowed a greater share of tenderness, than any of her other off spring; and his loss had caused her most affliction. The African, making observations on the grave, began to strip himself very expeditiously, assisted by ZEMBO; who seemed to recover from his blues; and by his activity and eagerness, manifested his expectation of soon seeing some fine sport.

Presently the two genii, or gentlemen, or whatever they were, turned towards the East, and performed certain antic prostrations; throwing handfuls of earth three times over their heads. Then returning to the tomb, they tore up the sods with ravenous fury; and soon drew out the last-mentioned son of the Lady, and threw him on the grass, beside the grave. ZEMBO fell as fiercely upon the corpse, as a hungry dog upon his dinner; but was arrested by the AFRICAN, who lent him a severe box on the ear, which sent him blubbering to a corner of the cemetery.

What added both to the mother's horrors and admiration, was, that the body of her child was perfectly fresh, and the olfactory nerves experienced no unsavoury sensation from its proximity; while its cheeks were diffused with so deep a tinge of scarlet, that they shone like ruddy fireballs in the darkness of the spot. Her husband drew a golden goblet from beneath a large stone; then, bending over the corse, he scooped out the heart, with his long and polished nails; and, having pressed the blood into the chalice, mingled with it some dark particles, gathered from the newly turned up earth. From the pure and scanty lymph, which gushed near by and flickered like a streak of quicksilvery-light in the moonbeam, he added a third ingredient of the potion. Then seizing his passive and trembling spouse by the throat, and presenting the unnatural mixture to her lips; he cried in a hollow voice, whose very inflection thrilled through each fibre of its victim,—"Swear, or if that is against your principles, affirm, by this dirty blood, —and bloody dirt;—by this watery blood,—and bloody water;—by this watery dirt, and dirty water;—that you will never disclose in any manner, aught of what you have seen and shall see this night. Call them all to witness your wish, that in the moment when you even conceive the thought of perjury, your bowels may burst out, and your bones rot! Swear and drink!"

The affrighted woman murmured, (as articulately as the iron gripe of the monster would suffer her,) that she was not thirsty; and had not breath enough to aspirate such a terrible conjuration. "No trifling;" roared the fiend, "you have not a moment to deliberate." But his bellowing and threats were vain; and he found to his mortification that he had gotten the wrong sow by the ear, or rather by the throat. She stuttered out, in the most pitiful accents, which would have softened any heart (but a Vampyre has none,) that though she was by no means partial to the delectable confectionary of the pharmacopeia, calomel and jalap, ipecacuanha, rhubarb, and tartar-emetic, she would rather take them all, collectively and individually, than the unchristian decoction he held against her teeth.

Foaming with madness, till the white slaver flowed down his sable limbs, the African hurled MRS. PERSONNE, DUBOIS, &c. &c. on the grave of her first husband, and stamping violently on the earth, it seemed to heave as with the throes of an earthquake. Immediately the tumuli yawned. The ponderous stones and slabs were shaken from their ancient sockets; and the ghastly dead, in uncouth attitudes, crawled from their nooks; with their hair curling in tortuous and serpent twinings; and their eyeballs of fire bursting from their heads; while, as they extended their withered arms, and tapering fingers, furnished with blood-hound claws, their gory shrouds fell in wild drapery around them, transiently revealing their forms, bloated as if to bursting, and often incarnadined with clotted blood, yet warm and dripping!!!

The Lady, (as those who have been in similar predicaments may suppose,) soon lost her recollection; not, however, before she had seen ZEMBO busily employed in tearing up the grave of her first husband; she saw herself surrounded by the spectres, and lost all consciousness.When reason and sense returned, she found herself in the same place; and it was also the midnight hour. She was laying by the grave of Mr. PERSONNE, and her breast was stained with blood. A wide wound appeared to have been inflicted there, but was now cicatrized. Imagine if you can, her surprise; when, by a certain carniverous craving in her maw, and by putting this and that together, she found she was a—VAMPYRE!!! and gathered from her indistinct reminiscences, of the preceding night, that she had been then sucked; and that it was now her turn to eject the peaceful tenants of the grave!

With this delightful prospect of immortality before her, she began to examine the graves, for subject to "a satisfy her furious appetite. When she had selected one to her mind, a new marvel arrested her attention. Her first husband got up out his coffin, and with all the grace so natural to his countrymen, made her a low bow in the last fashion, and opened his arms to receive her!

What were the emotions of this fond couple, when, after a lingering separation for sixteen years, they again embraced each other, with the ardour of an affection equal to their earliest transports, and which their long divorce served only to increase; tenderly inquiring into the state of each other's health; and the accidents which had befallen them during their disjunction. They forgot even their hunger and thirst; and sitting down on a tombstone, made a thousand inquiries; which, however, they related to family concerns, might not be as interesting to the reader as they were to the parties concerned.

Mr. PERSONNE, however, looked rather glum, when he learned that his Lady had been thrice married, since his decease. But she assured him, that she would never more tolerate the addresses of another suitor: and as for the two husbands, they were rotten enough by this time; as she was confident they had not attended the Vampyre Ball, on the preceding night. As for her sable spouse, she trusted that he would never again appear to interrupt their happiness. But while she was expressing this hope, the gentleman in question, (like his relation below, according to the old proverb,) came upon the ground, with ZEMBO. Mr. PERSONNE, having neither sword nor pistols at hand, armed himself with a gigantic thigh-bone; and warned the BLACK PRINCE to stand upon his guard as he meant to punish him severely.

But ZEMBO, rushing between the parties, raised his hands in a supplicating posture; while the generous monarch, making a Salam to his antagonist, begged him, keep himself quiet, and look behind him. They both turned round on this intimation, when, to the utter confusion of the Lady, her second and third husbands, Messieurs MARQUAND and DUBOIS, arose from the graves, where they had been lovingly deposited by the side of each other. They both advanced to salute their wife; but Mr. PERSONNE, brandishing his thigh-bone, warned them to stand off, as he had the first title to the Lady. Much confusion would have ensued, had not the African Prince interfered. He told the gentlemen that so delicate a point could only be settled in an honourable way; and proposed that Mr. MARQUAND and Mr. DUBOIS should first settle their difference in a personal encounter; after which Mr. PERSONNE might give the survivor gentlemanly satisfaction. To this all parties assented.

As they were already stripped, the combatants shook hands, to show their mutual good-will; and proceeded to action, without further ceremony. Mr. DuBois soon brought claret from Mr. MARQUAND; who, in returning the compliment, fibbed Mr. DUBOIS so severely in the bowels, that he lost his wind; and gasping for breath, smote the air on all sides, without any of his blows telling. He came to the ground, and his bones rattled as he fell. But soon recovering his breath, he made a desperate attack on Mr. MARQUAND'S sconce; and favoured him with so terrible a facer under the gills, that he fell incontinently like a bull smitten in his front; but entangling his own heels with those of Mr. DUBOIS, they both came simultaneously to the ground; striking their heads against different tombstones; and knocking out their own brains.

They rose again, refreshed like the giant of old, by their grappling with the earth, and all the better for the loss of their wits, which, indeed, was a mere trifle. But the AFRICAN, who had no time to see more sport, fixed them to the sod by his superior strength; and ZEMBO dexterously pinned them fast, by driving stakes through their hearts, with a large sledge hammer, (which he carried about his person for such emergencies.) During the operation, their roaring surpassed that which is performed by the Lioness, when bereft of her whelps; but as soon as they were fairly nailed to the counter, they lay motionless and breathless—a horrible pair of spectacles of sin and misery!

The AFRICAN assured the Lady, that she need never fear their second resurrection; and Mr. PERSONNE politely offered to settle their controversy, in any mode most agreeable to the PRINCE:—either to box with him on the spot, or appoint a meeting in future, with pistols, rifles, small or broad sword; or else they might toss up, who should set fire to a barrel of gunpowder. The PRINCE said that quarrelling was all nonsense, and offered his hand; but Mr. PERSONNE refused, saying, "Don't be too familiar, Blackey;" and renewing his threats of cracking him over the noddle with the thigh-bone.

The generous monarch pocketed the affront. "You have been," he said, "sufficiently rewarded, for the cruelties you practised upon my person, several years ago. I forgive you, my dear sir, what you performed, and intended to perform on me. Here is your son, who has grown considerably, as you may observe; and I assure you that his education has not been neglected. To his exertions last night you are indebted for your revivification. And as, you may remember, you were embalmed, you have kept quite sweet and fresh ever since your interment. Amiable and virtuous VAMPYRES! may you long enjoy that tranquillity and contentment, which your merit and accomplishments so eminently deserve! A vessel lies in the port, ready to sail for Europe in an hour. The Island is no longer a place for you. Here is money to pay your passages, and all I have to say, is, that the sooner you're off the better.—Farewell!" So saying he departed, without waiting for the acknowledgments of the party.

Mr. PERSONNE and his Lady, whom we shall again call by her first marriage name, did not exactly comprehend what their dingy benefactor meant, by bidding them take French leave of the Island, like pickpockets and outlaws; but, as they were yet wondering at their own existence, like Adam and Eve, the first day of their creation, and as they had reason to believe the PRINCE a potent magician, who could rouse the dead from their searments, and turn the planets from their courses; —for these reasons, they concluded to follow his bidding, without any impertinent scruples. But as the keen edge of their hunger had been whetted by delay, they would fain have taken supper, and digested a little something wherewithal to strengthen them, before they set out.

ZEMBO, who had filled his own breadbasket very lately, and was in no such urgent necessity, protested with all the vehemence which filial reverence would permit, against the unseasonable gratification of their unnatural craving; and recited with just emphasis and good discretion, an extract from Counsellor Phillips's harangue, about "the cannibal appetite of his rejected altar;" which his parents did not understand, and of course thought very sublime! But even this master-piece of mystical eloquence would have been delivered in vain; had not the boy given other reasons of such cogency, that they licked their lips—cast a longing, lingering look at the grave-yard,—and followed him without more opposition.

They prosecuted their nocturnal march, through closely woven and solemn groves; until they descended into a profound valley, where the light of the pale planet of magic adoration, streamed and quivered on serried files of bright armoury. The leader of the band seemed to have expected their arrival; and mutual tokens of recognition passed between him and ZEMBO. The whole company then set forward their array in silence:—

> No cymbal clash'd, no clarion rang,
> Still were the pipe and drum;
> Save heavy tread, and armour's clang
> The sullen march was dumb.

By continual descent, they seemed to have penetrated the bowels of a cavern, whose ramifications ran under the sea; as they heard a murmuring roar, as of the ocean, above their heads. The party, by the "nstructions of ZEMBO, dispersed themselves in different directions; until they had enclosed the interior of the rock where its largest chamber was, to speak catachrestically, so artfully concealed by nature, that no one, not instructed by an adept in its subterranean topography, could ever have detected the secret of its existence. It had been, in former days, a place of deposit and asylum for the Buccaniers; and its situation had been since known only to the Professors of the OBEAH art, who held here their midnight orgies.

Mr. and Mrs. PERSONNE, guided by their son, were

placed in a situation, where, through the crevices of the inner partition of the rock, they could observe what was passing in the interior.

It seemed, at first view, a vast hall of Arabian romance; supported by immense shafts, and studded with precious stones; so various and beautiful were the hues, which the different spars assumed, in the light of an hundred torches, blazing in every quarter, and illuminating the farthest recesses of the cave. The walls were decorated with other appendages, which added to the mystery, if not to the embellishment of the scene; being irregularly stained with blood; decorated with rude tapestry of many coloured plumage;—and stuccoed with the beaks of parrots;—the teeth of dogs, and alligators;—bones of cats;—broken glass and eggshells; plastered with a composition of rum and grave-dirt, the implements of NEGRO witchcraft!

At one extremity of the extensive apartment, on a kind of natural throne, sat several blackamoors in sumptuous Moorish apparel; whom, by their swollen forms, and remarkable eyes, Mrs. PERSONNE knew to be GOULS; and among whom she recognised her late husband. The whole range of this vast amphitheatre, sweeping from before the throne, was occupied by slaves, rudely attired, and imperfectly armed with clubs and missiles; a decent platoon of black-guards were posted be-fore the Vampyre monarchs; and, in the centre, a band of musicians performed an exquisite symphony. The soft strains of the MERRIWANG;—the lively notes of the DUNDO;—and the martial accompaniment of the GOOMBAY, made, with their united noises, a discordant harmony, whose powers the lyre of Orpheus could not equal; and which would certainly be enough to frighten all the hosts of Pandemonium. The oratorio being finished, the AFRICAN PRINCE arose, and making an obeisance to the company,—cleared his throat, and began to address them as follows:—"Gentlemen and Vampyres!"—but the VAMPYRES expressing their resentment against this breach of etiquette, he corrected himself: —" Vampyres and Gentlemen!"—but the NEGROES were no more willing to come last, than the Vampyres, and a loud growl accompanied by a slight hiss, again interrupted the orator. He was not, however, disconcerted, but like Mr. Burke, thundered out an iteration of the offensive sentence.

"Yes," said he, "I repeat it, Vampyres and Gentlemen? Shall not the immortal precede the mortal?— Shall not those whose diet surpasses the nectar and ambrosia of celestials, precede the ephemeral race, who fatten on the unclean juice of brutes,— the rank essence of esculent productions,—or the nauseous liquor of the distillery? (applause—hear! hear! and see-boy! from the Vampyres—groans from the negroes!) Gentlemen of colour! I appeal to yourselves; shall not the descendants of the Gods be named before the offspring of the earth-born image, whom Titan impregnated with celestial fire?—For Prometheus was the first Vampyre. You must all know, as you have undoubtedly read Æschylus, that the vulture, who preyed on his liver, was neither fish, flesh, nor fowl. He is called a dog, which makes him a quadruped;—he is represented as ερπων, creeping, which proves him an insect; and is said to have wings, which shows that he was a bird. Now, from this amphibious monster have descended the Crows,—the Jackalls,—and the Bloodhounds;—the pirate Bat of Madagascar,—and the man-killing Ivunches of Chili;—the Sharks;—the Crocodiles;—the Krakens;—the Horse-leeches;—the Cape-cod Sea Serpents;— the Mermaids;—the Incubi;—and the Succubi!!! (loud cheering from the Vampyres.) From Titan himself, descended the Cyclopes, and all other ancient and modern Anthropophagi; and, in lineal descent, the Moco tribe of our own EBOES, to whom I have the honour of being related. Those of you, too, are his posterity, who, after your deaths, return to your native land—the true Elysium; where the balmy bowl of the Coco, the soft bloom of the ANANA, and the coal-black beauties of the clime of love, shall for ever reward your fortitude, and steep in forgetfulness the memory of your wrongs. (hear! hear! from the negroes.) But none of these genera or species of our order, must longer engage your dignified and charitable attention. I come to ourselves, full- blooded—

unadulterated—immortal bloodsuckers!—To ourselves—whether Gouls,—or Afrits,—or Vampyres;— Vroucolochas,—Vardoulachos,—or Broucolokas—To ourselves—the terror of the living and of the dead, and the participants of the nature of both;—To ourselves—the emblems at once of corruption and of vitality;—blotted from the records of existence, and replenished to repletion with circulating life;—abandoned by the quick, and unrecognised by the dead:—'at once relics and relicts;— rocked on the bases of our own eternities;—the chronicles of what was—the solemn and sublime mementoes of what must be!' *unqualified approbation from both sides of the house*.) The estate of Vampyrism is a fee-tail, and may be docked in two different ways. The first mode is the sanguinary practice of perforating the subject with a stake; and this is final. The other is produced by the gentler operation of the narcotic potion you behold in this phial; by whose lenient and opiate influence, the individual is restored to the plight, in which he was previous to his death, or his becoming a Vampyre, and belongs to the OBEAH mysteries.

"But to come to the object of our present meeting. Sublime and soul-elevating theme!—The emancipation of the Negroes! —The consecration of the soil of ST. DOMINGO to the manes of murdered patriots in all ages!—No matter whether the bill of sale was scrawled in French or in English;—No matter whether we were taken prisoners, in a battle between the LEOPHARES and the JAKOFFS, or in a skirmish between the SAMBOES and the SAWPITS;—No matter whether we were bought for calico and cotton, or for gunpowder or for shot;—No matter whether we were transported in chains or in ropes—in a brig, or a schooner, or a seventy-four—the first moment we come ashore on ST. DOMINGO, our souls shall swell like a sponge in the liquid element;—our bodies shall burst from their fetters, glorious as a curculio from its shell;— our minds shall soar like the car of the æronaut, when its ligaments are cut; in a word, O my brethren, we shall be free!— Our fetters discandied, and our chains dissolved, we shall stand liberated,—redeemed,— emancipated,—and disenthralled by

the irresistible genius of UNIVERSAL EMANCIPATION!!!"
(*Unparalleled bursts of unprecedented applause!!!*) Such was the
report of this oration, taken down in short hand by ZEMBO;
of whose extraordinary sagacity so many proofs have been
exhibited; and who was never unprovided with materials for
any emergency. The fiery oratory of the Prince communicated
such inspiration to the auditors, that the whole mass of their
thick blood leaped up with the quickening pulse of anticipated
freedom; they danced and sung, with violent gesticulations,
like perfect Corybantes; but unfortunately, their Phyrricks
were interrupted by the glittering bayonets of the soldiery; who
poured in upon them from every quarter, and hemmed them
in, with a bristling chevaux-de-frise of steel. The Vampyres,
surprised but undaunted, unsheathed their sabres, and drew up
in a gallant style, as if determined to die game; being, indeed,
assured, that like so many Phœnixes, they would rise from their
own ashes, as often as they might be cut down.

A desperate conflict ensued, during which Mrs.
PERSONNE observed the phial, mentioned by the Prince,
lying on the ground; and very thoughtfully put it in her
ridicule. The slaves, seeing how the business was likely to termi-
nate, prudently sneaked off, while the attention of the military
was occupied by the Vampyres. The former were violently exas-
perated to find all their labour so unprofitable; since while they
themselves were wounded by every blow of their opponents,
the latter, like so many ninepins, were set up, as fast as they
were bowled down; bending to the storm, like masts on a
tempestuous ocean, and rising again upon the billow in
perpendicular triumph.

But, being instructed by ZEMBO, the soldiers pinioned
them as fast as they fell; and prevented their rising, by sitting in
great numbers on their bodies; though the task was somewhat
like that of detaining quicksilver beneath the fingers. The
PRINCE, however, still fought desperately. Brandishing a
huge scimitar in either hand, he swayed his arms like the sails
of a windmill; while limbs, heads, and bodies flew about him,
curvetting and dancing in the air; as when the ingenious Mr.

MAFFEY pulls to pieces a coach, or an old woman, children, chickens, friars, and petticoats dance about in wild confusion, till the artist's hand again brings order out of chaos:—Or, as when the renowned knight of the BED-CHAMBER, whose name eternal vases shall record, saw the ungenerous caricature on the wall, wielding a ponderous jug, he smote the innocent tables, chairs, and bed-posts, and strode victorious over the gory field: So fought the PRINCE; till being neatly pricked in the spine, unexpectedly, he soused (as Johannes Porco Latinus remarks) "in principia fundimentalia," and was immediately set upon by a host. So when a Gœtulian lion is pierced by the light bamboo, overpowered by the hunters, he struggles in his thrall like an Enceladus under Ætna, and dies at last with heart-wrung tears of anguish, and re- verberating roars of hatred!!!

Stakes were immediately procured, and the whole infernal fraternity securely disposed of: as their compeers, described by Homer,

> With burning chains fixed to the brazen floors
> And lock'd by hell's inexorable doors.

With their bellowings, the vast chambers of the subter-ranean rung like the caverns of Delphos, when the inflammable air was fired by the crafty priests. The Inhabitants of the Island started up from their slumbers in shuddering terror, and believed that an earthquake was rumbling beneath their feet.

Mr. and Mrs. PERSONNE and ZEMBO lost no time in trying the effects of the African's stolen prescription. Being thrown into a tranquil slumber they were conveyed to their plantation; and awoke the next morning, perfectly well, excepting slight colds in the head. Mr. PERSONNE, having been in status quo, for sixteen years, was now much younger than his lady; a circumstance, for which she was not at all sorry; and which he himself declared by no means displeased him. The remainder of their life was serene as a tropic night; —illu-mined by the mild effulgence of domestic love;—fanned by the soft aspirations of peaceful bosoms;—and enlivened by the fire-fly scintillations of rapture!!!

ZEMBO, to whose taste and ingenuity they were indebted for their happiness, and who was baptized with the Christian name of BARABBAS, after an uncle of his mother's, recorded what the reader has perused. One only circumstance, like one of those claps of thunder, frequently heard in the unclouded sky, passed over the tranquillity of their bosoms. Mrs. PERSONNE'S fourth husband's child was a mulatto, and of Vampyrish propensities; of which his mother and Mr. PERSONNE were never able entirely to cure him, having used up all the African's preparation.

The intelligent reader, (if any such there be,) will remember that this narrative commenced with the name of Mr. ANTHONY GIBBONS, of whom nothing has since been said; and whose adventures (to use a FORUM trope) "must remain buried in the bowels of futurity," until a more convenient opportunity. He is a lineal descendant from the last-mentioned mulatto; and the manuscript, which is now given to the public, was transmitted to him from his ancestors. He is a resident in Essex county, New-Jersey; and candour requires us to state, that he is no relation to his celebrated namesake at ELIZABETH-TOWN; as it is notorious to all who have had the pleasure of witnessing the size of the latter gentleman's waist, that he has too much bowels for so diabolical a profession; and it is to be hoped in charity, that though he is such a delicate morsel, when he is laid in the sepulchre of his fathers, he may not prove a titbit, to GLUT THE THIRST OF A VAMPYRE!!!

Moral.

In this happy land of liberty and equality, we are free from all traditional superstitions, whether political, religious, or otherwise. Fiction has no materials for machinery;—Romance no horrors for a tale of mystery. Yet in a figurative sense, and in the moral world, our climate is perhaps more prolific than any other, in enchanters,—Vampyres,—and the whole infernal brood of sorcery and witchcraft. The accomplished dandy, who in maintaining his horses,—his taylor, &c.—absorbs in the forced and unnatural excitement of his senseless orgies, the life-blood of that wealth which his prudent Sire had accumulated by a long devotion to the counter,—What is he but a Vampyre?

The fraudulent trafficker in stock and merchandize, who, having sucked the whole substance of an hundred honest men, is consigned for a few weeks to the sepulchre of the jail; and then, by the potent magic of an insolvent law, stalks forth, triumphant with bloated villany, more elated in his shameless resurrection to renew his career of iniquity and of disgrace,—what is he but a Vampyre? The corrupted and senseless Clerk, who being placed near the vitals of a moneyed institution, himself exhausted to feed the appetite of sharpers, drains, in his turn, the coffers he was appointed to guard,—is he not, I appeal to the Stockholders,—is he not a Vampyre?

Brokers, Country Bank Directors, and their disciples—all whose hunger and thirst for money, unsatisfied with the tardy progression of honest industry, by creating fictitious and delusive credit, has preyed on the heart and liver of public confidence, and poisoned the currents of public morals, are they not all Vampyres?

The whole tribe of Plagiarists, under every denomination; —The Critic, who. by eviscerating authors, and stuffing his own meagre show of learning with the pilfered entrails, ekes out his periodical fulmination against public taste;—the Forum Orator, who, without compunction, barbarously exenterates Burke, and Curran, and Phillips,—the Second- handed Lawyer,—Scholar,—Theologue,—who quote from quotations, and steal stolen property:—the Divine, who preaches Tillotson and Toplady;—what are they all but Vampyres?

The Empiric, who fills his own stomach, while he empties his shop into the bowels of the hypochondriac;—the Bibliopolist, "who guts the fobs" of the whole reading community, by ascribing to Lord Byron works which that author never saw; the philanthropic Contractor for the Army, who charges more for lime and horse-beef, than his quantum-meruit for the best provisions; who sets up his carriage and his palace, by blistering the mouths and destroying the intestines of thousands, — what are these but Vampyres?

The Professors and Disciples of Surgeon's Hall, who, when a fine fat corse is rolled out of the resurrectionist's budget, set up a howl of horrible transport, like the anthropophagous Caribs in Robinson Crusoe;—glut their gloating eyes with the pinguidity and unctuousness of the subject; and whet their blades like Shylock, impatient to attack the ilia,—what are they but Vampyres?

And I, who, as Johnson said of an hypochondriac Lady, "have spun this discourse out of my own bowels," and made as free with those of others—I am a VAMPYRE!

Vampyrism; a poem

Utrum horum mavis accipe.SOLOMON LANG & LAUNCELOT LANGSTAFF, Esquires.

GENTLEMEN, FROM the Gazette of August 17th, I am happy to learn, that you have entered into an alliance, offensive and defensive. The ties of kindred and the attraction of sympathy, one would think, ought to have brought about this union much sooner. You are, I believe, of one family;—although I am ignorant from whence LAUNCELOT has taken the Agnomen of STAFF: and I am equally unable to divine, why you have both docked the Nomen of your ancestors, which hath been written LANGEARS from time immemorial. Whatever may be your reasons for disowning your consanguinity to the great GENTILE family, the literary and political worlds rejoice, at least, in this consolidation of the talents of their two most distinguished members. The parity of intellect,—the similarity of taste,—the pungency of sarcasm possessed by both parties, justify the expectations formed by the public, from this conjunction of two such great luminaries. Both are imbued with that modest confidence, connected with the consciousness of superior talent. SOLOMON is formed, perhaps, of more impenetrable stuff: LAUNCELOT has more of the irritability and exquisite sensibility of genius.—Ira quidem communiter urit utrumque; but SOLOMON taketh the driest knocks with a good grace; LAUNCELOT is sooner thrown into a fever, and frets, to use a classic quotation of his own, "like a bear, with a sore head."—SOLOMON is the better grammarian: LAUNCELOT hath, occasionally, greater command of language. Solomon, as he states, composes ideas and types simultaneously, a la mode de Wooler; Launcelot has the advantage of seeing his ideas embodied in black and white, in their flight from his brains to the printing office.— LAUNCELOT the FIERY, may be likened to the mad ORESTES: SOLOMON the PATIENT, to the faithful PYLADES.— SOLOMON is original in his own way: LAUNCELOT purloins from Swift, and Rabelais and others. —

SOLOMON, pilloried in his own press, with no ally but the gray mare, bravely receives the missiles of the whole legion of editors; LAUNCELOT has only to open his mouth, or saw the air, or make a leg, on the literary stage; and all the gods of the Philadelphia gallery, pipe their shrill catcalls in discordant unison.—The castigation of both is equally dreadful. SOLOMON, with his "Good morning, Mr. Coleman," and "Rot the sarpent," condenses all his wrath into a laconic sarcasm: LAUNCELOT elaborates books, to the great terror and discomfiture of Gifford, Southey, and Scott. The Quarterly Reviewers received a death blow, because they could not find out the wit of the Scottish Fiddle; and the translator of Juvenal has never dared to show his face, since Mr. LANGSTAFF promulgated to the world, the secret of his origin. Poor Mr. Hall, the editor of the Port Folio,— because he criticised that Poem, (than which, in the language of Croaker, "nothing can be flatter or funnier;") according to the canons of Martinus Scriblerus,—said Hall has been severely bemauled for his temerity. Many a heart-burning hath he experienced, from the caustic of Salmagundi Redivivus—Godwot! —magni nominis umbra!—On the whole, "none but yourselves can be your parallels.

Allow me to dedicate the following rhymes to your firm; which will, I have no doubt, stand secure, amid all the present wreck of matters, and crashes of credit. Profound ignorance, bolstered by vanity, sits firmly on it own fundamental principles. Farewell, Gentlemen, accept the considerations of my high esteem—Fortunati ambo—si quid mea carmina possunt, Nulla dies unquam memori vos eximet aevo!-URIAH DERICK D'ARCY.

VAMPYRISM; A POEM

I.

IN this blest land, where valour burst
The links which bound his children erst,
And rent the vail whose darkness hid
Legitimacy's monstrous creed;—
Where all that since the world began
Had sway'd the sacred rights of man,
With ancient dreams had past away,
And bare in all its weakness lay;—
Here reason, in triumphal hour,
Asserted too her conquering power:
From mountain, valley, plain and flood,
She exorcised the shadowy brood.

II.

When freshening gales had swept the mists,
That wildly wreath'd the mountain crests,
No cloudy spectre o'er the storm
Reveal'd the terrors of his form;—
When evening breezes curl'd the wave

No wraiths disturb'd the wandering brave,—
When lost in darkness, down the side
Of craggy mount their path they tried,
And stunn'd by torrents deafening roar,
Downward were hurl'd, to rise no more;
Men said their balance they had lost,
But never laid it to a ghost.

III.

No more, around the guarded gold,
Their wake were pirates seen to hold;—
No elves the midnight circle tript;
No fairies lunar vigils kept;
Genii nor devils rose—except,
Indeed, that once in godly Salem,
Blue laws and preachings seem'd to fail 'em;
Bed bugs and rats their slumbers broke,
On Beelzebub they laid the joke;
Took brandy to expel the fiend,
Which answered quite another end!
Old ladies then to swim were taught,
In amorous league with Satan caught;—
And some were hang'd:—but now no more
'Tis fit to rake up that old sore.

IV.

Of late the pole its fiends has sent,
The 'tarnal Yankees to torment;
By water witchcraft long distrest,
In vain with all their might they *guest;*
Till when their *gumption* seem'd to fail
One captain got him by the tail;
But metamorphos'd, (such their story,)
The wizard gave the man the go-by
Turn'd out a tunny fish to be,

The "shallowest monster" of the sea.

V.

And now they swear with might and main,
That Monsieur Tonson's come again:
And Marshal Prince, his wife and daughters,
Off Nahant, saw him walk the waters.
The coachman there and Mrs. Prince
Got at the odd fish several squints;
But Mr. Prince, for weak his eye was,
Look'd at him through a mast-head spy-glass;
And took, lest men his word should doubt,
An ugly likeness of his snout,
With all the bumps the monster bore—
He says, thirteen—his wife, two more.

VI.

In Morristown we've heard a ghost
Wrought wonders to the people's cost.
'Tis not long since, on New Year's night,
The devil gave three bad boys a fright;
Who o'er their whiskey took to cursing,
Spoke disrespectfully of his person,
His government began to libel,
And on the back-log put the bible.—
But these things are of little moment,
Unworthy of a further comment.

VII.

Yet SUPERSTITION! though thy throne
Be rear'd in wilds and woods alone,
Where the rude wanderer of the glen
Invokes the souls of martial men;—
Adores the torrent thundering loud;

Calls on the spirits of the cloud;—
And o'er the black and bursting heaven,
Sees Ariouski's chariot driven;—
Yet, queen of terror's sheetedband!
Fiends worse than thine affright our land,
While, stalking from their ghastly homes,
The VAMPYRE host infuriate roams!

VIII.

Behold that EXQUISITE divine,
Fit to hang up for fashion's sign.
In classic mould his wig is shear'd—
SO SAUNDERS says—by all rever'd—
(Yet much, with deference, due I doubt
If Saunders' science could make out
Apollo's nob, if slic'd off well,
From J—n G. B—t's bust to tell—
Both are stuck up in the Academy
—
Yet for this query think not bad o' me.)
But to the Dandy—
'neath his chin
Hog's bristles fiercely fence him in;
One corset back his shoulders throws;
His bowels other bones enclose;
His *ample* chest is bullet proof,
With cotton cram'd and such like stuff;
And for his clothes—but here's enough.
For ere the printer's tardy imp,
Shall bid in type this doggrel limp,
The swifter ninth part of a man
Shall change the passing mode again;
And waists now short shall then be long.
All that's now right shall then be wrong!

IX.

How came that puppy by his gig?
What taught him how to look so big?
For this behind the measur'd board
His father scrap'd the growing hoard—
Like him the pyramids who rear'd,
To leave behind no name rever'd
For, on the bowels of the heap,
His revels shall this Vampyre keep;
Till vigils late—and generous wine,
And—things that suit no lay of mine;
Have left him soon to die and rot,
Be laugh'd at, pitied, and forgot!
His species and his line to trace,
And count the honours of his race,
Let Mr. Wynkoop soar as high,
As Scythia's Cynocephali,
And Mr. Langstaff dive as low
As he, and he alone, can go;"
Let this quote Greek—that crack stale jokes,
The theme is worthy of such folks.

X.

Lo! thro' the bustling world of trade,
What monsters march in long parade;
Gorg'd with the substance of a host,
Swelling they strut with empty boast;
The bubble burst, and credit fled,
The money'd quack proclaims them dead;—
Bailiffs in haste the corpse escort;—
The turnkey says his service short;—
Awhile in jail their bones repose,
Till lo! the dungeon doors unclose!
Insolvent laws, with potent spell,
Have wrought the wondrous miracle;
Their words of might the dead restore;

And even more bloated than before,
From that deep sepulchre, to prey
On all the gudgeons in his way,
Of shameless resurrection vain,
The VAMPYRE BANKRUPT stalks again!

XI.

Temples of Mammon! O beware
What priests the golden chalice bear!
And let not hands profane approach
The tempting, costly shrines to touch!
Have we not seen what secret stealth
Has suck'd the vitals of your wealth,
When the weak dupe, quite drain'd himself,
Grew hungry for the luscious pelf;
Nor did his secret orgies end,
Till fail'd a whole year's dividend.
And now once more in open air,
Have we not seen the Vampyre *pair*,
Stalk forth, from jails and juries free,
In all the pride of infamy?

XII.

O HERMES of these latter times,
I hail thee in unworthy rhymes!134
Great ALCHYMIST, whose art alone
Has found the philosophic stone!
Thou arch magician! to whose hand
Alone is given the hazel wand,
That finds the veins of glittering ores,
Great DOUSTERSWIVEL135 of conjurors!
What though thine art itself despair,
And all the pageant fade in air?
While harmless mobs thy doors assail,
And blustering butchers curse and rail,

Above thine own Flaminian136 roll'd,
Shall thy triumphal chariot hold
Its course majestical along,
Before the whole admiring throng!

XIII.

O JACOB! JACOB! thou art keen,
As thy great namesake;—him, I mean.
Who manag'd for himself to keep
The best of crafty Laban's sheep.
Immortal VAMPYRE of our age!
O might this unassuming page
Be read by all, whose fobs must bleed,
Thy ravenous appetite to feed,
Behind thy coach and four might I
Roll in an humbler tilbury;
Beneath thy wings might D'ARCY's name
Soar to the solar blaze of fame!

XIV.

Plumb from the giddy height I fall,
Amid whole herds of Vampyres small,
CRITICS, who worn out common place
With Author's pilfer'd entrails grace;

The FORUM spouter—barbarous Turk!
Who rips up Curran, Phillips, Burke,
And thunders forth bombastic centos,
Of wasted time the sad mementoes;
All those who QUOTE at second hand,
And what they quote don't understand;
The PARSON who in sleepy tone
Evangelizes Tillotson;
All PLAGIARISTS,—concise to be,—
Are GOULs of high or low degree.

XV.

The QUACK with brick dust who provides,
Wherewith to line his own insides;
Who fills up all his hungry chinks,
While to a ghost his patient shrinks;
THOMAS who vends as Byron's own
The works of doggrelists unknown;
Honest CONTRACTORS, who are able
To cheat both government and rabble;
Who, worthy of the scourge and gallows,
Set up their equipage and palace;
While blister'd mouths deep curses pour
And tortur'd soldiers writhe and roar,
Who eat the beef of horses dead,
And craunch corroding lime for bread—
These, as the sufferers all agree,
Are of the GOULE fraternity.

XVI.

There are whose tongues around them throw
The gall with which their hearts o'erflow,
Like those from old Medusa's head,
Where'er its venom'd drops are shed,
Earth's verdure fades;—rank poison springs;
Snakes hiss, and dragons spread their wings.
Pale Dian's hopeless votary old,
Crabb'd, ancient dames, and bachelors cold,
Nay e'en the blooming maid—will hie
To the foul feast of calumny;
On wisdom, worth, and reverend age,
Beauty and wit, they glut their rage;
And fondly hope, that as they tear
The limbs of murder'd character,
Their own fair fame shall prouder swell,

Fatten'd upon the feast of hell!

XVII.

There is a spot,144 unknown to fame,
Where Vampyres haunt their hold of shame
When ENVY left her noxious cave,
Along Passaic's winding wave,
(Though Ovid has this fact forgot,)
She linger'd by one cherish'd spot;
She left her benediction here,
The ground became for ever sere;
Infected by her scatter'd slime
And tainted to all after time;
Whoever tastes its baleful food,
A Vampyre longs to feed on blood—
The blood of honour, virtue free,
Fame, confidence and chastity!

XVIII.

But wouldst thou, in thy purpose bold,
The demon orgies foul behold—
Mark where the SONS of SURGEON'S HALL,
Upon their foul purveyor call;
And lo, the plunderer of the tomb
Brings up his budget in the room;
Rolls out, their ardent gaze before,
A huge, fat negress on the floor;
Then with a savage howl they roar!
Like cannibals, prepar'd to roast
Their pris'ners on some barbarous coast;
Like Shakspeare's Jew, the joyous band
Whet their keen blades with eager band;
While all the putrid limbs excite
Their foul and Vampyre appetite.—

XIX.

And what am I, whose spider skill
Has thus contrived this sheet to fill;
From my own bowels spun the lay,
Until I find no more to say?
Before to all I bid adieu,
Confess,—I AM A VAMPYRE TOO!

Note:

The following lines appeared in the Evening Post of August 14th: FOR THE EVENING POST.

To the anonymous Gentleman, *who says he* is *the author of the "Black Vampyre."*

"Ubi dolor, ibi digitus—one must needs scratch where it itches."—

— BURTON'S ANAT. OF MEL.

Dear sir, since jackall-like you prowl,
Preying on carrion in the dark,
Unseen, I only hear you howl,
And know you only by your bark;

I send my shot thus in the air,
Aimless, and eke uncharg'd by wit;
Yet knowing, it must fall somewhere,
And where it happens, it must hit.
Though thus like rotten-wood to shine,
Only through night's uncertain cloak,
With sickly lustre—I opine.
Is "Low Ambition's" stalest joke—

Yet men have always had strange ways,
Like thee, of picking up stray laurels,
When e'en like mine, the wither'd bays
Unworthy were of serious quarrels.

And from Vespusius' mighty theft
Even to thy lowest pitch of pride,
Thousands from other brows have rest
The wreaths, fate to their own denied.

So P—g's Muse, by Irving boosted,
Above the brush-wood scrambled soon;
High in the upper branches roosted,
And chanted something like a tune.

Now floundering in the bogs alone,
With sullen scream she frights our ears;
And all, with sympathetic groan,
Lament the boast of former years.

So at Commencement have I seen
Full many in borrow'd plumes array'd;
While but a scurvy show, I ween,
The motley mimickry display'd.

Shade of a shadow! now good night!
Ghost of a lie! invok'd in vain!
Flit through the dim uncertain light,
Be nothing—and thyself again!

-Uriah Derick D'arcy

LAUNCELOT, it appears, not relishing the great moral truth
alluded to in the above lines, inserted the following low-lived

scurrility, in the New-York Gazette of August 17th: *Fortunate Escape!*—The absence of the worthy editor of that "excellent journal" the Evening Post, already begins to be felt in the city. Several small dogs, supposed to be mad, taking advantage of their old enemy's back being turned, have lately ventured out, in spite of the vigilance of the police, and molested several citizens of good credit and reputation. We understand, that last Saturday afternoon, a small puppy, either mad or very angry, sallied out of the office of that "excellent journal" the New-York Evening Post, and snapped at a peaceable gentleman who was going about on his lawful occasions, but who, for reasons best known to themselves, is very much disliked by the little dogs. Luckily, being an exceeding158 small pug, he only reached the heel of the gentleman's boot, the which he gave a fearful wound, which obliged him to go immediately, not to a surgeon, but a cobbler. It is not ascertained whether the gentleman took occasion to kick him or not, but it is said the little animal ran back in the office, howling very much, and took shelter between Mr. B—'s legs.

P. S. The angry little dog wore a brass collar, on which was engraved the name of URIAH DERICK D'ARCY in large capitals.—

The public is warned *not* to beware of him.

The Death-Bride (aka The Dead Bride)

by Friedrich August Schulze

Friedrich August Schulze (1770-1849) was a German author who wrote under the pseudonym of Friedrich Laun. He wrote one novel and many stories, as well as edited "Book of Ghosts." Laun's interest in the supernatural led him to write "The Death-Bride," which as you can surmise from the title, is a story of the undead. It isn't strictly a vampire story, but it fits most of the criteria, and it found its way into an 1812 collection of weird tales, "Fantasmagoriana Volume 2."

The Death-Bride
by Friedrich August Schulze

Translated by Sarah Elizabeth Utterson

"She shall be such
As walk'd your first queen's ghost-"
Shakspeare.

The Death-Bride

THE summer had been uncommonly fine, and the baths crowded with company beyond all comparison: but still the public rooms were scarce ever filled, and never gay. The nobility and military associated only with those of their own rank, and the citizens contented themselves by slandering both parties. So many partial divisions necessarily proved an obstacle to a general and united assembly.

Even the public balls did not draw the *beau-monde* together, because the proprietor of the baths appeared there bedizened with insignia of knighthood; and this glitter, added to the stiff manners of this great man's family, and the tribe of lackeys in splendid liveries who constantly attended him, compelled the greater part of the company assembled, silently to observe the rules prescribed to them according to their different ranks.

For these reasons the balls became gradually less numerously attended. Private parties were formed, in which it was endeavoured to preserve the charms that were daily diminishing in the public assemblies.

One of these societies met generally twice a week in a room which at that time was usually unoccupied. There they supped, and afterwards enjoyed, either in a walk abroad, or remaining in the room, the charms of unrestrained conversation.

The members of this society were already acquainted, at least by name; but an Italian marquis, who had lately joined their party, was unknown to them, and indeed to every one assembled at the baths.

The title of *Italian* marquis appeared the more singular, as his name, according to the entry of it in the general list, seemed to denote him of Northern extraction, and was composed of so great a number of consonants, that no one could pronounce it without difficulty.

His physiognomy and manners likewise presented many singularities. His long and wan visage, his black eyes, his imperious look, had so little of attraction in them, that every one would certainly have avoided him, had he not possessed a fund of entertaining stories, the relation of which proved an excellent antidote to *ennui:* the only drawback against them was, that in general they required rather too great a share of credulity on the part of his auditors.

The party had one day just risen from table, and found themselves but ill inclined for gaiety. They were still too much fatigued from the ball of the preceding evening to enjoy the recreation of walking, although invited so to do by the bright light of the moon. They were even unable to keep up any conversation; therefore it is not to be wondered at, that they were more than usually anxious for the marquis to arrive.

"Where can he be?" exclaimed the countess in an impatient tone.

"Doubtless still at the faro-table, to the no small grief of the bankers," replied Florentine. "This very morning he has occasioned the sudden departure of two of these gentlemen."

"No great loss," answered another.

"To us—," replied Florentine; "but it is to the proprietor of the baths, who only prohibited gambling, that it might be pursued with greater avidity."

"The marquis ought to abstain from such achievements," said the chevalier with an air of mystery. "Gamblers are revengeful, and have generally advantageous connections. If what is whispered be correct, that the marquis is unfortunately implicated in political affairs—."

"But," demanded the countess, "what then has the marquis done to the bankers of the gaming-table?"

"Nothing; except that he betted on cards which almost invariably won. And what renders it rather singular, he scarcely derived any advantage from it himself, for he always adhered to the weakest party. But the other punters were not so scrupulous; for they charged their cards in such a manner that the bank broke before the deal had gone round."

The countess was on the point of asking other questions, when the marquis coming in changed the conversation.

"Here you are at last!" exclaimed several persons at the same moment.

"We have," said the countess, "been most anxious for your society; and just on this day you have been longer than usual absent."

"I have projected an important expedition; and it has succeeded to my wishes. I hope by to-morrow there will not be a single gaming-table left here. I have been from one gambling-room to another; and there are not sufficient post-horses to carry off the ruined bankers."

"And cannot you," asked the countess, "teach us your wonderful art of always winning?"

"It would be a difficult task, my fair lady; and in order to do it, one must ensure a fortunate hand, for without that nothing could be done."

"Nay," replied the chevalier, laughing, "never did I see so fortunate an one as yours."

"As you are still very young, my dear chevalier, you have many novelties to witness."

Saying these words, the marquis threw on the chevalier so piercing a look that the latter cried:

"Will you then cast my nativity?"

"Provided that it is not done to-day," said the countess; "for who knows whether your future destiny will afford us so amusing a history as that which the marquis two days since promised we should enjoy?"

"I did not exactly say *amusing*."

"But at least full of extraordinary events: and we require some such, to draw us from the lethargy which has over-whelmed us all day."

"Most willingly: but first I am anxious to learn whether any of you know aught of the surprising things related of the *Death-Bride*."

No one remembered to have heard speak of her.

The marquis appeared anxious to add something more by way of preface; but the countess and the rest of the party so openly manifested their impatience, that the marquis began his narration as follows:—

"I had for a long time projected a visit to the count Lieppa, at his estates in Bohemia. We had met each other in almost every country in Europe: attracted *hither* by the frivolity of youth to partake of every pleasure which presented itself, but led *thither* when years of discretion had rendered us more sedate and steady.—At length, in our more advanced age, we ardently desired, ere the close of life, once again to enjoy, by the charms of recollection, the moments of delight which we had passed together. For my part, I was anxious to see the castle of my friend, which was, according to his description, in an extremely romantic district. It was built some hundred years back by his ancestors; and their successors had preserved it with so much care, that it still maintained its imposing appearance, at the same time it afforded a comfortable abode. The count generally passed the greater part of the year at it with his family, and only returned to the capital at the approach of winter. Being well acquainted with his movements, I did not think it needful to announce my visit; and I arrived at the castle one evening precisely at the time when I knew he would be there; and as I approached it, could not but admire the variety and beauty of the scenery which surrounded it.

"The hearty welcome which I received could not, however, entirely conceal from my observation the secret grief depicted on the countenances of the count, his wife, and their daughter, the lovely Ida. In a short time I discovered that they still mourned the loss of Ida's twin-sister, who had died about a year before. Ida and Hildegarde resembled each other so much, that they were only to be distinguished from each other by a slight mark of a strawberry visible on Hildegarde's neck. Her room, and every thing in it, was left precisely in the same state as when she was alive, and the family were in the habit of visiting it whenever they wished to indulge the sad satisfaction of meditating on the loss of this beloved child. The two sisters had but one heart, one mind: and the parents could not but apprehend that their separation would be but of short duration; they dreaded lest Ida should also be taken from them.

"I did every thing in my power to amuse this excellent family, by entertaining them with laughable anecdotes of my younger days, and by directing their thoughts to less melancholy subjects than that which now wholly occupied them. I had the satisfaction of discovering that my efforts were not ineffectual. Sometimes we walked in the canton round the castle, which was decked with all the beauties of summer; at other times we took a survey of the different apartments of the castle, and were astonished at their wonderful state of preservation, whilst we amused ourselves by talking over the actions of the past generation, whose portraits hung in a long gallery.

"One evening the count had been speaking to me in confidence, on the subject of his future plans: among other subjects he expressed his anxiety, that Ida (who had already, though only in her sixteenth year, refused several offers) should be happily married; when suddenly the gardener, quite out of breath, came to tell us he had seen the ghost (as he believed, the old chaplain belonging to the castle), who had appeared a century back. Several of the servants followed the gardener, and their pallid countenances confirmed the alarming tidings he had brought.

"'I believe you will shortly be afraid of your own shadow,' said the count to them. He then sent them off, desiring them not again to trouble him with the like fooleries.

"'It is really terrible,' said he to me, 'to see to what lengths superstition will carry persons of that rank of life; and it is impossible wholly to undeceive them. From one generation to another an absurd report has from time to time been spread abroad, of an old chaplain's ghost wandering in the environs of the castle; and that he says mass in the chapel, with other idle stories of a similar nature. This report has greatly died away since I came into possession of the castle; but it now appears to me, it will never be altogether forgotten.'

"At this moment the duke de Marino was announced. The count did not recollect ever having heard of him.

"I told him that I was tolerably well acquainted with his family; and that I had lately been present, in Venice, at the betrothing of a young man of that name.

"The very same young man came in while I was speaking. I should have felt very glad at seeing him, had I not perceived that my presence caused him evident uneasiness.

"'Ah,' said he in a tolerably gay tone, after the customary forms of politeness had passed between us; 'the finding you here, my dear marquis, explains to me an occurrence, which with shame I own caused me a sensation of fear. To my no small surprise, they knew my name in the adjacent district; and as I came up the hill which leads to the castle, I heard it pronounced three times in a voice wholly unknown to me: and in a still more audible tone this strange voice bade me welcome. I now, however, conclude it was yours.'

"I assured him, (and with truth,) that till his name was announced the minute before, I was ignorant of his arrival, and that none of my servants knew him; for that the valet who accompanied me into Italy was not now with me.

"'And above all,' added I, 'it would be impossible to discover any equipage, however well known to one, in so dark an evening.'

"'That is what astonishes me,' exclaimed the duke, a little amazed.

"The incredulous count very politely added, 'that the voice

which had told the duke he was welcome, had at least expressed the sentiments of all the family.'

"Marino, ere he said a word relative to the motive of his visit, asked a private audience of me; and confided in me, by telling me that he was come with the intention of obtaining the lovely Ida's hand; and that if he was able to procure her consent, he should demand her of her father.

"'The countess Apollonia, your bride elect, is then no longer living?' asked I.

"'We will talk on that subject hereafter,' answered he.

"The deep sigh which accompanied these words led me to conclude that Apollonia had been guilty of infidelity or some other crime towards the duke; and consequently I thought that I ought to abstain from any further questions, which appeared to rend his heart, already so sensibly wounded.

"Yet, as he begged me to become his mediator with the count, in order to obtain from him his consent to the match, I painted in glowing colours the danger of an alliance, which he had no other motive for contracting, than the wish to obliterate the remembrance of a dearly, and without doubt, still more tenderly, beloved object. But he assured me that he was far from thinking of the lovely Ida from so blameable a motive, and that he should be the happiest of men if she but proved propitious to his wishes.

"His expressive and penetrating tone of voice, while he said this, lulled the uneasiness that I was beginning to feel; and I promised him I would prepare the count Lieppa to listen to his entreaties, and would give him the necessary information relative to the fortune and family of Marino. But I declared to him at the same time, that I should by no means hurry the conclusion of the affair by my advice, as I was not in the habit of taking upon myself so great a charge as the uncertain issue of a marriage.

"The duke signified his satisfaction at what I said, and made me give (what then appeared to me of no consequence) a promise, that I would not make mention of the former marriage he was on the point of contracting, as it would necessarily bring on a train of unpleasant explanations.

"The duke's views succeeded with a promptitude beyond his most sanguine hopes. His well-proportioned form and sparkling eyes smoothed the paths of love, and introduced him to the heart of Ida. His agreeable conversation promised to the mother an amiable son-in-law; and the knowledge in rural economy, which he evinced as occasions offered, made the count hope for an useful helpmate in his usual occupations; for since the first day of the duke's arrival he had been prevented from pursuing them.

"Marino followed up these advantages with great ardour; and I was one evening much surprised by the intelligence of his being betrothed, as I did not dream of matters drawing so near a conclusion. They spoke at table of some bridal preparations of which I had made mention just before the duke's arrival at the castle; and the countess asked me whether that young Marino was a near relation of the one who was that very day betrothed to her daughter.'

"'Near enough,' I answered, recollecting my promise.—Marino looked at me with an air of embarrassment.

"'But, my dear duke,' continued I, 'tell me who mentioned the amiable Ida to you; or was it a portrait, or what else, which caused you to think of looking for a beauty, the selection of whom does so much honour to your taste, in this remote corner; for, if I am not mistaken, you said but yesterday that you had purposed travelling about for another six months; when all at once (I believe while in Paris) you changed your plan, and projected a journey wholly and solely to see the charming Ida?'

"'Yes, it was at Paris,' replied the duke; 'you are very rightly informed. I went there to see and admire the superb gallery of pictures at the Museum; but I had scarcely entered it, when my eyes turned from the inanimate beauties, and were riveted on a lady whose incomparable features were heightened by an air of melancholy. With fear and trembling I approached her, and only ventured to follow without speaking to her. I still followed her after she quitted the gallery; and I drew her servant aside to learn the name of his mistress. He told it me: but when I expressed a wish to become acquainted with the father of this beauty, he said that was next to impossible while at Paris, as the family were on the point of quitting that city; nay, of quitting France altogether.

"'Possibly, however,' said I, 'some opportunity may present itself.' And I looked every where for the lady: but she, probably imagining that her servant was following her closely, had continued to walk on, and was entirely out of sight. While I was looking around for her, the servant had likewise vanished from my view.'

"'Who was this beautiful lady?' asked Ida, in a tone of astonishment.

"'What! you really did not then perceive me in the gallery?'

"'Me!'—'My daughter—!' exclaimed at the same moment Ida and her parents.

"'Yes, you yourself, mademoiselle. The servant, whom fortunately for me you left at Paris, and whom I met the same evening unexpectedly, as my guardian angel, informed me of all; so that after a short rest at home, I was able to come straight hither.'

"'What a fable!' said the count to his daughter, who was mute with astonishment.

"'Ida,' he added, turning to me, 'has never yet been out of her native country; and for myself, I have not been in Paris these seventeen years.'

"The duke looked at the count and his daughter with similar marks of astonishment visible in their countenances; and conversation would have been entirely at an end, if I had not taken care to introduce other topics: but I had it nearly all to myself.

"The repast was no sooner over, than the count took the duke into the recess of a window; and although I was at a considerable distance, and appeared wholly to fix my attention on a new chandelier, I overheard all their conversation.

"'What motive,' demanded the count with a serious and

dissatisfied air, 'could have induced you to invent that singular scene in the gallery of the Museum at Paris? for according to my judgment, it could in no way benefit you. Since you are anxious to conceal the cause which brought you to ask my daughter in marriage, at least you might have plainly said as much; and though possibly you might have felt repugnance at making such a declaration, there were a thousand ways of framing your answer, without its being needful thus to offend probability.'

"'Monsieur le comte,' replied the duke much piqued; 'I held my peace at table, thinking that possibly you had reasons for wishing to keep secret your and your daughter's journey to Paris. I was silent merely from motives of discretion; but the singularity of your reproaches compels me to maintain what I have said; and, notwithstanding your reluctance to believe the truth, to declare before all the world, that the capital of France was the spot where I first saw your daughter Ida.'

"'But what if I prove to you, not only by the witness of my servants, but also by that of all my tenants, that my daughter has never quitted her native place?'—

"'I shall still believe the evidence of my own eyes and ears, which have as great authority over me.'

"'What you say is really enigmatical,' answered the count in a graver tone: 'your serious manner convinces me you have been the dupe of some illusion; and that you have seen some other person, whom you have taken for my daughter. Excuse me, therefore, for having taken up the thing so warmly.'

"'Another person! What then, I not only mistook another person for your daughter; but the very servant of whom I made mention, and who gave me so exact a description of this castle, was, according to what you say, some other person!'

"'My dear Marino, that servant was some cheat who knew this castle, and who, God only knows for what motive, spoke to you of my daughter as resembling the lady.'

"'Tis certainly no wish of mine to contradict you; but Ida's features are precisely the same as those which made so deep an impression on me at Paris, and which my imagination has preserved with such scrupulous fidelity.'

"The count shook his head; and Marino continued:—

"'What is still more—(but pray pardon me for mentioning a little particularity, which nothing short of necessity would have drawn from me)—while in the gallery, I was standing behind the lady, and the handkerchief that covered her neck was a little disarranged, which occasioned me distinctly to perceive the mark of a small strawberry.'

"'Another strange mystery!' exclaimed the count, turning pale: 'it appears you are determined to make me believe wonderful stories.'

"'I have only one question to ask:—Has Ida such a mark on her neck?'

"'No, monsieur,' replied the count, looking steadfastly at Marino.

"'No!' exclaimed the latter, in the utmost astonishment.

"'No, I tell you: but Ida's twin-sister, who resembled her in the most surprising manner, had the mark you mention on her neck, and a year since carried it with her into the grave.'

"'And yet 'tis only within the last few months that I saw this person in Paris!'

"At this moment the countess and Ida, who had kept aside, a prey to uneasiness, not knowing what to think of the conversation, which appeared of so very important a nature, approached; but the count in a commanding tone ordered them to retire immediately. He then led the duke entirely away into a retired corner of the window, and continued the conversation in so low a voice that I could hear nothing further.

"My astonishment was extreme when, that very same evening, the count gave orders to have Hildegarde's tomb opened in his presence: but he beforehand related briefly what I have just told you, and proposed my assisting the duke and him in opening the grave. The duke excused himself, by saying that the very idea made him tremble with horror; for he could not overcome, especially at night, his fear of a corpse.

"The count begged he would not mention the gallery scene

to any one; and above all, to spare the extreme sensibility of the affianced bride from a recital of the conversation they had just had, even if she should request to be informed of it.

"In the mean time the sexton arrived with his lantern. The count and I followed him.

"'It is morally impossible,' said the count to me, as we walked together, 'that any trick can have been played respecting my daughter's death: the circumstances attendant thereon are but too well known to me. You may readily believe also, that the affection we bore our poor girl would prevent our running any risk of burying her too soon: but suppose even the possibility of that, and that the tomb had been opened by some avaricious persons, who found, on opening the coffin, that the body became re-animated; no one can believe for a moment that my daughter would not have instantly returned to her parents, who doted on her, rather than have fled to a distant country. This last circumstance puts the matter beyond doubt: for even should it be admitted as a truth, that she was carried by force to some distant part of the world, she would have found a thousand ways of returning. My eyes are, however, about to be convinced, that the sacred remains of my Hildegarde really repose in the grave.

"'To convince myself!' cried he again, in a tone of voice so melancholy yet loud that the sexton turned his head.

"This movement rendered the count more circumspect; and he continued in a lower tone of voice:

"'How should I for a moment believe it possible that the slightest trace of my daughter's features should be still in existence, or that the destructive hand of time should have spared her beauty? Let us return, marquis; for who could tell, even were I to see the skeleton, that I should know it from that of an entire stranger, whom they may have placed in the tomb to fill her place?'

"He was even about to give orders not to open the door of the chapel, (at which we were just arrived,) when I represented to him, that were I in his place I should have found it extremely difficult to determine on such a measure; but that having gone thus far, it was requisite to complete the task, by examining whether some of the jewels buried with Hildegarde's corpse were not wanting. I added, that judging by a number of well-known facts, all bodies were not destroyed equally soon.

"My representations had the desired effect: the count squeezed my hand; and we followed the sexton, who, by his pallid countenance and trembling limbs, evidently shewed that he was unaccustomed to nocturnal employments of this nature.

"I know not whether any of this present company were ever in a chapel at midnight, before the iron doors of a vault, about to examine the succession of leaden coffins enclosing the remains of an illustrious family. Certain it is, that at such a moment the noise of bolts and bars produces such a remarkable sensation, that one is led to dread the sound of the door grating on its hinges; and when the vault is opened, one cannot help hesitating for an instant to enter it.

"The count was evidently seized with these sensations of terror, which I discovered by a stifled sigh; but he concealed his feelings: notwithstanding, I remarked that he dared not trust himself to look on any other coffin than the one containing his daughter's remains. He opened it himself.

"'Did I not say so?' cried he, seeing that the features of the corpse bore a perfect resemblance to those of Ida. I was obliged to prevent the count, who was seized with astonishment, from kissing the forehead of the inanimate body.

"'Do not,' I added, 'disturb the peace of those who repose in death.' And I used my utmost efforts to withdraw the count immediately from this dismal abode.

"On our return to the castle, we found those persons whom we had left there, in an anxious state of suspense. The two ladies had closely questioned the duke on what had passed; and would not admit as a valid excuse, the promise he had made of secrecy. They entreated us also, but in vain, to satisfy their curiosity.

"They succeeded better the following day with the sexton, whom they sent for privately, and who told them all he knew:

but it only tended to excite their anxious wish to learn the subject of the conversation which had occasioned this nocturnal visit to the sepulchral vault.

"As for myself, I dreamt the whole of the following night of the apparition Marino had seen at Paris; I conjectured many things which I did not think fit to communicate to the count, because he absolutely questioned the connection of a superior world with ours. At this juncture of affairs, I with pleasure saw that this singular circumstance, if not entirely forgotten, was at least but rarely and slightly mentioned.

"But I now began to find another cause for anxious solicitude. The duke constantly persisted in refusing to explain himself on the subject of his previous engagement, even when we were alone: and the embarrassment he could not conceal, whenever I made mention of the good qualities that I believed his intended to have possessed, as well as several other little singularities, led me to conclude that Marino's attachment for Apollonia had been first shaken at the picture gallery, at sight of the lovely incognita; and that Apollonia had been forsaken, owing to his yielding to temptations; and that doubtless she could never have been guilty of breaking off an alliance so solemnly contracted.

Foreseeing from this that the charming Ida could never hope to find much happiness in an union with Marino, and knowing that the wedding-day was nigh at hand, I resolved to unmask the perfidious deceiver as quickly as possible, and to make him repent his infidelity. An excellent occasion presented itself one day for me to accomplish my designs. Having finished supper, we were still sitting at table; and some one said that iniquity is frequently punished in this world: upon which I observed, that I myself had witnessed striking proofs of the truth of this remark;—when Ida and her mother entreated me to name one of these examples.

"'Under these circumstances, ladies,' answered I, 'permit me to relate a history to you, which, according to my opinion, will particularly interest you.'

"'Us!' they both exclaimed. At the same time I fixed my

eyes on the duke, who for several days past had evidently distrusted me; and I saw that his conscience had rendered him pale.

"'That at least is *my* opinion,' replied I: 'But, my dear count, will you pardon me, if the supernatural is sometimes interwoven with my narration?'

"'Very willingly,' answered he smiling: 'and I will content myself with expressing my surprise at so many things of this sort having happened to you, as I have never experienced any of them myself.'

"I plainly perceived that the duke made signs of approval at what he said: but I took no notice of it, and answered the count by saying,

"That all the world have not probably the use of their eyes.

"'That may be,' replied he, still smiling.

"'But,' said I to him in a low and expressive voice, 'think you an uncorrupted body in the vault is a *common* phænomenon?'

"He appeared staggered: and I thus continued in an under tone of voice:—

"'For that matter, 'tis very possible to account for it naturally, and therefore it would be useless to contest the subject with you.'

"'We are wandering from the point,' said the countess a little angrily; and she made me a sign to begin, which I accordingly did, in the following words:—

"'The scene of my anecdote lies in Venice.'

"'I possibly then may know something of it,' cried the duke, who entertained some suspicions.

"'Possibly so,' replied I; 'but there were reasons for keeping the event secret: it happened somewhere about eighteen months since, at the period you first set out on your travels.

"The son of an extremely wealthy nobleman, whom I shall designate by the name of Filippo, being attracted to Leghorn by the affairs consequent on his succession to an inheritance, had won the heart of an amiable and lovely girl, called Clara. He promised her, as well as her parents, that ere his return to

Venice he would come back and marry her. The moment for his departure was preceded by certain ceremonies, which in their termination were terrible: for after the two lovers had exhausted every protestation of reciprocal affection, Filippo invoked the aid of the spirit of vengeance, in case of infidelity: they prayed even that whichever of the lovers should prove faithful might not be permitted to repose quietly in the grave, but should haunt the perjured one, and force the inconstant party to come amongst the dead, and to share in the grave those sentiments which on earth had been forgotten.

"The parents, who were seated by them at table, remembered their youthful days, and permitted the overheated and romantic imagination of the young people to take its free course. The lovers finished by making punctures in their arms, and letting their blood run into a glass filled with white champaigne.

"'Our souls shall be inseparable as our blood!' exclaimed Filippo; and drinking half the contents of the glass, he gave the rest to Clara."

At this moment the duke experienced a violent degree of agitation, and from time to time darted such menacing looks at me, that I was led to conclude, that in *his* adventure some scene of a similar nature had taken place. I can however affirm, that I related the details respecting Filippo's departure, as they were represented in a letter written by the mother of Clara.

"Who," continued I, "after so many demonstrations of such a violent passion, could have expected the denouement? Filippo's return to Venice happened precisely at the period at which a young beauty, hitherto educated in a distant convent, made her first appearance in the great world: she on a sudden exhibited herself as an angel whom a cloud had till then concealed, and excited universal admiration. Filippo's parents had heard frequent mention of Clara, and of the projected alliance between her and their son; but they thought that this alliance was like many others, contracted one day without the parties knowing why, and broken off the next with equal want of thought; and influenced by this idea, they presented their son to the parents of Camilla, (which was the name of the young beauty,) whose family were of the highest rank.

"They represented to Filippo the great advantages he would obtain by an alliance with her. The Carnival happening just at this period completed the business, by affording him so many favourable opportunities of being with Camilla; and in the end, the remembrance of Leghorn held but very little place in his mind. His letters became colder and colder each succeeding day; and on Clara expressing how sensibly she felt the change, he ceased writing to her altogether, and did every thing in his power to hasten his union with Camilla, who was, without compare, much the handsomer and more wealthy. The agonies poor Clara endured were manifest in her illegible writing, and by the tears which were but too evidently shed over her letters: but neither the one nor the other had any more influence over the fickle heart of Filippo, than the prayers of the unfortunate girl. Even the menace of coming, according to their solemn agreement, from the tomb to haunt him, and carry him with her to that grave which threatened so soon to enclose her, had but little effect on his mind, which was entirely engrossed by the idea of the happiness he should enjoy in the arms of Camilla.

"The father of the latter (who was my intimate friend) invited me before-hand to the wedding. And although numerous affairs detained him that summer in the city, so that he could not as usual enjoy the pleasures of the country, yet we sometimes went to his pretty villa, situated on the banks of the Brenta; where his daughter's marriage was to be celebrated with all possible splendour.

"A particular circumstance, however, occasioned the ceremony to be deferred for some weeks. The parents of Camilla having been very happy in their own union, were anxious that the same priest who married them, should pronounce the nuptial benediction on their daughter. This priest, who, notwithstanding his great age, had the appearance of vigorous health, was seized with a slow fever which confined him to his bed: however, in time it abated, he became gradually better and better, and the wedding-day was at length fixed. But, as if some secret power was at work to prevent this union, the worthy priest was, on the very day destined for the celebration of their marriage, seized with a feverish shivering of so alarming a nature, that he dared not stir out of the house, and he strongly advised the young couple to select another priest to marry them.

"The parents still persisted in their design of the nuptial benediction being given to their children by the respectable old man who had married *them*.—They would have certainly spared themselves a great deal of grief, if they had never swerved from their determination.—Very grand preparations had been made in honour of the day; and as they could no longer be deferred, it was decided that they should consider it as a ceremony of solemn affiance. At noon the bargemen attired in their splendid garb awaited the company's arrival on the banks of the canal: their joyous song was soon distinguished, while conducting to the villa, now decorated with flowers, the numerous gondolas containing parties of the best company.

"During the dinner, which lasted till evening, the betrothed couple exchanged rings. At the very moment of their so doing, a piercing shriek was heard, which struck terror into the breasts of all the company, and absolutely struck Filippo with horror. Every one ran to the windows: for although it was becoming dark, each object was visible; but no one was to be seen."

"Stop an instant," said the duke to me, with a fierce smile —His countenance, which had frequently changed colour during the recital, evinced strong marks of the torments of a wicked conscience. "I am also acquainted with that story, of a voice being heard in the air; it is borrowed from the 'Memoirs of Mademoiselle Clairon;' a deceased lover tormented *her* in this completely original manner. The shriek in her case was followed by a clapping of hands: I hope, monsieur le marquis, that you will not omit that particular in your story."

"And why," replied I, "should you imagine that nothing of a similar nature could occur to any one besides that actress?

Your incredulity appears to me so much the more extraordinary, as it seems to rest on facts which may lay claim to belief."

The countess made me a sign to continue; and I pursued my narrative as follows:

"A short time after they had heard this inexplicable shriek, I begged Camilla, facing whom I was sitting, to permit me to look at her ring once more, the exquisite workmanship of which had already been much admired. But it was not on her finger: a general search was made, but not the slightest trace of the ring could be discovered. The company even rose from their seats to look for it, but all in vain.

"Meanwhile, the time for the evening's amusements approached: fire-works were exhibited on the Brenta preceding the ball; the company were masked and got into the gondolas; but nothing was so striking as the silence which reigned during this *fête*; no one seemed inclined to open their mouth; and scarcely was heard a faint exclamation of *Bravo*, at sight of the fire-works.

"The ball was one of the most brilliant I ever witnessed: the precious stones and jewels with which the ladies of the party were covered, reflected the lights in the chandeliers with redoubled lustre. The most splendidly attired of the whole was Camilla. Her father, who was fond of pomp, rejoiced in the idea that no one in the assembly was equal to his daughter in splendour or beauty.

"Possibly to satisfy himself of this fact, he made a tour of the room; and returned loudly expressing his surprise, at having perceived on another lady precisely the same jewels which adorned Camilla. He was even weak enough to express a slight degree of chagrin. However, he consoled himself with the idea, that a bouquet of diamonds which was destined for Camilla to wear at supper, would alone in value be greater than all she then had on.

"But as they were on the point of sitting down to table, and the anxious father again threw a look around him, he discovered that the same lady had also a bouquet which appeared to the full as valuable as Camilla's.

"My friend's curiosity could no longer be restrained; he approached, and asked whether it would be too great a liberty to learn the name of the fair mask? But to his great surprise, the lady shook her head, and turned away from him.

"At the same instant the steward came in, to ask whether since dinner there had been any addition to the party, as the covers were not sufficient.

"His master answered, with rather a dissatisfied air, that there were only the same number, and accused his servants of negligence; but the steward still persisted in what he had said.

"An additional cover was placed: the master counted them himself, and discovered that there really was one more in number than he had invited. As he had recently, on account of some inconsiderate expressions, had a dispute with government, he was apprehensive that some spy had contrived to slip in with the company: but as he had no reason to believe, that on such a day as that, any thing of a suspicious nature would be uttered, he resolved, in order to be satisfied respecting so indiscreet a procedure as the introduction of such a person in a family *fête*, to beg every one present to unmask; but in order to avoid the inconvenience likely to arise from such a request, he determined not to propose it till the very last thing.

"Every one present expressed their surprise at the luxuries and delicacies of the table, for it far surpassed every thing of the sort seen in that country, especially with respect to the wines. Still, however, the father of Camilla was not satisfied, and loudly lamented that an accident had happened to his capital red champaigne, which prevented his being able to offer his guests a single glass of it.

"The company seemed anxious to become gay, for the whole of the day nothing like gaiety had been visible among them; but no one around where I sat, partook of this inclination, for curiosity alone appeared to occupy their whole attention. I was sitting near the lady who was so splendidly attired; and I remarked that she neither ate nor drank any thing; that she neither addressed nor answered a word to her neighbours, and that she appeared to have her eyes constantly fixed on the affianced couple.

"The rumour of this singularity gradually spread round the room, and again disturbed the mirth which had become pretty general. Each whispered to the other a thousand conjectures on this mysterious personage. But the general opinion was, that some unhappy passion for Filippo was the cause of this extaordinary conduct. Those sitting next the unknown, were the first to rise from table, in order to find more cheerful associates, and their places were filled by others who hoped to discover some acquaintance in this silent lady, and obtain from her a more welcome reception; but their hopes were equally futile.

"At the time the champaigne was handed round, Filippo also brought a chair and sat by the unknown. She then became somewhat more animated, and turned towards Filippo, which was more than she had done to any one else; and she offered him her glass, as if wishing him to drink out of it.

"A violent trembling seized Filippo, when she looked at him steadfastly.

"'The wine is red!' cried he, holding up the glass; 'I thought there had been no *red* champaigne.'

"'Red! said the father of Camilla, with an air of extreme surprise, approaching him from curiosity.

"'Look at the lady's glass,' replied Filippo.

"'The wine in it is as white as all the rest,' answered Camilla's father; and he called all present to witness it. They every one unanimously declared that the wine was white.

"Filippo drank it not, but quitted his seat; for a second look from his neighbour had caused him extreme agitation. He took the father of Camilla aside, and whispered something to him. The latter returned to the company, saying,

"'Ladies and gentlemen, I entreat you, for reasons which I will tell you presently, instantly to unmask.'

"As in this request he but expressed in a degree the general wish, every one's mask was off as quick as thought, and each face uncovered, excepting that of the silent lady, on whom every look was fixed, and whose face they were the most anxious to see.

"'You alone keep on your mask,' said Camilla's father to her, after a short silence: 'May I hope you will also remove yours?'

"She obstinately persisted in her determination of remaining unknown.

"This strange conduct affected the father of Camilla the more sensibly, as he recognised in the others all those whom he had invited to the *fête*, and found beyond doubt that the mute lady was the one exceeding the number invited. He was, however, unwilling to force her to unmask; because the uncommon splendour of her dress did not permit him any longer to harbour the idea that this additional guest was a spy; and thinking her also a person of distinction, he did not wish to be deficient in good manners. He thought possibly she might be some friend of the family, who, not residing at Venice, but finding on her arrival in that city that he was to give this *fête*, had conceived this innocent frolic.

"It was thought right, however, at all events to obtain all the information that could be gained from the servants: but none of them knew any thing of this lady; there were no servants of hers there; and those belonging to Camilla's father did not recollect having seen any who appeared to appertain to her.

"What rendered this circumstance doubly strange was, that, as I before mentioned, this lady only put the magnificent bouquet into her bosom the instant previous to her sitting down to supper.

"The whispering, which had generally usurped the place of all conversation, gained each moment more and more ascendancy; when on a sudden the masked lady arose, and walking towards the door, beckoned Filippo to follow her; but Camilla hindered him from obeying her signal, for she had a long time observed with what fixed attention the mysterious lady looked at her intended husband; and she had also remarked, that the latter had quitted the stranger in violent agitation; and from all this she apprehended that love had caused him to be guilty of some folly or other. The master of the house, turning a deaf ear to all his daughter's remonstrances, and a prey to the most terrible fears, followed the unknown (at a distance, it is true); but she was no sooner out of the room than he returned. At this moment, the shriek which they had heard at noon was repeated, but seemed louder from the silence of night, and communicated anew affright to all present. By the time the father of Camilla had returned from the first movement which his fear had occasioned him to make, the unknown was no where to be found.

"The servants in waiting outside the house had no knowledge whatever of the masked lady. In every direction around there were crowds of persons; the river was lined with gondolas; and yet not an individual among them had seen the mysterious female.

"All these circumstances had occasioned so much uneasiness to the whole party, that every one was anxious to return home; and the master of the house was obliged to permit the departure of the gondolas much earlier than he had intended.

"The return home was, as might naturally be expected, very melancholy.

"On the following day the betrothed couple were, however, pretty composed. Filippo had even adopted Camilla's idea of the unknown being some one whom love had deprived of reason; and as for the horrible shriek twice repeated, they were willing to attribute it to some people who were diverting themselves; and they decided, that inattention on the part of the servants was the sole cause of the unknown absenting herself without being perceived; and they even at last persuaded themselves, that the sudden disappearance of the ring, which they had not been able to find, was owing to the malice of some one of the servants who had pilfered it.

"In a word, they banished every thing that could tend to weaken these explanations; and only one thing remained to harass them. The old priest, who was to bestow on them the nuptial benediction, had yielded up his last breath; and the friendship which had so intimately subsisted between him and the parents of Camilla, did not permit them in decency to think of marriage and amusements the week following his death.

"The day this venerable priest was buried, Filippo's gaiety received a severe shock; for he learned, in a letter from Clara's mother, the death of that lovely girl. Sinking under the grief occasioned her by the infidelity of the man she had never ceased to love, she died: but to her latest hour she declared she should never rest quietly in her grave, until the perjured man had fulfilled the promise he had made to her.

"This circumstance produced a stronger effect on him than all the imprecations of the unhappy mother; for he recollected that the first shriek (the cause of which they had never been able to ascertain) was heard at the precise moment of Clara's death; which convinced him that the unknown mask could only have been the spirit of Clara.

"This idea deprived him at intervals of his senses.

"He constantly carried this letter about him; and with an air of wandering would sometimes draw it from his pocket, in order to reconsider it attentively: even Camilla's presence did not deter him.

"As it was natural to conclude this letter contained the cause of the extraordinary change which had taken place in Filippo, she one day gladly seized the opportunity of reading it, when in one of his absent fits he let it fall from his hands.

"Filippo, struck by the death-like paleness and faintness which overcame Camilla, as she returned him the letter, knew instantly that she had read it. In the deepest affliction he threw himself at her feet, and conjured her to tell him how he must act.

"'Love *me* with greater constancy than you did her,'— replied Camilla mournfully.

"With transport he promised to do so. But his agitation became greater and greater, and increased to a most extraordinary pitch the morning of the day fixed for the wedding. As he was going to the house of Camilla's father before it became dark, (from whence he was to take his bride at dawn of day to the church, according to the custom of the country,) he fancied he saw Clara's spirit walking constantly at his side.

"Never was seen a couple about to receive the nuptial benediction, with so mournful an aspect. I accompanied the parents of Camilla, who had requested me to be a witness: and the sequel has made an indelible impression on my mind of the events of that dismal morning.

"We were proceeding silently to the church of the Salutation; when Filippo, in our way thither, frequently requested me to remove the stranger from Camilla's side, for she had evil designs against her.

"'What stranger?' I asked him.

"'In God's name, don't speak so loud,' replied he; 'for you cannot but see how anxious she is to force herself between Camilla and me.'

"'Mere chimera, my friend; there are none but yourself and Camilla.'

"'Would to Heaven my eyes did not deceive me!'—'Take care that she does not enter the church,' added he, as we arrived at the door.

"'She will not enter it, rest assured,' said I: and to the great astonishment of Camilla's parents I made a motion as if to drive some one away.

"We found Filippo's father already in the church; and as soon as his son perceived him, he took leave of him as if he was going to die. Camilla sobbed; and Filippo exclaimed:—

"'There's the stranger; she has then got in.'

"The parents of Camilla doubted whether under such circumstances the marriage ceremony ought to be begun.

"But Camilla, entirely devoted to her love, cried:—'These chimeras of fancy render my care and attention the more necessary.'

"They approached the altar. At that moment a sudden gust of wind blew out the wax-tapers. The priest appeared displeased at their not having shut the windows more securely; but Filippo exclaimed: 'The windows! See you not, then, that there is one here who blew out the wax-tapers purposely?'

"Every one looked astonished: and Filippo cried, as he hastily disengaged his hand from that of Camilla,—'Don't you see, also, that she is tearing me away from my intended bride?'

"Camilla fell fainting into the arms of her parents; and the priest declared, that under such peculiar circumstances it was impossible to proceed with the ceremony.

"The parents of both attributed Filippo's state to mental derangement. They even supposed he had been poisoned; for an instant after, the unfortunate man expired in most violent convulsions. The surgeons who opened his body could not, however, discover any grounds for this suspicion.

"The parents, who as well as myself were informed by Camilla of the subject of these supposed horrors of Filippo, did every thing in their power to conceal this adventure: yet, on talking over all the circumstances, they could never satisfactorily explain the apparition of the mysterious mask at the time of the wedding *fête*. And what still appeared very surprising was, that the ring lost at the country villa was found amongst Camilla's other jewels, at the time of their return from church."

"'This is, indeed, a wonderful history!' said the count. His wife uttered a deep sigh: and Ida exclaimed,—

"'It has really made *me* shudder.'

"'That is precisely what every betrothed person ought to feel who listens to such recitals,' answered I, looking steadfastly at the duke, who, while I was talking, had risen and sat down again several times; and who, from his troubled look, plainly shewed that he feared I should counteract his wishes.

"'A word with you!' he whispered me, as we were retiring to rest: and he accompanied me to my room. 'I plainly perceive your generous intentions; this history invented for the occasion—'

"'Hold!' said I to him in an irritated tone of voice: 'I was eye-witness to what you have just heard. How then can you doubt its authenticity, without accusing a man of honour of uttering a falsehood?'

"'We will talk on this subject presently,' replied he in a tone of raillery. 'But tell me truly from whence you learnt the anecdote relative to mixing the blood with wine?—I know the person from whose life you borrowed this idea.'

"'I do assure you that I have taken it from no one's life but Filippo's; and yet there may be similar stories—as of the shriek, for instance. But even this singular manner of irrevocably affiancing themselves may have presented itself to *any* two lovers.'

"'Perhaps so! Yet one could trace in your narration many traits resembling another history.'

"'That is very possible: all love-stories are founded on the same stock, and cannot deny their parentage.'

"'No matter,' replied Marino; 'but I desire that from henceforth you do not permit yourself to make any allusion to my past life; and still less that you relate certain anecdotes to the count. On these conditions, and only on these conditions, do I pardon your former very ingenious fiction.'

"'Conditions!—forgiveness!—And do you dare thus to talk to *me?*—This is rather too much. Now take my answer: To-morrow morning the count shall know that you have been already affianced, and what you now exact.'

"'Marquis, if you dare—'

"Oh! oh!—yes, I dare do it; and I owe it to an old friend. The impostor who dares accuse me of falsehood shall no longer wear his deceitful mask in this house.'

"Passion had, spite of my endeavours, carried me so far, that a duel became inevitable. The duke challenged me. And we agreed, at parting, to meet the following morning in a neighbouring wood with pistols.

"In effect, before day-light we each took our servant and went into the forest. Marino, remarking that I had not given any orders in case of my being killed, undertook to do so for me; and accordingly he told my servant what to do with my body, as if every thing was already decided. He again addressed me ere we shook hands;—

"'For,' said he, 'the combat between us must be very unequal. I am young,' added he; 'but in many instances my hand has proved a steady one. I have not, it is true, absolutely killed any man; but I have invariably hit my adversary precisely on the part I intended. In this instance, however, I must, for the first time, *kill* my man, as it is the only effectual method of preventing your annoying me further; unless you will give me your word of honour not to discover any occurrences of my past life to the count, in which case I consent to consider the affair as terminated here.'

"As you may naturally believe, I rejected his proposition.

"'As it must be so,' replied he, 'recommend your soul to God.' We prepared accordingly.

"'It is your first fire,' he said to me.

"'I yield it to you,' answered I.

"He refused to fire first. I then drew the trigger, and caused the pistol to drop from his hand. He appeared surprised: but his astonishment was great indeed, when, after taking up another pistol, he found he had missed me. He pretended to have aimed at my heart; and had not even the possibility of an excuse; for he could not but acknowledge that no sensation of fear on my part had induced me to move, and baulk his aim.

"At his request I fired a second time; and again aimed at his pistol which he held in his left hand: and to his great astonishment it dropped also; but the ball had passed so near his hand, that it was a good deal bruised.

"His second fire having passed me, I told him I would not fire again; but that, as it was possible the extreme agitation of his mind had occasioned him to miss me twice, I proposed adjusting matters.

"Before he had time to refuse my offer, the count, who had suspicions that all was not right, was between us, with his daughter. He complained loudly of such conduct on the part of his guests; and demanded some explanation on the cause of our dispute. I then developed the whole business in presence of Marino, whose evident embarrassment convinced the count and Ida of the truth of the reproaches his conscience made him.

"But the duke soon availed himself of Ida's affection, and created an entire change in the count's mind; who that very evening said to me,—

"'You are right; I certainly ought to take some decided step, and send the duke from my house: but what could win the Apollonia whom he has abandoned, and whom he will never see again? Added to which, he is the only man for whom my daughter has ever felt a sincere attachment. Let us leave the young people to follow their own inclinations: the countess perfectly coincides in this opinion; and adds, that it would hurt her much were this handsome Venetian to be driven from our house. How many little infidelities and indiscretions are committed in the world and excused, owing to particular circumstances?'

"'But it appears to me, that in the case in point, these particular circumstances are wanting,' answered I. However, finding the count persisted in his opinion, I said no more.

"The marriage took place without any interruption: but still there was very little of gaiety at the feast, which usually on these occasions is of so splendid and jocund a nature. The ball in the evening was dull; and Marino alone danced with most extraordinary glee.

"'Fortunately, monsieur le marquis,' said he in my ear, quitting the dance for an instant and laughing aloud, "there are no ghosts or spirits here, as at your Venetian wedding.'

"'Don't,' I answered, putting up my finger to him, 'rejoice too soon: misery is slow in its operations; and often is not perceived by us blind mortals till it treads on our heels.'

"Contrary to my intention, this conversation rendered him quite silent; and what convinced me the more strongly of the effect it had made on him, was, the redoubled vehemence with which the duke again began dancing.

"The countess in vain entreated him to be careful of his health: and all Ida's supplications were able to obtain was, a few minutes' rest to take breath when he could no longer go on.

"A few minutes after, I saw Ida in tears, which did not appear as if occasioned by joy; and she quitted the ball-room. I was standing as close to the door as I am to you at this moment; so that I could not for an instant doubt its being really Ida: but what appeared to me very strange was, that in a few seconds I saw her come in again with a countenance as calm as possible. I followed her, and remarked that she asked the duke to dance; and was so far from moderating his violence, that she partook of and even increased it by her own example. I also remarked, that as soon as the dance was over the duke took leave of the parents of Ida, and with her vanished through a small door leading to the nuptial apartment.

"While I was endeavouring to account in my own mind how it was possible for Ida so suddenly to change her sentiments, a conference in an under tone took place at the door of the room, between the count and his valet.

"The subject was evidently a very important one, as the greatly incensed looks of the count towards his gardener evinced, while *he* confirmed, as it appeared, what the valet had before said.

"I drew near the trio, and heard, that at a particular time the church organ was heard to play, and that the whole edifice had been illuminated within, until twelve o'clock, which had just struck.

"The count was very angry at their troubling him with so silly a tale, and asked why they did not sooner inform him of it. They answered, that every one was anxious to see how it would end. The gardener added, that the old chaplain had been seen again; and the peasantry who lived near the forest, even pretended that they had seen the summit of the mountain which overhung their valley illuminated, and spirits dance around it.

"'Very well!' exclaimed the count with a gloomy air; 'so all the old idle trash is resumed: the *Death-Bride* is also, I hope, going to play her part.'

"The valet having pushed aside the gardener, that he might not still further enrage the count, I put in my word; and said to the count, 'You might at least listen to what they have to say, and learn what it is they pretend to have seen.'

"'What is said about the *Death-Bride?*' said I to the gardener.

"He shrugged up his shoulders.

"'Was I not right?' cried the count: 'here we are then, and must listen to this ridiculous tale. All these things are treasured in the memory of these people, and constantly afford subjects and phantoms to their imaginations.—Is it permitted to ask under what form?'—

"'Pray pardon me,' replied the gardener; 'but it resembled the deceased mademoiselle Hildegarde. She passed close to me in the garden, and then came into the castle.'"

"'O!' said the count to him, 'I beg, in future you will be a little more circumspect in your fancies, and leave my daughter to rest quietly in the tomb—'Tis well—'

"He then made a signal to his servants, who went out.

"'Well! my dear marquis!' said he to me.

"'Well?'

"'Your belief in stories will not, surely, carry you so far as to give credence to my Hildegarde's spirit appearing?'

"'At least it may have appeared to the gardener only—Do you recollect the adventure in the Museum at Paris?'

"'You are right: that again was a pretty invention, which to this moment I cannot fathom. Believe me, I should sooner have refused my daughter to the duke for his having been the fabricator of so gross a story, than for his having forsaken his first love.'

"'I see very plainly that we shall not easily accord on this point; for if my ready belief appears strange to you, your doubts seem to me incomprehensible.'

"The company assembled at the castle, retired by degrees; and *I alone* was left with the count and his lady, when Ida came to the room-door, clothed in her ball-dress, and appeared astonished at finding the company had left.

"'What can this mean?' demanded the countess. Her husband could not find words to express his astonishment.

"'Where is Marino?' exclaimed Ida.

"'Do *you* ask us where he is?' replied her mother; 'did we not see you go out with him through that small door?'

"'That could not be;—you mistake.'

"'No, no; my dear child! A very short time since you were dancing with singular vehemence; and then you both went out together.'

"'*Me!* my mother?'

"'Yes, my dear Ida: how is it possible you should have forgotten all this?'

"'I have forgotten nothing, believe me.'

"'Where then have you been all this time?'

"'In my sister's chamber,' said Ida.

"I remarked that at these words the count became somewhat pale; and his fearful eye caught mine: he however said nothing. The countess, fearing that her daughter was deceiving her, said to her in an afflicted tone of voice:—

"'How could so singular a fancy possess you on a day like this?'

"'I cannot account for it; and only know, that all on a sudden I felt an oppression at my heart, and fancied that all I wanted was Hildegarde. At the same time I felt a firm belief that I should find her in her room playing on her guitar; for which reason I crept thither softly.'

"'And did you find her there?'

"'Alas! no: but the eager desire that I felt to see her, added to the fatigue of dancing, so entirely overpowered me, that I seated myself on a chair, where I fell fast asleep.'

"'How long since did you quit the room?'

"'The clock in the tower struck the three-quarters past eleven just as I entered my sister's room.'

"'What does all this mean?' said the countess to her husband in a low voice: 'she talks in a connected manner; and yet I know, that as the clock struck three-quarters past eleven, I entreated Ida on this very spot to dance more moderately.'

"'And Marino?'—asked the count.

"'I thought, as I before said, that I should find him here.'

"'Good God!' exclaimed the mother, 'she raves: but the duke—Where is he then?'

"'What then, my good mother?' said Ida with an air of great disquiet, while leaning on the countess.

"Meanwhile the count took a wax-taper, and made a sign for me to follow him. A horrible spectacle awaited us in the bridal-chamber, whither he conducted me. We there found the duke extended on the floor. There did not appear the slightest signs of life in him; and his features were distorted in the most frightful manner.

"Imagine the extreme affliction Ida endured when she heard this recital, and found that all the resources of the medical attendants were employed in vain.

"The count and his family could not be roused from the deep consternation which threatened to overwhelm them. A short time after this event, some business of importance occasioned me to quit their castle; and certainly I was not sorry for the excuse to get away.

"But ere I left that county, I did not fail to collect in the village every possible information relative to the *Death-Bride;* whose history unfortunately, in passing from one mouth to another, experienced many alterations. It appeared to me, however, upon the whole, that this affianced bride lived in this district, about the fourteenth or fifteenth century. She was a young lady of noble family, and she had conducted herself with so much perfidy and ingratitude towards her lover, that he died of grief; but afterwards, when she was about to marry, he appeared to her the night of her intended wedding, and she died in consequence. And it is said, that since that time, the spirit of this unfortunate creature wanders on earth in every possible shape; particularly in that of lovely females, to render their lovers inconstant.

"As it was not permitted for her to appear in the form of any living being, she always chose amongst the dead those who the most strongly resembled them. It was for this reason she voluntarily frequented the galleries in which were hung family portraits. It is even reported that she has been seen in galleries of pictures open to public inspection. Finally, it is said, that, as a punishment for her perfidy, she will wander till she finds a man whom she will in vain endeavour to make swerve from his engagement; and it appears, they added, that as yet she had not succeeded.

"Having inquired what connection subsisted between this spirit and the old chaplain (of whom also I had heard mention), they informed me, that the fate of the last depended on the young lady, because he had assisted her in her criminal conduct. But no one was able to give me any satisfactory information concerning the voice which had called the duke by his name, nor on the meaning of the church being illuminated at night; and why the grand mass was chanted. No one either knows how to account for the dance on the mountain's top in the forest.

"For the rest," added the marquis, "you will own, that the traditions are admirably adapted to my story, and may, to a certain degree, serve to fill up the gaps; but I am not enabled to give a more satisfactory explanation. I reserve for another time a second history of this same *Death-Bride;* I only heard it a few weeks since: it appears to me interesting; but it is too late to begin to-day, and indeed, even now, I fear that I have intruded too long on the leisure of the company present by my narrative."

He had just finished these words, and some of his auditors (though all thanked him for the trouble he had taken) were expressing their disbelief of the story, when a person of his acquaintance came into the room in a hurried manner, and whispered something in his ear. Nothing could be more striking than the contrast presented by the bustling and uneasy air of the newly arrived person while speaking to the marquis, and the calm air of the latter while listening to him.

"Haste, I pray you," said the first (who appeared quite out of patience at the marquis's *sang-froid):* "In a few moments you will have cause to repent this delay."

"I am obliged to you for your affecting solicitude," replied the marquis; who in taking up his hat, appeared more to do, as all the rest of the party were doing, in preparing to return home, than from any anxiety of hastening away.

"You are lost," said the other, as he saw an officer enter the room at the head of a detachment of military, who inquired for the marquis. The latter instantly made himself known to him.

"You are my prisoner," said the officer. The marquis followed him, after saying Adieu with a smiling air to all the party, and begging they would not feel any anxiety concerning him.

"Not feel anxiety!" replied he whose advice he had neglected. "I must inform you, that they have discovered that the marquis has been detected in a connection with very suspicious characters; and his death-warrant may be considered as signed. I came in pity to warn him of his danger, for possibly he might then have escaped; but from his conduct since, I can scarely imagine he is in his proper senses."

The party, who were singularly affected by this event, were conjecturing a thousand things, when the officer returned, and again asked for the marquis.

"He just now left the room with you," answered some one of the company.

"But he came in again."

"We have seen no one."

"He has then disappeared," replied the officer, smiling: he searched every corner for the marquis, but in vain. The house was thoroughly examined, but without success; and the following day the officer quitted the baths with his soldiers, without his prisoner, and very much dissatisfied.

The End

Vampire

by Jan Neruda

Jan Neruda (1834-1891) was a Czech journalist and writer of numerous short stories. Neruda (who was a man, for the record) mainly wrote realistic stories about Prague, but he also penned this tale of a "vampire." We put it in quotes, because this isn't a typical vampire. Rather, it's about a ghoulish character who "sketches only corpses." We don't want to say too much and give away the ending, but this short story is a fun entry into the genre.

Vampire

by Jan Neruda

The excursion steamer brought us from Constantinople to the shore of the island of Prinkipo and we disembarked. The number of passengers was not large. There was one Polish family, a father, a mother, a daughter and her bridegroom, and then we two. Oh, yes, I must not forget that when we were already on the wooden bridge which crosses the Golden Horn to Constantinople, a Greek, a rather youthful man, joined us. He was probably an artist, judging by the portfolio he carried under his arm. Long black locks floated to his shoulders, his face was pale, and his black eyes were deeply set in their sockets. From the first moment he interested me, especially for his obligingness and for his knowledge of local conditions. But he talked too much, and I then turned away from him.

All the more agreeable was the Polish family. The father and mother were good-natured, fine people, the lover a hand-some young fellow, of direct and refined manners. They had come to Prinkipo to spend the summer months for the sake of the daughter, who was slightly ailing. The beautiful pale girl was either just recovering from a severe illness or else a serious disease was just fastening its hold upon her. She leaned upon her lover when she walked and very often sat down to rest, while a frequent dry little cough interrupted her whispers. Whenever she coughed, her escort would considerately pause in their walk. He always cast upon her a glance of sympathetic suffering and she would look back at him as if she would say: "It is nothing. I am happy!" They believed in health and happiness.

On the recommendation of the Greek, who departed from us immediately at the pier, the family secured quarters in the hotel on the hill. The hotel-keeper was a Frenchman and his entire building was equipped comfortably and artistically, according to the French style.

We breakfasted together and when the noon heat had abated somewhat we all betook ourselves to the heights, where in the grove of Siberian stone-pines we could refresh ourselves with the view. Hardly had we found a suitable spot and settled ourselves when the Greek appeared again. He greeted us lightly, looked about and seated himself only a few steps from us. He opened his portfolio and began to sketch.

"I think he purposely sits with his back to the rocks so that we can't look at his sketch," I said.

"We don't have to," said the young Pole. "We have enough before us to look at." After a while he added, "It seems to me he's sketching us in as a sort of background. Well —let him!"

We truly did have enough to gaze at. There is not a more beautiful or more happy corner in the world than that very Prinkipo! The political martyr, Irene, contemporary of Charles the Great, lived there for a month as an exile. If I could live a month of my life there I would be happy for the memory of it for the rest of my days! I shall never forget even that one day spent at Prinkipo.

The air was as clear as a diamond, so soft, so caressing, that one's whole soul swung out upon it into the distance. At the right beyond the sea projected the brown Asiatic summits; to the left in the distance purpled the steep coasts of Europe. The neighboring Chalki, one of the nine islands of the "Prince's Archipelago," rose with its cypress forests into the peaceful heights like a sorrowful dream, crowned by a great structure—an asylum for those whose minds are sick.

The Sea of Marmora was but slightly ruffled and played in all colors like a sparkling opal. In the distance the sea was as white as milk, then rosy, between the two islands a glowing orange and below us it was beautifully greenish blue, like a transparent sapphire. It was resplendent in its own beauty. Nowhere were there any large ships—only two small craft flying the English flag sped along the shore. One was a steamboat as big as a watchman's booth, the second had about twelve oarsmen, and when their oars rose simultaneously molten silver dripped from them. Trustful dolphins darted in and out among them and dove with long, arching flights above the surface of the water. Through the blue heavens now and then calm eagles winged their way, measuring the space between two continents.

The entire slope below us was covered with blossoming roses whose fragrance filled the air. From the coffee-house near the sea music was carried up to us through the clear air, hushed somewhat by the distance.

The effect was enchanting. We all sat silent and steeped our souls completely in the picture of paradise. The young Polish girl lay on the grass with her head supported on the bosom of her lover. The pale oval of her delicate face was slightly tinged with soft color, and from her blue eyes tears suddenly gushed forth. The lover understood, bent down and kissed tear after tear. Her mother also was moved to tears, and I—even I—felt a strange twinge.

"Here mind and body both must get well," whispered the girl. "How happy a land this is!"

"God knows I haven't any enemies, but if I had I would forgive them here!" said the father in a trembling voice.

And again we became silent. We were all in such a wonderful mood—so unspeakably sweet it all was! Each felt for himself a whole world of happiness and each one would have shared his happiness with the whole world. All felt the same—and so no one disturbed another. We had scarcely even noticed the Greek, after an hour or so, had arisen, folded his portfolio and with a slight nod had taken his departure. We remained.

Finally after several hours, when the distance was becoming overspread with a darker violet, so magically beautiful in the south, the mother reminded us it was time to depart. We arose and walked down towards the hotel with the easy, elastic steps that characterize carefree children. We sat down in the hotel under the handsome veranda.

Hardly had we been seated when we heard below the sounds of quarreling and oaths. Our Greek was wrangling the hotel-keeper, and for the entertainment of it we listened.

The amusement did not last long. "If I didn't have other guests," growled the hotel-keeper, and ascended the steps towards us.

"I beg you to tell me, sir," asked the young Pole of the approaching hotel-keeper, "who is that gentleman? What's his name?"

"Eh—who knows what the fellow's name is?" grumbled the hotel-keeper, and he gazed venomously downwards. "We call him the ."

"An artist?"

"Fine trade! He sketches only corpses. Just as soon as someone in Constantinople or here in the neighborhood dies, that very day he has a picture of the dead one completed. That fellow paints them beforehand—and he never makes a mistake —just like a vulture!"

The old Polish woman shrieked affrightedly. In her arms lay her daughter pale as chalk. She had fainted.

In one bound the lover had leaped down the steps. With one hand he seized the Greek and with the other reached for the portfolio.

We ran down after him. Both men were rolling in the sand. The contents of the portfolio were scattered all about. On one sheet, sketched with a crayon, was the head of the young Polish girl, her eyes closed and a wreath of myrtle on her brow.

THE END

The Skeleton Count, (or The Vampire Mistress)

by Elizabeth Caroline Grey

This "penny dreadful" is considered by some to be the first vampire story written by a woman. Penned by Elizabeth Caroline Grey (1798–1869), a prolific English author, this 1828 story involves a deal with the devil, romance - which was Grey's speciality - and everlasting life. It has two different titles, one of which focuses on the man, and one on the woman. This is a fun read.

The Skeleton Count

by Elizabeth Caroline Grey

Count Rodolph, after his impious compact with the prince of darkness, ceased to study alchemy or to search after the elixir of life, for not only was a long lease of life assured him by the demon, but the same authority had declared such pursuits to be vain and delusive. But he still dabbled in the occult sciences of magic and astrology, and frequently passed day after day in fruitless speculation, concerning the origin of matter, and the nature of the soul. He studied the writings of Aristotle, Pliny, Lucretius, Josephus, Iamblicus, Sprenger, Cardan, and the learned Michael Psellus; yet was he as far as ever from attaining a correct knowledge of the things he sought to unveil from the mystery which must ever envelope them. The reveries of the ancient philosophers, of the Gnostics and the Pneaumatologists, only served to plunge him into deeper doubt, and at length he determined to pass from speculation to experiment, and put his half-formed theories to the test of practice.

After keen study of the anatomy of the human frame, and many operations and experiments on the corpse of a malefactor who had been hanged for a robbery and murder, and which he stole from the gibbet in the dead of night, and conveyed to Ravensburg Castle, with the assistance of two wretches whom he had picked up at an obscure hostelry in the town of Heidel-berg, he resolved to exhume the corpse of some one recently dead, and attempt its reanimation. The formula of the necro-mancers for raising the dead did not suffice for their restoration to life, but only for a temporary revivification; but in an old Greek manuscript, which he found in the library of the castle, was an account of how this restored animation might be sustained by means of a miraculous liquid, for the distillation of which a recipe was given.

Count Rodolph gathered the herbs at midnight, which the Greek manuscript prescribed and distilled from them a clear gold-coloured liquid of very little taste, but most fragrant odour, which he preserved in a phial. Having discovered that a peasant's daughter, a girl of singular beauty, and about sixteen years of age, had died suddenly, and was to be buried on the day following that on which he had prepared his marvelous restorative, he set out on that day to Heidelberg to obtain the assistance of the fellows who had aided him in removing the corpse of the malefactor from the gibbet, and then returned to Ravensburg Castle, to prepare for his strange experiment.

At the solemn hour of midnight he departed secretly from the castle by a door in the eastern tower, of which he retained the key in his own possession, and bent his step to the church-yard of the neighbouring village. It was a fine moonlight night, but all the rustic inhabitants were in the arms of Morpheus, the leaden-eyed god of sleep, and the violator of the sanctity of the grave gained the church-yard unperceived. He found his hired associates waiting for him in the shadow of the wall, which was easily scaled, and being provided with shovels and a sack to contain the corpse, they set to work immediately. The fresh broken earth was soon thrown off from the lid of the coffin, which the resurrectionists removed with a screw-driver, and then the dead was disclosed to their view.

The corpse of the young maiden was lifted from its narrow resting place, and raised in the arms of the ungodly wretches whom Rodolph had hired, who deposited the inanimate clay on the margin of the grave, which they hastily filled up, and then proceeded to enclose in the sack the lifeless remains of the beautiful peasant girl. Having removed every trace of the sacrilegious theft which they had committed, one of them took the sack on his shoulders, and when he was tired his comrade relieved him, and in this manner they reached the castle. Count Rodolph led the way up the narrow stairs which led to his study chamber in the eastern turret, and having deposited the corpse upon the floor, and received their stipulated reward, the two resurrectionists were glad to make a speedy exit from a place which popular rumour began to associate with deeds of darkness and horror.

Having lighted a spirit lamp, which cast a livid and flickering light upon the many strange and mysterious objects which that chamber contained, and made the pale countenance of the corpse appear more ghastly and horrible, Count Rodolph proceeded to denude the body of its grave-clothes, which he carefully concealed, lest the sight of them, when the young maiden returned to life might strike her with a sudden horror which might prove fatal to the complete success of his daring experiment. He then placed the corpse in the centre of a magic circle which he had previously drawn upon the floor of the study, and covered it with a sheet. He had purchased some ready-made female apparel in the town of Heidelberg, and these he placed on the table in readiness for the use of the young girl, whom he felt sanguine of resuscitating.

Bertha had been, as was evidenced by her stark and cold remains, a maiden of surpassing symmetry of form and loveliness of countenance; no painter or sculptor could have desired a finer study, no poet a more inspiring theme. As she lay stretched out upon the floor of the study she looked like some beautiful carving in alabaster, or rather like a waxen figure of most artistical contrivance. Her long black hair was shaded with a purple gloss like the plumage of the raven, and her features were of most exquisite proportion and arrangement. But now her angelic countenance was livid with the pallid hue of death, the iron impress of whose icy hand was visible in every lineament.

Count Rodolph then took in his hand a magic wand, one end of which he placed on the breast of the corpse, and then proceeded to recite the cabalistic words by which necromancers call to life the slumbering tenants of the grave. When he had concluded the impious formula, an awful silence reigned in the turret, and he perceived the sheet gently agitated by the quivering of the limbs, which betokened returning animation. Then a shudder pervaded his frame in spite of himself, as he perceived the eyes of the corpse slowly open, and the dark dilated pupils fix their gaze on him with a strange and stolid glare.

Then the limbs moved, at first convulsively, but soon with a stronger and more natural motion, and then the young girl raised herself to a sitting posture on the floor of the study, and stared about her in a wild and strange manner, which made Rodolph fear that the object of his experiment would prove a wretched idiot or a raving lunatic.

But suddenly he bethought him of the restorative cordial, and snatching the phial from a shelf, he poured down the throat of the resuscitated maiden a considerable portion of the fragrant gold colored fluid which it contained. Then a ray of that glorious intellect which allies man to the angels seemed to be infused into her mind, and beamed from her dark and lustrous eyes, which rested with a soft and tender expression on the handsome countenance of the young count. Her snowy bosom, from which the sheet had fallen when she rose from her recumbent position on the floor, heaved with the returning warmth of renewed life, and the Count of Ravensburg gazed upon her with mingled sensations of wonder and delight.

As the current of life was restored, and rushed along her veins with tingling warmth, the conscious blush of instinctive modesty mantled on her countenance, and drawing the sheet over her bosom, she rose to her feet, with her long black hair hanging about her shoulders, and her dark eyes cast upon the floor. Count Rodolph then directed her attention to the clothing which he had provided, so sanguine of complete success had the daring experimentalist been, and then he withdrew from the study while the lovely object of his scientific care attired herself.

When the Count of Ravensburg returned to his study, Bertha was sitting before the fire, attired in the garments he had provided for her, and he thought that he had never beheld a more lovely specimen of her sex. She rose when he entered, and kissed his hand, as though he were a superior being, and would have remained standing, with head bowed upon her bosom, as if in the presence of a being of another world, had he not gently forced her to resume the seat from which she had risen, and inquired tenderly the state of her feelings upon a return to life so strange and wonderful. But he found that she retained no remembrance of a previous existence, and all her feelings were new and strange, like those of Eve on bursting into conscious life and being from the hand of the Omnipotent. In her mysterious passage from life to death, and from death to new life, she had lost all her previous ideas and convictions, all her experience of the past, all that she had ever acquired of knowledge; and had become a child of nature, simple and unsophisticated as a denizen of the woods, with all the keen perceptions and untrained instincts of the untutored savage.

The young girl had braided up her flowing tresses of glossy blackness, and on her cheeks dwelt color that might test a painter's skill, so rich yet delicate its hue, like the rosette tinge of some rare exotic shell, or that which a rose would cast upon an alabaster column. The young count felt himself irresistibly attracted towards the maiden, whom his science had endued with such a mysterious and preternatural existence, and she, on her part, regarded the handsome Rodolph with the wild, yet tender passion of frail humanity, mingled with the gratitude and devotion which she deemed due to one who stood to her in the position of her creator.

Thus the feelings which had so rapidly sprung up in her heart towards the only being of whom she had any conception, partook of a nature of a religious idolatry, but mingled with the grosser feelings of earth, like those which agitated in the bosom of the vestal whose sons founded Rome, or the virgin of Shensi who was chosen from among all the women of the celestial empire to become the mother of the incarnate Foh.

'Thou art gloriously beautiful, my Bertha!' exclaimed the enamored count, pressing her in his arms. 'Say that thou wilt be mine, and make me thy happy slave; thou should'st be loving as thou art lovable, beautiful child of mystery!'

'Love thee!' returned Bertha, a soft and tender expression dwelling in the clear depths of her dark eyes. 'I adore thee, my creator; my soul bows itself before thee, yet my heart leaps at thy glance, though I fear it is presumptuous for the work of thy hands to look on thee with eyes of love.'

'Sweet, ingenuous creature!' cried the Count of Ravensburg, kissing her coral lips and glowing cheeks. 'It is I who should worship thee! Thou art mine, Bertha, now and for ever. Henceforth I live only in thy smile!'

'For ever! Shall I remain with thee for ever? Oh, joy incomparable! My heart's idol, I adore thee!' and the beautiful Bertha wound her white arms about his neck, and pressed her lips to his, for in the new existence which she now enjoyed her feelings knew no restraint, and she yielded to every impulse of her ardent nature.

'Come, my Bertha,' said the enraptured Rodolph, 'this solitary turret must not be thy world; come with me, thy Rodolph, and be the mistress of Ravensburg Castle, as thou art already of its owner's heart.'

Passing his arm around the taper waist of the mysterious maiden, Rodolph took up the lamp, and quitting the eastern turret, they proceeded with noiseless steps to his chamber, where the first faint blush of day witnessed the consummation of their desires, nor did the torch of Hymen burn less brightly because no priest blessed their nuptial couch.

The presence in Ravensburg Castle of this young girl, which Rodolph, with that contempt for the opinion of the world which usually marked his actions, took no pains to conceal, became the engrossing topic of conversation in the servants' hall throughout the day, and as Rodolph had never before indulged in any intrigue, either with the peasant girls of the neighbouring village or the courtesans of Heidelburg, the circumstance seemed the more remarkable. But the beautiful Bertha seemed quite unconscious of the equivocal nature of her position in reference to the young count, and though her views of human nature became every moment more enlarged with the sphere of her existence, she still regarded Rodolph as a being of superior mold.

When night again drew his sable mantle over the sleeping earth, Rodolph and the mysterious Bertha sought their couch, and never had shone the inconstant moon on a pair so well matched as regarded physical beauty, or we may add as regarded their strange destiny — one gifted with almost superhuman powers of mind, yet in a few days to undergo so horrible a transformation, and far removed by that strange fate from ordinary mortals; the other endowed with such singular beauty yet doomed to the dreadful existence of one who had passed the boundaries of the grave, and returned to life!

With sonorous and solemn stroke the bell of the castle clock proclaimed the hour of midnight, and then Bertha slowly raised herself from her lover's body and slipping from the bed, attired herself in a half-unconscious state, and stole noiselessly from the room.

Her cheeks were pale, and her eyes had the wild and stolid glare which Rodolph had observed when she awakened from the slumber of the grave; she quitted the castle, and after gazing around her, as if uncertain which way to go, she proceeded towards the village.

She stopped opposite the nearest cottage, and then advanced to the window, and shook the shutters; the fastenings being insecure, they opened with little trouble, and a broken pane of glass enabled Bertha to introduce her hand, and remove the fastenings of the window. Then she cautiously opened the window, and entered the room — she ascended the stairs on tiptoe, and entered a chamber where a little girl was in bed and fast asleep. For a moment she shuddered violently, as if struggling to repress the horrible inclination which is the dread condition of a return to life after passing the portals of death, and then she bent her face down to the child's throat, her hot breath fanned its cheek, and the next moment her teeth punctured its tender skin, and she began to suck its blood to sustain her unnatural existence!

For such is the horrible destiny of the vampire race, of whom we have yet further mysteries and secrets to unfold; and such a being was she whom Count Rodolph had taken from the grave to his bed!

Presently the child awoke with a fearful scream, and its father, leaping from his bed in the next room, hurried to her succor, but Bertha rushed past him in the dark, and escaped from the house. The peasant found the little girl much frightened, and bleeding at the throat; but she had suffered no vital injury, and having ascertained this fact, he snatched up his match-lock, and hurried after the aggressor.

'A vampire!' exclaimed the peasant, turning pale with horror, as he distinctly saw, by the light of the moon, a young female hurrying from the village at a rapid pace.

The man gave chase to the flying Bertha, and gradually gaining ground, came within gun shot, just as she reached the shelving banks of the river, when he raised his weapon to his shoulder, and fired. The report echoed along the banks of the Rhine, and Bertha screamed as the ball penetrated her back, and tumbled headlong into the stream. The peasant hastened back to the village, satisfied that the horrible creature was no more, and the corpse of the vampire floated on the surface of the moonlit river.

The moon was that night at the full, and shed a flood of pearly light over the picturesque scenery of the Rhine, which, throughout its whole course, is a panorama of scenic beauty, every bend revealing some object interesting either for its historical reminiscences or legendary associations. There was the village, but now the scene of a horrible outrage — the castle, thrown into alternate light and shadow by the passing of the light fleecy clouds over the face of the moon — the town of Heidelberg, sloping from the Castle of the Palatine, and spanning the river with its noble bridge — and the Rhine, here shaded by the dark rocks which overhung the opposite bank, and there reflecting the silver light of the moon. The corpse of the vampire floated down the stream for some distance, and then it became arrested in its course by the bending of the river, and lay partly out of the water on the shelving bank.

And now commenced another scene of strange and startling interest — another phase in the fearful existence of the vampire bride! For as the beams of the full moon fell on the inanimate form of that being of mystery and fear, sensation seemed slowly to return, as when the magic spells of the Count of Ravensburg resuscitated her from the grave; her eyes opened, her bosom rose and fell with the warm pulsations of returning life; her limbs moved spasmodically, and then she rose from the bank, and shuddering at the recollection of what had occurred to her, she wrung the water from her saturated garments, and ran towards the castle at a pace accelerated by fear.

Having admitted herself into the castle, she sought the count's chamber with noiseless steps, and having taken off and concealed her wet clothes, she returned to his bed without his being aware that she had ever quitted it. The count was surprised to find that his mistress took no refreshment throughout the day, but he was led to consider it as one of the natural laws of her strange existence, and thought no more about it.

But in the village, the utmost excitement prevailed when it became known that the cottage of Herman Klans had been visited by a vampire during the night, and his little daughter bitten by the horrible creature. All day long the cottage of the mysterious visitation was beset by the wondering villagers, who crossed themselves piously, and wondered who the vampire could have been, and the services of the priest were called into requisition to prevent the little blue-eyed Minna becoming a vampire after death, as is supposed to be the case with those who have the misfortune to be bitten by one of those horrible creatures, just as a person becomes mad after the bite of a mad dog or cat.

According to the terms of the compact which had been

entered into between Count Rodolph and the demon, its conditions did not come into operation until seven days after the signing of the dreadful bond, and as day after day flew on, Rodolph dreaded the necessity of acquainting Bertha with the terrible transformation which he must nightly undergo. But he knew how impossible it would be to keep his hideous and appalling metamorphosis a secret from his mistress, and he reflected that if he made her the confidant of his terrible fate it would be the more likely to remain unknown to the rest of the world. He accordingly nerved his mind to the appalling revelation which he had to make, and on the seventh day after his compact with Lucifer, he disclosed to her his awful secret.

'Bertha,' said he, in a sad and solemn tone, 'I am about to entrust thee with a terrible secret; swear to me that thou wilt never divulge it.'

'I swear,' she replied.

'Know, then,' continued the count, lowering his voice to a hoarse whisper, 'that, by virtue of a compact with the infernal powers of evil and of darkness, I am endowed with a term of life and youth amounting almost to the boon of immortality but to this inestimable gift, there is a condition attached which commences this night, and which I almost tremble to impart to thee.'

'Fear not, my Rodolph!' exclaimed his beautiful mistress, twining her round white arms about his neck, 'thy Bertha can never love thee less, and her soul the rather clings to thee more intensely for the preternatural gift which links thy destiny more closely to my own. For mine, too, is a strange and fearful existence, which I owe to thee, and therefore shall I cling to thee the more fondly for the kindred doom which allies us to each other while it lifts us far above ordinary mortals.'

'Then prepare thy ears for a dread revelation, Bertha,' returned the Count of Ravensburg. 'Each night of my future existence, at the hour of sunset, my doom divests me of my mortal shape, and I become a skeleton until sunrise on the morn ensuing. Now, thou knowest all, my Bertha, and be it thy care to prevent the dreadful secret from becoming known.'

'It shall, my brave Rodolph!' exclaimed Bertha, her eyes glittering with a strange expression, as she thought of the facility which her lover's strange doom would allow for her nocturnal absences from the castle. 'No eye but mine shall witness thy transformation, and I will watch over thee until thy return to thy natural shape.'

'Thanks, my Bertha!' returned Rodolph, embracing her. 'The hour draws nigh when I must relinquish for the night my mortal form; come, love, to our chamber, and see that no prying eye beholds the ghastly change.'

Bertha and her lover accordingly repaired to their chamber, and when the luminary of day sank below the horizon, leaving the traces of his splendor on the western sky, the Count Rodolph shrunk to a grisly skeleton, and fell upon the bed. Bertha shuddered as she witnessed the horrid transformation, and they lay down on the bed until midnight, the necessity of secrecy overcoming any repugnance she might otherwise have felt to the horrible contiguity of the skeleton, but when the castle clock proclaimed the hour of midnight with iron tongue, she rose from the bed, and locking the door of the chamber which contained so strange a guest, she stole from the castle to sate her unnatural appetite for human blood.

The moon rode high in the heavens on that night of unfathomable mystery and horror, and her silver beams shone through the chamber-window of Theresa Delmar, one of the loveliest maidens in the village of Ravensburg, revealing a snowy neck, and a white and dimpled shoulder, shaded by the bright golden locks which strayed over the pillow. The maiden's blue eyes were concealed by their thin lids and their long silken fringes, and her snowy bosom gently rose and fell beneath the white coverlet as the thoughts which agitated her by day, mingled in her dreams at night. Silence reigned in the thatched cottage, and throughout the village was only occasionally broken by the barking of some watchful house-dog.

But soon after midnight the silence was broken by a slight noise at the chamber window as if someone was endeavoring to obtain an entrance, and the flood of moonlight which streamed upon the maiden's bed was obscured by the form of a woman standing on the windowsill. Still Theresa slumbered on, nor dreamed of peril so near, for the woman had succeeded in opening the window, and in another moment she stood within the room.

With slow and cautious step she softly approached the bed whereon the maiden reposed so calmly, little dreaming how dread a visitant was near her couch, and then she shuddered involuntarily as she bent over the sleeping girl, and her long dark ringlets mingled with the masses of golden hair which shaded the white shoulder, and the partially exposed bosom of Theresa Delmar. Her lips touched the young girl's neck, her sharp teeth punctured the white skin, and then she began to suck greedily, quaffing the vital fluid which flowed warm and quick in the maiden's veins, and sapping her life to maintain her own!

Still Theresa awoke not, for the puncture made in her throat by the teeth of the horrible creature was little larger than that which would be made by a leech, and the vampire sucked long and greedily, for her long abstinence from blood had sharpened her unnatural appetite. Suddenly Theresa awoke with a start, doubtless caused by some unpleasant transition in her dreams, but she did not immediately cry out, for she felt no pain, and as yet she was scarcely conscious of her danger. But in a few seconds she was thoroughly awake, and her surprise and horror may be more easily imagined than described, when she found bending over her, and sucking her blood, the horrible creature that had but a few nights previously attacked Minna Klaus, and which the child's father thought he had destroyed.

Spell-bound by the glittering eyes of the vampire, she lay without the power to scream, until the appalling horror of her situation became too great for endurance, her quivering nerves were strung to their utmost power of extension, and a wild shriek burst from her lips. Even then the horrible creature did not leave its hold, but continued to suck from her palpitating veins the crimson current of her life, until footsteps were heard hastily approaching the chamber, and the lovely Theresa, whose screams seemed to have broken the fascination which had bound her in its thrall, struggled so violently that Bertha was compelled to relinquish her horrid banquet. Springing to the window, she effected her escape, just as heavy blows resounded on the door of the chamber, and her affrighted victim sank insensible on the bed.

'What is the matter, Theresa? Open the door!' exclaimed her terrified parents; but they received no answer.

Then Delmar broke open the door, and he and his wife rushed into the room and found their daughter lying insensible on the bed, with spots of blood on her throat and bosom, and the window wide open.

'The vampire has come to life again, and has attacked our Theresa!' exclaimed her mother. 'See the blood-marks on her dear neck! Raise the village, Delmar, to pursue the monster.'

'Oh, dear! where am I? Has it gone, mother?' inquired Theresa, as she recovered from her swoon, and gazed in a frightened manner round the room.

'Yes, it has gone now, dear,' said her mother. 'What was it like?'

'Aye, what was it like?' added old Delmar. 'Perhaps it was not the same one that neighbor Klans shot at the other night.'

'Oh, yes! it was a young woman, and as much like Bertha Kurtel as ever one pea was like another,' replied the young girl, shuddering.

'Holy virgin!' exclaimed her mother, crossing herself with a shudder. 'Bertha Kurtel a vampire, and returned from the grave to prey upon our Theresea! Oh, horrible!'

Delmar hurriedly dressed himself, and catching up an axe, he hastened to call up Klans and others to pursue the vampire, and in a few minutes the whole village was in commotion. About twenty men armed themselves with whatever weapon came first to hand, and followed the direction which the vampire had taken when chased by Herman Klans on a former occasion. They searched every bush all round the village, to which they returned at sunrise without having found any trace of the object of their search. Delmar found his daughter somewhat faint from fright and loss of blood, but not otherwise injured by the vampire's attack. The greatest excitement prevailed in that usually quiet village, and all the morning, groups of men stood about the little street, or clustered round Delmar's cottage, conversing in low and mysterious whispers of the dreadful visitation which the village had a second time received.

'What a shocking thing it would be if a pretty girl like Theresa Delmar was to become a vampire when she dies,' observed one. 'And who knows what may happen now she has been bitten by one of those horrible creatures?'

'And poor little Minna Klaus,' said another.

'Ah, and we do not know how long the list may be if we do not put a stop to it,' added one of the rustic group. 'I have heard Father Ambrose say that they generally attack females and children.'

'Who can it be? that is what I want to know,' said old Klaus. 'Why, Theresa declares it was just like Bertha Kurtel,' returned another, shaking his voice to a whisper.

'Bertha Kurtel!' repeated a youth who had loved her who once bore that name. 'Bertha a vampire! impossible.'

'It is easily ascertained,' observed the gruff voice of the village blacksmith. 'We have only to take up the coffin and see if she is in it, as she ought to be. If we do not find her we shall know what's o'clock.'

'If it was not for her parents' feelings I really should like to be satisfied whether it is Bertha,' remarked old Delmar.

'Feelings!' repeated the smith, in a surly tone. 'Have we not all got our feelings? Are we to have our wives and children attacked in this manner, and all turned into vampires, and let other people's fine feelings prevent us from having satisfaction for it?'

'There is something in that,' observed Delmar, scratching his head with an air of perplexity.

'I would make one if anybody else would go,' said Herman Klaus, after a pause.

'And I will be another,' exclaimed the smith, looking

around him. 'Now who will go and have a peep in the church-yard to see whose coffin is empty?'

Several expressed themselves ready, and others following their example the smith proceeded to the churchyard, backed by about twenty of the most resolute of the villagers, to reenact the scene which had taken place there but a few nights since. On arriving at the churchyard the smith and another immediately set to work to throw the earth out of the grave, which was soon accomplished, and amid the most breathless silence the smith proceeded to remove the lid of the coffin.

'Look here, neighbors,' said he, turning pale in spite of himself. 'The lid has been removed, and the coffin is empty!'

'So it is!' exclaimed Herman Klaus.

'Then is it not plain that Bertha is the vampire — the horrible creature that sucked the blood of Theresa Delmar and little Minna Klans?' said the smith, looking round upon the throng which had been swelled during the work of exhumation by idlers from the village.

'But where is she now? that is the question,' observed Herman Klans.

'This must be investigated,' said the smith. 'We must keep watch for the vampire, and catch it; then we must either burn it, or drive a stake through the creature's body, for they say those are the only methods that will effectually fix a vampire.'

The wondering group of peasants returned to the village, and great was the grief of the Kurtels at the horrible discovery that their daughter had become a vampire, and the youth who had so loved Bertha in her human state became delirious on hearing the confirmation of the suspicion which Theresa's assertion had first excited. The ordinary occupations of the villagers were entirely neglected throughout the day, and nothing was talked of but vampires and werewolves, and other human transformations more terrific and appalling than any recorded in the metamorphoses of Ovid. Towards the evening the venerable seneschal of the Count of Ravensburg arrived in the village and had an interview with the Delmars, after which he visited the cottage of Herman Klans, and a vague rumor spread like wildfire from house to house, to the effect that the vampire was an inmate of Ravensburg Castle.

The communication made by the seneschal to Delmar and Klans was to the effect that, on the morning following the interment of Bertha Kurtel, a young female exactly resembling her in form, features, voice, and every individual peculiarity, had appeared in a mysterious manner at the castle, and had resided there ever since in the capacity of the count's mistress. No one knew who she was, where she came from, or how she obtained admission into the castle; and the occurrences in the village having reached the ears of the count's retainers and domestics, accompanied with the suspicion that the vampire was the revived Bertha Kurtel, the seneschal had hastened to the village to report his observations. The abstinence of the count's mistress from food was deemed corroborative of the suspicion that she was a vampire, and the seneschal's report caused the utmost excitement among the villagers. Symptoms of hostile intentions soon became visible, and in less than half an hour, more than a hundred men were proceeding in a disorderly manner towards the castle, armed with every imaginable weapon, and swearing to put an end to the vampire.

Count Rodolph and his beautiful mistress were sitting at a window which commanded a view of the road for some distance, the small white hand of Bertha locked in that of her lover, and whispering words of tenderness and love, when their attention was attracted by a disorderly mob approaching from the village.

'What can this mean?' said Rodolph, rising.

'Oh, this is what I have dreaded!' exclaimed Bertha, turning pale, and clasping her hands in a terrified manner: 'your studies have caused you to be suspected of necromancy, my Rodolph, they come to attack the castle.'

'I fear thou art right, dearest,' said the count: 'but we will give them a warm reception. Ho! a lawless mob menaces the castle with danger: make fast the gates; bar every door; bid my retainers man the battlements to repel the attack.'

'And sunset is approaching,' exclaimed Bertha, with a meaning glance at her lover.

'Do thou retire, sweet love, to thy chamber,' said Rodolph; 'fear not for me; I bear a charmed life, and neither sword nor shot will avail against it. If this lawless rabble be not dispersed when the dread moment comes all hope will be lost, and they shall behold the grisly change. Perhaps they may be struck with a sudden panic, and we may be enabled to fly into another country.'

Bertha retired after embracing the count, and shut herself up in her chamber. Preparations were immediately made to resist the attack of the insurgent villagers, who continued to advance upon the castle, yelling like savages, and breathing vengeance against the vampire mistress of Count Rodolph.

'Down with the vampire!' was the hoarse and sullen cry which rolled like distant thunder from a hundred throats, and then the mob drew up before the castle gates, and the smith struck them heavily with his ponderous hammer.

The count took an arquebuse and fired at the mob, very few of whom were provided with fire-arms; one of the peasants was wounded, and with a shout of rage and defiance a volley of shot, arrows, and stones was directed against the beleaguered castle. The smith continued to batter away at the gate, aided by several stalwart fellows with axes, and though several of the mob were killed by the fire of the men-at-arms, those who were endeavoring to force the gate were protected by the overhanging battlements, and continued to ply their implements with unwearied energy.

Could Rodolph turned pale, and shuddered as he listened to the wild cries of the assailants, not from fear, for apart from his invulnerability he was inaccessible to that feeling, but from the horrible ideas engendered from these shouts, having reference to the beautiful Bertha Kurtel. Had her resuscitation from the grave endowed her with the horrible nature of the vampire? Could that lovely creature sustain her renewed existence with the blood of her former companions? Horrible! yet, had she not hinted at something of the kind when he revealed to her the horrors of his own strange doom? It must be so, then; and he shuddered violently at the appalling idea.

'Down with the vampire!' was still the menacing cry which rose from the assailants, who at length succeeded in breaking down the gates, and rushed tumultuously into the court-yard, shouting and brandishing their weapons.

Undismayed by the fire from the battlements, they commenced an attack on the doors and windows of the castle, and now they were all crowded in the courtyard, Count Rodolph thought the moment favorably for a sally. Drawing his sword, and commanding a score of his armed retainers to follow him, he suddenly opened a door leading into the court-yard, and fell furiously on the flank of the assailants. For a moment they were thrown into confusion, but they quickly rallied, when Count Rodolph and his little party were surrounded and compelled to act on the defensive. The ruddy beams of the setting sun were already purpling the distant hills when the peasants marched upon the castle, and as his broad disk sank below the horizon, the aspect of the Count of Ravensburg suddenly underwent a marvelous change, and much as the insurgents had wondered to see arrows glance off from his body, and their swords rebound as if their stroke fell on a giant oak, how much greater was their astonishment when they beheld him suddenly transformed into a fleshless skeleton!

'It is some devise of Satan! — he is a sorcerer!' cried the stalwart smith, brandishing his huge hammer. 'Come on, mates — down with the vampire!'

'Down with the vampire!' echoed from the mob, and the count's retainers giving way on all sides, as much appalled as the peasants at this horrible metamorphosis, the assailants rushed into the castle by the open door, and marched from room to room, looking in every closet and under every bed, while the terrified Bertha flew from one apartment to another, until she at length sought refuge in the highest apartment of the eastern turret, that chamber which had witnessed her return from death to her renewed state of strange and horrible existence. She had locked and bolted the door of the study, but what availed these obstacles against a furious mob, animated by their success in gaining the castle, and bent upon destruction and revenge? The door cracked, yielded, was forced open, and several men rushed into the little chamber.

'Here she is! — here is the vampire!' cried the foremost, and despite her piercing shrieks and earnest supplications for mercy, the wretched Bertha was dragged out of the study, with her long black hair hanging in wild disorder about her shoulders, and her beautiful countenance pale with overpowering terror.

'Mercy, indeed! What mercy can we feel for a vampire?' cried the peasants, and the terrified creature was dragged down the turret stairs by one or two of the boldest, for few would venture to come in contact with the dreaded being.

As they reached the foot of the stairs a volume of smoke rolled along the passage, and the crackling of burning wood told them that some of their companions had set fire to the castle.

'Now what shall we do with the vampire?' said her remorseless captors.

'Throw her into the Rhine!' suggested one.

'Tie her up and shoot at her!' said another.

'What will be the use of that?' objected a third. 'Nothing but fire or a sharp stake will destroy a vampire. Let us shut her up in the castle, and burn her to ashes!'

'Yes, yes! burn the vampire!' shouted a score of voices.

'No, no! — I say, no!' cried the smith. 'Let us carry her to the churchyard, put her in her coffin again, and peg her down with a stake, so that she can never rise again.'

The suggestion of the smith was approved of, and the wretched Bertha was half-dragged and half-carried, more dead than alive, towards the village church. The flames were bursting forth from all parts of the castle when the lawless spoilers left it, and a red glow hung over its ancient towers; the work of destruction was rapid, and in a few hours naught but the bare and blackened walls were left standing.

On the destroyers of Ravensburg Castle reaching the

churchyard, the almost lifeless form of Bertha Kurtel was dragged to the grave, which had been left open, and flung rudely into the coffin. Then a sharp pointed stake was produced, which had been prepared by the way, and the smith plunged it with all the force of his sinewy arms into the abdomen of the doomed vampire. A piercing shriek burst from her pale lips as the horrible thrust aroused her to consciousness, and as her clothes became dabbed with the crimson stream of life, and the smith lifted his heavy hammer and drove the stake through her quivering body, the transfixed wretch writhed convulsively, and the contortions of her countenance were fearful to behold. Thus impaled in her coffin, and while her limbs yet quivered with the last throes of dissolution, the earth was replaced and rammed down by the tread of many feet.

But those strange and terrible scenes were not yet ended. A young peasant of equal curiosity and boldness, and who had been engaged in the attack upon the castle and the horrible tragedy which followed it, was anxious to know more of the strange affair of the skeleton, which had been left in the court-yard where it fell, none of the villagers caring to interfere with so ghastly an object. He therefore stole away a little before midnight, and went towards the castle, where the fire was dying out, though a fiery glow was still reflected from the moldering embers of beams and rafters. He advanced cautiously through the broken gates of the castle, and shuddered slightly as he perceived the skeleton of the Count of Ravensburg still lying on the pavement of the courtyard.

He determined to watch until daylight, and see what became of the grisly relics of mortality, which a few hours before had been the young and handsome Count of Ravensburg. The hours passed slowly on from midnight to the dawn of another day, and when the rising sun tinged the eastern sky with crimson and gold, a strange spectacle was witnessed by the solitary watcher in the court-yard of Ravensburg Castle.

The skeleton rose slowly from the pavement, and assumed the form of Count Rodolph, just as he appeared at the moment preceding his transformation on the evening before. A cold perspiration bedewed the brow of the peasant, and his hair stood erect with terror, on witnessing this sudden metamorphosis. The count looked up at the dilapidated walls and towers of his castle, and shuddered violently, and crossing the court-yard, passed through the broken gate.

The peasant then hastened to the village, and reported what he had seen, which was a source of much marvel to the rustic inhabitants. The story of the skeleton count, and his vampire mistress, quickly spread all over Germany, but the villagers were no more molested by vampires, for Bertha Kurtel was securely fixed in her coffin, and no ill effects ensued from her attacks upon Theresa Delmar and little Minna Klans.

The End

Aylmer Vance
and the Vampire

BY ALICE ASKEW AND CLAUDE ASKEW

This is the first book in a series of supernatural stories written by the prolific husband-and-wife team of Claude and Alice Askew. Aylmer Vance is an investigator of weird things and reminds us of the modern-day "Dresden Files." Alice (1874-1917) and Claude (1865-1917) wrote this vampire story in 1914, and if you enjoy it, be sure to look up further tales of Aylmer Vance.

Aylmer Vance and
the Vampire

by Alice Askew and Claude Askew

Aylmer Vance had rooms in Dover Street, Piccadilly, and now that I had decided to follow in his footsteps and to accept him as my instructor in matters psychic, I found it convenient to lodge in the same house. Aylmer and I quickly became close friends, and he showed me how to develop that faculty of clairvoyance which I had possessed without being aware of it. And I may say at once that this particular faculty of mine proved of service on several important occasions.

At the same time I made myself useful to Vance in other ways, not the least of which was that of acting as recorder of his many strange adventures. For himself, he never cared much about publicity, and it was some time before I could persuade him, in the interests of science, to allow me to give any detailed account of his experiences to the world.

The incidents which I will now narrate occurred very soon after we had taken up our residence together, and while I was still, so to speak, a novice.

It was about ten o'clock in the morning that a visitor was announced. He sent up a card which bore upon it the name of Paul Davenant.

The name was familiar to me, and I wondered if this could

be the same Mr Davenant who was so well known for his polo playing and for his success as an amateur rider, especially over the hurdles? He was a young man of wealth and position, and I recollected that he had married, about a year ago, a girl who was reckoned the greatest beauty of the season. All the illustrated papers had given their portraits at the time, and I remember thinking what a remarkably handsome couple they made.

Mr Davenant was ushered in, and at first I was uncertain as to whether this could be the individual whom I had in mind, so wan and pale and ill did he appear. A finely-built, upstanding man at the time of his marriage, he had now acquired a languid droop of the shoulders and a shuffling gait, while his face, especially about the lips, was bloodless to an alarming degree.

And yet it was the same man, for behind all this I could recognize the shadow of the good looks that had once distinguished Paul Davenant.

He took the chair which Aylmer offered him—after the usual preliminary civilities had been exchanged—and then glanced doubtfully in my direction. 'I wish to consult you privately, Mr Vance,' he said. 'The matter is of considerable importance to myself, and, if I may say so, of a somewhat delicate nature.'

Of course I rose immediately to withdraw from the room, but Vance laid his hand upon my arm.

'If the matter is connected with research in my particular line, Mr Davenant,' he said, 'if there is any investigation you wish me to take up on your behalf, I shall be glad if you will include Mr Dexter in your confidence. Mr Dexter assists me in my work. But, of course—.'

'Oh, no,' interrupted the other, 'if that is the case, pray let Mr Dexter remain. I think,' he added, glancing at me with a friendly smile, 'that you are an Oxford man, are you not, Mr Dexter? It was before my time, but I have heard of your name in connection with the river. You rowed at Henley, unless I am very much mistaken.'

I admitted the fact, with a pleasurable sensation of pride. I was very keen upon rowing in those days, and a man's prowess at school and college always remain dear to his heart..After this we quickly became on friendly terms, and Paul Davenant proceeded to take Aylmer and myself into his confidence.

He began by calling attention to his personal appearance. 'You would hardly recognize me for the same man! was a year ago,' he said. 'I've been losing flesh steadily for the last six months. I came up from Scotland about a week ago, to consult a London doctor. I've seen two—in fact, they've held a sort of consultation over me—but the result, I may say, is far from satisfactory.

They don't seem to know what is really the matter with me.'

'Anaemia—heart' suggested Vance. He was scrutinizing his visitor keenly, and yet without any particular appearance of doing so. 'I believe it not infrequently happens that you athletes overdo yourselves—put too much strain upon the heart—'

'My heart is quite sound,' responded Davenant. 'Physically it is in perfect condition. The trouble seems to be that it hasn't enough blood to pump into my veins. The doctors wanted to know if I had met with an accident involving a great loss of blood—but I haven't. I've had no accident at all, and as for anaemia, well, I don't seem to show the ordinary symptoms of it. The inexplicable thing is that I've lost blood without knowing it, and apparently this has been going on for some time, for I ye been getting steadily worse. It was almost imperceptible at first—not a sudden collapse, you understand, but a gradual failure of health.'

'I wonder,' remarked Vance slowly, 'what induced you to consult me? For you know, of course, the direction in which I pursue my investigations. May I ask if you have reason to consider that your state of health is due to some cause which we may describe as super-physical?'

A slight colour came to Davenant's white cheeks.

'There are curious circumstances,' he said in a low and earnest tone of voice. 'I've been turning them over in my mind, trying to see light through them. I daresay it's all the sheerest folly—and I must tell you that I'm not in the least a superstitious sort of man. I don't mean to say that I'm absolutely incredulous, but I've never given thought to such things—I've led too active a life. But, as I have said, there are curious circumstances about my case, and that is why I decided upon consulting you.'

'Will you tell me everything without reserve?' said Vance. I could see that he was interested.

He was sitting up in his chair, his feet supported on a stool, his elbows on his knees, his chin in his hands—a favourite attitude of his. 'Have you,' he suggested, slowly, 'any mark upon your body, anything that you might associate, however remotely, with your present weakness and ill-health?'

'It's a curious thing that you should ask me that question,' returned Davenant, 'because I have got a curious mark, a sort of scar, that I can't account for. But I showed it to the doctors, and they assured me that it could have nothing whatever to do with my condition. In any case, if it had, it was something altogether outside their experience. I think they imagined it to be nothing more than a birthmark, a sort of mole, for they asked me if I'd had it all my life. But that I can swear I haven't. I only noticed it for the first time about six months ago, when my health began to fail. But you can see for yourself.'

He loosened his collar and bared his throat. Vance rose and made a careful scrutiny of the suspicious mark. It was situated a very little to the left of the central line, just above the clavicle, and, as Vance pointed out, directly over the big vessels of the throat. My friend called to me so that I might examine it, too. Whatever the opinion of the doctors may have been, Aylmer was obviously deeply interested..And yet there was very little to show. The skin was quite intact, and there was no sign of inflammation. There were two red marks, about an inch apart, each of which was inclined to be crescent in shape. They were more visible than they might otherwise have been owing to the peculiar whiteness of Davenant's skin.

'It can't be anything of importance,' said Davenant, with a

slightly uneasy laugh. 'I'm inclined to think the marks are dying away.'

'Have you ever noticed them more inflamed than they are at present?' inquired Vance. 'If so, was it at any special time?'

Davenant reflected. 'Yes,' he replied slowly, 'there have been times, usually, I think perhaps invariably, when I wake up in the morning, that I've noticed them larger and more angry looking. And I've felt a slight sensation of pain—a tingling—oh, very slight, and I've never worried about it. Only now you suggest it to my mind, I believe that those same mornings I have felt particularly tired and done up—a sensation of lassitude absolutely unusual to me. And once, Mr Vance, I remember quite distinctly that there was a stain of blood close to the mark. I didn't think anything of it at the time, and just wiped it away.'

'I see.' Aylmer Vance resumed his seat and invited his visitor to do the same. 'And now,' he resumed, 'you said, Mr Davenant, that there are certain peculiar circumstances you wish to acquaint me with. Will you do so?'

And so Davenant readjusted his collar and proceeded to tell his story. I will tell it as far as I can, without any reference to the occasional interruptions of Vance and myself.

Paul Davenant, as I have said, was a man of wealth and position, and so, in every sense of the word, he was a suitable husband for Miss Jessica MacThane, the young lady who eventually became his wife. Before coming to the incidents attending his loss of health, he had a great deal to recount about Miss MacThane and her family history.

She was of Scottish descent, and although she had certain characteristic features of her race, she was not really Scotch in appearance. Hers was the beauty of the far South rather than that of the Highlands from which she had her origin. Names are not always suited to their owners, and Miss MacThane's was peculiarly inappropriate. She had, in fact, been christened Jessica in a sort of pathetic effort to counteract her obvious departure from normal type. There was a reason for this which we were soon to learn.

Miss MacThane was especially remarkable for her wonderful red hair, hair such as one hardly ever sees outside of Italy—not the Celtic red—and it was so long that it reached to her feet, and it had an extraordinary gloss upon it so that it seemed almost to have individual life of its own.

Then she had just the complexion that one would expect with such hair, the purest ivory white, and not in the least marred by freckles, as is so often the case with red-haired girls. Her beauty was derived from an ancestress who had been brought to Scotland from some foreign shore—no one knew exactly whence.

Davenant fell in love with her almost at once and he had every reason to believe, in spite of her many admirers, that his love was returned. At this time he knew very little about her personal history. He was aware only that she was very wealthy in her own right, an orphan, and the last representative of a race that had once been famous in the annals of history—or rather infamous, for the MacThanes had distinguished themselves more by cruelty and lust of blood than by deeds of chivalry. A clan of turbulent robbers in the past, they had helped to add many a blood-stained page to the history of their country.

Jessica had lived with her father, who owned a house in London, until his death when she was about fifteen years of age. Her mother had died in Scotland when Jessica was still a tiny child..Mr MacThane had been so affected by his wife's death that, with his little daughter, he had abandoned his Scotch estate altogether—or so it was believed—leaving it to the management of a bailiff—though, indeed, there was but little work for the bailiff to do, since there were practically no tenants left. Blackwick Castle had borne for many years a most unenviable reputation.

After the death of her father, Miss MacThane had gone to live with a certain Mrs Meredith, who was a connection of her mother's—on her father's side she had not a single relation left.

Jessica was absolutely the last of a clan once so extensive that intermarriage had been a tradition of the family, but for which the last two hundred years had been gradually dwindling to extinction.

Mrs Meredith took Jessica into Society—which would never have been her privilege had Mr MacThane lived, for he was a moody, self-absorbed man, and prematurely old—one who seemed worn down by the weight of a great grief.

Well, I have said that Paul Davenant quickly fell in love with Jessica, and it was not long before he proposed for her hand. To his great surprise, for he had good reason to believe that she cared for him, he met with a refusal; nor would she give any explanation, though she burst into a flood of pitiful tears.

Bewildered and bitterly disappointed, he consulted Mrs Meredith, with whom he happened to be on friendly terms, and from her he learnt that Jessica had already had several proposals, all from quite desirable men, but that one after another had been rejected.

Paul consoled himself with the reflection that perhaps Jessica did not love them, whereas he was quite sure that she cared for himself. Under these circumstances he determined to try again.

He did so, and with better result. Jessica admitted her love, but at the same time she repeated that she would not marry him. Love and marriage were not for her. Then, to his utter amazement, she declared that she had been born under a curse —a curse which, sooner or later was bound to show itself in her, and which, moreover, must react cruelly, perhaps fatally, upon anyone with whom she linked her life. How could she allow a man she loved to take such a risk? Above all, since the evil was hereditary, there was one point upon which she had quite made up her mind: no child should ever call her mother —she must be the last of her race indeed.

Of course, Davenant was amazed and inclined to think that Jessica had got some absurd idea into her head which a little reasoning on his part would dispel. There was only one other possible explanation. Was it lunacy she was afraid of? But Jessica shook her head, She did not know of any lunacy in her family. The ill was deeper, more subtle than that. And then she told him all that she knew.

The curse—she made us of that word for want of a better—was attached to the ancient race from which she had her origin. Her father had suffered from it, and his father and grandfather before him. All three had taken to themselves young wives who had died mysteriously, of some wasting disease, within a few years. Had they observed the ancient family tradition of intermarriage this might possibly not have happened, but in their case, since the family was so near extinction, this had not been possible.

For the curse—or whatever it was—did not kill those who bore the name of MacThane. It only rendered them a danger to others. It was as if they absorbed from the blood-soaked walls of their fatal castle a deadly taint which reacted terribly upon those with whom they were brought into contact, especially their nearest and dearest.

'Do you know what my father said we have it in us to become?' said Jessica with a shudder.

'He used the word vampires. Paul, think of it—vampires—preying upon the life blood of others.'.And then, when Davenant was inclined to laugh, she checked him. 'No,' she cried out, 'it is not impossible. Think. We are a decadent race. From the earliest times our history has been marked by bloodshed and cruelty. The walls of Blackwick Castle are impregnated with evil—every stone could tell its tale, of violence, pain, lust, and murder. What can one expect of those who have spent their lifetime between its walls?'

'But you have not done so,' exclaimed Paul. 'You have been spared that, Jessica. You were taken away after your mother died, and you have no recollection of Blackwick Castle, none at all. And you need never set foot in it again.'

'I'm afraid the evil is in my blood,' she replied sadly, 'although I am unconscious of it now.

And as for not returning to Blackwick—I'm not sure I can help myself. At least, that is what my father warned me of. He said there is something there, some compelling force, that will call me to it in spite of myself. But, oh, I don't know—I don't know, and that is what makes it so difficult. If I could only believe that all this is nothing but an idle superstition, I might be happy again, for I have it in me to enjoy life, and I'm young, very young, but my father told me these things when he was on his death-bed.' She added the last words in a low, awe-stricken tone.

Paul pressed her to tell him all that she knew, and eventually she revealed another fragment of family history which seemed to have some bearing upon the case. It dealt with her own astonishing likeness to that ancestress of a couple of hundred years ago, whose existence seemed to have presaged the gradual downfall of the clan of the MacThanes.

A certain Robert MacThane, departing from the traditions of his family, which demanded that he should not marry outside his clan, brought home a wife from foreign shores, a woman of wonderful beauty, who was possessed of glowing masses of red hair and a complexion of ivory whiteness—such as had more or less distinguished since then every female of the race born in the direct line.

It was not long before this woman came to be regarded in the neighbourhood as a witch. Queer stories were circulated abroad as to her doings, and the reputation of Blackwick Castle became worse than ever before.

And then one day she disappeared. Robert MacThane had been absent upon some business for twenty-four hours, and it was upon his return that he found her gone. The neighbourhood was searched, but without avail, and then Robert, who was a violent man and who had adored his foreign wife, called together certain of his tenants whom he suspected, rightly or wrongly, of foul play, and had them murdered in cold blood. Murder was easy in those days, yet such an outcry was raised that Robert had to take to flight, leaving his two children in the care of their nurse, and for a long while Blackwick Castle was without a master.

But its evil reputation persisted. It was said that Zaida, the witch, though dead, still made her presence felt. Many children of the tenantry and young people of the neighbourhood sickened and died—possibly of quite natural causes; but this did not prevent a mantle of terror settling upon the countryside, for it was said that Zaida had been seen—a pale woman clad in white—

flitting about the cottages at night, and where she passed sickness and death were sure to supervene.

And from that time the fortune of the family gradually declined. Heir succeeded heir, but no sooner was he installed at Blackwick Castle than his nature, whatever it may previously have been, seemed to undergo a change. It was as if he absorbed into himself all the weight of evil that had stained his family name—as if he did, indeed, become a vampire, bringing blight upon any not directly connected with his own house..And so, by degrees, Blackwick was deserted of its tenantry. The land around it was left uncultivated—the farms stood empty. This had persisted to the present day, for the superstitious peasantry still told their tales of the mysterious white woman who hovered about the neighbourhood, and whose appearance betokened death—and possibly worse than death.

And yet it seemed that the last representatives of the MacThanes could not desert their ancestral home. Riches they had, sufficient to live happily upon elsewhere, but, drawn by some power they could not contend against, they had preferred to spend their lives in the solitude of the now half-ruined castle, shunned by their neighbours, feared and execrated by the few tenants that still clung to their soil.

So it had been with Jessica's grandfather and great-grandfather. Each of them had married a young wife, and in each case their love story had been all too brief. The vampire spirit was still abroad, expressing itself—or so it seemed—through the living representatives of bygone generations of evil, and young blood had been demanded as the sacrifice.

And to them had succeeded Jessica's father. He had not profited by their example, but had followed directly in their footsteps. And the same fate had befallen the wife whom he passionately adored. She had died of pernicious anaemia—so the doctors said—but he had regarded himself as her murderer.

But, unlike his predecessors, he had torn himself away from Blackwick—and this for the sake of his child. Unknown to her, however, he had returned year after year, for there were times when the passionate longing for the gloomy, mysterious halls and corridors of the old castle, for the wild stretches of moorland, and the dark pinewoods, would come upon him too strongly to be resisted. And so he knew that for his daughter, as for himself, there was no escape, and he warned her, when the relief of death was at last granted to him, of what her fate must be.

This was the tale that Jessica told the man who wished to make her his wife, and he made light of it, as such a man would, regarding it all as foolish superstition, the delusion of a mind overwrought. And at last—perhaps it was not very difficult, for she loved him with all her heart and soul—he succeeded in inducing Jessica to think as he did, to banish morbid ideas, as he called them from her brain, and to consent to marry him at an early date.

'I'll take any risk you like,' he declared. 'I'll even go and live at Blackwick if you should desire it. To think of you, my lovely Jessica, a vampire! Why, I never heard such nonsense in my life.'

'Father said I'm very like Zaida, the witch,' she protested, but he silenced her with a kiss.

And so they were married and spent their honeymoon abroad, and in the autumn Paul accepted an invitation to a house party in Scotland for the grouse shooting, a sport to which he was absolutely devoted, and Jessica agreed with him that there was no reason why he should forgo his pleasure.

Perhaps it was an unwise thing to do, to venture to Scotland, but by this time the young couple, more deeply in love with each other than ever, had got quite over their fears. Jessica was redolent with health and spirits, and more than once she declared that if they should be anywhere in the neighbourhood of Blackwick she would like to see the old castle out of curiosity, and just to show how absolutely she had got over the foolish terrors that used to assail her.

This seemed to Paul to be quite a wise plan, and so one day, since they were actually staying at no great distance, they motored over to Blackwick, and finding the bailiff, got him to show them over the castle.

It was a great castellated pile, grey with age, and in places falling into ruin. It stood on a steep hillside, with the rock of which it seemed to form part, and on one side of it there was a precipitous drop to a mountain stream a hundred feet below. The robber MacThanes of the old days could not have desired a better stronghold.

At the back, climbing up the mountainside were dark pinewoods, from which, here and there, rugged crags protruded, and these were fantastically shaped, some like gigantic and misshapen human forms, which stood up as if they mounted guard over the castle and the narrow gorge, by which alone it could be approached.

This gorge was always full of weird, uncanny sounds. It might have been a storehouse for the wind, which, even on calm days, rushed up and down as if seeking an escape, and it moaned among the pines and whistled in the crags and shouted derisive laughter as it was tossed from side to side of the rocky heights. It was like the plaint of lost souls—that is the expression Davenant made use of—the plaint of lost souls.

The road, little more than a track now, passed through this gorge, and then, after skirting a small but deep lake, which hardly knew the light of the sun so shut in was it by overhanging trees, climbed the hill to the castle.

And the castle! Davenant used but a few words to describe it, yet somehow I could see the gloomy edifice in my mind's eye, and something of the lurking horror that it contained communicated itself to my brain. Perhaps my clairvoyant sense assisted me, for when he spoke of them I seemed already acquainted with the great stone halls, the long corridors, gloomy and cold even on the brightest and warmest of days, the dark, oak-panelled rooms, and the broad central staircase up which one of the early MacThanes had once led a dozen men on horseback in pursuit of a stag which had taken refuge within the precincts of the castle. There was the keep, too, its walls so thick that the ravages of time had made no impression upon them, and beneath the keep were dungeons which could tell terrible tales of ancient wrong and lingering pain.

Well, Mr and Mrs Davenant visited as much as the bailiff could show them of this ill-omened edifice, and Paul, for his part, thought pleasantly of his own Derbyshire home, the fine Georgian mansion, replete with every modern comfort, where he proposed to settle with his wife. And so he received something of a shock when, as they drove away, she slipped her hand into his and whispered:

'Paul, you promised, didn't you, that you would refuse me nothing?'

She had been strangely silent till she spoke those words. Paul, slightly apprehensive, assured her that she only had to ask —but the speech did not come from his heart, for he guessed vaguely what she desired.

She wanted to go and live at the castle—oh, only for a little while, for she was sure she would soon tire of it. But the bailiff had told her that there were papers, documents, which she ought to examine, since the property was now hers—and, besides, she was interested in this home of her ancestors, and wanted to explore it more thoroughly. Oh, no, she wasn't in the least influenced by the old superstition—that wasn't the attraction—she had quite got over those silly ideas. Paul had cured her, and since he himself was so convinced that they were without foundation he ought not to mind granting her her whim.

This was a plausible argument, not easy to controvert. In the end Paul yielded, though it was not without a struggle. He suggested amendments. Let him at least have the place done up for her—that would take time; or let them postpone their visit till next year—in the summer—not move in just as the winter was upon them.

But Jessica did not want to delay longer than she could

help, and she hated the idea of redecoration. Why, it would spoil the illusion of the old place, and, besides, it would be a waste of money since she only wished to remain there for a week or two. The Derbyshire house was not quite ready yet; they must allow time for the paper to dry on the walls.

And so, a week later, when their stay with their friends was concluded, they went to Blackwick, the bailiff having engaged a few raw servants and generally made things as comfortable for them as possible. Paul was worried and apprehensive, but he could not admit this to his wife after having so loudly proclaimed his theories on the subject of superstition.

They had been married three months at this time—nine had passed since then, and they had never left Blackwick for more than a few hours—till now Paul had come to London—alone.

'Over and over again,' he declared, 'my wife has begged me to go. With tears in her eyes, almost upon her knees, she has entreated me to leave her, but I have steadily refused unless she will accompany me. But that is the trouble, Mr Vance, she cannot; there is something, some mysterious horror, that holds her there as surely as if she were bound with fetters. It holds her more strongly even than it held her father—we found out that he used to spend six months at least of every year at Blackwick—months when he pretended that he was travelling abroad. You see the spell—or whatever the accursed thing may be—never really relaxed its grip of him.'

'Did you never attempt to take your wife away?' asked Vance.

'Yes, several times; but it was hopeless. She would become so ill as soon as we were beyond the limit of the estate that I invariably had to take her back. Once we got as far as Dorekirk —that is the nearest town, you know—and I thought I should be successful if only I could get through the night. But she escaped me; she climbed out of a window—she meant to go back on foot, at night, all those long miles. Then I have had doctors down; but it is I who wanted the doctors, not she.

They have ordered me away, but I have refused to obey them till now.'

'Is your wife changed at all—physically?' interrupted Vance.

Davenant reflected. 'Changed,' he said, 'yes, but so subtly that I hardly know how to describe it. She is more beautiful than ever—and yet it isn't the same beauty, if you can understand me. I have spoken of her white complexion, well, one is more than ever conscious of it now, because her lips have become so red—they are almost like a splash of blood upon her face. And the upper one has a peculiar curve that I don't think it had before, and when she laughs she doesn't smile—

Do you know what I mean? Then her hair—it has lost its wonderful gloss. Of course, I know she is fretting about me; but that is so peculiar, too, for at times, as I have told you, she will implore me to go and leave her, and then perhaps only a few minutes later, she will wreathe her arms round my neck and say she cannot live without me. And I feel that there is a struggle going on within her, that she is only yielding slowly to the horrible influence—whatever it is—that she is herself when she begs me to go, but when she entreats me to stay—and it is then that her fascination is most intense—oh, I can't help remembering what she told me before we were married, and that word'—he lowered his voice-'the word "vampire"—'

He passed his hand over his brow that was wet with perspiration. 'But that's absurd, ridiculous,' he muttered; 'these fantastic beliefs have been exploded years ago. We live in the twentieth century.'

A pause ensued, then Vance said quietly, 'Mr Davenant, since you have taken me into your confidence, since you have found doctors of no avail, will you let me try to help you? I think I may be of some use—if it is not already too late. Should you agree, Mr Dexter and I will accompany you, as you have suggested, to Blackwick Castle as early as possible—by tonight's mail North. Under ordinary circumstances I should tell you as you value your life, not to return—'. Davenant shook his head. 'That is advice which I should never take,' he declared. 'I had already decided, under any circumstances, to travel North tonight. I am glad that you both will accompany me.'

And so it was decided. We settled to meet at the station, and presently Paul Davenant took his departure. Any other details that remained to be told he would put us in possession of during the course of the journey.

'A curious and most interesting case,' remarked Vance when we were alone. 'What do you make of it, Dexter?'

'I suppose,' I replied cautiously, 'that there is such a thing as vampirism even in these days of advanced civilization? I can understand the evil influence that a very old person may have upon a young one if they happen to be in constant intercourse —the worn-out tissue sapping healthy vitality for their own support. And there are certain people—I could think of several myself—who seem to depress one and undermine one's energies, quite unconsciously, of course, but one feels somehow that vitality has passed from oneself to them. And in this case, when the force is centuries old, expressing itself, in some mysterious way, through Davenant's wife, is it not feasible to believe that he may be physically affected by it, even though the whole thing is sheerly mental?'

'You think, then,' demanded Vance, 'that it is sheerly mental? Tell me, if that is so, how do you account for the marks on Davenant's throat?'

This was a question to which I found no reply, and though I pressed him for his views, Vance would not commit himself further just then.

Of our long journey to Scotland I need say nothing. We did not reach Blackwick Castle till late in the afternoon of the following day. The place was just as I had conceived it—as I have already described it. And a sense of gloom settled upon me as our car jolted us over the rough road that led through the Gorge of the Winds—a gloom that deepened when we penetrated into the vast cold hall of the castle.

Mrs Davenant, who had been informed by telegram of our arrival, received us cordially. She knew nothing of our actual mission, regarding us merely as friends of her husband's. She was most solicitous on his behalf, but there was something strained about her tone, and it made me feel vaguely uneasy. The impression that I got was that the woman was impelled to everything that she said or did by some force outside herself—but, of course, this was a conclusion that the circumstances I was aware of might easily have conduced to. In every other aspect she was charming, and she had an extraordinary fascination of appearance and manner that made me readily understand the force of a remark made by Davenant during our journey.

'I want to live for Jessica's sake. Get her away from Blackwick, Vance, and I feel that all will be well. I'd go through hell to have her restored to me—as she was.'

And now that I had seen Mrs Davenant I realized what he meant by those last words. Her fascination was stronger than ever, but it was not a natural fascination—not that of a normal woman, such as she had been. It was the fascination of a Circe, of a witch, of an enchantress—and as such was irresistible.

We had a strong proof of the evil within her soon after our arrival. It was a test that Vance had quietly prepared. Davenant had mentioned that no flowers grew at Blackwick, and Vance declared that we must take some with us as a present for the lady of the house. He purchased a bouquet of pure white roses at the little town where we left the train, for the motorcar has been sent to meet us..Soon after our arrival he presented these to Mrs Davenant. She took them it seemed to me nervously, and hardly had her hand touched them before they fell to pieces, in a shower of crumpled petals, to the floor.

'We must act at once,' said Vance to me when we were descending to dinner that night. 'There must be no delay.'

'What are you afraid of?' I whispered.

'Davenant has been absent a week,' he replied grimly. 'He is stronger than when he went away, but not strong enough to survive the loss of more blood. He must be protected. There is danger tonight.'

'You mean from his wife?' I shuddered at the ghastliness of the suggestion.

'That is what time will show.' Vance turned to me and added a few words with intense earnestness. 'Mrs Davenant, Dexter, is at present hovering between two conditions. The evil thing has not yet completely mastered her—you remember what Davenant said, how she would beg him to go away and the next moment entreat him to stay? She has made a struggle, but she is gradually succumbing, and this last week, spent here alone, has strengthened the evil. And that is what I have got to fight, Dexter—it is to be a contest of will, a contest that will go on silently till one or the other obtains the mastery. If you watch, you may see. Should a change show itself in Mrs Davenant you will know that I have won.'

Thus I knew the direction in which my friend proposed to act. It was to be a war of his will against the mysterious power that had laid its curse upon the house of MacThane. Mrs Davenant must be released from the fatal charm that held her.

And I, knowing what was going on, was able to watch and understand. I realized that the silent contest had begun even while we ate dinner. Mrs Davenant ate practically nothing and seemed ill at ease; she fidgeted in her chair, talked a great deal, and laughed—it was the laugh without a smile, as Davenant had described it. And as soon as she was able to she withdrew.

Later, as we sat in the drawing-room, I could feel the clash of wills. The air in the room felt electric and heavy, charged with tremendous but invisible forces. And outside, round the castle, the wind whistled and shrieked and moaned—it was as if all the dead and gone MacThanes, a grim army, had collected to fight the battle of their race.

And all this while we four in the drawing-room were sitting and talking the ordinary commonplaces of after—dinner conversation! That was the extraordinary part of it—Paul Davenant suspected nothing, and I, who knew, had to play my part. But I hardly took my eyes from Jessica's face. When would the change come, or was it, indeed, too late!

At last Davenant rose and remarked that he was tired and

would go to bed. There was no need for Jessica to hurry. We would sleep that night in his dressing-room and did not want to be disturbed.

And it was at that moment, as his lips met hers in a good-night kiss, as she wreathed her enchantress arms about him, careless of our presence, her eyes gleaming hungrily, that the change came.

It came with a fierce and threatening shriek of wind, and a rattling of the casement, as if the horde of ghosts without was about to break in upon us. A long, quivering sigh escaped from Jessica's lips, her arms fell from her husband's shoulders, and she drew back, swaying a little from side to side.

'Paul,' she cried, and somehow the whole timbre of her voice was changed, 'what a wretch I've been to bring you back to Blackwick, ill as you are! But we'll go away, dear; yes, I'll go, too. Oh, will you take me away—take me away tomorrow?' She spoke with an intense earnestness—unconscious all the time of what had been happening to her. Long shudders were convulsing her frame. 'I don't know why I've wanted to stay here,' she kept repeating. 'I hate the place, really—it's evil—evil.'

Having heard these words I exulted, for surely Vance's success was assured. But I was to learn that the danger was not yet past.

Husband and wife separated, each going to their own room. I noticed the grateful, if mystified glance that Davenant threw at Vance, vaguely aware, as he must have been, that my friend was somehow responsible for what had happened. It was settled that plans for departure were to be discussed on the morrow.

'I have succeeded,' Vance said hurriedly, when we were alone, 'but the change may be a transitory. I must keep watch tonight. Go you to bed, Dexter, there is nothing that you can do.'

I obeyed—though I would sooner have kept watch, too—watch against a danger of which I had no understanding. I went to my room, a gloomy and sparsely furnished apartment, but I knew that it was quite impossible for me to think of sleeping. And so, dressed as I was, I went and sat by the open window, for now the wind that had raged round the castle had died down to a low moaning in the pinetrees—a whimpering of time-worn agony.

And it was as I sat thus that I became aware of a white figure that stole out from the castle by a door that I could not see, and, with hands clasped, ran swiftly across the terrace to the wood. I had but a momentary glance, but I felt convinced that the figure was that of Jessica Davenant.

And instinctively I knew that some great danger was imminent. It was, I think, the suggestion of despair conveyed by those clasped hands. At any rate, I did not hesitate. My window was some height from the ground, but the wall below was ivy-clad and afforded good foothold. The descent was quite easy. I achieved it, and was just in time to take up the pursuit in the right direction, which was into the thickness of the wood that clung to the slope of the hill.

I shall never forget that wild chase. There was just sufficient room to enable me to follow the rough path, which, luckily, since I had now lost sight of my quarry, was the only possible way that she could have taken; there were no intersecting tracks, and the wood was too thick on either side to permit of deviation.

And the wood seemed full of dreadful sounds—moaning and wailing and hideous laughter.

The wind, of course, and the screaming of night birds—once I felt the fluttering of wings in close proximity to my face. But I could not rid myself of the thought that I, in my turn, was being pursued, that the forces of hell were combined against me.

The path came to an abrupt end on the border of the sombre lake that I have already mentioned. And now I realized that I was indeed only just in time, for before me, plunging knee deep in the water, I recognized the white-clad figure of the woman I had been pursuing. Hearing my footsteps, she turned her head, and then threw up her arms and screamed. Her red hair fell in heavy masses about her shoulders, and her face, as I saw it in that moment, was hardly human for the agony of remorse that it depicted.

'Go!' she screamed. 'For God's sake let me die!'

But I was by her side almost as she spoke. She struggled with me—sought vainly to tear herself from my clasp—implored me, with panting breath, to let her drown.

'It's the only way to save him!' she gasped. 'Don't you understand that I am a thing accursed? For it is I—I—who have sapped his life blood! I know it now, the truth has been revealed to me tonight! I am a vampire, without hope in this world or the next, so for his sake—for the sake of his unborn child—let me die—let me die!'.Was ever so terrible an appeal made? Yet I—what could I do? Gently I overcame her resistance and drew her back to shore. By the time I reached it she was lying a dead weight upon my arm. I laid her down upon a mossy bank, and, kneeling by her side, gazed intently into her face.

And then I knew that I had done well. For the face I looked upon was not that of Jessica the vampire, as I had seen it that afternoon, it was the face of Jessica, the woman whom Paul Davenant had loved.

And later Aylmer Vance had his tale to tell.

'I waited', he said, 'until I knew that Davenant was asleep, and then I stole into his room to watch by his bedside. And presently she came, as I guessed she would, the vampire, the accursed thing that has preyed upon the souls of her kin, making them like to herself when they too have passed into Shadowland, and gathering sustenance for her horrid task from the blood of those who are alien to her race. Paul's body and Jessica's soul—it is for one and the other, Dexter, that we have fought.'

'You mean,' I hesitated, 'Zaida the witch?'

'Even so,' he agreed. 'Hers is the evil spirit that has fallen like a blight upon the house of MacThane. But now I think she may be exorcized for ever.'

'Tell me.'

'She came to Paul Davenant last night, as she must have done before, in the guise of his wife.

You know that Jessica bears a strong resemblance to her ancestress. He opened his arms, but she was foiled of her prey, for I had taken my precautions; I had placed That upon Davenant's breast while he slept which robbed the vampire of her power of ill. She sped wailing from the room—a shadow—she who a minute before had looked at him with Jessica's eyes and spoken to him with Jessica's voice. Her red lips were Jessica's lips, and they were close to his when his eyes were opened and he saw her as she was—a hideous phantom of the corruption of the ages. And so the spell was removed, and she fled away to the place whence she had come—'

He paused. 'And now?' I inquired.

'Blackwick Castle must be razed to the ground,' he replied. 'That is the only way. Every stone of it, every brick, must be ground to powder and burnt with fire, for therein is the cause of all the evil. Davenant has consented.'

'And Mrs Davenant?'

'I think,' Vance answered cautiously, 'that all may be well with her. The curse will be removed with the destruction of the castle. She has not—thanks to you—perished under its influence. She was less guilty than she imagined—herself preyed upon rather than preying. But can't you understand her remorse when she realized, as she was bound to realize, the part she had played? And the knowledge of the child to come—its fatal inheritance—'

'I understand.' I muttered with a shudder. And then, under my breath, I whispered, 'Thank God!'

The End